W9-CHS-348

Praise for Brenda Minton and her novels

"Minton's characters are well crafted."
—*RT Book Reviews*

"A lovely romance."
—*RT Book Reviews* on *The Cowboy's Family*

"[A] satisfyingly emotional story."
—*RT Book Reviews* on *The Cowboy's Courtship*

"This easy, sensitive story…is quite touching.
Don't miss [it]."
—*RT Book Reviews* on *His Little Cowgirl*

BRENDA MINTON

The Cowboy's Family
&
The Cowboy's Homecoming

HARLEQUIN® LOVE INSPIRED® CLASSICS

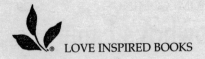

LOVE INSPIRED BOOKS

Recycling programs for this product may not exist in your area.

ISBN-13: 978-0-373-20873-9

The Cowboy's Family & The Cowboy's Homecoming

Copyright © 2018 by Harlequin Books S.A.

The publisher acknowledges the copyright holder of the individual works as follows:

The Cowboy's Family
Copyright © 2011 by Brenda Minton

The Cowboy's Homecoming
Copyright © 2011 by Brenda Minton

www.Harlequin.com

Printed in U.S.A.

CONTENTS

Brenda Minton lives in the Ozarks with her husband, children, cats, dogs and strays. She is a pastor's wife, Sunday-school teacher, coffee addict and is sleep deprived. Not in that order. Her dream to be an author for Harlequin started somewhere in the pages of a romance novel about a young American woman stranded in a Spanish castle. Her dreams came true, and twenty-plus books later, she is an author hoping to inspire young girls to dream.

Books by Brenda Minton

Love Inspired

Bluebonnet Springs

Second Chance Rancher
The Rancher's Christmas Bride

Martin's Crossing

A Rancher for Christmas
The Rancher Takes a Bride
The Rancher's Second Chance
The Rancher's First Love
Her Rancher Bodyguard
Her Guardian Rancher

Lone Star Cowboy League: Boys Ranch

The Rancher's Texas Match

Lone Star Cowboy League

A Reunion for the Rancher

Visit the Author Profile page
at Harlequin.com for more titles.

THE COWBOY'S FAMILY

Thou hast turned for me my mourning into dancing:
Thou hast put off my sackcloth,
and girded me with gladness.
—*Psalms* 30:11

To my readers.
And especially to Julie, for your prayers,
your thoughtfulness and your insight.
To Stephanie Newton, for those
last minute critiques!

Chapter One

Why had she thought this was a good idea, cleaning house for Wyatt Johnson? Rachel Waters cut the engine to her car and stared up at the big, brick home that Wyatt had built over the winter. She pushed her sunglasses to the top of her head as she mulled the reasons for being here. First of all, she'd agreed to this as a favor to Ryder and Andie. Second, she struggled with the word *no*.

There were plenty of reasons not to be here. She didn't need the money. She didn't need the headache.

She especially didn't need the heartache.

And Wyatt Johnson had heartache written all over his too-handsome face. Heartache was etched into his eyes. It was the whisper of a smile on his lips. It hovered over his lean features when he picked up his girls from the church nursery, hugging them but saying little to her or the other nursery workers.

So what had she gone and done? As if she didn't have enough to occupy her time, Rachel had agreed when Ryder Johnson asked her to clean the house his brother Wyatt had built on land across the road from the origi-

nal Johnson ranch house, the house Ryder and his wife
Andie now called home.

Rachel eyed the brick, French country-style home.
The windows were wide, the porch was brick and stone.
The landscaping was professionally done, but the flow-
ers were being choked out by weeds.

It was a far cry from the parsonage she'd shared with
her parents for the last year; since her dad took the job
as pastor of the Dawson Community Church. Their little house could fit into this one five times. But the parsonage was immaculate. If her father could get hold
of these gardens, he could do wonders with the place.

Oh, well, she couldn't put it off forever. She hopped
out of her car. A border collie bounded toward her, tail
wagging. The animal, black-and-white coat clean and
brushed, rolled over at her feet. Rachel leaned to pet
the dog's belly.

"So, at least you get some attention, huh, girl?"

That wasn't fair. Wyatt tried, she was sure he tried.
But his girls often came to church with ragged little braids and mismatched clothes. Not that the girls
seemed to mind. They smiled and hugged him, and
then waited for him to pick them up again.

Rachel cast a critical gaze over the lawn and the
house. The barns and fences surrounding the place were
well-kept. The horses grazing in the fields gleamed in
the early spring sunshine. She'd spent a lifetime dreaming of a place like this.

She walked up the patio steps and knocked on the
back door. She stood there for a long time, looking
out over the fields, talking aimlessly to the dog. She
knocked again. From inside she heard children talking
and the drone of the television.

She knocked a third time.

Finally footsteps headed her way and a male voice said something about the television show they were watching. She stepped back and the door opened. Wyatt Johnson stared at her, his dark hair longish. His brown eyes with flecks of dark green were fringed with long lashes. Gorgeous eyes and a gorgeous man. She nearly groaned. He stared at her and then looked down. Two little heads peeked out at her. Molly, age three, and Kat, age two. Molly had told her that she'd be turning four in a few of weeks.

"Can I help you?" Wyatt didn't move, didn't invite her in. He just stared, as if he didn't have a clue who she was. Six months he'd been home. Six months she'd held his girls and read them stories. Sundays had flown by and each week he'd signed the girls in, signed them out and she'd asked how he was doing.

She was the invisible Rachel Waters. He was probably trying to decide where he knew her from.

"I'm here to clean," she explained, and she managed to smile.

"Clean?"

She held up the bucket she'd taken from her car and the tub of cleaning supplies. "Clean your house. Ryder hired me."

"He didn't say anything to me."

"No, he probably didn't. Surprise!" She smiled at the girls. They giggled. At least they thought she was funny.

Kat, hands pudgy, her smile sweet, pushed against Wyatt and slipped outside. Rachel wasn't invisible to Kat. Or to Molly.

"We have crayons."

"That's wonderful, Kat. Are you coloring a picture?"

Kat nodded. "For Mommy. Daddy said we could mail it to heaven."

"That's a lovely idea." That was the heartache in his eyes. Rachel didn't look up because she didn't want to see his pain. His story was his, private, that's how he'd kept it. She understood. She had her own stories.

Molly remained behind Wyatt, but she moved a little and peeked out from behind his legs. "I like coloring flowers."

"I think flowers are one of my favorite things, Molly. It's April, we'll have lots of flowers blooming very soon."

Rachel glanced up. Wyatt hadn't moved. He just stared for a long minute and then he shook his head and let out a long sigh. It sounded a lot like someone giving up. It didn't seem as if he'd changed his mind about her, though, because he didn't move an inch.

"I don't think we need help with the house."

Rachel peeked past him and her nose wrinkled. "I disagree."

He glanced back over his shoulder and shrugged. "It isn't that bad."

"It is bad." Molly waved a hand in front of her nose. "It's smelly bad. That's what Uncle Ryder said when he came home last week from the rodeo circus."

"Circuit." Wyatt corrected and then his gaze was back on Rachel. "I don't need help with the house."

He leaned against the door frame, faded jeans, bare feet and a T-shirt. She took a step back, putting herself out of his personal space and back into her own.

"Ryder already paid me." And she didn't like backing down. "I have a few hours free today, no time tomorrow. I'm not going to take his money and not do the job."

"Ryder should have checked with me. The girls and I were about to clean."

"After Daddy traces our hands and then does bank stuff." Molly supplied the information with all the innocence of an almost-four-year-old.

"Sounds like fun." Rachel stood on the porch, sun beating down on her back. Wyatt continued to stare and she felt fifteen and overweight. She wasn't, but that look took her back about fifteen years to a place in her life that she really didn't want to return to.

"Honestly, Rachel, we don't need a housekeeper."

"Sorry." She smiled and took a step forward. Ryder and Andie had warned her that he'd be stubborn about this.

"Yeah, I'm sure."

"So, I can come in?" Rachel glanced at her watch. She really didn't have all day.

Wyatt, tall and cowboy lean, shrugged and stepped back. He waved her in and she was pretty sorry she'd ever agreed to do this. Dishes covered the counters and the sink overflowed. Toys were scattered across a floor that hadn't seen a mop in, well, it looked like a long time.

"I guess it's a mess." Wyatt smiled a little and scooped up Kat to settle her on his shoulders. "We haven't really paid much attention."

She wanted to ask how he could not pay attention but that insult piled up on top of a dozen other things she wanted to say to him. His daughters were still in their pajamas and he hadn't shaved in days. This wasn't a life; this was hiding from life.

Wyatt had been home for more than six months and from what she'd seen, he hadn't done a thing to step back into life here, other than church on Sundays and meals at the Mad Cow. Oh, and he'd bought horses. He always had his girls in tow, though. She had to give him credit for that.

He couldn't match an outfit for anything, but he loved Molly and Kat.

So this was how his brother planned on pushing him back into the dating world. She was probably clueless and really thought this was about cleaning the house. Wyatt planned a few choice words for Ryder as Rachel Waters stepped away from him and leaned to talk to Kat, dusting his daughter's hands off in the process. The back of Rachel's shirt came up a little and he couldn't look away.

He must have made a sound because she straightened and shifted her shirt back into place. Her face was a little pink and she glanced away from him as she pulled her dark, curly hair into a ponytail. She continued to ignore him and he couldn't stop thinking about a butterfly tattoo at the waist of her jeans. Did the church nursery worker have secrets?

A little late he remembered to be resentful. His younger brother had a habit of pushing his way into people's lives and shoving his ideas off on them. Rachel cleaning the house was Ryder's idea.

Wyatt kept his own ideas to himself, the way he'd been doing for the last few months. He didn't have time or energy to worry about Rachel or what Ryder was up to.

"I guess if you're here to clean, have at it." He nodded in the direction of the kitchen. He'd put a lot of thought into building this house. Granite countertops, stainless steel appliances and tile floors. It should have gleamed. Instead it looked like a bunch of teenagers had ransacked the place.

He hadn't meant to reminisce, but he remembered his parents' kitchen after it had been ransacked by Wyatt, Ryder and their friends. He and Ryder hadn't been easy to raise. Not that their parents had done a lot of raising; more like they'd just turned them loose and told them to do whatever, as long as they didn't land in jail.

Rachel looked around the kitchen, her mouth open a little. Yeah, it was pretty bad. He didn't have time to do everything. The girls came first, then the farm, then business. Last, and probably least, the house.

"Need anything?" he asked, turning his attention back to Rachel Waters.

"No, thanks. If you don't mind, I'll get started." She smiled, a wide smile that settled in dark brown eyes.

"I don't mind. I'll be in the office with the girls. Don't worry about upstairs."

"Seriously? Wyatt, your brother paid me a lot. I really don't want to do a halfway job."

Kat was tugging on his hand, wanting him to help her finish drawing a pony. He glanced down at his daughter and then back to the woman standing a short distance away. She was already moving around the kitchen, picking up trash and tossing it, putting dishes next to the sink. Long curls were held in a ponytail and she wore flip-flops with her jeans.

The shoes made a flap-flap sound on the tile floors that distracted him for a second, until she cleared her throat.

"Upstairs, Wyatt?"

He glanced up, meeting brown eyes and a hint of a

strawberry-glossed smile. Molly's hand slid into his and he squeezed lightly, holding her close, grounded by her presence and shifted back to reality by her shoulder against his leg.

Eighteen months of holding it together, just trying to be a dad and trying to make sense of life, and now this. This, meaning Rachel Waters and the sudden realization that he was still a man. He blinked a few times, surprised that he'd noticed anything other than the broom she held in her hand. When was the last time he'd noticed a woman's lips? Or her hair?

He'd seen her at church every Sunday, though. It wasn't the first time he'd noticed her, her smile, her laugh. It wasn't the first time she'd taken him by surprise.

"Yeah, sure, go ahead. The bedrooms are fine, though. The girls clean their own. Kind of." He grinned down at his daughters because that cleaning part was an exaggeration. "Anyway, there are a couple of bathrooms up there."

"Good, I'll clean those, too." She grabbed a broom and swept at his feet. "Scoot, now."

Scoot. Molly was already pulling him toward the hall. He glanced back at Rachel. She had turned on the CD player hidden under the upper cabinets and in moments Sara Evans was singing about a runaway teen leaving the suds in the bucket and the clothes hanging on the line.

As his daughters led him down the hall to the office, he could hear the chorus of the song and Rachel singing along. Her voice got a little louder on the line about wondering what the preacher would preach about on Sunday. He shot a look back in the direction of the kitchen, but the wall blocked her from sight.

Kat was dragging him into the office, jabbering about ponies and wondering when she would get one of her own. She was two. He considered reminding her of that fact, but she'd been reminded more than once.

For the next couple of hours the girls colored pictures and he went over farm accounts and receipts for taxes that had to be filed. The vacuum cleaner rumbled overhead. Rachel was still singing. She was always singing. Even when he picked the girls up in the nursery at church he could hear her singing to them.

He should be glad about that, that someone sang to them, someone soft and feminine. And she laughed, all the time. At least with the kids she laughed. He tried to remember the last time he'd really laughed. He watched his daughters trade crayons and he remembered. Kat had done something that made him laugh. They laughed more than they had six months ago. Far more than they had a year ago.

He shook his head and glanced back at numbers blurring on the ledger he'd been staring at for the last hour. Ryder had just about let the ranch run into the ground. Not financially, just upkeep, the things that required sitting still.

His cell phone rang and he reached for it, distracted. Wendy's mom's voice said a soft hello. Mother-in-law? Did he still call her that? She was still grandmother to his girls. A week didn't pass that she didn't call to check on them. More than once a month she and William, her second husband, drove up from Oklahoma City to visit.

He didn't want to sound paranoid, but he thought it was more like spying. It was Violet's way of making sure he was surviving and that her granddaughters were being taken care of. He didn't really blame her. There had been a few months when he hadn't been sure if he was going to make it.

"Violet, how are you?"

"I'm fine, of course. The question is, how are you?" The southern accent should have been sweet and maternal. Instead it held about a dozen questions pertaining to his sanity.

Which was just fine.

"Good, Violet. The girls are coloring pictures and we're getting ready to eat lunch." He glanced at his watch and winced. It was past time for lunch.

"Isn't it a little late for lunch?" She never missed a thing. He smiled.

"A little, but we ate a late breakfast." That probably didn't sound better, but he wasn't going to lie to her.

"Right. Well, I thought I'd come up this week, just to…"

"Check up on us?"

"Of course not. Wyatt, you know we love you and the girls. I miss…"

Broken sentences. He held back the sigh. In the last eighteen months they'd talked in broken sentences, half-finished thoughts and unspoken accusations.

"I miss her, too." He finished the sentence for her.

"So, about this week?"

It wasn't a good week for a visit. He leaned back in his chair and stared out the window at the overgrown lawn. He needed to hire a lawn service. "Sure, Violet, I'll be here."

The vacuum cleaner stopped.

"What's that noise?" Violet asked.

"Ryder hired a housekeeper."

"Oh. Well, that's good."

"I guess it is."

"And a cook?"

Of course it came back to cooking. He smiled a little. "I don't need a cook."

She didn't respond for a minute. "Okay, Wyatt. Well, I'll call and let you know what day I'll be up."

No, she wouldn't. He slipped the phone back in his pocket knowing full well she'd launch a sneak attack when he least expected it.

He leaned to kiss Molly on the top of her head. "You girls stay here for a second. I'm going to talk to Miss Rachel and then we'll blow up our balloons. Later we'll go to town."

To the store for groceries and a cookbook for dummies. Maybe he could learn to cook before Violet showed up.

Molly shot him a narrow-eyed look. Kat ignored him. The girls were like night and day. Molly was her mother all over, but she looked like him. Kat looked like Wendy. They both had dark hair, but Kat's was a little lighter and she had Wendy's light brown eyes. It was getting easier to stare into eyes that reminded him of his wife.

He hurried up the stairs and met Rachel in the hallway. She picked up her bucket of cleaning supplies and then smiled at him. Perspiration glistened on her brow and her hair was a little damp. But the upstairs smelled clean for the first time in a long time.

The windows gleamed at either end of the hall and there were no cobwebs clinging to the ceiling. Maybe a housekeeper wasn't such a bad idea. It might be a great idea. But he didn't know if Rachel Waters was the one he wanted. She wore faded jeans and had the tiniest butterfly at the small of her back. Shouldn't a housekeeper wear something more…housekeeperish?

He pictured Alice from *The Brady Bunch*. Or the robot maid from *The Jetsons*. Yeah, that's what a housekeeper should look like. A housekeeper should make PB and J sandwiches and smell like joint cream, not wildflowers.

"Is there anything else I need to do?" She stood in the center of the hallway, the bucket in her hand, and he'd lost it for a minute.

"No, nothing else." He glanced around. "It looks great, though."

"I'm glad you approve. Listen, I know this isn't what you wanted, but if you ever need me to come over again, just call. I can even watch the girls if you need time away."

Time away from his girls. He needed that less than anything. He needed them with him, all the time. He didn't ever want them to be alone and afraid again. She didn't know that, though. There were details that no one knew but Wyatt, Andie and a few others. He'd left Florida to escape those memories. Florida, where he and Wendy had been in youth ministry after college.

"Thanks, I appreciate that. I don't usually leave them, other than in the church nursery. But I do have to head out in a few minutes and I wanted to make sure Ryder paid you enough."

"He did." She brushed strands of damp hair back from her face. "Are you sure you don't want me to stay with the girls?"

"No, I'll take them. I'm just going to the store."

Because he had separation anxiety and so did they.

It was about the least manly statement he could think of to make, so he didn't. He glanced out the window, which gleamed and the fingerprints the girls had put on the glass were gone.

She smiled. "Okay, but the offer stands."

"Thanks."

Rachel headed down the stairs with the bucket. He followed. Her shirt stayed carefully in place. He kind of hoped…and then again, he didn't. He shook his head and worked hard to pull it together.

She stopped at the bottom of the stairs. The girls ran out of the office, pigtails and sunshine. His sunshine. He hugged them both close. But they broke out of his arms and ran to Rachel. She didn't hesitate, just pulled them close and hugged them as she kissed the tops of their heads.

His phone rang again, not a moment too soon because he needed the distraction from the scene in front of him. Rachel walked away with his girls. He watched them as he raised the phone to his ear.

"Wyatt, how did you like your surprise?" Ryder laughed from five hundred miles away.

"Thanks."

"Is she done cleaning?"

"Yeah, the house looks great. I'm going to think of a nice surprise for you when you get back."

"You should be more appreciative. You have a clean house and a pretty woman to clean it."

"I wouldn't talk like that in front of my wife if I was you."

"She knows I only have eyes for her. But you, on the other hand…"

"Ever heard of the word *subtle,* little brother?"

Ryder laughed, louder, longer. Wyatt held the phone away from his ear.

"I guess subtle has never been my thing," Ryder admitted.

"Listen, I have to go shopping. Remind me that I owe you for this. And the payback won't be pleasant."

Rachel walked toward him, the laughter gone from her dark eyes and he didn't even know why. He couldn't let that be his problem. He had enough girl problems. One was two and the other was almost four. They were more than enough to keep him busy and keep him guessing.

"I'm going now." She stared straight at him, her gaze unwavering. She had a few freckles on suntanned cheeks.

"Okay, well, thank you." He didn't have time for this. "Look, I appreciate what you did. The place looks great. I just…"

"Don't need a housekeeper?"

He shrugged off the sarcasm in her tone. They both knew that he needed a housekeeper. What he didn't need was that little smile of hers making him feel as if he needed a housekeeper and an intervention.

"Yeah, I don't need a housekeeper." It hadn't been what he'd planned to say, but it worked.

What he really didn't need was someone who smelled like spring and who reminded him of everything he'd lost.

Chapter Two

Rachel drove away from the Johnson ranch and she was pretty glad to see it in her rearview mirror. She wanted to be a good distance away before the girls released the balloons with messages to their mother. It wouldn't have done anyone any good to have Rachel crying by their side.

She really should have known that she wouldn't be able to do this, spend more time with them, and stay detached. After years of considering herself a real pro at detachment, two little girls and a cowboy were going to be her downfall. The signs had been pretty obvious. The girls had been in the nursery and her preschool Sunday school class for six months and it had been way easy to fall in love with them.

Of course Wyatt wasn't included in those emotions. She felt sorry for him, nothing else. After hearing his conversation with Ryder, she knew he felt about the same for her.

It shouldn't matter to her what he thought. At twenty-nine, when she finally knew who she was and what she wanted out of life, Wyatt Johnson's opinion shouldn't matter. But old feelings of inadequacy didn't care what she thought of herself now. Those old emotions had a way of pushing to the surface when she least needed them.

So what? She would never be homecoming queen and guys like Wyatt Johnson always laughed behind her back.

It didn't matter anymore. She wasn't the fat girl in school or the rebel in the back of a police car trying to prove to people that she wasn't the good little preacher's kid.

She knew who she was, and who God wanted her to be. She worked in children's ministry, helped when her mother's lupus flared, and she loved her life in Dawson.

All of those pretty sermons to herself didn't take away a sudden desire for a big, fat chocolate bar. Or brownies with ice cream. She reached for her purse and dug her hand through the side pocket for a pack of gum. As she drove she managed to get a stick of peppermint gum out of the package.

She shoved the gum in her mouth and chewed, trying to pretend it helped the way chocolate helped. It didn't.

Forget Wyatt, she had other things to do. She was supposed to work for Etta Forrester that afternoon. Etta designed and sewed a line of tie-dye clothing that she sold to specialty boutiques around the country. Etta made sundresses, skirts, pants, tops and even purses. Rachel worked for her a couple of days a week, more if Etta needed. With Etta's granddaughter, Andie, married to Ryder Johnson and Andie's twin, Alyson, married to Jason Bradshaw, Etta had more need for help these days.

She drove down the road and pulled into Etta's driveway. The bright yellow Victorian with the lavender wicker furniture on the wide porch managed to lift Rachel's spirits. Etta stood on the porch with a watering can in her hand and a floppy hat covering her lavender-gray hair. She waved as she poured water on the flowers. Last week she'd made a trip to Grove and she'd come home with a truck load of plants for the baskets and flower gardens.

Rachel parked under the shade of an oak tree and stepped out of her car. As she walked up the wide steps of the porch, Etta put down the watering can and pulled off her gardening gloves. Her nails were long, painted purple and never chipped. It was a mystery how Etta could take care of this farm, make her clothing and always be perfectly manicured.

The one time Rachel asked how she did it, Etta laughed and said, "Oh, honey, life teaches those little skills."

Rachel doubted it. She always felt about as together as a pair of old shoes falling apart at the seams. She couldn't paint her nails without smudging at least one. And her hair. The only good thing that had ever happened to her hair was a ponytail holder.

"Good to see you, honey." Etta slipped an arm around Rachel's shoulders. "I thought we'd have tea out here before we get started on those T-shirts."

"Tea sounds wonderful."

"You look about wrung out. Did you clean Wyatt's house today?"

Rachel nodded and picked dead blooms off the petunias.

Etta lifted her sunglasses and stared hard. "Well, tell me how it went."

"The place was definitely a mess." She shrugged and

kept plucking blooms, tossing them over the rail into the yard. "And so is Wyatt."

"Oh, he isn't such a mess. He just needs a little time." Etta lifted the little watch she wore on a chain around her neck. "Goodness, speaking of time. I'm going to keep watering. Do you want to bring the tea out?"

"I can do that."

Etta had lowered the sunglasses. The big rhinestone encrusted frames covered half her face. "And try not to look so down in the mouth, honey. You're going to depress me and you know I don't depress easily."

Rachel smiled. "Is that better?"

"Not much." Etta laughed and went back to watering.

"I'll be back in a few."

"I'll be here."

The dog that had been sleeping under a tree started barking as Rachel fixed the tea tray. She picked up the wooden tray and headed down the hallway to the front door. The door was open and a breeze lifted the curtains in the parlor. Voices carried on that breeze.

"So you think you're going to learn to cook something more than canned spaghetti and hamburgers?" Etta laughed and said something else that Rachel didn't hear.

She stopped at the screen door and looked out. Etta was standing on the sidewalk and Wyatt stood next to her. Etta's skirt flapped in the breeze. Wyatt had taken off his hat and held it behind his back. They were both facing the opposite direction and didn't see Rachel.

"It can't be that hard to learn, Etta. I've got to show Violet that I'm capable."

"Of course you're capable." Etta turned and waved when she saw Rachel. "There's Rachel with my tea.

Well, have a seat and while you have tea, I'll look for a cookbook."

"I appreciate it, Etta, but I don't have time for tea. The girls are waiting in the truck. We're going grocery shopping."

Etta argued, of course she did. "Well, get the girls out."

Wyatt laughed, white teeth flashing in a kind of hot smile. He shook his head. "I'm not getting them out of the truck. If I do, I'll never round them up and get them back in the truck. I just thought rather than taking my chance with any old cookbook I found in the store, I'd see if you had one that spelled it all out."

Etta held the rail and walked up the steps, Wyatt following. "I'll see what I have. Something with casseroles would be best."

"If I can throw the whole meal in one pan, I guess that would be the best thing."

"You ought to know how to cook, Wyatt. It isn't like you're a kid."

"I never thought much about it, Etta." His neck turned a little red. "I guess I always thought…"

Etta's eyes misted and she patted his arm. "I'll be right back. I'll pick you out a couple and you'll be cooking us dinner in no time."

After Etta walked away, Rachel didn't know what to say. She hadn't been at a loss for words in years. Probably about twenty-eight of them. Her mom liked to tell people that she was talking in complete sentences when she was two and that she'd been talking ever since.

But at that moment she was pretty near speechless and so was Wyatt Johnson.

"My mother-in-law is coming to visit." He had placed

the cowboy hat back on his head. He leaned against the rail of the porch, tall and confident. His boots were scuffed and his jeans were faded and worn in spots.

How many people would guess that the Johnson brothers had part ownership of a bank in Tulsa and subdivisions named after their family? She only knew those things because Andie, Wyatt's sister-in-law and Etta's granddaughter, had told her. Andie had married Ryder Johnson before Christmas and their twin babies were due in a month or so.

"I see." She nearly offered to help, and then she didn't. She'd already told him she'd clean or watch the girls. He'd rejected both offers.

"She's worried that I'm not coping." His smile lifted one corner of his mouth and he shrugged. "I guess it won't hurt me or the girls to have a home-cooked meal once in a while."

"I imagine it won't." Rachel poured her tea. "Do you want a cup?"

"No, thanks. I like my tea on ice and out of a glass that holds more than a swallow."

She smiled and listened for Etta's footsteps. Etta would give him a long lecture if she heard him demean her afternoon tea ritual.

It was a few minutes before Etta appeared, her arms holding more than a few cookbooks. "Here's a few to get you started."

"That's a half dozen, Etta, not a few."

"Well, you can find what you really like this way."

He took the books from her arms. "Thanks, Etta. Rachel, see you at church."

He nodded to each of them and walked down the steps.

The truck was pulling down the driveway when Etta laughed a little and whistled. "That's tension you could cut with a knife."

"What?" Rachel nearly poured Etta's tea on the table.

"The two of you, circling like a couple of barn cats. I'm no expert, but I think it's called chemistry."

"I think it's called, Wyatt knows that everyone, including his brother, is trying to push me off on him."

"And would that be such a bad thing?" Etta sat down on the lavender wicker settee.

"I'm not sure, but I think he believes it probably would be."

"What about you?"

Rachel sipped her tea and ignored the question. Etta smiled and her brows shot up, but Rachel didn't bite. No way, no how was she chasing after Wyatt Johnson or any other man, for that matter. She'd done her chasing, she'd had her share of fix-ups, and she'd learned that it worked better to let things happen the way they were supposed to happen.

Or not. But she had decided a long time ago that being alone was better than pushing her way into the life of the wrong person.

It had been two days since Rachel cleaned and his house still looked pretty decent. Wyatt stood in the kitchen with its dark cabinets, black granite countertops and stainless steel appliances. A chef's kitchen for a guy who had to borrow cookbooks because he couldn't make mac and cheese. That was pretty bad.

He hadn't planned it, but Rachel was front and center in his mind again. She was a strange one. First glance and he would have thought she had all the confidence in the world. But the other day on Etta's porch, there had been something soft and kind of lost in her expression, in those dark eyes of hers.

Not that it was any of his concern.

He dropped bread into the toaster and started the coffeemaker. Excited voices and little feet pattering overhead meant the girls were up. His day was about to start.

At least he'd had fifteen minutes to himself. That didn't happen often these days. It hadn't happened much in the last eighteen months. Since Wendy left him.

He stopped in front of the kitchen window and looked out. For a minute he closed his eyes and remembered that he used to pray. He used to believe that with Wendy he could build a life far from this ranch and the chaos of his childhood. He opened his eyes and shook his head. Prayer these days was abbreviated. It went something like: *God, get me through another day.*

That would have to do for now. It was all he had in him, other than anger and guilt.

Eighteen months of trying to figure out what he could have done differently. He was still trying to come to terms with the reality that he couldn't have done anything more than he'd done. Wendy had made a choice.

The choice to leave him and their daughters. She wrote a note, opened a bottle of sleeping pills and she'd left them for good.

Eighteen months of wondering what he could have done to stop her from going away.

He breathed in deep and it didn't hurt as much as yesterday, even less than a month ago. He was making it. He had to make it—for the girls. He had to smile and make each day better for them. And he calculated that he had about two minutes before they hit the kitchen, ready for breakfast. Two minutes to pull it together and make this day better.

On cue, they rushed in, still in their pajamas. Man, they made it easy to smile. He leaned to hug them and pulled them up to hold them both. He brushed his whiskered cheek against Kat and she giggled.

"What are we going to do today, girlies?"

"Get a pony!" Kat shouted and then she giggled some more.

"Nope, not a pony." He kissed her cheek.

"Let Miss Rachel clean again." Molly's tone was serious but her smile was real, her eyes shining. She knew how to work him.

He sat both girls on the granite-topped island that sat in the center of the kitchen. "Miss Rachel? Why do you want her to clean?"

He liked the idea of a clean house, but he was determined to find a nice grandmotherly type. He wanted control top socks and cookies baking in the oven. It sounded a lot less complicated than Miss Rachel I've-Got-Secrets Waters.

Kat sighed, as if he couldn't possibly be her dad or he would understand why they picked Rachel. She leaned close. "She hugs me."

"She draws pictures and sings." Molly crossed her arms and her little chin came up. "She has sheep."

"I'm sure she does. But she's really busy with church and helping Miss Etta."

"She doesn't mind cleaning." Molly was growing up and her tone said that she had a handle on this situation.

"Look, girls, she just cleaned for us that one time. Uncle Ryder hired her." He reached into the cabinet under the island and pulled out a cereal box. Add that to his list for the day. He needed to go to the store again. Even though he'd had a list, he'd forgotten a lot. "How about cereal?"

"And a pony?" Kat grinned and her eyes were huge.

A pony. Would it work to buy himself a break from this?

"Maybe a pony." He was so weak. "But first we have to eat breakfast and then we need to go outside and feed the horses and cows we already have."

He lifted them down from the counter and sat them each on a stool at the island.

"You girls are getting big."

Molly. He shook his head because she wasn't just big, she acted like an old soul, as if she'd had to learn too much too soon. And she had.

Most of it he doubted she remembered. If she did, the memories were vague. But she remembered being afraid. He knew she remembered that.

He took bowls out of the cabinet and set one in front of each girl and one for himself. He opened the cereal cabinet door again and looked at the half-dozen boxes. "Chocolate stuff, fruity stuff or kind-of-healthy stuff?"

The girls giggled a little.

"That does it, you get kind-of-healthy today. I think you've had way too much sugar because you're both so sweet." He grabbed the box and then reached for the girls and held them, kissing their cheeks. "Yep, sweet enough."

Normal moments, the kind a dad should share with his daughters. Eighteen long months of going through the motions, but they were all coming back to life. They were building something new here, in this house. They would have good memories. He hadn't expected to have something good for his family here, in Dawson. His own dad hadn't provided that for him and Ryder.

But he wasn't his dad. He guessed he learned something from his dad's mistakes. Like how to be faithful. And how to be there.

His phone rang and he answered it as he poured cereal into three bowls. Two partially filled and his to the top. He talked as he poured milk and dug in a drawer for spoons. When he hung up both girls were looking at him.

"I have to go pick up something for Uncle Ryder." He ate his cereal standing across the counter from the girls.

"A pony?" Kat giggled as she spooned cereal into her mouth. Milk dribbled down her chin and her brown eyes twinkled.

"No, a bull."

"We can go?" Molly didn't touch her cereal and he knew, man, he knew how scared she was. He was just starting to get over it, *he* hadn't been a two-year-old kid alone with a mommy who wouldn't wake up.

That kind of fear and pain changed a person. Molly was watching him, waiting for him to be the grown-up, the one who smiled and showed her that it was okay to be happy.

"Of course you can go." He took a bite of cereal and she followed his example. She even smiled. He let out a sigh that she didn't hear.

Fifteen minutes later he walked out the back door with them on his heels. Today they'd slipped back into the old pattern of leaving dishes on the counter and dirty clothes on the floor in the bedroom. He didn't have time to worry about it right now. He'd barely had time to pull on his boots and find his hat.

Horses saw him and whinnied. The six mares in the field closest to the house headed toward their feed trough. He whistled and in the other field about a dozen horses lifted their heads and headed toward the barn, ready for grain.

A quick glance over his shoulder confirmed that Kat and Molly were close behind him. They weren't right on his heels now, but they were following, grabbing up dandelions and chasing after the dog.

He turned away from the girls and headed for the fence. He watched for a chestnut mare. She walked a short distance behind the others. Her limp was slight today. She'd gotten tangled in old barbed wire out in the field. Sometimes a good rain washed up a lot of junk from the past.

This mare had stepped into that junk one day last week after a gully washer of a rain. He'd found her with gashes in her fetlock and blood still oozing from the wound. She headed for the fence and him, the extra attention over the last week had turned her into a pet.

A car driving down the road honked. He turned to wave. The red convertible slowed and pulled into his drive. The girls hurried to his side, jabbering about Rachel's car. He had worked hard at building a safe life for his girls.

What was it about Rachel that shook it all up? He glanced down at his girls and they didn't look too scared.

He tossed the thought aside. Rachel was about the safest person in the world. She was a Sunday school teacher and the preacher's daughter.

So what part of her life had been crazy enough for butterfly tattoos?

* * *

Rachel had meant to drive on past the Johnson ranch, but the girls waving dandelions had done it for her. She had seen them from a distance, first noticing the horses running for the fence and then spotting Wyatt and his girls. She had slowed to watch and then she'd turned.

As she pulled up to the barn she told herself this was about the craziest thing she'd done since… She had to think about it and one thing came to mind. The tattoo.

She'd thought about having it removed, but she kept it to remind herself to make decisions based on the future and not the moment. So what in the world was she doing here, at Wyatt Johnson's? He probably wanted her around as much as she wanted to be there.

This was definitely a spontaneous decision and not one that was planned out. Stupid. Stupid. Stupid.

The girls dropped the dandelions and raced across the lawn, the dog at their heels. As she pushed her door open, Molly and Kat were there, little faces scrubbed clean and smiles bright. No matter what, he'd done a great job with the girls, even if he did seem to be color-blind. That had to be the reason the girls never seemed to have an outfit that matched.

This time they were in their pajamas.

"What are you girls up to?"

"We're going with Daddy." Molly held tight to her hand.

Wyatt had disappeared. Into the barn, she decided. She could hear him talking and heard a door shut with a thud. He walked back out, his hat pulled down to block the sun from his face. He had a bag of grain tossed over his shoulder, his biceps bulging.

She let the girls tug her hands to follow him. He

stopped at a gate and unlatched it with his free hand. Cattle were at a trough, waiting. From outside the fence she watched him yank the string on the top of the bag and pour it down the length of the trough. He walked back with the empty bag. After closing the gate he tossed the bag into a nearby barrel.

And then he was staring at her. The hat shaded his face, but it definitely didn't hide the questions in his dark eyes. And she didn't have answers. What could she tell him, that her car suddenly had a mind of its own? But she'd have to think of something because the girls were pulling her in his direction.

"What are you up to today?" He pulled off leather gloves and shoved them in the back pocket of his jeans.

She didn't have an answer. The girls were holding her hands and she was staring into the dark eyes of a man who had been hurt to the deepest level. And survived. Those eyes were staring her down, waiting for an answer.

She was on his territory. She'd never felt it more than at that moment, that territorial edge of his. He protected the ones he loved.

"I saw the girls and I realized you might not know about our church picnic Wednesday evening. Instead of our normal service, we're roasting hot dogs and marshmallows."

It wasn't a lie, she had forgotten to remind him. He seemed to need reminding from time to time. He had a degree in ministry and yet church seemed to be something he forced himself to do. She got that. She had done her share of avoiding church, too.

He'd actually been in youth ministry until eighteen months ago.

"Sounds like fun." He glanced at his watch.

"I should go. Listen, if you need anything, any more help around here…"

"Right, I'll let you know."

She should have known better than to think he'd want to talk. A momentary glitch in her good sense had made her believe that he might want a friend. But then, he probably had friends. He'd grown up here.

"See you two Wednesday." Time to walk away.

Kat grabbed her hand. "Come and see my frog."

"Kat, you don't have a frog." Wyatt reached for her but Kat pulled Rachel the other direction and two-year-olds were pretty strong when they had their mind set on something.

"I have a frog." She didn't let go and Rachel didn't have the heart to tell her no. She went willingly in the direction of an old log.

"Is that where your frog lives?"

"There are millions of frogs." Kat dropped to her knees and pushed the chunk of wood. Sure enough, little frogs hopped out. Actually, they were baby toads. She didn't correct the toddler.

"Wow, Kat, there are a bunch of them." Rachel kneeled next to the child. "Do you have names for them?"

Kat nodded. "But I don't 'member."

"I think they're beautiful. I bet they like living under this log."

Kat nodded, her eyes were big and curls hung in her eyes. Rachel pushed the hair back from the child's face and Kat smiled. A shadow loomed over them. Kat glanced up and Rachel turned to look up at Wyatt. He was smiling down at his daughter. The smile didn't include Rachel.

He had a toe-curling smile, though, and she wanted her toes to curl. Which was really just plain wrong.

"Kat, we have to go, honey." He got hold of Molly's hand. "I have to finish feeding and you two need to be getting ready to jump in the truck."

"We're getting a pony." Kat patted Rachel's cheek with a dirty hand that had just released a toad back to its home under the log.

"Are you?" She looked up and Wyatt shook his head.

"We're picking up a bull."

"I see." Rachel stood and dusted off her jeans. "I could stay here with them, Wyatt."

She had offered the other day and he'd said no, so why in the world was she offering again? Oh, right, because she loved, loved, loved rejection. And to make it better, she loved that look on his face when his eyes narrowed and he looked at her as if she had really fallen off the proverbial turnip truck.

He took in a breath and she wondered why it was so hard for him to leave them. "No, they can go with me."

"But we could stay, and Miss Rachel could help us draw pictures." Molly bit down on rosy lips and big tears welled up in her eyes. "I always get carsick."

"I'm sorry, I shouldn't have said anything."

"That's a thought." Wyatt picked up his little girl. "Molly, you're going with me."

She nodded and rested her head on his shoulder.

"I'll see you later." Rachel brushed a hand down Molly's little back.

Yes, driving up here had been the wrong thing to do. She leaned to kiss Kat's cheek and then she walked away. She had a life. She had things to do today. She definitely didn't need to get tied up in the heartache that was Wyatt Johnson's life.

She made it to her car without looking back.

Wyatt put Molly down and he held tight to Kat's hand because he had a feeling that if he let go, she was going to run after Rachel. Molly was looking up at him, as if she was wondering why in the world he wasn't the one running after her new favorite person.

He needed this as much has he needed to hit his thumb with a hammer. If God would give him a break, he'd get the hammer and hit his thumb twice.

He wasn't going to run after a woman, not one who made more trouble in his life. And that's what she was doing. She was causing him a lot of trouble. She was upsetting the organized chaos of his life with her sunny personality and cute little songs.

She was getting in her car and Kat was next to him, begging him to stop her. He stared at the preacher's daughter in jean shorts and a T-shirt. Not for himself, for Kat. Man, he didn't need this. He let go of his daughter's hand and went after Rachel. Yelling when she started her car. Waving for her to stop when she put it in reverse.

The radio was blasting from the convertible. She loved music. He shook his head because today she was listening to Taylor Swift and a song about teen romance gone wrong. He really didn't need this.

She had stopped and she turned the radio down and waited for him to get to her. This was proof that he'd do anything for his girls. He'd even put up with Miss

Merry Sunshine for a couple of hours if it made Molly and Kat smile.

When he reached the car she turned and lifted her sunglasses, pushing them on top of her head. He realized that her eyes were darker than he'd thought, and bigger. They were soft and asked questions.

"The girls really want you to go with us. I thought it might help. They'll be bored if this takes too long."

She just stared at him.

"I'll pay you," he offered with a shrug that he hoped was casual and not as pathetic as he imagined.

She laughed and the sound went through him. "Pay me?"

"For watching them."

She was going to make him beg. He shoved his hat down a little tighter on his head and then loosened it.

"You don't have to pay me. It would be kind of fun to see that bull. Is it one they'll use for bull riding?"

"Yeah, probably."

"Fun. Where should I park?"

He pointed to the carport near the barn. "That'll keep it a little cooler. I have to finish feeding and the girls have to get dressed."

"Can I help?"

Hadn't she helped enough?

"No, I can do it." He walked away because it was a lot easier than staying there to answer more of her questions. He knew it probably seemed rude, but she didn't have a clue.

She didn't know that he was rebuilding his family and that it took every bit of energy he had. Everything he had went to his girls, into making them smile and making their lives stable.

As he walked into the barn he glanced back. She leaned to talk to Kat. Curls fell forward, framing her face, but a hand came up to push her hair back. She smiled and leaned to kiss his daughter on the cheek. And then the three of them, Rachel, Kat and Molly, headed into the house.

He walked into the shadowy interior of the barn and flipped on a light. He breathed in the familiar scents. Cows, horses, hay and leather. He could deal with this. He couldn't deal with Mary Poppins.

Chapter Three

If it hadn't been for Kat and Molly she wouldn't have climbed into this truck and taken a ride with Wyatt. But the girls, with their sweet smiles and tight hugs, they were what mattered. Little girls should never hurt. They shouldn't hide their pain in cheesecake or think their self-worth depended on the brand and size of their jeans.

Oh, wait, that had been her, her childhood, her pain.

"You aren't carsick, are you?" Wyatt's voice was soft, a little teasing. Yummier than cheesecake. And she hadn't had cheesecake in forever.

She glanced his way and smiled. "I don't get carsick."

"Good to know. The girls do. Not on roads like this, fortunately."

"We keep a trash can back here." Molly informed her with the voice of young authority. Rachel heard the tap, tap of a tiny foot on plastic.

She looked over her shoulder at the two little girls on the bench seat behind her. Kat's eyes were a little droopy and she nodded, her head sagging and then bouncing up. Molly looked as if she had a lot more to say but she was holding back.

Poor baby girls. Wyatt loved them, but there was an empty space in their lives that a mom should have filled. And they wouldn't even have memories of her as they grew older. They would have pictures and stories their dad told.

If he told stories. She chanced a quick glance in his direction and thought he probably didn't tell stories about the wife he'd lost. He probably had a boat load of memories he wished he could lose.

"Here we are." He flipped on the turn signal and smiled at her as he pulled into a gated driveway. "Can you pull through and I'll open the gate?"

"I can open the gate." She reached for the door handle and opened it, ignoring his protests. It was a lot easier to be outside away from him. A soft breeze blew in warm spring air and she could hear cattle at a nearby dairy farm.

She loved Oklahoma. Growing up she'd lived just about everywhere, but mostly in bigger towns and cities. She'd never felt like she belonged. Maybe because she had always been the pastor's kid, poor in wealthy subdivisions, trying to fit in. Or maybe because deep down she'd always wanted to be a country girl.

She had wanted to jump out of trucks and open gates. She had studied about sheep, wool and gardening. Pitiful as it sounded, she'd watched so many episodes of *The Waltons,* she could quote lines. She couldn't think about it now without smiling.

The truck eased through the gate and stopped. She pushed the gate closed and latched the chain. When she climbed back into the truck, Wyatt wasn't smiling.

"I said I'd get it." He shifted into gear and the truck eased forward again.

"I don't mind."

"No, you don't."

Oh, no, he hadn't! She shot him a look. "I'm not five. I don't mind opening gates. I really don't have to *mind* you."

His brows went up. He reached for the hat he'd set on the seat next to him and pushed it back on his head. The chicken wasn't going to comment. She glanced back at the girls and smiled. Kat was sleeping. Molly stared out the window, her eyelids drooping.

Wyatt parked next to the barn, still silent. But when she glanced his way, she saw the smile. It barely lifted the corners of his mouth, but it was there.

"This shouldn't take long." He opened his door and paused. "I think you and the girls can get out and look around."

"Thanks, we'll do that. If you think I can handle it. After all, I'm five."

"You're not five. You're just…" He shook his head and got out of the truck. He didn't say anything else. He opened the back door of the truck and motioned for the girls to get out. He set each of them on the ground and then glanced back in at her. "Getting out?"

"Yeah, I'm getting out."

She'd been crazy to stop at his house. She was still trying to figure it out. He smiled at something Kat said. Oh, that's right, now she remembered. It was that smile. She wanted him to smile like that at her.

"Wyatt, good to see you."

She turned to face the man who'd spoken. He stood outside the barn and everything about him said "rancher." From his dusty boots to his threadbare jeans, he was a cowboy. His skin was worn and suntanned, making deeper lines around his mouth and crinkles at his eyes. His hair was sun-streaked brown. He winked at her.

"Jackson, I'm surprised to see you here. I thought your brother was meeting me." Wyatt stepped toward the other man, hand extended.

"Yeah, he's at the bank. You know, he's Mr. Workaholic."

"Got it. So what are you doing these days?"

"Oh, trying to stay away from trouble. But most of the time, trouble just seems to find me." He smiled at Rachel. "Hi there, Trouble."

Heat climbed her cheeks.

"Jackson Cooper, meet Rachel Waters. Her father is the pastor of the Dawson Community Church."

If Wyatt had used that introduction to put the other man in his place, Jackson Cooper didn't look at all embarrassed. "If our pastor's daughter looked like you, I might just get right with God."

Wyatt wasn't smiling. "Okay, let's look at the bull."

"You gonna ride him?" Jackson laughed.

"I doubt it."

"Chicken?" Jackson Cooper obviously didn't know about backing down. She thought it might be a family trait; not backing down. She had heard about the Coopers. There were about a dozen of them: biological and adopted.

"Nope, just smarter than I used to be. I haven't been on a bull in a half-dozen years and I don't plan on starting again."

"There's a lot more money in it these days," Jackson continued, his smile still in place.

"Plenty of money in raising them, too." Wyatt turned

to his daughters. "You girls stay with Rachel and I'll be back in a few minutes."

The men left them and Rachel smiled down at the girls. "I think we should make clover chains."

One last glance over her shoulder. Wyatt picked that moment to stop and watch them, to watch his girls. Rachel turned away.

"Nice bull." Young, but definitely worth the money the Coopers were asking. Wyatt watched the young animal walk around the corral. He was part Brahma, long and rangy with short legs. He'd been used in local rodeos last year and was already on the roster for some bigger events.

"Want me to get a bull rope and chaps?" Jackson leaned over the corral, a piece of straw in his mouth.

"No, I think we know what he'll do. And we know where you live if he doesn't."

"He'll go out of the chute to the right for about four spins and then switch back and spin left. He's got a belly roll you won't believe."

"Your brother, Blake, told Ryder that he isn't mean." Wyatt continued to watch the bull. The animal pushed at an old tire and then stomped the dusty ground.

"He's never hurt anyone. But he's a bull, Wyatt. They're unpredictable, we both know that."

"Yeah, I know we do." They'd lost a friend years ago. They'd been teenagers riding in junior events when Jimmy got killed at a local event.

"That was a rough one, wasn't it?" Jackson's sister had dated Jimmy.

"Yeah, it was rough." He brushed away the memories. "Do I write you a check?"

"Sure. So, is she your nanny?" Jackson nodded in the direction of Rachel Waters. She was in the large yard and the girls were with her. They were picking clover and Rachel slipped a chain of flowers over Molly's head.

Wendy should have been there, doing those things with their daughters. He let out a sigh and refocused on the bull. It took a minute to get his thoughts back on track. Jackson didn't say anything.

"No, she isn't." Wyatt pulled the checkbook out of his back pocket. "I like the bull, Jackson. I don't like your price."

Jackson laughed. "Well, now, Wyatt, I don't know that I care if you like my price or not."

"He isn't worth it and you know it."

"So what do you think would make him worth it?" Jackson's smile disappeared. Yeah, that was the way to wipe good-natured off a guy's face, through his bank account.

"I've been thinking of adding Cooper Quarter Horses to our breeding program. I'd like one of your fillies." His gaze swept the field and landed on a small herd of horses. One stuck out, but it wasn't quite what he'd planned to ask for. "And that pony."

"You want a pony. Shoot, Wyatt, I'll throw in the pony. We'll have to talk about the horse, though. This bull's daddy was Bucking Bull of the Year two years in a row. He isn't a feedlot special."

"Okay, let's talk." Wyatt let his gaze slide to where the girls were still playing with Rachel. Kat was sitting on the grass, a big old collie next to her. Molly and Rachel were spinning in circles.

They needed her. The thought settled so deep inside of him that it ached. His girls needed Rachel. Maybe more than they needed him. He couldn't make chains with clover or even manage a decent braid in their hair.

"Do you think she'd go out with me?" Jackson walked over to the gate and tugged it open. "I mean, if you're not interested."

"I'm not interested." Wyatt walked through the gate, sidestepping a little snake that slid past. "I'm not interested, but I think maybe you're not her type. Shoot, I'm probably not her type either."

"Yeah, well, I always had this idea that when I settle down it'd be with a woman like her, the kind that goes to church on Sundays and probably makes a mean roast." Jackson shot him a smile. "Yeah, a guy would live right with a wife like her."

"Right." He'd had enough of this talk. "Let's take a look at the pony first. How old?"

"Ten. He was my niece's. But Tash is getting older and Greg bought her a bigger horse."

"I don't want to take someone's pony."

"He's just eating grass and getting fat."

Wyatt stopped in front of the paint pony. It was a pretty thing, brown and white spotted with a black mane and tail. The pony lifted its head from the clover that it was munching on and gave him a look.

"He isn't mean?"

"Never seen him be mean."

Wyatt knew all about horse traders and lines like that. He wasn't about to take Jackson Cooper's word for it. He patted the fat pony and leaned against him, holding his mane to keep him close.

"Yeah, but I want a little more reassurance than that, Jackson. This is for my kids."

Jackson walked up and lifted a leg to settle it over

the pony's back. His normal smile had disappeared and he was all serious. "Wyatt, I might be a lot of things, but I can tell you this: I wouldn't get a kid hurt. This pony is the safest one you'll find. I broke him myself and I wouldn't be afraid to let my own kids on him. If I had a kid."

Wyatt nodded and he didn't take his eyes off the pony. Even with part of Jackson's weight on his back, the little pony hadn't moved, hadn't been distracted from the clover he was tugging at. He didn't even startle when shouts from the gate meant that he'd been spotted by the girls.

The girls were on the gate, standing midway up, waving. Rachel stood next to them, her smile as big as theirs. He wondered if she was still dreaming of having a pony someday? He'd known girls like her his whole life. Wannabe cowgirls. He used to like them. They were fun on a Friday night at a rodeo in Tulsa. They were easy to impress and soft to hold.

That had been a lifetime and another Wyatt Johnson ago. Before. His life fell into two slots. Before Wendy, and after. The first half had been full of hope and promise. The second was about getting it back.

He was just standing there, staring, when Jackson waved them into the field. They yelled and before Rachel could open the gate, they were running toward him. The little pony looked up, watching, dark ears pricked forward. Yeah, he'd do for a first pony.

Rachel caught up with the girls halfway across the field and spoke to them. He watched them settle and reach for her hands. One on each side of her.

Jackson whistled and shook his head, laughing a little. Wyatt shot him a sideways glance and shoved his hands in his pockets.

"Keep it to yourself, Jackson."

"I'm just saying…"

"Yeah, I know what you're saying." He wasn't blind.

And then the girls were there, Rachel standing quietly behind them. They were all hands, reaching for the pony, saying it was the prettiest pony ever. Jackson Cooper looked as if he had created the thing himself and set it in front of them with a ribbon.

"Be careful, girls." Rachel moved closer and her hand went out, reaching to brush through the pony's mane.

"What do you think, girls? Would this be a good pony?" Wyatt wanted to be the hero. He'd been fighting the pony conversation for a while. They were still little, still needed to be held and couldn't brush their teeth alone. He'd been on horses his entire life, but that was different. When it came to his girls, it was different.

Molly nodded. "This is a perfect pony named Prince."

"Actually, his name is…" Jackson grinned. "His name is Prince."

Rachel smiled at him. Wyatt lifted his hat and settled it back in place. "We'll take him. And a filly."

"Let's talk price." Jackson looped a bit of rope around the pony's neck. "Can you girls lead Prince back to the barn so we can load him in the trailer?"

Molly was nodding, her hands moving in anticipation, but Jackson handed the lead rope to Rachel. Wyatt started to tell them to be careful, but he clamped his mouth shut. He hadn't been real good at letting go lately. It wasn't easy, letting someone else take care of Molly and Kat. It wasn't easy watching them with someone who was not their mother.

But they needed this. They needed to let go of him once in a while.

His good intentions almost came undone when halfway to the gate Rachel stopped, picked up Molly and then Kat and placed them on the back of that pony. Kat was in front and Molly wrapped her arms around her sister. Rachel stood close to them.

"Might as well breathe and let it go, Wyatt." Jackson laughed and slapped him on the back. "Two things are going to happen. They're going to grow up, and that woman's probably going to get under your skin."

Wyatt didn't smile. He watched as Rachel led the pony with his girls on it through the gate and then he settled his attention back on Jackson Cooper and the filly he wanted.

And he repeated to himself that Rachel Waters wasn't going to get under his skin.

Chapter Four

Stupid moment number twelve. Or maybe twelve thousand? That's what Rachel thought of volunteering to ride along with Wyatt and the girls to get that bull. And it was even worse standing in the shade watching Wyatt unload the pony from the trailer. He had hauled the pony and his new filly home. He'd left the bull for Jackson Cooper to trailer for him.

The girls stood next to Rachel, waiting for their dad to give the all clear. They fidgeted in one spot because they knew better than to run at the pony.

Wyatt led the filly, a dark bay two-year-old, into the barn. The horse pranced alongside him, her black tail waving like a banner. The filly dipped her head a few times and whinnied to horses in the field who answered back with shrill whinnies to the new girl in town.

Wyatt walked out of the barn a few minutes later. The filly was still inside, her shrill whinny continued. Wyatt pulled off his hat and swiped his brow with his arm. The girls were tugging on Rachel's hands, but she didn't let go. Somehow she managed to stand her ground.

He had told them to wait. She was more than willing to do what he asked. She was content to stay in one spot and watch as he stepped back into the trailer to retrieve the pony.

The second he stepped out of the trailer with the pony the girls started to jabber. Kat was pulling on her hand. Rachel leaned and picked the child up. When she looked up, Wyatt watched, his smile gone, his expression unreadable. He turned away and led the pony to the small corral next to the barn.

He closed the gate and tied the lead rope to the pole fence. "Come on over."

She put down Kat and the girls ran toward him. He held up his hand and they slowed to a walk. Rachel followed because it was time to say goodbye. It had been a good day. The girls were wonderful. Wyatt was a wonderful dad who loved his daughters.

He probably thought Rachel could be a decent friend.

She'd had a lifetime of being the best friend, the girl that guys called when they wanted a pal to hang out with. Funny that when she lost weight all of those best friends started looking at her in a different way.

Wyatt untied the lead rope. "If you want to hold her, I'll get the bridle and saddle."

"I can do that." So much for the quick escape. She took the rope and their fingers touched. She looked up, into dark eyes that held hers for a long moment. She looked away, back to the girls. Things that were easy.

Kat and Molly had climbed up on the bottom pole of the fence. They reached through and little fingers found the pony's mane.

"I'll be right back." Wyatt glanced from her to his

daughters and then he walked away, disappearing through the side door of the barn.

And she should do the same. She should tell him she had things to do today. She needed to clean her room or weed the garden. There were plenty of things she could have been doing.

It might be a good idea for her to go home and spend time in prayer.

When he came back with the tiny saddle and bridle, she opened her mouth to explain that she should go. But he smiled and she stayed.

She stayed and held the little pony as Wyatt lifted Kat and Molly onto his back. They rode double the first time, so that neither of them could say they got to ride first. Rachel stood by the gate watching as he led them around the corral. Kat was shaking the reins she held in her little hands, trying to make the pony run. Molly had her arms wrapped around her sister's waist and her smile was huge.

Wyatt lifted Molly off the saddle and put his hat on Kat's head. The black cowboy hat fell down over the child's eyes. She didn't mind. She had a pony.

Molly trudged across the arena and stopped next to Rachel. The little girl watched her sister ride the pony around the arena and as they got close, Molly started to bounce up and down.

"Might want to stand still, sweetie. We don't want to startle the pony," Rachel warned.

"Daddy said he didn't think a train going through would make him scared."

"He's a pretty special pony."

Molly looked up, her smile still splitting her little

face. She nodded and continued to bounce as Wyatt headed their way with Kat in the saddle.

As he pulled one daughter down and lifted the other, Rachel stood close. "I should go now. Thank you for letting me go with you today."

Wyatt took the hat off Kat's head and placed it on Molly's. He turned to Rachel, his smile still in place. The hair at the crown of his head was flat from wearing the hat.

"Thanks for going. Are you sure you don't want a turn?" He teased with an Oklahoma drawl and a half smile.

"No, I think probably not. My feet would drag on the ground and the poor pony would need a chiropractor."

"I doubt that." He handed the reins to Molly. "Hold tight, kiddo."

"Have fun with the pony." Rachel leaned to kiss Kat's cheek and she waved to Molly the cowgirl. "See you at church Wednesday."

She turned to walk away, but Wyatt touched her arm, stopping her. She smiled because he looked as surprised as she did. His hand was still on her arm, warm and rough against her skin.

"All joking aside, I really do appreciate you going with us today. I know the girls loved having you along."

She shrugged and his hand slid off her arm. "I enjoyed it as much as they did."

And then she stood there, unmoving. The moment needed an escape route, the kind posted in hotel rooms. It should read: In case of emergency, exit here.

Wyatt remembered the Wednesday evening bonfire fifteen minutes before it started. He pulled into the parking lot of the church and the fire was already going, and people were gathered around in lawn chairs. He killed the engine on his truck and glanced in the backseat.

"Oh, man, we really should have done something with your hair." But the girls' hair had been the last thing on his mind as they rushed out the door.

He'd spent the day working the new bull, bringing it into the chute and bucking it out with a dummy on its back. He knew that it would buck, he just wanted to see for himself what they'd gotten themselves into. In the next week or two he'd take him over to Clint Cameron's and let some of the teens that hung out over there give him a try.

But the bull aside, he'd also had to put out a fire in the kitchen. A cooking experiment had gone very wrong. Good thing he'd remembered the Wednesday evening bonfire. He smiled at the girls. Both had dirty faces, pigtails that were coming undone and boots with their shorts. He was pretty sure this was a real fashion catastrophe.

At least they were at church. He got out and opened the back door for the girls. They clambered down from the truck, jumping off the running board and then heading off to join Rachel and the other kids.

She was the pied piper of girls, big and small. Teenagers followed her around, talking as she worked. Sometimes she gave them jobs to do. As he stared she glanced quickly in his direction.

"She's our bonus."

He turned and Etta smiled at him.

"What does that mean?" He shoved his keys in his pocket and walked across the big lawn with Etta. He thought to offer her his arm, but she would have laughed and told him she was able to walk on her own steam.

"I mean, we got a great pastor and pastor's wife and Rachel is the bonus. She does so much in the church. Our youth and children's ministries have doubled. That's why Pastor Waters is thinking of hiring a youth minister."

"I'm not interested."

"In Rachel you mean?" Etta smiled and headed in the other direction.

"You know what I mean." He called out after her. She turned and waved, ornery as ever. And he loved her. He thought back to the hard times in his life. She had been there, getting him through every one of them. She'd even flown down to Florida after Wendy died. She'd stayed a month, helping with babies, helping him to breathe.

"Wyatt."

This time it was Jason Bradshaw and his wife Alyson. The happy couple headed is his direction. There was too much romance going on in this town for his comfort.

"How are you two?"

"Good. I'm glad to see you here. We're going to have music after we eat. We can always use another guitar, if you have yours."

"I left it here last week." Wyatt scanned the yard for his girls.

He saw them in the playground. Molly had just gone down the slide. Kat had her arms around Rachel's neck and was being carried to the swing.

"Then I'll find you when we're ready to get started." Jason followed the direction of his gaze and smiled.

"Sounds good. I need to check on the girls."

"Right, check on the girls." Jason laughed and shot a pointed look in the direction of Rachel Waters.

Wyatt ignored the insinuation. He headed across the lawn toward the playground. Rachel sat on a bench, Molly in front of her. She had ponytail holders in her mouth and a brush in her hand. When he got close enough she looked up and smiled.

"Do you mind?"

He shook his head. "No."

But he did mind. For reasons he didn't get, he minded. It might have been about her, or about himself, maybe it was about Wendy, but he minded.

She scooted and he got that it was an offer. He could sit down and let people say what they wanted or he could walk away. And people would still talk. It wouldn't be malicious, the talk. No, it would be pure Dawson. Everyone would be hoping to fix him.

Option one seemed like the best bet. He sat down next to her. Kat hurried to him and climbed on his lap. Her hair had already been fixed. He hadn't noticed from across the lawn.

Molly sat quietly. She never sat that still for him. Rachel talked about their pony, talked about s'mores and ran the brush through his daughter's tangled brown hair. When it was smooth she pulled it back, brushed it smooth again and held it tight. She had placed the ponytail holders on her wrist and she took them off, wrapping them around the ponytail, holding it firm at the crown of Molly's head.

"There you go, sweetie." Rachel kissed her cheek.

"You make it look easy."

She smiled at the comment. "It takes practice. You'll get the hang of it."

He wasn't so sure.

After cooking hot dogs and marshmallows in the fire, Rachel sat with the kids, making a circle around Jason, Wyatt and some others. The men started with a few praise songs and then switched to contemporary Christian music. The teens clapped and sang along.

Molly and Kat climbed into her lap, both of them snuggling close. She held them tight and pretended it didn't hurt. But it did. The other children had gone off to their mommies.

Molly and Kat had turned to her while their daddy sang. She wrapped them in an extra blanket her own mother had brought and the two dozed in her lap. Firelight flickered. The songs were softer, sweeter. She closed her eyes and listened.

When she opened her eyes her gaze sought another, connecting, holding. Wyatt looked away first, shifting his gaze down, to the strings of his guitar.

Etta moved from her chair and joined Rachel on the ground. She lowered herself onto the blanket and reached for Kat.

"Let me help you with that little sweet thing." Etta held the child close. "I do love these babies."

"Me, too." Rachel exhaled and a chill swept up her back. The night was getting cooler, the air was damp. The fire was burning out and the heat no longer reached where she sat.

"We should wrap this up." Jason Bradshaw put his drum down and looked around. The crowd had seriously disappeared. "Wow, where'd everyone go?"

"It's almost ten o'clock," Alyson informed him, smiling, her eyes revealing that she adored him.

"Wow." Jason leaned to kiss his wife.

Wyatt stood up, putting his guitar back in the case. He carried it to where she sat and leaned it against a chair. He towered over her and she breathed easier when he knelt next to them.

"Thank you for watching them for me."

Rachel held Molly close. "They were watching me."

"Let me get her and then I'll come back for Kat."

"I have an idea. You take her, I'll take Kat from Etta and carry her over for you."

He stared down at her and after a minute he nodded. But he had that look on his face, the same one as the other day when she'd opened the gate.

He took Molly from her arms, leaning in, his head close to Rachel's. She waited for him to move away before she stretched her legs and then stood. Etta smiled up at her, brows arching. But she didn't comment. Rachel loved that the other woman knew when to keep her thoughts to herself. Sometimes.

Rachel took Kat and held her in one arm. She extended her free hand and Etta took it, pulling herself to her feet.

"That ground isn't as soft as it used to be." Etta kissed Kat's cheek and hugged Rachel. "See you in a few days, Rachel Lynn."

"Let me know if you need me sooner."

"Will do, honey." And then Etta headed for Alyson.

Rachel headed toward the parking lot with Kat. When she reached Wyatt's truck Molly was already buckled in and his guitar case was in the front seat. He opened the driver's side back door and reached for

Kat. His hands slid against Rachel's arms. He caught her gaze, held it for a second and then moved away.

Rachel backed up a few steps. "They're easy to love."

He smiled at that. "Yeah, they are."

She took another step back, trying not to think too much. He leaned against his truck, always the cowboy in his faded jeans and worn boots. He had on a ball cap tonight, though, no cowboy hat.

Time to make her escape.

"I'll see you in a few days." She backed up, tripping over the curb.

A hand shot out, grabbing her arm, steadying her. He laughed a little and winked. "You might want to work on that walking thing."

"Yeah, I might."

He let go of her arm. "Good night, Rachel."

She watched him drive away and then she hurried back to the leftover embers of the fire.

Chapter Five

Wyatt never would have imagined that one little pony would be so much trouble. But a few days after they brought Prince home, Wyatt was starting to see what he'd done. The night before, the girls had ridden the poor little animal until sunset. Wyatt had finally insisted they go inside and eat something quick before they crashed.

This day had been more of the same. The sun wasn't going down, but it was suppertime and the girls were hungry and beat. He wasn't too far behind them. Wyatt herded them into the laundry room, trying to ignore the massive pile of laundry that needed to be done. He kicked off his boots as the girls sat on the floor and pulled theirs off.

"What are we gonna eat?" Molly sat on the floor, her arms crossed over her raised knees. "Are you gonna cook?"

The cookbooks. He bent to help Kat get her left boot off. Her cheeks were a little pink from the sun and her hair was tangled from the wind. They needed a bath and an early bedtime.

"I can try another recipe. I have hamburger."

Molly covered her face. "Not hamburgers."

Kat imitated her sister. "Not burgers."

"I don't mean hamburgers. I'll cook something *with* hamburger." He picked them up and walked into the kitchen. He put the girls down and Molly looked around, her face nearly as pink as her sister's. She opened the cabinet with cereal.

They'd had cereal the night before. And the night before that they'd eaten at the Mad Cow. He'd never been much of a cook. For the first year or so it hadn't seemed to matter. He'd been numb and food had just been food. Ryder had shaken him out of that way of thinking.

He really needed a housekeeper. He needed someone who could cook. He glanced at his girls sitting on the stools where they were waiting for him to cook something wonderful. Molly's braids were coming undone. She pulled it loose. They needed someone who could put ribbons in their hair.

Rachel Waters's image interrupted his thoughts and he pushed it aside as he reached into a drawer for the apron he'd bought a few days ago. He tied it around his waist and winked at his girls. They giggled and Kat covered her eyes.

Rachel Waters was not on the short list of people he could hire. He wasn't going to let her do this to him. She wasn't going to be traipsing around the place, smelling it up with her perfume, invading his peace and quiet.

"Okay, we need food."

"We need Rachel," Molly said, the voice of reason. He wasn't convinced. He had an apron. He could cook.

"Why do we need Rachel?" He stood next to his oldest daughter. Her arms wrapped around his waist and she held him close.

"She sings."

"Right, she sings." He didn't know if that qualified her to be their housekeeper. They needed a grandmotherly woman who knitted scarves. Yeah, that would be perfect.

"I'm hungry." Kat rubbed sleepy eyes with her pudgy fists.

"Right, and I'm cooking." Something quick and easy. He opened the casserole cookbook and found a recipe that included tater tots, soup and hamburger. Man, what could be easier than that?

Molly stared, her expression skeptical as he tossed the thawed hamburger into a heated pan and then turned on the oven to preheat. He glanced at the cookbook. To four hundred degrees.

"I can do this, Mol, I promise."

"Promise?" Kat covered her eyes again and peeked between her fingers.

"Kat, it isn't going to be that scary. Why don't you go wash up and it'll be ready soon."

Kat was drooping like some of the plants in the den. He guessed he had about ten minutes to get something in her before she crashed. They'd been having so much fun on the pony he hadn't paid attention to the time.

Eighteen long months of trying to make the right decisions. Eighteen months of wondering what he could have done to change the course of their lives. He should have noticed something that day when he left Wendy and the girls for a youth retreat.

He stirred the hamburger until it turned brown.

Instead of noticing the look in Wendy's eyes, he'd

kissed her goodbye and wondered why she held him so long before he walked out the door. Even now, eighteen long months later, the memory shook him. He started to slam his fist into the wall, but the girls were there, watching. They kept him sane. They kept him being a dad and living his life.

They kept him in church when he would have liked to walk away. They kept him from being so angry that he couldn't go on.

"Hey, you girls going to go clean up?"

He turned and Kat's head was on the granite top that covered the kitchen island. A chef's kitchen for a guy who could barely manage a bowl of cereal. Pretty crazy.

When he talked to the contractor last fall, he had this idea that a great kitchen would inspire him to cook. Instead, it inspired him to spend as much time as possible in the barn.

Molly stared up at him, her dark eyes seeing too much. She wasn't even four years old. She needed to chase butterflies and ride ponies, not spend her days worrying about her dad or what they'd feed her little sister. He hugged her.

"We can have cereal, Daddy," she whispered in his ear.

"No, we're not going to have cereal. We're going to have a casserole. Kat can nap while I cook." He glanced at the clock. It was almost seven. "Let's go wash your hands and I'll put your sister on the couch. We'll straighten up while the casserole cooks."

"You're a bad cleaner, Daddy." Molly leaned her head on his shoulder. "And you even burned our grilled cheese."

"I know, pumpkin, but tonight will be better. I have a cookbook."

Fifteen minutes later the smoke detector was going off and Kat was screaming the house down. He ran down the hall to grab a broom and he knocked the offending alarm off the ceiling. Smoke filled the kitchen and someone was banging on the back door.

Just what he needed. No reason to call and warn a person that you planned to visit.

"Come in." He could hear the girls crying. The upstairs smoke detector was now going off and the back-door banged shut.

"Do I need to call the fire department?"

He was pouring baking soda on the flaming hamburger meat when his mother-in-law appeared at his side and sat a lid on the fiasco that was supposed to be dinner. His baking soda had already worked to put out the flames. He'd remembered that much from something he'd read years ago.

"Grandma." Molly and Kat in unison ran to Violet and hugged her legs. She hugged them back.

"Girls, get your shoes on, we're going to the Mad Cow." He ignored Violet and smiled at his daughters. And he hated ignoring Violet. She'd been more of a parent to him than the two he'd been stuck with at birth.

"This was their dinner?" Violet stood and flipped on the exhaust fan before opening the window over the sink. "Honestly, Wyatt, this isn't what I wanted to see when I showed up here."

"Well, Violet, I'm not sure what to tell you. Accidents happen."

"Of course they do."

Okay, so she was making him feel like a ten-year-old kid who had gotten caught writing on the bathroom wall. He jerked off the apron and tossed it on the counter. "Look, Violet, we're fine. The girls are fine."

"I know you're fine." She fiddled with the diamond rings on her left hand. "I'm not here to grade your progress. I'm here to see you."

"I didn't know you were going to be here today."

"I wanted to surprise the girls." Her arms were around his daughters again.

"I see." It felt like some kind of snap inspection.

"Let's take the girls to the diner and later we can talk."

"Talk about what, Violet?" He shot a look past her, to his daughters and he smiled a little softer smile. "You girls go find shoes and wash your hands and faces before we go."

Molly took Kat by the hand and led her out of the kitchen, down the hall. He could hear their little girl jabber and once they were out of earshot, he turned his attention back to Violet. He hadn't noticed before that she had dark circles under her eyes and more gray in her dark hair than the last time he'd seen her.

But then, he wasn't the most observant guy in the world.

"What is it we're going to talk about?" he reminded her when she didn't say anything.

"About the girls coming to spend time with me."

"Violet, I'll bring the girls to see you. Maybe in a week or two. We'll spend a couple of nights." He knew that wasn't what she wanted.

He pretended it was as he walked out the door to the laundry room and slid his feet into his boots. Violet followed him. She didn't belong here. She wore designer dresses and diamonds. Wendy had worn jeans and T-shirts.

A jacket on the hook next to his hat caught his attention. Not his jacket. He closed his eyes and remembered Rachel taking it off and hanging it there. Man, for a minute he almost felt at ease.

He glanced away, not wanting Violet to notice that jacket. It didn't mean anything, but it would imply a lot. He didn't want that hornet's nest opened, especially when there was nothing to know.

"You know that isn't what I mean. I don't want a day visit, Wyatt." Violet was a small woman with a will the size of Mount Rushmore. "I want to take the girls, maybe for the summer. I think you need time to get your head on straight. You can't do this, taking care of them, the house and the ranch, alone. I know you're trying, but you need help."

Anger simmered and he couldn't look at her. If his head hadn't been on straight, as she'd implied, he would have lost it right at that moment. He reached for his hat and shoved it down on his head. What he really wanted to do was walk out the door. If it hadn't been for his girls he might have.

"I'm together, Violet. I'm not a perfect parent. My cooking skills are pretty limited, but I'm doing what counts. I'm here every single day taking care of my girls. I'm the person making their breakfast and the guy who tucks them in at night."

Tears welled up in Violet's eyes. "I know you're a good dad. But I also think that maybe you're suffering and that isn't good for my granddaughters."

He turned away from his mother-in-law and rested

a hand on the door, sucking in deep breaths, trying to keep it together before she had a real case against him.

"I'm not letting you take my girls."

"Wyatt, I didn't say I wanted to *take* them. I want to give you a break. Maybe you can find a housekeeper, someone to help with cooking and laundry? They're my granddaughters and I'm worried, that's all."

His daughters. He started to remind her of that fact, but footsteps in the hallway stopped him. He looked past Violet and smiled at Kat and Molly.

Molly's nose scrunched and her eyes narrowed as she looked from her father to her grandmother and he wondered how much she'd overheard, or if she'd heard any of it. Maybe she sensed the problem. Either way, he wasn't going to let her be a part of this.

Violet picked up her purse. She opened her mouth and he shot her a look that stopped her from saying more.

"Let's go, girls. We're going to the Mad Cow and I bet Vera will cook us up something special."

"Fried bologna sandwich?" Molly's eyes lit up and Violet gasped.

Wyatt picked up his two girls, one in each arm and walked through the back door, leaning against it to hold it open for his mother-in-law. She wasn't smiling and he didn't know if it was because she'd given up or was planning a new strategy. Maybe she was still trying to get over the idea of fried bologna?

A housekeeper, she'd said. As if he hadn't given it a lot of thought. But the one person that kept coming to mind was the last person he needed in his home on a daily basis.

Violet stood there for a moment, not walking through

the door. He didn't have a clue what she expected from him. Maybe she wanted him to promise to send the girls with her, or maybe she expected him to cave on the subject of a housekeeper.

She walked out the door and he made the worst decision he figured he'd made in years.

"Okay, Violet, I'll hire a housekeeper." He let the door close and he followed her down the steps to her car. She'd won. He didn't know how, but he did know that this was a victory for his mother-in-law.

A warm breeze whipped the sheets on the clothesline. In the bright light of the full moon, Rachel unpinned the clothes she'd hung up earlier and pulled them down. She folded the crisp sheets, holding them to her face to breathe in the outdoor scent. They smelled like clover and fresh air.

The clip-clop of hooves on the paved road caught her attention. She looked into the dark and wondered who was lucky enough to be riding tonight. It was a beautiful evening with a clear sky and a light breeze that promised rain, but not yet.

She stood in the dark holding a pillow case she'd pulled down from the line and whispering for her dog to stay still. The German shepherd stayed at her side but he growled low, a warning for anyone who came too close.

The horse stopped and then the clip-clop continued. Instead of going down the road it was coming up the drive, hooves crunching on gravel. She grabbed the dog's collar.

"Laundry this late at night?" Wyatt's voice called from the dark shadows.

"Riding this late at night?"

He rode closer and the moonlight caught his face and the big gray that he rode. She shivered and felt the chill of the breeze against her arms.

"I had to get out of the house."

"Who's with the girls?" It came out like an accusation. She hadn't meant that. "I'm sorry, that's none of my business."

"No, it isn't." He sat steady on the horse that shifted a little and pawed the ground. "My mother-in-law."

"Oh, I see." But she didn't. She didn't know Wyatt, not really. She didn't know his life, other than caring about the girls and hearing about his wife's death. He didn't really share personal details.

She got that, because neither did she. Too many times in the past when she'd shared, it had been recycled and used against her.

"She showed up this evening." He swung down off the horse, landing lightly on the ground and holding the reins as he stood there.

Unsure. She was surprised to see him unsure. He should have looked confident standing there next to that horse. She wondered if it was about his mother-in-law. His hand went up, catching hold of the horse's bridle. The big animal pushed at his arm and Wyatt held him tight.

"I'm sure the girls are happy to see her." She held on to the laundry basket with one arm and with her left hand she kept hold of the dog that growled a low warning.

"They were. Unfortunately I was in the process of burning the house down when she showed up." Wyatt reached up and pulled something off his saddle. Her jacket that she'd left at his house. "I thought you might need this."

He dropped it in the laundry basket on top of the sheets she'd just folded. And then he stood there. She looked up, caught him watching her. It was hard to breathe when he did that.

"Would you like to go for a ride?" He said it so easy and nothing was that easy. No word fit him better than complicated. Everything about him fit into that box.

His mother-in-law was at his house and he was riding in the dark. That meant something other than "nice night for a ride."

But a moonlight ride with Wyatt Johnson seemed to trump the fear of complications and whatever was going on with him. Her gaze shifted to the tiny parsonage that she shared with her parents. Her mom was inside knitting. She'd had a rough day, a rough month. Rachel's dad was working on Sunday's sermon.

"We won't be gone long." Wyatt moved a little closer.

"I shouldn't. I have more laundry to do."

He laughed a little. "Are you always the good daughter?"

No, she wasn't.

Cynthia was the good one. That fact didn't hurt the way it once had. Life changed. Cynthia was married and had a family. Rachel lived with her parents, making sure their mother stayed healthy. It was an easy choice to make. Stay with her parents, help with their ministry and take care of them. Leaving wasn't an option, not when her brother and sister both lived on the other side of the country.

Her gaze landed on Wyatt's dusty boots and slid up. When she reached his face, he was smiling. And he winked. She nearly dropped the laundry basket and in her shock, she let go of the dog. Wolfgang jumped away from her. His tail wagged and he made a beeline for Wyatt.

"Hey now, you're a big old dog." His hand went out and the dog dropped on his belly. "And he's friendly."

"He isn't supposed to be."

"Oh, you want him to attack me?" Wyatt grinned again.

"No, but I don't want him to lose his edge. He's a guard dog."

"Right." Wyatt continued to rub the dog behind the ears. "So, you want to go? I can't be gone too long."

Rachel bit down on her bottom lip and then she nodded.

"Okay, let me take Wolfgang in and I'll put on boots."

"Flip-flops are okay."

"Right, so you can laugh at the city girl who wore the wrong shoes to go riding."

"Okay, I'll stand out here and hold on to Gatsby."

She laughed. "Gatsby."

"Oh, laughter from the woman with a dog named Wolfgang?"

She whistled and Wolfgang trotted to her side. "I'll be right back."

As she walked through the back door, letting it bang softly behind her, Rachel heard her dad on the phone. She glanced at the clock, surprised that he'd have a call this late at night. Hopefully no one was hurt or sick. Late calls were almost never a good thing. She peeked into the living room. Her mom was still sitting in the recliner next to the window, the lamp glowing soft light and her hands working the knitting needles as the scarf in her lap grew.

"Hey, I'm going riding with Wyatt Johnson." Rachel sat the basket of laundry on a chair and used what she hoped was a casual, it's-really-nothing voice.

Her mom glanced up. Gloria Waters always looked serene. Rachel envied that about her mother. She envied that her mom and sister could eat cake and never gain an ounce. And yeah, she knew that envy was wrong. But there were days she could really use a piece of cake.

Or maybe the whole cake. And that was the problem.

"Riding with Wyatt?" Gloria put her knitting down. "Okay, well, be careful."

What had she expected her mom to say? That she couldn't go? Rachel smiled. She was a dozen years past the time when her parents made decisions for her. And yet she still checked with them.

Her father's voice carried from his office. "I'm not sure if we're interested, Bill. I know we've talked about that. Let me pray on this…"

His voice faded. Rachel couldn't breathe for a second because she'd heard similar conversations in the past. She hadn't expected it now. She shifted her gaze to her mom and got a shrug, nothing more.

"What's going on?"

"I'm not sure. Your dad missed a call from Bill and he called him back."

Rachel nodded.

Her mom picked up her knitting again as if it didn't matter. Maybe it didn't. Maybe it was another door opening, another one closing. But she didn't want this door closed.

"I should go. Wyatt is waiting."

She walked out the back door still wearing her flip-flops. It wasn't cold but the air was damp and the breeze blew against her bare arms. She shrugged into the jacket that Wyatt had given her before she went inside.

"Ready to go?" Wyatt looked down at her feet. "I was kind of joking about shoes. Do you have boots?"

"I do. I'm sorry." She glanced back at the house.

"It isn't a big deal. You can wear those." His booted foot went into the stirrup and he swung into the saddle. He reached for her hand. "Come on."

She hesitated and then she grasped his hand. Strong fingers wrapped around hers. It felt like a lifeline.

Chapter Six

Wyatt grasped Rachel's hand and her fingers wrapped tight around his. It was easier to think about riding than to think about the lost look on her face when she walked out of the house. She had looked pretty close to shell-shocked.

"Put your foot in the stirrup." He moved his left foot and she slid her foot into the stirrup. "And up you go."

He pulled and she swung her right leg up and over, landing behind him. The horse sidestepped and then settled. Her foot was out of the stirrup. He slid his foot back into place and glanced back at her.

"Ready?"

She nodded but didn't say anything. Three minutes in the house shouldn't have done this to her. Maybe she'd had a day like his?

Gatsby headed down the road at an easy clip, his gait smooth, his long stride eating up the ground and putting distance between them and the parsonage. Rachel was stiff behind him, holding the saddle rather than wrapping her arms around his waist.

"Where are we going?" Her voice trembled a little. She was close to his back but didn't touch him.

"Nowhere, just riding. I haven't done this in years. Since Violet is at the house I decided to get out and clear my head."

He was taking steps. The girls were with Violet. They were fine. He was fine. Rachel Waters was sitting behind him, and he thought he could hear a quiet sob as the horse's hooves pounded the pavement.

"We've got land down here. I'm going to cut across the field and hit a dirt road that will take us back to your place."

She didn't answer.

The gate was open and he rode Gatsby through the entrance. They hadn't put livestock on this place since last fall. The grass was growing up and in a month or so they'd cut it for hay.

The moon was almost full and the silver light that shone down on the field was bright. The grass blew and the moonlight caught the blades, turning them silvery green. Wyatt slowed the horse to an easy walk. Behind him, Rachel sighed. He hoped she'd relaxed a little.

They rode through the field. Wyatt felt the presence of the woman behind him, even though she hadn't touched him. He'd been impulsive in his life, but this one had him questioning what in the world he'd done. He'd planned on taking a ride and clearing his head. It wasn't often that he had a few minutes alone. Instead of being alone, he had Rachel Waters on the back of his horse.

Out of the corner of his eye he saw a flash of something running through the grass. The horse must have seen it at the same time. The animal jumped a little, knocking Rachel forward. Wyatt held the reins steady and tightened his legs around the animal's middle.

"Easy there, Gats. It's a nice night for a ride, but I'm not looking for a big run."

Rachel's arms were now tight around his waist. He smiled and remembered high school, pretending a car had died or run out of gas on a back road. He kind of figured he could spur Gatsby just little and send the animal running across the field, and keep Rachel Waters holding tight.

Instead he eased up on the reins but kept the horse at a steady walk. "He's fine, just startled. I think that was a coyote."

"I think so, too." Rachel's cheek brushed his back and then was gone. But her hands were still at his waist.

"So what happened back at the house?" He eased into the conversation the same way he eased his way into the saddle of a green broke horse.

"Why don't you tell me what happened with your mother-in-law?"

He glanced back and then refocused on the trail that was overgrown from years of neglected riding. Rachel readjusted behind him. Her arms slipped from his middle and her hands grabbed the sides of his shirt.

"Okay, rock, paper, scissors." He turned sideways in the saddle and held his hand out.

She shook her head but she smiled and held her hand out.

"Fine. One, two, three." She cut his paper with scissors.

He groaned. "Me first. Great. My mother-in-law isn't positive I'm fit to be a parent right now."

She didn't respond.

"You still back there?" He glanced back, pushing his hat up a little to get a better look at the woman behind him.

"I'm here." And then a sweet pause with her hands on his waist. "She's wrong."

"Thanks." He spurred Gatsby a little and the horse picked up his pace. "He'll be a good horse when we're done breaking him."

"Done breaking him!"

"Yeah, he hasn't ridden double before tonight. In a few weeks we're going to start him on roping."

"Great, I'm practice."

No, not practice, he wanted to tell her. But she was a soft, easy way to slip back into life. He hadn't thought about dating too much, about any other woman taking Wendy's place. It still wasn't the direction he planned to take, but life was pulling him back in.

"You're not practice. You're helping me." He assured her, smiling as the words slipped out, meaning more than she would understand.

"Oh, so I can add horse trainer to my résumé?"

That's right, they were talking about the horse being broke to ride double, not about his dating life.

"Yeah, and since I spilled it, I think it's your turn to talk."

No answer. They rode for a few minutes in total silence. No, not total silence, tree frogs sang and a few night birds screeched. Her arms slid around his waist again. Her chin brushed his shoulder.

"I really can't talk about it. It has to do with my dad and the church."

The years in Florida doing youth ministry weren't that far behind him. He got that she couldn't talk. But whatever had happened, it'd upset her. He leaned back a little, turning his head. It caught him by surprise, that she was so close. His cheek brushed hers and she moved back.

A Justin McBride song filled the night air. Wyatt groaned and reached into his pocket for his phone. It was Violet. He answered and in the background he could hear Molly crying. He'd been wrong, to take off like this, to leave them.

"I'll be home in five minutes." He spoke softly to his mother-in-law, offered more assurances and slid the phone back into his pocket. "Mind going back to my place?"

She shook her head, but he wondered. If he was her, he'd probably mind. Man, even he wasn't crazy about going back. It wasn't about his girls. It was about not wanting to face Violet, not with Rachel on the back of his horse.

It took less than five minutes to get from the field to the dirt road and back to Wyatt's house. Rachel held tight as the horse covered the ground in an easy lope. She tried hard not to think about falling off at the pace they were going.

Falling off or facing Wyatt's mother-in-law? She had to wonder a little about which one would be worse. Falling off would leave more marks. She wasn't that stupid.

"You okay back there?" Wyatt's voice was raspy and way too sexy.

"I'm good." Ugh, she was horrible.

He chuckled, his sides vibrating under her arms. "Of course you are. I promise, Violet isn't dangerous. She's overprotective of the girls. I guess I am, too. Maybe that's why we clash on a regular basis."

"They're your girls, of course you're protective. I don't think you're over…" She sighed.

"I'm overprotective." He glanced back at her. "It's okay, I can handle it. There are reasons, Rachel."

"But sometimes…"

"No, not sometimes." He reined in the horse. "Okay, sometimes. I know Molly needs to be able to separate from me. The hour or so a week that she's in the nursery has helped."

"I can see that she's doing better." Without knowing all of the reasons why Molly was afraid, it was hard to help her.

She held on as he cut through a ditch and up the driveway to his house. It looked as if every light in the house was on.

Nerves twisted a funny dance in her stomach as he pulled the horse to a quick stop next to the back door. He didn't wait for her to slide off. Instead he swung his right leg over the horse's neck and jumped off, leaving her sitting on the back of the saddle.

The door opened as she was sliding forward into the saddle, grabbing the reins as the horse started to side-step. He calmed the minute she held the reins. Wyatt took the steps two at a time and met his mother-in-law and Molly as they walked out the back door. Molly held her arms out to him, no longer crying, just sobbing and hiccupping a little into his shoulder.

"I'm here." He spoke softly to his daughter.

"She woke up and you were gone." Violet, a woman with soft features and hair that framed a face that was still young.

"I shouldn't have left."

His mother-in-law shook her head. "Wyatt, there are going to be times that you have to leave."

Rachel sat on the horse, waiting for them to remember her. She didn't want to be the witness to their pain. She didn't want to be the bystander who got in the way. Violet remembered her presence and turned to stare.

Emotions flickered across the woman's face. Anger, sorrow, it was difficult to tell exactly what Violet thought about Rachel's presence.

"I should go." She didn't really mean to say it out loud. She slid to the ground, still holding the reins. "It isn't far. I can walk."

Wyatt, still holding Molly, came down the steps. "Don't be ridiculous. I'll drive you home, Rachel. Molly and I can drive you home."

"Rachel?" Violet walked to the edge of the porch. "Are you the Rachel that my granddaughters talk about nonstop?"

"I'm Rachel."

"Wyatt said you cleaned his home last week. Are you interested in the job on a permanent basis?"

Rachel shot Wyatt a look and she wondered if that was what this night ride had been about. Had his mother-in-law put him on the spot and he'd used Rachel as his get-out-of-jail card because she had cleaned one time?

"She makes the house smell good," said Molly, suddenly talkative. Rachel smiled at the little girl.

"Well, that sounds perfect to me." Violet smiled at her granddaughter. "Do you cook?"

Rachel nodded because she had no idea what to say. She avoided looking at Wyatt because he probably looked cornered. She knew that she felt pretty cornered. Cleaning Wyatt's house once did not make her a housekeeper and nanny.

"Perfect." Violet looked from Rachel to Wyatt. "When do you want her to start?"

"Violet, this is something Rachel and I need to discuss."

"Well, the two of you talk and I'll go check on Kat."

Rachel thought about reminding them that she was still there, still a grown-up who could make her own decisions, but the conversation ended and Violet went inside looking like a woman who had solved a national crisis.

"That went well." He walked down the steps, still holding Molly, toward Rachel. Wyatt took the leather reins from Rachel. "Let me unsaddle him and I'll drive you home."

"I can walk. Or call my dad." She hugged herself tight, holding her jacket closed against the sudden coolness in the wind.

Wyatt turned, pushing his hat back. He shook his head. "You aren't walking. You're not calling your dad. I'm driving you home. Right, Mol?"

Molly nodded against his shoulder. She looked so tiny in her pink pajamas and her dark hair tangled around her face. The security light caught her in its glow and her little eyes were open, a few stray tears still trickling down her cheeks.

"I'm sorry that Violet put you on the spot."

"I understand." She stepped closer. "Do you want me to take her while you unsaddle Gatsby?"

He dropped a kiss on his daughter's brow and nodded. Molly held out her arms. Rachel didn't know why it mattered so much to her, but it did. In her heart it mattered that this little girl would reach out to her. It changed everything.

It even changed that truck ride home, sitting with Molly between them and the stereo playing softly. It changed the way she felt when Wyatt said goodbye and then waited until she was in the house before he backed out of the driveway, the headlights flashing across the side of the house.

And then she refocused because her parents were still up, still discussing something that could change her life forever.

Wyatt turned up the radio as he headed down the drive and back to his house. Molly was in the seat next to him, curled over against his side. Her breathing had settled into a heavy pattern that meant she'd fallen back to sleep.

When he pulled up his driveway he could see Violet in the living room, watching for him to come back. His house. His life. His kids. Violet was their grandmother.

As much as he cared for her, he didn't care for facing off with her tonight.

He definitely didn't like her trying to make decisions for him. Decisions such as hiring Rachel Waters to be his housekeeper. There were plenty of women out there who could do the job. Women with loose housedresses and heavy shoes. That seemed pretty close to perfect.

He stopped the truck and got out, lifting Molly into his arms and carrying her up the back steps. Violet met him. She pushed the door open and he stepped into the laundry room, kicking off his boots, still holding his daughter tight.

"You're dating her?" Violet followed him through the kitchen.

Man, he needed peace and quiet, not this. He needed to put his daughter to bed and think before he got hit with twenty questions. He wasn't dating.

He'd gone for a ride to clear his head and for whatever reason he'd let that ride take him straight to Rachel. It wasn't like he'd planned it.

"I'm going to put my daughter in bed, Violet."

He glanced back and she stood in the hallway, her eyes damp with tears but she wasn't angry. He let out a sigh and walked up the stairs to the room Molly and Kat shared. Twin beds painted white, pastel quilts with flowers and butterflies. It was the perfect room for little girls to grow up in. Until they started fighting like barn cats and needed their own space.

That wasn't something he wanted to think about, their growing up. He hoped they would always be close. He didn't want to think about them in their twenties, having one major fight and pulling away until...

He didn't want to go back and he wasn't going to let his girls be him and Ryder.

He put his daughter in her bed and pulled the quilt up to her chin. She opened her eyes and smiled softly, raising a hand to touch his cheek. Sleepy eyes drifted closed again and he kissed her cheek. "Love you, Molly."

"Love you, Daddy." She smiled but her eyes didn't open.

"I'm downstairs if you need me." He walked to the door. "I'm not going anywhere."

As he walked downstairs, he felt as if he was about to face the judge. Violet was waiting in the den. The TV was turned off. She put down her book, a book he knew she hadn't opened. He took off his hat and shoved a hand through his hair. And he stood there in the middle of the living room, unsure.

"What's going on, Wyatt?"

"There's nothing going on, Violet. I'm being a dad to my daughters and I'm raising horses with Ryder." He sat down on the couch and rubbed a hand over his face because he was a grown man and he really didn't feel the need to answer her questions. But he owed her something. "I'm not dating Rachel Waters. She's the pastor's daughter and she takes care of the girls when they're in the church nursery. She teaches their preschool Sunday school class."

"I see. Well, she's very pretty."

"Right." Was that a trick statement?

"Wyatt, someday you'll want to date again. You'll move on. That's okay."

He closed his eyes because it seemed like a real good way to avoid this discussion. Instead he got smacked upside the head with a vision of Rachel Waters. Facing Violet was easier than facing the image taunting him behind closed eyes.

Never in his wildest dreams would Violet have been the person telling him to move on.

"Hire her, Wyatt. She'd be perfect for the girls. They need someone like her in their lives."

"They have me." He twisted the gold band on his finger. Someday he would have to take it off. "No one can replace Wendy."

"She was my daughter, Wyatt. I think I know that no one can replace her. But I lost a husband once and I do know that we can't stop living."

"I haven't stopped living." Okay, maybe he had for a while.

He hadn't expected it to hurt when the grief started to fade and life started to feel like something he wanted to live again. Moving on felt like cheating.

"Wyatt, you're a good dad. You were a good husband."

He had wondered for a long time and never been able to ask if she blamed him. He sure blamed himself. He still couldn't ask.

"It's the hardest thing in the world, moving forward. But…" What else could he say? Moving forward meant accepting.

She leaned and patted his arm. "Don't beat yourself up too much for having good days."

She had lost her husband years ago. Wendy's dad had died at work. A sudden heart attack that took them all by surprise. A few years ago Violet had remarried. He admired her strength, even if she did try to run his life from time to time.

"If you don't hire Rachel, do you have any thoughts on who you would like to hire?" Violet picked up her purse and dug through it, pulling out a small tablet and pen.

"Someone capable." He pictured Rachel and brushed the thought aside to replace it with a more suitable image. "Someone older."

Violet laughed a little and wrote down something about unattractive older woman. Now she was starting to get it.

Chapter Seven

The new lambs frolicked next to their mothers. Rachel leaned against the fence and watched, smiling a little. And smiling wasn't the easiest thing to do, not after the previous evening's conversation with her parents.

This was her place, Dawson, this house and the sheep she raised. Working for Etta, that was another place where she fit. Finally, at twenty-nine she fit.

That meant something because growing up she'd been the misfit, the overweight rebel always compared to her older sister. Cynthia had been the pretty one, the good one. Rob, her older brother, had been the studious one.

Rachel had set out to prove that she had a mind of her own.

"Thinking?" Her dad appeared at her side.

She glanced at him, wondering when he'd gotten those lines around his eyes and that gray in his hair. As a kid, she'd always imagined him young and capable. She'd never imagined her mother in bed for days, fighting a lupus flare-up that attacked her joints and caused fatigue that forced her to rest more often.

Parents weren't supposed to age.

"Yes, thinking."

"Rachel, if we get this church, you don't have to go."

She stepped back from the fence and turned to face him.

"If you go, I go."

"I know that's how you feel, but we also know how you feel about Dawson. In all of the years of moving, there's never been a town that became your home the way this town has. We want you to be happy."

"I'd be happy in Tulsa."

"No, you won't. But we will. We love the city and we need to live closer to the hospitals and doctors. We're not getting any younger."

She didn't want to have this conversation. She turned back to the small field with her six ewes and the three babies that had been born so far this spring.

"You're not old."

Her dad laughed. "No, we're not, but there are things we need to consider. Promise me you'll pray about this. I don't want you to make this decision based on what you think we need."

"I'll pray." She sighed and rested her arms on the top of the gate. "When do they want you to take the church in Tulsa?"

"Six weeks. And remember, nothing is set in stone, not yet."

"But that isn't a lot of time for the church here to find a pastor."

"It isn't, but there are men here who should pray about stepping into the role. Sometimes God moves us so that others can move into the place where He wants them."

"True." She turned to face him. "But then I question why He brought us here just to move us."

"To everything there is a season, a purpose. God doesn't make mistakes, Rachel. If we're here for a year, there's a purpose in that year."

"I know you're right." She stepped away from the gate. "I have to run into town to get grain. Do you want lunch from the Mad Cow?"

"No, we're going to have sandwiches." He kissed the top of her head the way he'd done when she was a kid. He hadn't changed that much. He still wore dress slacks and a button-up shirt. He still parted his hair, though thinning, on the side.

He was still the person she turned to when she needed advice. And sometimes she recognized that her parents were a crutch. They were her safe place. This was easier than getting hurt again.

She drove the truck to town. Not that she couldn't put feed in the back of her convertible, but she liked the old farm truck her dad had bought when they moved to Dawson. When she'd thought this would be the last move.

She'd been moving her entire life. From place to place, in and out of lives. She'd learned not to get too close. Either the friends would soon be gone, or they'd find out she was human, not at all the perfect preacher's kid.

But she was no longer a kid. And this time she'd gotten attached.

She parked in front of the black-and-white painted building that was the Mad Cow Café. It was early for the lunch crowd. That meant time to sit and talk to Vera, the owner. Maybe they could have a cup of coffee together.

A truck pulled in next to hers. She glanced quick to the right and nearly groaned. Wyatt Johnson in his big truck. He saluted with two fingers to his brow and grinned. That cowboy had more charm than was good for him.

Or anyone else, for that matter.

She guessed it would be pretty obvious if she backed out of her parking space and went on down the road, so she opened the door and grabbed her purse. Wyatt met her at the front of the truck. The girls weren't with him.

"How are you?" He pulled off the cowboy hat and ran a hand through hair that was a little too long. Dark and straight, it looked soft. She thought it probably was soft.

"I'm good. Where are the girls?"

"Andie and Ryder are home after a trip to the doctor in Tulsa. Andie is on the couch for the next month or so till the babies come, and she thought the girls could keep her entertained."

"That'll be good for all three of them."

"Yeah, it is."

"And your mother-in-law?" She walked next to him, his stride longer than her own.

"Interviewing housekeepers."

"Oh."

It shouldn't hurt, that he was going to pick someone else. Of course she didn't want a full-time job as anyone's housekeeper. She didn't even know that they'd be here for her to take such a job.

"It will make things easier," he explained it in a way that made her wonder if he wanted to convince himself.

"Of course it would."

"Do you have any suggestions?" He opened the door to the Mad Cow and she stepped in ahead of him, brushing past him, trying hard not to look at him, to look into those eyes of his, to not see the faded jeans, the scuffed boots or the buckle he'd won at Nationals back when he team roped. Before marriage, before horse training. He still roped in local events.

A few weeks ago she had watched from the bleachers. She had watched him smile and avoid the women who tried to get his attention. Those women rode horses and they understood his world.

She was still breaking in boots she'd bought when they moved to Dawson. And now she'd have to put them back in the closet like most forgotten dreams. She'd pack them up with childhood books, love letters she'd never sent and pictures of ranch houses she'd dreamed of owning.

Wyatt was a cowboy. He was the real deal. He even held the door open and pulled out a chair for her when Vera pointed them to a table in the corner.

And he did it because it was what men in Dawson did. It was the way they lived. Her heart ached clean through and she told herself it wasn't about him, it was about leaving.

"You know, I'm not used to seeing you without a smile on your face." He drew her back with that comment and she managed a smile. "Oh, that's not better."

She laughed. "Sorry, just a lot on my mind. What about Ernestine Douglas?"

"What? Ernestine's smile?"

She laughed at the pretend shock on his face. "As a housekeeper."

"I hadn't thought about her. Yeah, I might give her a call."

"She'd be great with the girls. Her kids are grown and gone."

Vera approached, dark hair shot through with silver, knotted at the back of her head and covered with a net. She wiped wet hands on her apron and pulled an order pad out of the pocket.

"What can I get you kids today?"

Wyatt laughed, "Vera, I wish I was still a kid. If I was twenty again I'd ride a few bulls and then take Rachel off to Tulsa for a wild night."

Vera tsk'd. "Wyatt Johnson, you're talking about our preacher's daughter. She teaches Sunday school and watches over your babies in the nursery."

"Yeah, but in this dream, we're still young and crazy. Remember?" Wyatt winked at Rachel and picked up the menu. "What's special today?"

Vera pointed at the white board on the wall near the register. "My special cashewed chicken, and the pile of nothing you're trying to feed us."

"Vera, Vera, I guess you won't give a guy a break."

"Not a chance."

He laughed and ordered the cashewed chicken. Rachel ordered a salad. But she wanted that cashewed chicken. She had always wanted what she shouldn't have, the things that weren't good for her. Fried chicken, chocolate and the cowboy sitting across from her. The last was new on the list of things she shouldn't want and couldn't have.

Wyatt watched Rachel pick at the salad she'd ordered. Lettuce with chopped-up turkey and ham and barely a dab of dressing. He felt kind of guilty digging into the plate of fried chicken chunks over rice that covered his plate, the special gravy oozed over the side and dripped onto the table. Cashews and chopped green onions topped it off.

The way he looked at it, skinny women ought to eat something fried every now and then. He grabbed the saucer from under her coffee cup and scraped some of his chicken onto it.

"What are you doing?" She put her fork down and wiped her mouth.

"Feeding you. If you haven't got the sense to eat some of Vera's cashewed chicken, I'm going to help you out."

"But I don't want it."

"Oh, yes, you do." He grinned, hoping she'd smile and look a little less cornered. Man, what was it about this woman? She didn't eat. She had a butterfly tattoo. She had secrets.

He had two little girls who needed him to stay focused.

He reached for his iced tea and the band on his left hand glinted, a reminder. And guilt. Because he still wore a ring that symbolized forever with a woman who was gone.

But her memory wasn't.

He sighed and Rachel lowered her fork. Her eyes were dark, soulful. She didn't smile but her eyes changed, softened. "You okay?"

"I'm fine. So, are you going to try the cashewed chicken?"

Rachel picked up her fork and took a bite. Her eyes closed and she nodded.

"It's as good as people say." Her eyes opened and

she flashed him a smile. "And you Johnson boys are as wicked as they say."

"We're not really wicked." He wanted to hug her tight because she was dragging him past a hard place in his life and she didn't even know it. "We're just on the edge a lot of the time."

"Temptation."

"Reformed."

The door opened. The lunch crowd was piling in. While they'd been talking the parking lot had filled up with farm trucks, a tractor or two and a few cars. He knew about everyone in Dawson and he figured Rachel did as well.

"We're about to get caught."

Rachel shrugged, "Yeah, that's life in Dawson. I love it here."

She sounded as if that meant something.

"You know, if you need to talk, I know how to keep a secret."

Her smile was sweet. She wasn't a girl from Dawson, but she fit this place, this world. From her T-shirt to her jeans, she was fitting in. But maybe that's what she did. The life of a preacher's kid wasn't easy. They moved a lot, changed towns, changed schools and changed friends.

Maybe she knew how to become the person each town or church expected her to be? Did that mean she wasn't who he thought she was? That left him kind of unsettled.

"I need to go. I don't want to leave the girls too long. They…" He stood up and dropped a few bills on the table for their lunch and Vera's tip. "The girls worry if I'm gone too long."

Rachel stood up. "Wyatt, if you need anything, I'm here."

Man, he could think of a list of things he needed. He needed to keep his life together. He took a step back. He really wasn't ready for this.

The Johnson brothers weren't the only temptation in town.

Trouble was looking him in the eyes and it was about time he made the great escape. He and Ryder had done a lot of that in their younger days. They had experience. They knew how to race through a hay field to escape an angry dad. They knew how to escape the county deputy on a dirt road. Not exactly life lessons he was proud of.

He touched the brim of his hat. "Thanks for recommending someone. I'll call Mrs. Douglas."

"Right, that's a good idea."

"Or you could take the job? The girls would love that."

"I don't think so."

"Yeah, of course."

He bumped into a chair as he backed away from her and a few of the guys called out names and other things he didn't really want to deal with.

The only good idea right now was to escape Rachel Waters, maybe spend some time at Ryder's knocking the tar out of the punching bag still hanging in the old hay barn. Their dad had put that thing up years ago. He had taught them one decent lesson in life, other than how to make money. He'd taught them the art of boxing.

And right now felt like a pretty good time to go take a few swings at an inanimate object.

There were a list of reasons why. Wendy's memory, tugging him back in time and pushing him to think about how he'd let her down. His girls hurting and needing their mom. Rachel Waters with brown eyes and a butterfly tattoo, offering to be there for him but rejecting a job offer to take care of his girls.

Thoughts of Rachel felt a lot like cheating.

Thirty minutes after he left the Mad Cow he was in the barn behind Ryder's house. He had spent fifteen minutes in that hot, dusty barn slamming his fists into the frayed and faded bag that hung from the rafters.

"Trying to hurt someone?"

Wyatt punched the bag and then grabbed it to keep it from swinging back at him. He turned, swiping his arm across his brow. Boxing in boots and jeans, not the most effective form in the world.

Ryder stood in the doorway, sunlight behind him. They'd taken a few swings at each other over the years. The last time had been about something crazy, a woman that Ryder had hurt. It shouldn't have mattered to Wyatt—he hadn't known her. But Ryder had left a trail of broken hearts in his reckless wake.

They hadn't talked for over a year after that fight.

"No, just exercising." Wyatt stepped away from the punching bag.

Ryder grinned and shook his head. "Right, and that's why you were in town having lunch with Rachel Waters."

"That's why I don't like this town." Wyatt walked past Ryder, into the warm sunlight. At least there was a breeze. He didn't put his hat back on but stood there for a minute, cooling down.

"Yeah, people talk. Most of the time they're talking

about me. Or at least they used to. Kind of nice to have you being the target of the gossip."

Wyatt walked on, toward his truck. "How's Andie?"

"Itching to get out of bed. The church brought a truckload of frozen meals for us and a few of the ladies cleaned the house. Rachel came over yesterday and brought a pie."

"Of course she did."

"Want a glass of tea or a bottle of water?" Ryder had stopped and that forced Wyatt to stop and turn around.

"Nope, I need to get home to the girls. Violet is trying to find a housekeeper-slash-nanny for us. I'm leaving it up to her, but I want to keep an eye on things."

"Wyatt, I know you're still angry or hurt. I know this messed you up, but it's time…"

Wyatt took a step in Ryder's direction. "Don't tell me when it's time, little brother. You think because you're married and finally getting it together, you have it all figured out. You don't have a clue how I feel."

Man, *he* didn't even know how he felt. So being angry with Ryder, wanting to shove him into the dirt, probably wasn't the right reaction. He sighed and took a step back, tipping his hat to shade his face.

"I'm sorry, Ryder. But let me figure this out, if you don't mind."

"Got it. But I wanted you to know," Ryder looked down and turned a little red. "We're praying for you."

That was a change for his brother. Ryder was now the one with the stronger faith. That was another thing Wyatt was working on getting back. He'd walked away from the ministry and spent a long year blaming God. He'd spent the last six months working through that and trying to find peace.

"Ryder, I appreciate that."

Ryder grinned. "Yeah, do you appreciate how hard it was to say?"

They both laughed.

"Yeah, cowboys from Dawson don't have a lot of Dr. Phil moments."

"Ain't that just about the truth?" Ryder slapped him on the back. "See you later. If I don't get in there, she'll be climbing the curtains."

Wyatt watched his brother walk away and then he headed for his truck. He sat behind the wheel for a minute, letting things settle inside him and watching as Rachel Waters jogged down the driveway and away from his house.

Now what in the world was that all about?

Chapter Eight

Friday night lights had a different meaning in Dawson, Oklahoma, than it did in Texas. Friday nights in Dawson meant the local rodeo at the community arena. Trucks and trailers were scattered in the field that served as a parking lot and cars parked in the small lot that used to be gravel, but the rain had washed it out last fall and so now it was dirt, grass and some gravel.

Wyatt's truck and trailer were parked near the pens where livestock were ready for action. There were a half-dozen bulls, a small pen of steers and a few rangy horses. Someone had dropped off a few sheep for the kids' mutton bustin' event.

The youth group from Community Church was busy cooking hamburgers on a grill as a fundraiser for their trip to Mexico. Pastor Waters had asked him to think about going as a counselor. He wasn't ready for that but he'd agreed to pray.

Maybe soon, though.

He watched the crowds file in, taking seats on the old wooden bleachers. His girls were with Violet. She should be there by now. She'd stayed at home to make more calls to prospective housekeepers. He had thought about stopping her. He had managed just fine all this time, so why did he need someone now?

He wasn't sure he liked the idea of a stranger in his home, taking care of his kids, cooking their meals. The one thing about Violet, she was determined. She'd informed him she had one woman that seemed to be perfect for the job. Great.

"Hey, are you competing tonight?" Ryder walked through the pen of steers, his jeans tucked into boots that were already caked with mud.

The rain they'd had that morning had cooled the air and left the arena pretty soupy. It had also brought a lot of rocks to the surface inside the arena.

"I'm going to rope with Clint Cameron. How's Andie?"

Ryder shuddered. "Not a good patient. You know she doesn't like to sit still. But she'll do it for the girls. Etta is with her tonight."

Twins. Wyatt shook his head and laughed a little. In less than a month his brother was going to be daddy to not one, but two babies. It had taken Andie and those babies to settle Ryder.

"She'll survive it. I'm not sure about you." Wyatt slapped his brother on the back. "You getting on a bull tonight?"

"Andie said if I get on a bull and break my leg, she'll break my neck. Think she means it?"

"Yeah, she probably does."

He glanced toward the bleachers again, looking for his girls. He spotted Violet, but not the girls. He scanned the area around her and didn't see Molly or Kat. Ryder was still talking, but Wyatt held up a hand to stop him.

"I have to go find the girls."

"Aren't they with Violet?"

"They were supposed to be." Wyatt stepped around his brother. "I'll be back."

"Do you want me to help you look?"

"No, I've got it. You stay here in case they show up over here. Maybe they gave her the slip."

He walked on the outside of the arena, ignoring a few people who called out to him and sidestepping puddles left behind by the downpour.

A child yelled. He glanced toward the refreshment stand and his heart hammered hard. Molly and Kat, each holding a corn dog. And Rachel Waters standing next to them. He stopped and then moved quick to get out of the way of a few riders about to enter the arena for the opening ceremony.

The horses moved past him and he had to search again for Rachel and the girls. They were standing a short distance away. Molly laughed and Rachel wiped her cheek. Kat was shoving fries in her mouth. Ketchup had dripped down the front of her plaid shirt and her jeans had dirt on the knees. Her pink boots were almost brown from dirt and mud. His little girl.

Rachel looked up and her smile froze when she saw him. He headed in their direction with anger and some other emotion having a doggone war inside him. Why were his girls with Rachel, not Violet?

Man, seeing her with his girls, seeing them smile like that. Come to think of it, he wasn't even sure he was angry, just confused.

"You have my girls." He spoke as softly as he could, not raising his voice, but it wasn't like he was happy.

"I do." Rachel touched each of their heads. She wasn't eating a corn dog. "I pulled in right after they did. When we got inside the gate, the girls asked Violet for something to eat. I was heading this way, so I told her I'd get them something. Is that okay?"

"Of course it is." He said the words like it was easy and didn't matter.

Rachel remained a few feet away, shifting back and forth on city-girl boots, her jeans a little too long. Her T-shirt said something about joy. A few curls sprang rebelliously from the clip that held her hair in a ponytail.

"I'll take them back to Violet."

"Let them finish eating and I'll take them back with me. They want to see the calves and the sheep."

"Okay." She bent and dropped a kiss on the top of Molly's head and then she hugged Kat. "I'll see you later."

"Why don't you come with us? I'll show you the horse I traded for this morning." He didn't know if she cared about a horse. But he did know that he wanted to keep his daughters smiling.

And the smile he got in return, her smile, kind of shattered his world a little. It also made him regret not thinking this through more carefully.

The girls finished their corn dogs and tossed the sticks in the trash. Rachel wiped their hands with a napkin and then their mouths. Wyatt stood back, like a bystander, observing. She made it all look so easy.

But nothing was simple, not even the way she twisted his emotions. She had somehow hijacked his life and he didn't think she even knew it.

"Let's go." She smiled at him, her hands holding tight to Kat and Molly.

* * *

The girls led Rachel as they followed Wyatt back to pens on the north side of the arena. Cattle mooed low and a few sheep bleated their dislike of the muddy pens. A horse whinnied and someone laughed loud. Rachel followed that sound to the source.

The source happened to be tall and wiry with sandy brown hair that curled just a little and a big smile that flashed in a suntanned face. Black framed glasses somehow made his angular features look studious.

He was one of the Cooper brothers, she couldn't remember which. It surprised her to see him at a local event. He was a bullfighter for the professional bull riding events across the country. Tall and wiry, he made his living jumping in front of bulls and taking the shots to keep the bull riders safe.

She knew a daredevil when she saw one. And a flirt.

He lived up to his reputation, jumping one of the fences to land in front of her. Wyatt turned, his smile dissolving when the unknown Cooper took off his hat and bowed in front of her.

"Pleasure to meet you, ma'am." His accent was a little heavy. Andie had told her that she thought he used his Russian heritage to woo the ladies and that his accent hadn't been as heavy a few years back.

She smiled because he was cute and she wasn't interested.

Wyatt appeared at her side. She shivered a little because he didn't appear to be in a great mood. Nor did he appear to be too patient.

"See you later, Travis." He nodded curtly.

The younger man laughed and mumbled something

about striking out before he climbed back over the fence to finish saddling his horse.

"He's always up to something." Wyatt led them through a crowd of men and then to his truck and trailer. A pretty chestnut, deep red with white socks, was tied to the back of his trailer.

"He's beautiful." Rachel ran a hand down the horse's sleek neck.

"I thought so. I bought him at the auction the other night. People are dumping horses like crazy."

"I heard that they're being abandoned on government land."

Wyatt nodded. "This guy belonged to some folks over by Grove. They had to sell all of their livestock."

"I had planned on getting a horse." She stroked the fine boned face of the gelding. His ears pricked forward and he moved to push his head against her arm.

"Planned. You still could. If you decide to get one, I can take you to the auction and we can find you a good deal."

"Thanks, but..." She sighed and focused on the horse, much easier than looking at the cowboy leaning against the horse's saddle where he'd placed his two little girls. His arm was around Molly's back, holding her in place.

"But?"

"But I think right now isn't the right time for me to buy a horse." She smiled and pretended it didn't hurt. "I should go. Do you want me to take the girls back to Violet?"

"First name basis with my mother-in-law?"

"She took me to lunch today." She admitted with a fading sense of ease.

"That's great. Well, I do love to know that my life is being arranged for me." He lifted the girls down and then he put them in the back of his truck. "Stay there and don't get down. There are too many hooves back here and not enough people paying attention."

When he headed her way, Rachel shivered a little. She'd seen that stormy look on his face before. His dark eyes pinned her to the spot where she stood. He untied his horse, still staring at her.

"Rachel, I take care of my girls. I might not be the best cook in the world and maybe my house gets messy, but I haven't let them down. I hope you know that."

"Of course I do." She wanted to touch his arm, to let him know that she wasn't the enemy. She kept her hands to herself. "Violet knows you're a good dad. She's only trying to help. Maybe it's misguided, but…"

"I get that." He led the horse away from her. "I have to get in the arena to ride pickup. Can you take the girls back to Violet?"

"I can. And for what it's worth, I'm sorry."

He tipped his hat and rode off, the horse splattering mud as his big hooves bit into the ground. She stood there for a minute and then she turned to the girls. They were sitting on the tailgate of the truck, waiting. They knew better than to get down. She smiled at them and the two smiled back. They looked sweet in their plaid shirts, jeans and little boots.

Violet must have dressed them. She smiled and reached for their hands. "Let's head back to Grandma and watch the rodeo."

Rachel led the girls back through the crowd of cowboys. A few were zipping up their Kevlar vests in preparation for the bull rides. Bulls moved through the pens and a couple of the big animals were being run into chutes.

Adam MacKenzie stood next to Jason Bradshaw. They were watching one of the bulls, a big gray animal that snorted and when he shook his head, he sent a spray of slime flying through the air.

Kat giggled and wiped her cheek.

"Hey, girls." Jason lifted his hand and Molly high-fived him. "You having fun with Miss Rachel?"

Kat nodded big and smiled. "She could live with us."

Heat crawled up Rachel's cheeks. Jason and Adam laughed but they were definitely curious, she could see it in widened eyes and raised brows.

"Wyatt is thinking about hiring a housekeeper," she explained. "I'm *not* applying for the job."

"Oh, then that makes perfect sense." Jason was married to Etta's granddaughter, Alyson. Ryder's wife Andie was Alyson's twin.

Rachel smiled at Jason and kept walking, a little girl on each side of her.

A person didn't have to go far in Dawson to find people who were somehow related. Andie had told her it made dating in Dawson a real challenge. The reason Andie had explained that to her was because she wanted Rachel to know that she shouldn't have a difficult time finding someone to date in Dawson. At least she wasn't anyone's cousin.

At the time it had been funny. Now, not so much. If the church in Tulsa called, she would be gone by the end of June. Once again she had been smart not to get too attached.

Of course, she was just lying to herself. The two little girls holding her hands as they headed for the bleachers happened to be proof that she had gotten attached. The fast beating of her heart when she turned to watch Wyatt rope a bull that refused to leave the arena could probably be called serious evidence.

When they reached Violet, she smiled at the girls and patted the bench next to her. "Come on, girls, time to sit and watch."

A rider was already flying out of the gate on the back of a big white bull. The ride didn't last three seconds. The bull twisted in a funny arc, jumped and spun back in the other direction. Rachel held her breath as the rider flew through the air and landed hard on his back.

"Who was that?" Rachel leaned to ask Jenna who sat on the bench in front of her.

"I think it was one of the Coopers. I can't keep them all straight."

It must have been because Travis Cooper hopped in front of the bull, distracting it while Jackson ran through the gate to the fallen rider. Rachel bit her lip hard and watched, waiting for the rider to move, waiting as the medics hurried into the arena.

A leg moved, then an arm. The cowboy sat up. Rachel released her breath. The crowd erupted in applause. The cowboy lifted his hat as he stood, but then he went limp and his brothers lifted him and carried him from the arena.

"I have a love–hate relationship with this sport," Jenna MacKenzie said. She looked back and shook her head as she made the quiet comment. "I know why they do it. And then I wonder why they do it."

Rachel's gaze traveled to the back of the arena, to the rider holding his horse back from the fray, waiting for the next rider out of the chute. His rope was coiled, ready in case of emergency. He was all cowboy in a white hat, his button-up shirt a deep blue. She remembered the silver cross dangling from a chain around his neck.

If she didn't care, it wouldn't hurt to leave.

But she did care. Kat cuddled close, leaning and then curling on the bench to rest her head on Rachel's lap. Violet handed her a blanket. Kat carried that blanket everywhere, even to the nursery on Sunday.

Rachel dropped it over the little girl who dozed, thumb in her mouth. Molly was still bright-eyed, watching another bull being loaded into the chute. A rider on the catwalk prepared to settle himself on the animal's back.

But it all lost importance because Kat was curled next to her asleep. Rachel stroked the child's hair and Kat cuddled closer. By the time saddle broncs were run into the chutes for that event, Kat had climbed into her arms.

Nothing had ever felt as sweet, or hurt so much. It reminded her of waking up with the tail end of a wonderful dream still fresh on her mind and realizing it had just been a dream.

The cowboy who owned that dream was on his horse, taking the part of pickup man for the saddle bronc event. He glanced up at them, nodding and touching the brim of his hat. Molly waved big. He waved back, grinning. Oh, that grin. In his dark tanned face it flashed white and crinkled at the corners of his eyes. She didn't have to see the details because it had been imprinted in her mind.

His gaze settled on Rachel and Kat. She smiled

and nodded. But then his attention returned to the task at hand.

Tension knotted in Rachel's lower back. Maybe due to the child in her arms, having to sit so straight, or the stress of watching men take risks on wild animals. Or maybe because Wyatt Johnson unraveled her a little, making her feel undone and kind of crazy.

She tried to remember the last time a man had made her feel that way. It had to have been when she was fourteen and Andy Banks was the star football player who lived next door. He had been nice when they walked to school together. But one day she'd heard him in the hall talking about her weight and how he thought she had a crush on him. It had turned into a big joke for him, something to laugh about behind her back.

It no longer hurt, but it was something she still remembered. That kind of pain left a scar.

It made it hard to believe in a smile.

But that girl was long gone. That girl had learned to eat healthy and exercise. After losing fifty pounds she'd seen Andy again and he hadn't recognized her. He'd actually smiled and flirted.

Rachel pushed back against those old feelings because she was the person God had created her to be. Fat or skinny, she was His. She knew who she was, and where she was going. She wasn't the person those kids had teased or the girl who had rebelled trying to find herself.

Instead she was the person who had taken control of her life. She had started believing in herself, who she knew she was and stopped believing the lies that were whispered behind her back.

Jenna reached back and touched her hand. "Wyatt's sweet."

Rachel nodded but she didn't know what to say, not when her own thoughts were still in a chaotic jumble and his mother-in-law had just left for a few minutes to stretch her legs.

"Yes, he really loves his girls."

Jenna laughed a little, "Okay, sure, that's what I meant."

Rachel knew what Jenna meant but she didn't comment. Instead she watched Wyatt ready his horse to run it up alongside the saddle bronc as the cowboy on the bucking animal made a leap and landed on the back of the pretty chestnut gelding Wyatt had bought at the auction. The cowboy immediately slid to the ground and headed back to the gate as the judge called out his score.

She was way too old for crushes. When Violet returned, Rachel made up an excuse why she had to leave. It wasn't really an excuse. She had a lot to do tomorrow and she didn't want to get to bed too late.

She kissed the girls goodbye and eased down the bleachers to the ground. Wyatt turned, nodding when he saw her on the grassy area next to the arena. She smiled back, trying to pretend the moment meant nothing to her.

The choir had taken their seats when Wyatt walked through the back doors of the church Sunday and found a seat near the front of the sanctuary. He'd taken the girls from the preschool Sunday school class to the preschool nursery. No Rachel in nursery this morning. His gaze scanned the front of the church, remembering she was in the choir.

She had taken her seat on the left side of the stage with the other altos. Her choir robe was red and white. She stood as the song leader hurried onto the stage. Her hands were already clapping the beat of a fast-paced song. As he stood there like an idiot, her gaze shifted. She smiled big and waved a little.

He hadn't felt so completely tongue-tied since seventh grade and Cora Mason, a ninth grader, had thought he was pretty cute. She had teased him for a couple of weeks and then informed him that he was too young. He wasn't twelve anymore.

And the preacher's daughter wasn't too old for him or a flirt. She laughed and sang a song about joy. He had to refocus, from Rachel to the music. The music invaded his spirit, pushing the darkness from the corners of his soul.

It was easy to find faith here. This church, Pastor Waters, it all worked together to make a difference in a heart that had been ready to turn itself off to anything other than anger and bitterness. There were moments when he started to feel alive again, as if he could turn it all around. He had been thinking about the teens in this church, not having a youth leader. Everyone scrambled to find activities that kept them out of trouble and gave them options on weekends when there wasn't much to do in Dawson other than get in trouble.

As the choir switched to a more worshipful song, Wyatt closed his eyes. He sang along, listening for one voice. But another spoke to his heart, this one said to trust.

When he opened his eyes the choir was walking off the stage. Rachel hurried out the side door. He smiled because he knew that she would be going back to the nursery. No one could ever accuse of her of sitting by, waiting for someone else to do the work.

Her mother, often fighting sickness, sat behind the piano. She had days when she couldn't make it to church, but when she did make it, she played the piano and taught a Sunday school class.

People made choices every day, how to deal with pain, what to do with anger. He remembered back to being a kid in church and the anger over his dad's affairs. He had been angry when the affairs were made public, but he hadn't blamed God. He'd blamed the person responsible, his father. Ryder had blamed God.

Eighteen months ago, Wyatt had been the one blaming God.

He leaned back in the pew and listened to the sermon. It took concentration to hear the words, but as he listened something in that sermon sounded like goodbye. It had to be his imagination. By the time the sermon ended, he was sure of it. It was just a sermon about moving on in life, making choices, following God. That wasn't a goodbye.

The congregation wasn't in a hurry to leave, but Wyatt had two girls waiting to be picked up from the nursery. He shook a few hands and moved past a crowd that seemed like it might pull him into a long conversation. When he reached the back door, Pastor Waters stopped him.

"No church tonight, Wyatt, but I wanted to talk to you if you have time."

"This evening?"

"If that's okay."

Wyatt glanced at his watch. Violet had stayed home

to fix a roast and he had a horse that needed one more day under the saddle before his owner picked him up.

"Seven o'clock okay?"

Pastor Waters nodded. "Sounds good. I'll meet you here."

"Good. I'd better get my kids."

Wyatt hurried down the hall to the nursery. He peeked in and his girls were the last to be picked up. Rachel leaned to tie Molly's shoes. Wyatt waited, not saying anything. He watched as she made the loop and then hugged his little girl. Kat turned and saw him.

"Daddy!"

"Hey, kiddo." He leaned over the half door and picked her up. Little arms wrapped tight around his neck. "Did you have fun?"

Kat nodded, "We made Nose Ark."

"Noah's ark! Cool beans!"

"And there were lions and they roared," Kat continued. "And fish."

"Fish on the ark?"

Kat nodded, pretty serious about the whole thing. "And Rachel said we could fish."

He glanced over his daughter's head and made eye contact with Rachel. She bit down on her bottom lip and shrugged a little. Nice way to look innocent.

Chapter Nine

Rachel smiled at Molly. The little girl stood next to her, looking first to Wyatt and then back to Rachel, her eyes big. Rachel smiled at Wyatt, too, ignoring that he looked a little put out. "You can go, too."

"Where are you going fishing?" He leaned against the door frame, still holding Kat.

She knew this had to be difficult. For the last six months he'd kept them pretty close. Now Violet was pushing him to get a housekeeper and Rachel wanted to take them off fishing.

"To the lake. I have permission to fish off a dock that belongs to one of our church members. It's a pretty day and…"

She was rambling. He did that to her, and she really resented that he managed to undo her ability to hold it together. He was just a man. A man in jeans, a dark blue polo and boots. His hair was brushed back from his face, probably with his hand. And he'd shaved for once. His cologne drifted into her space, a fresh, out-doorsy scent.

Right, just a man.

So why couldn't she focus and act like the adult she was? He was leaning, hip against the door frame, watching her, his dark eyes a little wicked, sparkling with something mischievous; as if he knew that she wanted to step closer.

One of the Sunday school teachers appeared behind him, opening her mouth to say something. Maria, just a few years older than Rachel, looked from Wyatt to Rachel and then she scurried away mumbling that she'd catch up with her later. That left her, Rachel, stuck in a quagmire of emotion she hadn't been expecting.

She climbed out of the emotional quicksand and got it together.

"If it isn't a good day…" She had been so sure of herself that morning when the idea hit.

So much for the butterfly on her back serving as a reminder to think before acting. If she'd followed that rule she would have allowed him to sign his girls out, and she'd have driven on to the lake alone. Alone was much less complicated than this moment with Wyatt.

"It actually is a good day." He glanced out the window, and she followed his gaze to blue skies and perfectly green grass. "It's a perfect day. I have a young horse that I need to work before his owner picks him up. I think Violet is leaving so it would be good to work him without the possibility of little girls racing across the yard."

"Good, then this works for both of us." She felt a funny sensation in her stomach. "I'll pack a lunch and we'll make a day of it."

"Is it Frank Rogers's dock?"

"It is."

"Good, I just like to know where they are."

"We can go?" Molly jumped up and down. "And take our swimsuits?"

"If your daddy says it is okay. I'll go to our house and make sandwiches while you take them home to get play clothes. Swimsuits, if you don't mind them getting in the water."

"If you keep them in the shallow water."

"I think we can manage." She watched him leave with the girls and then she packed up her bag and headed out. This felt good, spending time with the girls. She had wanted to do it since they showed up in Dawson, but up till now he hadn't looked as if he would agree to let them go.

But today she would teach them to fish. And she wouldn't think about not being here at the end of the summer.

Two hours later, although fishing was her plan, she realized fishing was the last thing the girls wanted. Try as she might, Rachel couldn't get them settled down next to her on the dock's wooden bench. Instead they were running back and forth, sticking their feet in the water.

Kat wrestled with her life jacket, wishing, over and over again, that she could take it off. Finally she sat down next to Rachel, her little head hanging as she fiddled with the zipper.

"Leave it on, Kat." Molly lectured in a voice far older than a three-, almost four-year-old.

"I'm big enough."

Rachel smiled and shook her head at the statement.

"I tell you what, girls, let's skip rocks. And maybe we can wade." She looked around, spotting the perfect way to kill time. "Or we could take a ride on the paddleboat!"

Both girls let out squeals of delight. Who needed to catch fish, when there was something as fun as a paddle boat? She tightened the life jacket that Kat had managed to loosen and lifted her into the boat. Molly went in the seat next to her. Rachel untied the fiberglass boat and settled into the empty seat next to the girls. She started to peddle and the little boat slid away from the dock.

Waves rolled across the surface of the lake making it rough going for one person pedaling against the wind. But the girls didn't mind. Rachel looked down at the two little girls, their faces up to the sun and eyes closed against the breeze.

They were quite a distance from shore when she turned and headed them back toward the dock. Kat leaned against her, groggy, her thumb in her mouth. Rachel leaned back, her arms relaxed behind the two little girls.

It was moments like this she ached for a child of her own. She wanted to be someone's wife, the mother of their children.

A few years ago she had started to doubt that dream.

Her sister, Cynthia, had chided her for martyrdom. She said Rachel was giving up her life to take care of their parents. Rachel shrugged off that accusation. It wasn't martyrdom, not really. It wasn't even guilt, not anymore. It had started out that way, but over the years, when no handsome prince appeared, she stopped believing that there would be one for her.

Cynthia had a house in the suburbs. Rachel had boxes that she kept in the closet for the next move.

She didn't want to think about moving again, not

now with the girls next to her. If they moved, it would hurt in a way that no move had ever hurt before. She leaned to kiss Kat on the top of her head.

Time to push these thoughts from her mind and enjoy this day. She didn't know for certain that her dad would take a new church. He never made a decision without prayer. And Rachel was praying, too. Because she didn't want to leave Dawson.

The horse stood stiff-legged with Wyatt in the saddle. He really didn't want to get thrown today. He should have stopped when he finished working the other horse, but this one couldn't be put off. He gave the horse a nudge with his heels. The leather of the saddle creaked a little as the horse shifted. Wyatt settled into the saddle and the gelding took a few steps forward. He pushed his hat down a little because he wasn't about to lose a brand-new hat.

A car pulled up the drive and honked. Great.

The horse let loose, bucking across the arena, jerking him forward and then back. Wyatt tightened his legs around the horse's middle and held tight. Man, he really didn't like a horse that bucked.

Eventually the animal settled and Wyatt held him tight. The horse stood in the center of the arena, trembling a little and heaving.

"Sorry, Buddy, I'm still back here. You aren't my first trip to the rodeo." He nudged the horse forward and they walked around the arena.

They did a few laps around the arena, the horse jarring him with a gait somewhere between a walk and trot. Wyatt nodded when his mother-in-law approached the fence. He'd thank her later for the ride he hadn't really wanted to take.

At least the horse had calmed down and they would end this training session with the gelding remembering that Wyatt had remained in the saddle. Horses kept those memories. If they got a guy on the ground, they remembered. If you gave up on them, they remembered. If you stuck, they remembered.

He rode up to the gate and leaned to open it. A little more of a lesson than he'd planned, but the gelding didn't dump him. Instead he backed and then slid through the open gate with Wyatt still in the saddle.

"I'm so sorry, Wyatt." Violet smiled a little and shrugged. "I didn't even think."

He swung his leg over and slid to the ground. "Normally it wouldn't matter. He's just greener than most. The people bought him as a yearling and kept him in the field for the next two years. He hadn't been trailered or had a halter on until we brought him over here."

"And you're already riding him?"

"We've done a couple of weeks of ground work to get him to this point."

"I see." But she didn't. Violet wasn't country. She had never been on a horse. A half-dozen years ago Wyatt had still been hitting rodeos and Violet had seen it as a waste of time.

He'd quit after that year, the year he won the buckle he'd always wanted. He quit to focus on ministry, on his wife and family.

The dog ran out of the barn and barked. Another car was coming up the drive. He groaned a little. Just what he needed, Violet and Rachel here at the same time. Rachel pulled up and his girls climbed out of her car.

"She took them fishing." He explained, because Violet had been gone when he got back from church. She'd left a note that she'd be back in the afternoon and she'd spend another night before going home.

"That's good, Wyatt." Violet didn't cry, but man, her eyes were overflowing.

"They love being around her."

"Yes, they do. And she's a lovely young woman." She smiled at him as if that statement meant more. She was making a point he really didn't want pointed out.

"Violet, she isn't…"

Rachel was too close and the girls were running toward him with a stringer of perch. He shook his head and let it go. Violet could believe what she wanted. He let his gaze slide to the woman in question, to a smile that went through him with a jolt. Her hair was pulled back in a tangled mass of brown curls and her eyes sparkled with laughter.

Violet could believe what she wanted, he repeated in his head as his attention slid back to his girls, to what really mattered.

"Did you girls have fun?" He took the string of fish and hugged the girls close. Molly and Kat wrapped their arms around him.

"We fished and waded and paddled a boat." Molly smiled a big smile. Her wounded spirit was healing. He smiled up at Rachel, knowing she was partially to thank for that. Rachel and time were healing their hearts. Kat's and Molly's, not his.

His didn't feel quite as battered, but he thanked time, not Rachel. Oh, and the faith that he'd held on to, even when he hadn't realized he was clinging to it like a life raft.

"They had lunch and on the way home took a short nap."

"Thank you." Wyatt straightened from hugging the girls, a little stiff from the wild ride he'd taken a few minutes ago. "I guess I should get inside and get cleaned up. I'm supposed to be at the church this evening to meet with your dad."

Rachel glanced at her watch. "I have a meeting, too. But first I'm going to drive up and see if Andie needs anything."

He nodded and watched her walk away. The girls were telling him all about fishing and the lake. He shifted his focus from them for just a moment to watch Rachel get in her car. She waved as she drove away, the top down on her car.

"Wendy would have liked her." Violet spoke softly and he couldn't meet her gaze. His mother-in-law liked Rachel Waters.

So where did that leave him? It left him staring after a little red convertible. The dog had come out of the barn and chased her down the drive. At least Wyatt had more sense and dignity than that.

Rachel pulled up the long drive to Andie and Ryder's house. She did a double take when she spotted a plane parked near the barn. What in the world?

She got out of her car, still looking at the plane and ignoring the border collie that ran circles around her, barking and wagging its black-and-white tail to show that the barking was meant to be friendly. She reached to pet the dog and then walked up the sidewalk to ring the doorbell.

Etta opened the door before Rachel could actually

push the bell. The older woman looked beautiful as always with every hair in place and makeup perfectly applied. Today she wore jean capris and a T-shirt, no tie-dye.

"Hey, girl, what are you doing out here?" Etta motioned her inside.

"I took Molly and Kat fishing, then thought I'd stop and see if Andie needs anything."

Etta laughed. "She needs something all right. She needs off that couch. She's driving us all crazy. It's spring and she can't stand being inside."

"I hear you talking about me," Andie yelled from the living room.

Etta's brows shot up and she smiled a little, then motioned Rachel inside. She walked to the wide door that led into the living room.

Poor Andie, pregnant with twins, flat on the couch. The other option was the hospital. She waved Rachel in.

"Contrary to popular belief, I don't bite." Andie rolled on her side. "And do not call the media and tell them there is a whale beached in Dawson."

"You look beautiful."

Andie growled a little and sighed. "Right."

"It'll be worth it…"

Andie waved her hand. "I know, I know."

"And it won't take you long to get back to your old self. With babies, of course."

"It's frightening." Andie's eyes shadowed. "Honestly, Rachel, it really is scary. Ryder and I are just learning to be responsible for ourselves, and we're going to be responsible for two little people, for making sure they grow up to be good adults. We're going to be responsible for their health, for their well-being, for their spiritual life."

"I'm sure God is going to have a little hand in it."

"Of course. And hopefully He'll get us past the mistakes we're going to make."

Rachel sat down in the chair next to the couch. "Train up a child in the way they should go."

"And when they are teens they'll rebel and give you gray hair." Andie laughed and the shadows dissolved.

"Right. I think I gave my parents more than their share of gray hair during my rebellious years."

"I can't picture it, you as a rebel."

Rachel sat back in the chair and thought about it. "I don't know if it was rebellion or just trying to find a place where I felt included."

"You?"

"Me. My sister, Cynthia, was the pretty cheerleader. Rob was studious. I was overweight and never felt like I fit in. I was always the poor pastor's daughter in secondhand clothing, lurking at the back of the room."

"I'm sorry, Rach. I wish you could have grown up here."

"Me, too. But I went through those things for a reason. I can relate to feeling left out, afraid, unsure of who I'm supposed to be. When I tell the kids at church that this stuff is temporary, they believe me."

"I love you, Rachel Waters." Andie reached for her hand. "The girls at church are lucky to have you. And before long maybe we'll also have a new youth minister?"

"Dad has interviewed a few people but he hasn't

landed on the right person." Actually, her dad believed the right person was in their church and just not ready for the job. Not yet. Not until his own heart healed.

"What about Wyatt?"

"I'm not sure if he's ready."

"No, I mean, what *about* Wyatt?" Andie's smile changed and her eyes twinkled with mischief. "He's pretty hot."

"He's pretty taken and your brother-in-law."

"Taken?"

Humor and laughter faded. Andie's head tilted to the side and she waited.

"He still wears his wedding band."

"Of course. I think he hasn't thought to take it off." Andie grimaced a little. "These two are really doing the tango in there."

"Do you need me to get Etta or Ryder?"

Andie shook her head. "Nope, not yet. It's just occasional kicks and a few twinges. When the contractions really hit, I won't be this calm."

Rachel left a few minutes later. As she drove down the drive and turned back in the direction of Dawson, her thoughts turned again to Wyatt Johnson.

He was a complication. She smiled because it was the first time she'd found the perfect label for him. Complication.

How did people deal with a complication like that, one that made them forget convictions, forget past pain, made them want to take chances?

It seemed easy enough. Stay away. That was the key to dealing with temptation, resist it. Turn away from it. Not toward it.

She'd learned to resist the lure of chocolate cake, so surely she could learn to resist Wyatt Johnson. After all, she really, really loved chocolate cake.

Chapter Ten

It felt pretty strange, walking out of church with the sun setting, and his girls not with him. Wyatt reached into his pocket for his keys. He waved goodbye to Pastor Waters and headed for his truck.

Slowly, little by little, he was getting back to his life. Or at least the life he now had. That included faith. He could deal with life, with being alive.

Pastor Waters had helped him through the anger part of his grief. Wyatt had been working through the questions that had haunted him, kept him up at night.

Why had God allowed Wendy to take those pills? Why hadn't God stopped her from getting them, or stopped her from taking them? Why hadn't God sent someone to keep her from doing that to them? To herself?

Wyatt exhaled, but it didn't hurt the way it once did. He stopped at his truck but didn't get in. Instead he walked to the back of the truck and put the tailgate down. A few minutes alone wasn't going to hurt him. The girls were good with Violet.

He sat on the tailgate.

God hadn't stopped Wendy from breaking his heart. He closed his eyes and man, the anger still got to him. It was easier to be mad at God than to be mad at Wendy. She had made a choice. She had gone to a doctor who hadn't known about her depression, got pills Wyatt hadn't known about and had taken those pills.

After counseling. After prayer. After it seemed that she was doing better.

She'd made a choice to ignore the voice that probably tried to intervene, telling her to stop, to call someone, to give God a chance. God had been there the day she took those pills, probably pleading in His quiet way, trying to get her attention. And she'd made a choice.

Wyatt had to let go of blaming himself and God. He had to let go of blaming her. She'd been far sicker than any of them realized. She'd been hurting more than he knew.

A voice, real, clear, fresh, carried across the lawn of the church. He opened his eyes and listened to her sing. Rachel. He couldn't see her but he saw her car on the other side of the church. He hadn't realized she was still there.

He listened carefully to words that were far away. She was singing about falling down in the presence of God.

After a few minutes there was silence. The door of the church thudded closed. He watched as she walked down the sidewalk, away from him, not even realizing he was watching. He smiled a little because when no one was watching, she had a fast walk, almost a skip. She had changed from shorts and a T-shirt to a dress and cowboy boots.

A few minutes later he listened as she tried to start

her car. The starter clicked but the engine didn't turn over. So much for casual spying without getting caught. He hopped down from the back of the truck and headed her way.

She sat behind the wheel of the convertible, the top down. When she spotted him she looked surprised and a little smile tilted her mouth.

"Problem?" He leaned in close and her scent wrapped around him. Oriental perfume, peppermint gum and wild cherry lip gloss.

"No, not really." She turned the key again.

"Really?"

She bit down on her bottom lip and shook her head. "The alternator has been making a funny noise. Dad said it was about to go."

"Oh. That isn't something I can fix."

"Really?" Sarcasm laced her tone and he laughed.

"Really." He opened her car door. "But I can give you a ride home."

"Thank you." She stepped out of the car. Up close the dress had tiny flowers and she was wearing a jean jacket over it. He was used to seeing her in jeans. She reached into the back of the car for her purse and the bag she carried each week. He knew it usually contained cookies and craft projects for the nursery. On Wednesdays she worked with teen girls. She was always busy.

He took the bag from her hands. "Let me carry that for you."

She smiled and let him take it. "I didn't expect you to still be here."

"I had a meeting with your dad."

"Oh, that's right."

He wondered if she knew, but he doubted she did.

Pastor Waters wasn't the type to talk, not even to his family, about church business or counseling sessions.

"Have you had dinner?" He opened the passenger-side truck door for her and she climbed in.

"No."

"I would take you out, but the only thing open is the convenience store. How about a slice of pizza and a frozen slush?" He stood in the door of the truck, waiting for her answer.

She finally nodded. "Sounds good."

No, it sounded like trouble. But he'd offered and now he had to follow through. He shut her door and then he whistled low and walked around to climb in on his side.

He started his truck and backed out of the parking space. A quick glance right and Rachel was staring out the window, her hands in her lap, fingers clasped. He smiled because he hadn't expected her to be nervous.

The smile faded pretty quickly when he realized he felt a little like wringing his own hands. What was he, sixteen? Not even close. He was double that and then some. But when was the last time he'd been alone with a woman who wasn't his wife? Other than his mother-in-law or Andie, when he drove her to the doctor once a couple of months back, it had been a long time.

At least he still knew the basics. Open the door for her. Buy her a nice dinner. Or the closest thing to a nice dinner. Walk her to the door when he took her home.

Kiss her good-night?

He shifted gears and cruised down the back road that led the few blocks to the convenience store. The evening was warm and humid. He rolled down the windows and wind whipped through the cab of the truck.

Rachel continued to stare out the window. She

reached up to hold her hair in place as it blew around her face. They passed a few houses and people in their yards turned to wave. Well, at least everyone in town would know tomorrow that he'd been spotted with Rachel Waters.

Good or bad, it would get around.

"Want me to roll up the window?"

She shook her head and finally turned to look at him, smiling a little. She had a dimple in one cheek, and he noticed for the first time that her hair glinted with hints of auburn. He was a man, he wasn't supposed to remember details.

"I love this time of year."

He downshifted and turned into the parking lot of Circle A convenience store. "Yeah, me, too."

The timbre of his voice was low and husky, reminding her of fingers in her hair. Rachel swallowed at a thought that felt a little dangerous to a woman who had always been pretty happily single.

The metal building that housed the Circle A was lit up inside and out. Cars were lined up at the gas pumps and several trucks were stopped at the edge of the paved lot; teenagers hanging out on a Sunday night.

"This town never changes." Wyatt shook his head as he made the observation.

"Is that bad?"

"No, not really. I guess it's good to find a place that isn't moving too fast." He pulled the key from the ignition. "Do you want to eat at one of the booths inside?"

Orange plastic seats and bright fluorescent lights. That would just draw attention to them. "I'd rather eat out here."

"I guess we could be like the kids and sit on the tailgate."

Why that appealed to her, she didn't have a clue. But it did. She dug around in the handful of teenage memories she'd held on to and not one of them included sitting on the tailgate with a cowboy. Every woman should have that memory.

"Sounds like fun."

He shot her a look and smiled. His eyes were dark and his skin was tanned from working in the sun. He pushed the white cowboy hat back a little, giving her a better view. Who needed the Seven Wonders of the World if they could sit in a truck with Wyatt Johnson?

"So, are you coming in?"

She nodded and reached for her door handle. This was getting ridiculous, getting lost in daydreams that should have faded when she was sixteen, wanting things she'd thought she'd never have, with a man who clearly wasn't looking.

Butterfly, don't fail me now. She smiled a little as she closed the truck door and met him on the sidewalk. They didn't hold hands and he didn't put a guiding hand on her back. This wasn't a date, just two people having pizza.

Because her car hadn't started. She reminded herself that he was just being kind. When they circled the building and walked up to the sliding glass doors on the front of the building, their reflection greeted her. A man in jeans and a cowboy hat, a woman in a dress and boots. They looked like a nice couple, she thought.

Reminder—not a couple, just a nice guy who offered to take her home. Handsome, sweet and just a friend.

The cool air of the convenience store and the aroma

of convenience foods greeted them as they walked through the doors. A few kids stood around the soda fountain, talking, laughing and being kids. Wyatt's hand touched her back and he guided her to the counter where food warmed beneath lights and pizza circled on a display wheel.

"Pepperoni or sausage?" Wyatt asked, too close to her ear. She shivered a little and shrugged. He smiled at the girl behind the counter. "Three slices of each."

She started to object but kept her mouth closed. The girl in the red apron smock opened the plastic door and slid slices of pizza into a box.

"I can get our drinks," Rachel offered. "Do you really want a slushy?"

He grinned, the way Kat grinned when she was up to something. And a slushy wasn't exactly an act of rebellion. But on him, it appeared that way. His grin was a little lopsided and his dark eyes flashed.

"I want all three flavors."

She grimaced. "For real?"

"For real."

It sounded disgusting to Rachel, but if he really wanted to do that to himself, more power to him. She held his cup under each nozzle and grabbed a bottle of water for herself. When she returned he was at the register. He eyed her water but didn't comment.

Not until they were back outside sitting on the tailgate of his truck.

"Water, seriously?"

"I like water." She took a slice of pizza from the box.

And then there was silence as they ate and watched teenagers horsing around. One girl tried too hard. Rachel sighed because she remembered trying too hard.

She remembered chasing the boys, grabbing them, laughing too loud.

"Another slice?" He held out the box but she shook her head.

"Two is enough for me."

He set the box down next to him and nodded at the teenagers. "That really takes me back."

"Yeah, me, too." Rachel leaned against the side of the truck bed. "But I bet we have different memories. You were that boy, the one with the swagger and the grin."

A boy in jeans, a T-shirt and boots, with the big truck and the bigger smile.

He grinned and tipped his hat back. "Yeah, I guess I was."

"I was that girl." She pointed to the girl who was grabbing the boys and staggering just a little. Rachel wanted to rescue her, to pull her out of the crowd and tell her to love herself.

Closing her eyes, it was too easy to be that girl, to feel so insecure, to want so much to be loved and not getting that it really did have to start with accepting herself. She really hadn't gotten it, that she couldn't force people to love her.

"You okay?" The words were soft and a hand touched hers.

Rachel opened her eyes and smiled. "Just remembering."

"What's wrong with that girl?" Wyatt didn't look at the girl. He watched her instead. She shrugged and avoided what she knew would be a questioning look, but she felt his gaze on her, felt his intensity. "She looks like she's having fun."

"She isn't having fun. She's trying to find someone who will love her."

He didn't respond. She turned to look at him, smiling because she hadn't meant to delve that deeply into the past.

"That was you?"

"That was me."

"I can't imagine."

"I've gone through some changes since then." Another reason for the butterfly, a reminder that life has a way of changing things. Every season brings something new.

She hopped down from the back of the truck. "We should go."

He nodded, agreeing. Instead of commenting, he grabbed their trash and carried it to the barrel at the corner of the store. Rachel opened her door to get into the truck, but she shot one last look back at the kids. They had a beach ball, bouncing it in the air from person to person. Another truck pulled in. More kids got out. The young girl she had watched raced around the crowd, frantically trying to be a part of something.

A deep ache attached itself to Rachel's heart, remembering that person she'd left behind. But when Wyatt got behind the wheel, she questioned if she really had, or was that insecure girl still hiding inside her, wanting the love that Rachel insisted she really didn't need.

The lights of the parsonage glowed a soft yellow from behind gauzy curtains. A motion light in the backyard came on as Wyatt pulled the truck to a stop. He shifted into neutral and set the emergency brake. Rachel was already reaching for the door handle.

He should let it end that way, with her getting out, him letting her walk up to the door. But a butterfly tattoo and the hurt look that had flicked across her features as they'd sat eating their pizza kept him from listening to common sense.

Later he would regret this moment, he knew he would. He would regret not listening to the part of him that wanted to remain detached. Instead he got out of the truck and met her as her feet hit the ground.

"I can help you get your car to the garage tomorrow."

"Dad can take care of it." Her eyes were huge in the dusky night.

Another moment that he'd have to think about later: looking a little too long into those eyes. But looking into her eyes didn't begin to compare to the need to hold her. His hands were shoved into his pockets and he fought the part of himself that didn't want to get back in that truck and drive away.

She sighed and her lips parted, not an invitation, he didn't think. No, she was probably going to say something. She probably should tell him to back off or hit the road. Either of the two would work.

A thinking man would have given her a chance to say one of those two things. An idiot cowboy like him didn't always think things through. Sometimes guys like him just had no sense at all and they acted.

That's what he did, he acted, freeing his hands from his pockets and tangling them into masses of brown curls that smelled like wild flowers. He breathed deep as he leaned toward her. He hovered for a second, giving her one last chance to send him packing. When she didn't, he touched his lips to hers.

For a long second she didn't react, but then she

moved and her hands touched his arms. He drank her in, steadying himself with one hand on the truck door behind her. Man, she was sweet. The kiss was sweet. Her hands moved to his back, holding him close. That was sweet.

He pulled back, resting his forehead against hers because he couldn't really breathe. Or think.

And then reality came rushing back in, hitting him full force with a load of guilt and remorse. Those shouldn't be the emotions a man felt after a kiss. She deserved more than a guy tied to the past.

"I'm sorry." He whispered close to her ear, wanting to pull her back into his arms. Instead of giving in, this time he stepped back.

"Yeah, I knew you would be." Pain flickered across her features, hard to miss, even in the dark.

"What do you mean?" He jerked off his hat and swiped a pretty shaky hand through his hair.

Her expressions changed to compassion. She reached for his hand. "I just kissed a married man."

He pulled his hand loose from hers, too aware of the wedding ring he'd never taken off, and aware of the message it sent. He shoved his hat back on his head and took a few smart steps back.

It hurt to breathe and hurt worse to think about her words. She hadn't moved away from his truck until that moment and as she stepped past him, she paused to touch his cheek, her smile was soft and sweet.

"I know you loved her. You really don't have to explain or apologize."

"Yeah, I do." He said the words too late. She was halfway to the house and he was standing there like a fool. Her dog ran out of the house, past her to him. The big shepherd circled him a few times, growling. Her whistle called the animal off.

The drive home didn't take near long enough. He had two minutes to get it together. He felt like he needed two hours. Or two days. A man didn't kiss a woman like that and just walk off.

Rachel was the kind of woman looking for forever, not stolen moments at the end of the night. And Wyatt didn't know if he'd ever want to do forever again. But he did have to think about the future and about the ring still on his finger.

As he parked, lights flashed off in the upstairs room that belonged to his girls. He sat in his truck and watched as other lights came on. Violet waiting for him to come home.

He needed to get his act together. He leaned back in the seat and stared at the barn, at the glimmer of moon peeking through the clouds. At stars glittering in the clear patches of sky.

For eighteen months he'd been asking himself the question he had wanted to ask Wendy. Why had she left them? He let out a tight sigh that came from so deep inside him that it ached. Had she stopped loving them? Had she been unable to love them? He rubbed a hand across his face, clearing his vision.

It was wrong to blame her. He'd even come to terms with the fact that he couldn't blame himself. Now he had to come to terms with the fact that she wasn't coming back. Guilt, accusations, anger—none of that would bring her back.

He put his hands on the steering wheel and the gold band on his left hand glinted. He raised his hand and shook his head. Maybe it was time to let her go, to move on with his life.

Or maybe it wasn't. He'd deal with one thing at a time.

It took a minute to get the ring off, twisting and sliding it over his knuckles. His finger felt bare. His heart felt even worse. He slipped the ring into his pocket and opened the door of the truck.

Violet walked out the back door. He walked across the yard, his vision blurred. He took in a deep breath and let it go.

When he walked up the steps of the porch, Violet gave him space. She followed him inside and instead of asking questions she started a pot of coffee. Good thinking, because it looked like it might be a long night.

When she turned, her eyes were misty and her smile trembled on her lips. "Are you okay?"

"I am. Thank you for staying with the girls while I helped Rachel out."

"Where else would I be? Wyatt, you didn't stop being my family when…" She bit down on her bottom lip and blinked a few times. "You're my kid. Those are my sweet granddaughters up there. You're all I have left of Wendy, and I don't ever want that to end. No matter what happens in the future, I hope to always be your mom."

He hugged her and she eventually pulled away and reached for a tissue, pulling it from the box on the counter. She wiped her eyes and smiled.

"Violet, I thank God every single day for you and you'll always be in our lives."

"That's good to know because I can really be a pain sometimes and I need people who will put up with me."

He laughed, and pulled two cups from the cabinet over the coffeepot. Violet sighed a little and he turned.

"You took off your ring."

He looked at his left hand and nodded. "Yeah, I did."

Because of Rachel Waters. He didn't have to explain that to Violet. He guessed she probably knew. She probably understood better than anyone else in his life. Maybe even better than he understood it himself.

Chapter Eleven

The dog slid through the door ahead of Rachel. She kicked off her shoes and pushed them up against the wall. She dropped her purse next to them. She hadn't come in right away. After that moment in the yard with Wyatt, she had needed a few minutes to clear her mind and get it together before she faced her parents.

As if she was still fifteen and trying to hide something.

She was twenty-nine and really not a child.

In reality she was a long, long way from childhood and innocence. She sat down at the kitchen table and moved a few pieces of the puzzle that had been there for days, unfinished. The painted faces of kittens on cardboard were scattered, unrecognizable. She found an edge and slid it into place.

Her life was just as scattered, just as in pieces as that puzzle. She had kissed Wyatt Johnson. Her parents had decided to take the church in Tulsa and she couldn't tell anyone until the formal announcement. She had to bury the pain of moving and leaving this place behind.

She had to leave Wyatt and the girls. She hadn't

expected that to be the part that hurt the most. She hadn't expected to feel anything for Wyatt other than sympathy.

Surprise. The feelings were unexpected after years of holding back and waiting for God to bring someone into her life. She moved another puzzle piece and a ring on her own finger glinted in the soft light of the kitchen. A purity ring that she'd put on after some very bad relationship choices.

She had made a promise to wait for God to bring someone into her life. She had made a promise to herself to stop pursuing and to wait for someone who loved her enough to pursue her. She figured the fact that she was nearly thirty said it all.

"Hey, kiddo, how's your car?" Her dad stood in the doorway, the tie from earlier in the day gone, but he still looked like Pastor Waters. She smiled and pushed the other chair out with her foot, an invitation.

"It'll have to go to the garage. The alternator finally gave up and died."

"I'll have it towed to Grove tomorrow."

"Thanks, Dad."

"What's up?"

"Nothing."

Robert Waters crossed the room and sat down across from her. She smiled up at him because this was a scene that had played out a lot in their lives, the two of them together with a puzzle between them. He started moving pieces and she did the same.

"This move isn't what you want, is it?" He looked up, smiling a little. "You don't have to go."

"I know that. I want to go."

He pushed a piece of the puzzle into place and they

finally had an entire kitten. She was allergic, so this was the closest she got to fuzzy felines.

"Rachel, promise me you'll tell us the truth. If you don't want to leave, you shouldn't. You know that Etta would gladly let you stay with her."

"I know that, but Etta isn't my family."

"No, she isn't." He piled up gray puzzle pieces that went to the gray kitten she was working on. Rachel reached and took one that might fit.

"Dad, I'm okay with this." She smiled because she was okay. It wasn't her first move and she knew that moves were never easy. But she was okay. She would adjust.

She was used to leaving places, leaving people. Doing the right thing didn't always mean the right thing felt good. Sometimes doing the right thing was difficult.

Her dad stood up. Before he walked away, he leaned to kiss the top of her head. "Your mom said to tell you good-night and she loves you."

"Right back at her." She reached for his hand to stop him from walking away. "Don't worry about me."

"I always do. That's part of being a parent. We want our children to be happy."

She nodded but this time she didn't answer. She didn't know how to respond to being happy. Her heart had gone into rebellion and suddenly wanted something she knew she couldn't have.

The best way to get her heart into check was to explain to it that she had just experienced something that everyone experiences: a good-night kiss. It had been nothing more and nothing less, just a kiss at the end of a sweet evening with a man who might possibly be a friend.

To make it anything more than that was a mistake. Like telling him he was still wearing his wedding ring. She cringed a little because it wasn't her place to point that out to him, not a man who had been kindness itself. He had kissed her good-night. It wasn't as if he'd proposed.

Wyatt Johnson was sweet and gorgeous. He wasn't looking for long-term.

She moved another piece of puzzle into place and got up to go to bed. Tomorrow she'd apologize.

The crazy gelding jumped sideways and lurched. Wyatt held tight, wrapping his legs around the animal's belly. If he'd been paying attention instead of thinking about holding Rachel last night, maybe he wouldn't have been in this position. The horse beneath him shook his head and hunched again. Wyatt held tight, waiting. The horse settled into a jarring trot across the arena.

He'd be glad to send this one back to his owner. If it wasn't for the fact that he liked to tell people he'd never met a horse he couldn't break, he'd probably send the horse back today.

He glanced to the side, making sure the girls were still on the swing. They were. As he watched, Molly jumped up and started waving. He caught a glimpse of an old truck. Molly waved and ran.

The horse unleashed on him, bucking across the arena. Hooves beat into the hard-packed dirt of the arena. Wyatt pushed his hat down and held tight, his teeth gritted against the jolt that set him a little back in the saddle. The horse lurched again, this time nearly getting him off the side.

He barely made it back into the saddle when the

crazy animal's head went down and his back end went up. Wyatt felt himself leave the seat and go airborne over the horse's head. He heard Molly scream and then he hit the ground.

Pain shot through his back and head. He rolled over on his back and worked to take a deep breath. He bent his knees and blinked a few times to clear his brain.

This couldn't be happening.

Rachel yelled his name. Good way to be calm, Rachel. He shook his head. The girls were screaming. He rolled to his belly and made it to his knees. Oh, yeah, he'd been here before, sucking in a breath that hurt like crazy.

"I guess this is a bad time to tell you I saw a few of your cows out on the road?"

The voice came from his left. He rolled his head that way and tried to smile. But smiling hurt, too. He was way too old for getting thrown.

"Yeah, this might be a bad time."

"Want help?" Rachel reached for his arm. He gritted his teeth and pushed himself to his feet with her hand holding him steady.

"Daddy?" Molly's voice trembled. He blinked and focused on her face, just behind Rachel.

"I'm okay, sugar bug." He drew in a deep breath. "Wow."

"Should I call…" Rachel bit down on her bottom lip and shrugged a little.

An ambulance. Good not to say it around the girls and panic them more than they were. He shook his head and regretted it because it felt like it unhinged his brain a little.

"You can call Greg Buckley and tell him to come and

get that crazy horse of his. I'm done with that animal."
He'd been fighting that crazy buckskin every time he
got in the saddle.

"You think?" She smiled and his girls followed her
example. "What about those cows?"

"Daddy, are you broke?" Molly stared up at him,
eyes full of unshed tears.

"Nah, of course not."

Violet headed their way, picking through the dirt
and rocks with high heels that he would have laughed
about if he'd been able to laugh. "Do you want me to
drive you to the hospital?"

She'd been packing her stuff, getting ready to go
home. Now he had other concerns.

The girls. He sucked in a breath that hurt like crazy.
And crazy wasn't the word he really wanted to say. A lot
of other words came to mind. He leaned on the fence,
draping his arms over the top rail. The girls.

He shifted to look at Rachel.

"Could you stay with the girls?"

"Of course I can. Or I can drive you."

"No, Violet can take me." What he didn't need or
want to do was lean on Rachel. Literally. He didn't want
to be in pain in front of her. It didn't do a guy's ego any
good to have to lean on a woman to make it to the car.

"Daddy?" Molly stared up at him, brown eyes wide.

"I'm fine, Mol. You stay with Rachel and I'll be
home later."

"Do you need help?" Rachel had stayed next to
him, smelling soft and sweet. And she was asking if
he needed help.

Even if it killed him, he wasn't going to lean on
anyone.

"I'm fine." He touched Molly's cheek and she smiled. "Be good."

She nodded and grabbed Kat's hand. "We will."

He never had a doubt. But would she be afraid?

"Okay, let's go." One last deep breath, and then he headed for Violet's car with steady steps that said he would be fine.

Violet walked next to him. "You're such a tough guy."

"Yeah, well, we wouldn't want the girls to see me cry." He gritted the words out from clenched teeth.

"Are you really going to cry?" Violet teased as she opened the passenger-side door.

He waved at Rachel and the girls. "Not on your life, Violet."

"You cowboys think you're so tough."

Yeah, that's exactly what he thought.

Violet slid behind the wheel of the Cadillac and turned the key. As she shifted into reverse, she glanced his way. "How badly are you hurt? No lies this time."

"I haven't lied yet." He leaned back into the soft leather seat. He wished his truck felt this good. "Maybe ribs, maybe my back."

"How are you going to take care of the girls when I leave? You've vetoed every applicant I've interviewed. What do we do now?"

"I can take care of my girls, Violet."

"I know you can, but this changes things."

"You have me in the ICU and I haven't even made it to the E.R."

"I'm thinking of all the possibilities."

"Well, I'm not. I'm fine and I'll be home by dinner. I have a birthday party to plan. Molly will be four next week."

"I know. I had planned on going home to get a few things done and coming back before then."

"And you can still do that." He closed his eyes and counted to twenty.

As he counted he heard her phone dialing. He opened his eyes and waited.

"Rachel, this is Violet. Oh, no, honey, we haven't made it to Grove. No, but I need a favor. I'm taking John Wayne to the E.R., but he's probably going to need help when I leave. I haven't hired anyone because he's picky. I know you have a lot going on, but if you could take the job temporarily." Short pause and he wanted to jerk the phone out of Violet's hand. "Just for a month or until we can find someone."

"Violet." He whispered what she should have seen as a warning. She smiled at him and kept talking.

"That's great, honey. I'll write you a check when we get back. Or when I get back. Right, just keep the house clean, cook some meals and make sure the girls have clothes that match."

"I can dress my kids." He pushed the button to recline the bucket seat. "Women."

Because of a woman he'd taken his ring off last night. It was all connected: the kiss, her words and removing his wedding ring. He just didn't want to draw the lines, not at the moment.

Maybe it was just about letting Wendy go. Maybe it was about Rachel. Right now he needed a shot of something and a lot less thinking going on in his scrambled brain.

Chapter Twelve

"What do we do with that horse?" Rachel looked down at the girls. The two of them shrugged. Of course they didn't know. They were two and four. Or almost four.

Molly was about to have a birthday. Rachel worried her bottom lip thinking about that special occasion and the possibility that Wyatt would stay in the hospital. Okay, horse first, cows in the road second. Or maybe the cows should be first.

She pulled the phone from her pocket and called Ryder.

"Ryder." He answered with his name and he sounded stressed and frazzled.

"Ryder, it's Rachel. Listen, Wyatt got thrown and Violet is taking him to the E.R."

"Oh, that's just what I need."

Okay, not the response she expected. "Ryder, you guys have cows out, just a few hundred feet down from your drive. And I have this horse here, the one that dumped him, and..."

"Rachel, I'm sorry, I can't. Andie's having contractions. I'm flying her to Tulsa."

In the background she heard Andie yell that she wasn't getting in a plane with him. Rachel smiled and waited for the two to argue it out and remember that she was on the phone.

"Rachel, I'll call Jason and see if he can put those cows in. Can you handle the horse?"

"I don't know. I can try."

She looked at the horse in the arena. The buckskin stood at the far corner. He needed the saddle and bridle removed and he needed to be put in the field. Or maybe a stall. She wondered which one.

"If you can't get him, call Jason or Adam."

"Okay. Is there anything I can do for you and Andie?"

"Pray."

The conversation ended and she was on her own. Rachel looked at Molly and Kat. No help there. They both looked pretty nervous. Molly's dark eyes overflowed with tears.

"I want my daddy."

"I know, honey." Rachel squatted in front of the girls. "I know you're worried about your daddy. He's fine. Remember when he left, he was talking. He even walked to the car. He's fine."

"He'll come home." Molly sobbed and rubbed her eyes.

"Of course he will." This wasn't normal fear. Rachel hugged the girls close. "He'll be fine. And while he's gone, we'll be fine. We'll get that silly horse taken care of and if we need to, we'll put the cows in. We can do that, can't we?"

Keep them busy. That's all she knew to do.

But it meant walking into the arena with a horse she didn't trust. She straightened, trying to look taller, and gave the horse a look. As if that would do any good. A hand tugged on hers.

"You aren't gonna ride him." Molly wide-eyed and maybe a little impressed.

"No, honey, I'm not. I'm going to unsaddle him and—" she bit down on her bottom lip, "—I'm going to put him in a stall."

Molly grabbed her hand and with her other hand she grabbed hold of Kat. "We'll go with you."

"I appreciate that, Molly, but I think I should go in alone."

It sounded like a movie, as if they were going into a house with monsters, or some horrible villain. It was a horse, a tan horse with a black mane and tail. Just a small little horse. Well, maybe not so small.

"You girls wait out here." She handed Molly her phone. She didn't say to call 9-1-1 if something happened. Instead she smiled as if she was brave and not shaking in her shoes.

She whistled, kind of. The horse shot her a disinterested look. Okay, she was used to that look. He must be a man. She smiled at her joke and kept walking. The horse didn't move.

"Buddy, it would help me out if you'd play nice."

The horse reached his nose under the bottom rail of the fence and nibbled at a few blades of grass. Rachel walked up to him, talking softly, saying a few prayers under her breath. Did horses smell fear? She really hoped not.

She reached for the reins that had been dragging on

the ground. The horse snorted and raised his head. He jerked away from her but she held tight.

"Listen, horse, I'm not a cowgirl like Jenna and Andie, but I do know how to hold on tight. I am not going to let you win."

The buckskin edged close and snorted, blowing grass and grain all over the front of her shirt. "Oh, that's real nice."

She held both reins and led the horse back to the barn. He plodded along behind her as if he was Kat's little pony. She rubbed his neck as they walked.

"So now you're going to be nice?"

For a brief moment she relaxed but then she remembered how it felt when she watched Wyatt go flying from the horse's back. She didn't want to remember how it felt to watch him hit the ground and stay there, motionless.

From across the arena she heard her phone ring. She glanced back. Molly held it up.

"Go ahead and answer it. Tell them I'll call back." She didn't want to yell, to startle the horse.

She had decided the best course of action was to unsaddle him, take off his bridle and leave him in the arena. She could get him a bucket of water and hay.

First, the saddle. She wrapped the reins in a hook on the wall of the barn and the horse stood perfectly still. She pulled the girth strap loose and eased off the saddle. He moved away from her and she thought about how easy it would be for him to turn and kick.

Instead of thinking about that, about possibilities, she unbuckled the strap on the bridle and pulled it over his ears and off his head. The horse stood for a moment, a little unsure. Finally he backed away from her and turned to trot to the other side of the arena.

She had done it. Now to take care of the girls. She turned as a truck pulled up the drive. Jason Bradshaw. He hopped out of the truck and headed her way, his big smile making things feel better.

"You got him unsaddled." Jason opened the gate for her. "I'll put him in a stall and feed him for you."

"What about the cows in the road?"

Jason picked up Kat and tickled her until she laughed. "I put them back in and fixed a loose section of fence. Have you heard anything yet?"

"Not yet. I don't think they've had time." She glanced at the girls because she didn't want to have this conversation in front of them.

Jason sat Kat on the back of Rachel's truck. He motioned for her to walk with him. Rachel followed. The cowboy, his red hair cut short, had a smile that made everyone feel better.

"Rachel, do you know about the girls?"

"I'm not sure what you mean."

Jason rubbed his jaw. He glanced from her to her truck where the girls were waiting. "This should be up to Wyatt, but there's something you should know. In case Wyatt doesn't get home tonight, you need to understand that Molly gets pretty upset when he isn't here."

"I'm not sure if you should tell me something that Wyatt hasn't told me."

"He'd want you to know. For the sake of his girls. Molly and Kat were with Wendy. They were alone until he got home that afternoon and found them."

And she got it in a way that ached so deep inside her she didn't know if she could draw in a breath. She thought about those two little girls alone with their mother. But Wendy wouldn't have been with them. She took the pills and left them alone.

Rachel turned away from Jason because it was too much to know this secret about the wife that Wyatt had loved. Still loved.

But he'd taken off his wedding ring. She'd noticed it as she'd helped him up. She wondered if it had been about the kiss or what she'd said. Or had it been something he'd been working up to and he finally realized it was time?

"I should take them inside and fix their dinner."

Jason walked with her back to the truck. "He doesn't tell people because it's Wendy's memory. He doesn't want that to be what people think about when they remember her."

"I understand."

Jason lifted Molly and Kat out of the back of the truck. He gave them each a hug as he set them on the ground. "You girls help Miss Rachel. She's going to stay with you until your daddy gets home."

"Will he come home tonight?" Molly held on to his hand.

"I'm not sure, Molly. He might come home tonight. Or maybe tomorrow. Either way, he'll be fine and so will you. Rachel is going to stay with you."

She was staying. She smiled at the girls. They looked at her, both wide-eyed and full of trust. Of course she was staying.

It was after midnight when Wyatt walked through the front door of his house. He had eased up the front steps because two steps were easier than five or six when a guy had a few cracked ribs and a couple of pulled muscles. Oh, yeah, and a concussion.

He didn't remember, but the horse must have landed a good kick in his side as he went down.

Violet walked behind him. Poor Violet, he guessed she really wanted to go home after a week of the drama in Dawson. He smiled because she hadn't said too much. She'd actually been pretty terrific, fighting with the doctor when they wanted to keep him overnight.

No way could he leave his girls overnight. He knew the look of terror in Molly's eyes when she thought he wasn't coming home. He remembered eighteen months ago walking through the front door and finding her in the playpen with Kat. The two had been red-faced, eyes swollen from crying and nearly breathless from sobbing. That memory would never leave him.

"Wyatt, you have to let your mind rest." Violet touched his arm. "I know that look on your face. I know what you're thinking. The girls are fine. I've never seen them better."

"I know." He took careful steps into the living room. He'd sleep on the couch tonight instead of climbing the stairs.

But the living room was occupied. He stopped in the doorway. Molly and Kat slept on the couch. Rachel slept curled up in the chair near the couch. A fire, only embers, glowed in the fireplace. It felt good and smelled good. The temperature outside had dropped after a late-evening storm rolled through. The fire was pretty inviting.

Yeah, right, the fire.

"This is sweet." Violet touched his shoulder. "Now where are you going to crash?"

"The sofa in my office." He didn't move, though. Either because it hurt too bad or, he looked at the girls and at Rachel Waters, it hurt too bad. He smiled at Violet. "What about you?"

"I'll stay up with you."

"You should get some sleep." He nodded toward the stairs. "Go, Violet, I'll be fine."

"I'll stay up with him." A sleepy voice from the living room interrupted their conversation. Rachel stretched and sat up. "I've been sleeping for a few hours. You go to bed, Violet."

He really didn't need a babysitter. He considered arguing, but he didn't have the strength and he knew he'd never win against two women. Rachel was already on her feet, a blanket around her shoulders.

Blame it on painkillers or a concussion, but he wanted to say things he wouldn't be able to take back in the morning.

"He has to be woken up every hour." Violet explained what the doctor had told them. He kept his mouth shut, glad she'd stepped in and kept him from making a complete fool of himself.

"I can do that." Rachel stood, folding the blanket that she'd had over her.

"I really don't need a keeper. This isn't my first concussion or the first time I've cracked a few ribs." What he didn't want to admit was that it hadn't hurt as bad as this the last time.

"Right." Rachel smiled at Violet who said good-night and then retreated up the stairs. He watched her go and then he was alone with temptation itself. She smiled at him, completely unaware of how beautiful she was standing in that spot with just a sliver of moonlight coming through the window and the warm embers from the fire reflecting the auburn highlights in her hair.

Yeah, guys weren't always clueless.

"I'm not sure if this is right or wrong." He eased a step in her direction and braced a hand against the doorway.

"What?"

"This." He reached for her hand and pulled her close. She stood in front of him, unmoving, unblinking, staring at him as if he'd lost his mind. Maybe he had. Maybe the horse had knocked him silly. Maybe it had knocked sense into him. Whatever it was, he didn't want to think too deeply, not yet.

"This." He whispered it again and leaned, touching his lips to hers. She was so sweet, like cherry soda on a hot summer day. She was his first time driving alone, the first horse he owned, the first time he'd ever felt free. She was everything and more.

She healed his heart with that kiss. She made him feel things he hadn't expected, had never felt.

And she scared the daylights out of him. He moved his hand from her arm to her back and he held her close, trying to breathe, trying to get it right and trying to convince himself to let her go.

Eventually she stepped back. Her lips parted and she shook her head. "No."

"No." Did he want to argue with her or agree? He wasn't sure.

"This isn't what you want." She smiled a little. "This is about feeling vulnerable and alone. This isn't about us. This is something you have to work through, on your own."

He looked a little deeper and saw her pain. It shimmered in her eyes and he remembered the other night on the tailgate of his truck when she'd talked about girls trying too hard to be loved.

Her story. Man, he wanted her stories.

"You should lie down." She swallowed and looked away.

"I should." He laughed and it hurt like crazy. "I think I might need help."

"The sofa in the office."

"Yeah." Cowboy up, Wyatt, he told himself. A guy couldn't impress a woman if he had to lean on her just to make it to a chair. Casual would work. He draped his arm around her shoulders.

"That's a lame move." She left it there, though.

"It's all I could think of right now." He walked next to her, pretty thankful for a strong woman who felt soft and smelled sweet.

"Stop sniffing my hair." She whispered the warning as they walked through the office door.

"Sorry."

She laughed and shook her head. "My dog has more manners."

"Not possible."

"I'm sure of it." She stopped in front of the couch and slid out from under his arm.

With her hands holding his arms, she held tight while he lowered onto the couch, trying hard not to groan. He gritted his teeth instead. She smiled, not the kind of smile that meant sympathy.

He really wanted sympathy. A nice pillow, a soft blanket and maybe a glass of water. She didn't look as if she planned to play nursemaid. More than anything she looked like someone about to escape.

He was the guy who needed to let her go because that made sense. Getting tangled up in this didn't. He'd seen tangled up before. He'd doctored a horse for a week because it hadn't had the sense to stay out of barbed wire.

Yeah, he had more sense than that horse.

Chapter Thirteen

He looked pitiful, miserable actually. His dark hair was a mess, hanging across his forehead. The top two buttons of his shirt were gone and he still wore the jeans he'd been wearing when he hit the ground. Rachel stood for a moment, unsure of what to do next. Her internal alarm sounded, telling her to find the nearest exit and leave him to his own devices. But she had promised to stay with him, and Violet looked worn out. The girls were sleeping in the living room.

"You should take your boots off and I'll find a pillow and blanket." Good first step.

He grinned and shook his head, "Honey, I'd love to take off my boots, but I don't think I can lean down."

Okay, she didn't need this. Instead of discussing, she knelt and reached for the heel of one boot. She slid it off and reached for the other. "Your feet stink."

He laughed a little, but she heard the grimace of pain. "Yeah, I bet they do. Thank you for taking one for the team."

She looked up, mid-pull. He was watching her. She looked away quickly and finished the second boot. As she stood up, he wrapped his legs around hers, right at her knees, and held her in front of him.

His smiled changed from soft to rotten, lifting at one corner. No, no, no. Rachel didn't want this thin strand of emotion connecting them. She didn't want to get tied into this when he was having fun, or using her to get past something.

She'd been used before and it wasn't going to happen again.

"I'm going to get you a pillow." She stepped out of the circle of his legs and moved to the door. "Ice water?"

He nodded and she left the room, walking down the darkened hallway to the kitchen. Her heart hammered in her chest and she worked to get a deep breath.

"Okay, God, give me strength." She pulled a glass out of the cabinet and instead of heading for the fridge, she looked out the window, watching trees blown by a south wind and paper fluttering end over end across the lawn. Another storm was blowing up. Clouds were eating up the dark sky, blotting the moon and the twinkling stars.

Give her strength. More than that, help her find peace. Help her to not rush into a relationship with someone who was emotionally tied up and working past his grief.

She filled the glass with ice and water. Now to find a pillow and blanket. She had seen them the day she cleaned, in a closet off the main bathroom. She flipped on the light, dug around in the closet and headed back down the hall.

He was sleeping when she returned to the office. Stretched out on the couch, one foot on the floor and his arm flopped over his face. It would be good if he stayed asleep. She put the glass down and unfolded the blanket.

"I'm not cold." He moved his arm and there was no smile. His chest expanded with a heavy sigh. "I'm scared to death."

"Why?"

She couldn't have this conversation standing. She pulled a chair close to the couch and sat down. He reached for her hand, holding it, looking at it, running his fingers over hers. He had rough, warm hands. The hands of a cowboy, a rancher.

"Wyatt, it's just a concussion. Right?"

He smiled up at her, still holding her hand. "I'm not afraid of that. I'm afraid of you. I'm scared to death to feel what I feel. I'm not ready."

Slam. She drew in a shaky breath and pulled her hand from his. Be afraid of death, she wanted to tell him. Be afraid of the dark. Be afraid of anything, but not her.

But wasn't she scared to death of him, of being used, of being rejected?

She looked up, gathering strength and trying to find God. All of those words and then to hear that he wasn't ready. She reached for the pillow.

"You'll want this." She waited for him to lean forward and she slid it under his head. "And now, I should go."

"But…"

"I'm not leaving. I'm going in with the girls. These are not the words I want to hear in the middle of the night." She felt wrung out, exhausted, run over. "I'll be back in an hour. If you need me, I'm across the hall."

"Rachel?"

She shook her head as she walked out the door and back to the living room where the girls were sleeping.

She couldn't respond, instead she brushed away tears and buried her face in the pillow she'd been using earlier in the evening.

Nothing had ever hurt this bad. He wasn't ready. She wondered if he would ever really be ready. The awkward teenager she had been taunted her, telling her she'd never be the person he moved on with.

Tonight she fought back. God hadn't made her an awkward teenager. She was more than that. She knew that He didn't create mistakes. Every inch of her was designed by God.

The young girl who had wanted nothing more than to stay in one house was designed by Him. The teenager who had turned to chocolate and cheesecake, later to a reckless crowd of friends, and the twenty-year-old who had finally gotten it right, they were all the same person, His creation, fearfully and wonderfully made. It had just taken her a while to figure it out and to stop fighting who she was. It had taken her a while to trust Him with her life.

It had taken her a while to be comfortable in her own skin and to love herself enough to stop punishing herself.

Tonight the girl who wanted to be loved was fighting tooth and nail, wanting to believe a cowboy like Wyatt Johnson could really, really love her someday.

And maybe her parents' plan to move had come at just the right time. Maybe this move was designed to protect her heart.

Wyatt cracked one eye and saw two little girls leaning close, whispering for him to wake up. After a long night of hourly wake-up calls, this time waking up felt great, even if he didn't know how to take a deep breath and his head ached as if he'd been hit with a sledge-hammer. At that moment it was all about Molly and Kat leaning over him, studying his face with worried little expressions.

"Daddy, are you awake?" Molly leaned, her nose close to his. "Because we didn't know if you would wake up."

He wrapped them both in one arm and pulled them to him. "I'm definitely awake. And I love you both."

"Grandma left." Kat kissed his cheek. "And said you had to be good and listen to us and to Rachel."

"Rachel?"

Molly nodded, all serious and wide-eyed. "Rachel told Grandma she'd be our nanny and clean our house. And she already cooks good."

"Really?" He smiled, even though it hurt.

"She doesn't need books to make pancakes. They aren't even frozen first."

"Really?" He growled and pretended to get her arms. "Can she do that?"

Molly shook her head. "She doesn't have whiskers, Daddy."

Now that was something he did know. "You're right about that. Now help me up and we'll go see about that bad ol' buckskin."

"Rachel unsaddled him."

"That's good." They each had hold of a hand and he groaned as they pulled him to a sitting position. "Man, I'm sore."

"Grandma said you've been run over by a truck, but it was just a horse."

"She meant I feel like I've been run over by a truck."

Kat held on to his hand. "Mean old horse."

"Yeah."

They led him down the hall. The aroma of bacon lingered in the air. He hoped there was some left for him. On top of that, the house smelled clean. He glanced at the clock. It was just after nine in the morning. A clean house and breakfast. Not too shabby.

Rachel walked out of the laundry room carrying a mop bucket. Her hair was braided and she had changed into shorts and a T-shirt. He knew now that she jogged nearly every day. He'd seen her a few times in the last couple of weeks.

"Seems like I might be Rip Van Winkle. Everything changed while I was sleeping." Including her, his feelings and his house.

He ambled into the kitchen, working on casual when he felt as cagey as a penned-up cur dog. He poured himself a cup of coffee and took a piece of bacon from the plate near the stove. When he turned around she was in the kitchen, taking up space, moving around as if she belonged there.

It shouldn't bother him, that Violet had hired her, but it did. He wanted to choose the person who came into his home. He wanted to choose someone who didn't smell so stinking good and who didn't look prettier than a rodeo queen, even in those faded shorts and a T-shirt.

"I'll make you pancakes." She had the fridge door open, blocking her from his view. Molly, not even four, was sitting on a stool smiling at him as if she knew way more than he was saying.

He shot his daughter a look and she giggled. The fridge door closed and Rachel's eyes narrowed as she stared at him. It took him a second but he worked up to innocent and shrugged, as if he didn't know what his kid was all about.

"Sit down and I'll fix your breakfast."

He pulled out a stool next to Kat. Okay, maybe this wasn't so bad. What could possibly be bad about sitting here watching her in his kitchen?

"I should feed the animals before I eat breakfast."

She turned, a spatula in her hand. "I took care of it."

"You fed?" He didn't feel like smiling now.

"No, I called Ryder. Of course he's in Tulsa with Andie, but he sent Jason over to take care of things. And Jackson Cooper…"

He raised a hand to stop her. She flipped the pancakes and he had to wait a second for her to get back to him. This was getting a little crazy. He was feeling pretty crazy on the inside.

Emotions should be gradual, not wildfire, spreading every which way. But he didn't think emotions came in gradual increments. Pain—Bang. Grief—Bang. Anger—Bang. Now this—Bang. He didn't want to put a name on it.

Oh, wait, maybe jealousy. He lifted his coffee cup and took a few drinks. She flipped pancakes onto a plate and set it in front of him with butter and syrup.

"Jackson doesn't need to come over here. I can manage things myself." He jabbed a knife into the butter and spread it over the tops of the pancakes.

"Right."

"Yeah, right. Cracked ribs and a concussion, that's it, Rachel. I really don't need all this help." He wasn't some namby-pamby sissy. He'd been bucked off more bulls than he could count. He'd been thrown by horses. He'd been run over and stepped on.

"Fine, you can call Jackson and tell him you can do it yourself."

Okay, that made him sound like a three-year-old tackling a flight of stairs by himself. He chewed on pancakes that were so good he forgot to be mad.

Instead of anger, he felt a big urge to hug her. Molly giggled again. He looked down and she laughed harder.

"What's so funny?"

She giggled more. "You're funny, Daddy. You're not mad, you're happy."

Well, that just about beat all.

He kissed her cheek. "You're right, Molly Doodle, I'm happy."

As he finished the plate of pancakes, he watched Rachel move around his kitchen. He was happy. Bang. Just like that.

Being happy should have been something he grabbed hold of and thanked the good Lord above for. Instead he questioned it, a lot like the Israelites had questioned everything God did for them in the wilderness.

And on top of that, he felt guilty. The bad thing about guilt is that it undid happy.

He finished the pancakes and got up to carry the plate to the sink. Rachel took it from his hands with a smile.

"I can get it."

She rinsed it off and put it in the dishwasher. "So can I."

"Fine. I'm going to go outside and check on that buckskin. Did Jason call to see if they would pick him up?"

"I think they're getting him this evening."

He nodded and then he backtracked to the fact that

she'd mentioned Ryder and he hadn't really paid attention. He blamed it on the concussion.

"What was that about Ryder?"

"Andie was having contractions. Ryder flew her to Tulsa yesterday. They called earlier and she's resting. The contractions slowed down, but they think it will be in the next day or two."

"Ryder, a dad. That's going to be fun to watch."

"He's ready for it. He has you."

Now what did he say? He stood there, aching from the inside out thanks to cracked ribs and some deep bruises. He tried for casual and leaned hip against counter, arms crossed in front of him. Rachel's narrowed gaze went from his chest to his face. She cocked her head to the side.

"I'm going outside." He eased across the kitchen.

"Don't do too much too soon," she warned softly.

"I'm not. I can't stay in the house."

"I know." She picked up the bottle of pills he'd left on the counter and tossed it. He caught it.

"I don't need these. I don't want to feel sleepy all day."

"If you're sleeping you won't be doing something you shouldn't do."

He laughed because what he was thinking and what she was thinking were two different things. Maybe she had a point. Maybe drugging him was the best thing for both of them.

"Rachel, I'll take a few aspirins, not these. And I am going outside to check on things."

She shrugged and walked away. "Suit yourself."

Right, he would suit himself. Kat and Molly were sitting on their stools watching him and watching Rachel. He brushed a hand through his hair and smiled at his girls.

He'd pick getting thrown from a horse every single day of the week over the mess Violet had made of his life by hiring Rachel Waters.

Rachel started her car and leaned back in the seat, catching her breath while the top went back on the convertible. She reached for her sunglasses to fight the sun. She was going home for a few hours and later she'd return to Wyatt's to fix dinner for him and the girls.

One last glance back at the house and she pulled onto the road and headed home. She had chores to do there, too. She had her sheep. Her mom would need help with laundry. There was plenty to keep her busy.

Including packing. As she pulled into the garage she thought about that, about packing things up again. This time she really didn't want to go. And what would she tell Wyatt? What would she say to the girls, to Molly and Kat?

Complicated. Life was very complicated. She closed her eyes and thought about that, and she tried to grab hold of God's perspective. To Him it wasn't all that complicated. She had to trust His plan.

He hadn't opened all of these doors and brought her here for no reason. Maybe He had planned for them to be here just to help Wyatt and the girls through this difficult time. And when she left, there would be someone else to help.

Maybe Wyatt would find his way back to faith and take a job in the church.

The door to the house opened and her mom smiled. "How was the first day?"

Rachel rolled her eyes heavenward. "Not easy. A sick man is a difficult man."

"That's how they are. And he just called."

"Called here? Is he okay?"

"I think your cell phone battery must be dead. He said it went right to voice mail."

"Oh, it might be." She pulled it from her pocket. Sure enough, dead. "What did he want?"

"Andie's having the babies. He wondered if you would ride with them to Tulsa. He didn't say it, but I wonder if he isn't supposed to drive?"

"Probably not, but he isn't going to give up that information." She didn't want to go. Her emotions were wrung out and what she really wanted was to stay home and be safe. Home with her parents, no pressure, no difficult thoughts to sort out.

"Do you want your dad to drive them?"

"No, I can do it. It's just that I know we need to start packing. I planned on helping you for a few hours."

Rachel's mom stopped her, putting a hand on her arm. "Rachel, I can pack. Your dad has already started. We've done this so many times, I think we know how to get it done."

"But you need my help."

"Tonight Wyatt and the girls need you."

More people needing her. She didn't really know if that's what she wanted for her life. And when she left, what then?

Not that he couldn't replace her with someone just as capable, maybe more so. There were plenty of people looking for jobs and several in the area who would be great with the girls.

"I'll call him and see what's going on. But I need to

change clothes and get cleaned up." She'd been cleaning and cooking all day. No one would want to sit in a truck with her for an hour.

Cooped up in a truck. With Wyatt.

Not exactly the thought she needed while trying to convince herself that she needed to do this. Of course she wanted to, though. Andie might be having the babies. That was something Rachel didn't want to miss out on.

Thirty minutes later she parked next to Wyatt's garage, under the carport. He walked out of the barn as she got out of the car and reached in for her overnight bag. She watched him walk toward her, limping a little, a tiny bit stiff. He pushed his hat back and smiled.

"Nice to see you again."

"Yes, again. Do I need to get the girls ready to go?"

"I think probably. Molly is upstairs packing a bag. She's going to be four this weekend, so she's positive she can do it. I'm sure she'd let you help out, though." He pulled off his hat, smiling. "She said I can't help."

She knew he wasn't a lot of help in the clothing department, but he probably didn't need to hear that from her. But the birthday, that definitely needed to be discussed.

"Her birthday. Have you ordered a cake?"

"No, I planned to do it tomorrow." He rubbed his cheek and half smiled. "I'm not good at birthdays. Worse at buying their clothes. I really stink at the girl stuff."

Slow, steady breath. "I can help. I can even bake the cake, if you'd like."

"I'm keeping you from your life. What about Etta? I

know you've had things to do that haven't gotten done because of us."

"Etta is having a slow period. She calls when she needs help."

"So this isn't taking you away from something else?"

"Not really." Just packing and telling this life good-bye. That happened to be something else she wasn't ready to tell him. Her dad would share the news with the congregation Sunday. She planned on telling Wyatt before then. She didn't want him to hear it from the pulpit, from her dad.

"Rachel, if you have other things to do, I really can do this alone."

She smiled. "I don't mind. And while we're in Tulsa we can shop for birthday presents and summer clothes for the girls."

"Now that's a good idea. You probably know how to match things."

"Maybe a little better than you."

He leaned against her car, smiling.

"I should go inside."

He edged away from the car that she thought had probably been holding him up. "We'll leave as soon as I get finished feeding. Adam is going to feed tomorrow."

"I'll make sure things are closed up inside the house."

He flashed her another smile. "Thanks."

Leaving had never been easy. This time it would feel like tearing her heart out. She watched him walk away, a little slower but still with that confident cowboy swagger.

He would never know what these weeks meant to her or how much it hurt to go. What difference would it make if he did?

She only had to remind herself what he'd said last night. How could she forget? He'd kissed her silly and then said he wasn't ready.

Chapter Fourteen

❧

Wyatt stared through the window into the NICU at the two little girls, Ryder and Andie's babies. They were close to five pounds each, but Amelia needed oxygen and they were watching Annette. Two more A names. He shook his head, a little in awe over the whole situation.

His little brother was a daddy.

Molly and Kat stood on a stool and watched their little cousins. He couldn't help but think about their births. Molly's had been a happy occasion. But Kat's birth… He wrapped an arm around a little girl who had never really had her mother. Wendy had tried. He knew she'd tried. What a rough few years.

And lately? Things were changing. The weight on them wasn't as heavy. The girls smiled more.

The common denominator happened to be in the other room with Andie, hugging her, praying with her. He'd said his own prayers on the drive here, that the babies would be safe and healthy.

He tugged down on his hat, because he wasn't about to cry. But man, his eyes burned. Little babies did that to a guy. A hand slapped his back. He grimaced, cringing a little.

"Oh, sorry about that." Ryder grinned and pointed to his little girls. "Aren't they something?"

"Yeah, hard to believe you could make something that pretty."

"Don't make me have to take you outside and whoop you, not today." Ryder draped an arm over Wyatt's shoulder. "They look like Andie. Ain't that something?"

"Yeah, funny how that works." He glanced down at his own girls and saw their mother in them. He still had her, in them, in their smiles, their eyes. In Kat's spunky nature. In Molly's laugh.

"We're going to have to get busy and have some boys to protect these girls." Ryder smiled into the NICU window. "Yep, I'm starting to see why the Coopers had all them kids."

"I guess having the boys is up to you."

"Ah, come on, you could have a little boy in the next year or two."

Wyatt shook his head and gave his brother a look. "Ryder, I don't even know where you're going with this conversation. But let's just stick with the idea that you're married and before you know it, you'll have a son. Poor kid."

"I think Andie isn't going to want to have another one for a while." Ryder's smile softened. Andie had done that, turning him from a boy to a man. "Wendy's gone, Wyatt."

"I think I know that." He looked around. The girls had wandered back to the sitting area and weren't paying attention to their uncle Ryder.

"I know you do. No one knows it better than you. But seriously, Wyatt, it's okay to find someone else."

"Right."

Heels on the tile floor. He turned and smiled at the woman walking toward him. Her hair hung in loose curls that framed her face. She smiled a little, her eyes misty and her lips trembling. She bit down on her bottom lip and blinked a few times.

Babies did that to people. Not to him, of course. He turned back to the window, the babies that were wiggling and scrunching up those wrinkled little faces. He'd always said babies weren't really as pretty as people said. He was rethinking that.

"Aren't they beautiful?" Rachel peeked over his shoulder, her chin touching, resting on him.

"Yeah, they sure are." He caught her reflection in the mirror. She backed away but she still stared at those babies. Twin girls with downy soft, blond hair.

"You guys staying the night in Tulsa?" Ryder glanced from Wyatt to Rachel, smiling. Wyatt shot him down with a look.

"Yeah, we've got a couple of hotel rooms. Molly already informed me she's staying in the room with Rachel."

Kat was hugging Rachel's leg. He figured he'd lost her, too. And it was okay. He was fine with that. He was kind of losing himself, too.

"We're going shopping tomorrow," Molly piped up, smiling big with tired eyes. Wyatt picked her up and she wrapped her arms around his neck. Man, this was what life was all about.

"I'm going to have that." Ryder had the look of a man who had just gotten it.

"Yeah, this is it, Ryder. Good times and bad, it's all about this." Wyatt hugged his daughter and rubbed his cheek against hers. "This is what makes it all worth it."

"I have to go see Andie." Ryder blinked a few times.

Wyatt slapped him on the back and then he turned to Rachel. Ryder was already down the hall, turning the corner. Wyatt slipped an arm around Rachel's waist and, as if she knew, she took Molly.

He took a good deep breath and kept his arm around the woman at his side. Sometimes it just felt good to have someone to lean on. He remembered last night, holding her, teasing her.

"What now?" He didn't really know what he meant by that. "Something to eat? Shopping?"

Rachel held Molly and Kat walked next to her. Both girls were dragging. "Both, if they don't fall asleep in the car."

"Right." He held his arms out to Kat. "Come on, Kat, I can carry my girl."

She grabbed his hands and he picked her up. Rachel smiled but she didn't say anything. Yeah, fine, it wasn't as easy as it should have been. But Kat's arms clung to him and she buried her face in his shoulder.

Yeah, it was all worth it.

After shopping with two toddlers, Rachel's feet hurt and she was ready for a cup of coffee on the balcony of her room. She kissed Molly and tucked the blanket in close. The child wrapped sweet arms around Rachel's neck and smiled.

"I love you, Molly."

"I love you."

Rachel's heart melted. She leaned to kiss the little

forehead again. Kat, next to Molly in the queen-size bed, slept soundly. She'd fallen asleep as soon as they got her into her jammies and tucked her in.

"Go to sleep." She tucked Molly's blankets again. "I'll be sitting on the balcony and I'll leave the door open a crack."

"You won't leave?"

"I won't leave. Promise. I'll be on the balcony and I'll be here with you in the morning."

Molly nodded and smiled.

One last kiss on the cheek and Rachel walked away. She poured herself a cup of coffee and stirred creamer and sugar in it. When she turned, Molly's eyes were closed. Sleeping already. Rachel smiled and walked quietly past the bed toward the glass doors that led to the balcony.

A movement on the balcony caught her attention. Wyatt. They had separate rooms but shared a balcony. He stood at the wrought iron railing, leaning against the support post that ran from the floor to the upstairs balcony. When she opened the door, he turned.

"It's a nice night," he commented as he turned back to the view of the skyline.

She nodded, but he probably wasn't paying any attention. It had been that kind of day, the kind that wrung a person out and left them empty. The babies, the memories and she was positive he was in more pain than he let on. It hadn't been an easy day.

"Coffee?"

He shook his head. "No, thanks, too late at night."

She sat down and held the cup in her hands. Tulsa evenings were beautiful. It was a little warm, a little humid and traffic honked on the city streets. She put her feet up on the chair next to the one she sat in.

Wyatt left the rail and sat next to her. He moved slower but broken ribs didn't seem to be something that slowed him down. He told her it wasn't the first time he'd cracked a few ribs and probably wouldn't be the last.

She sipped her coffee and he rubbed his shoulder and neck. Try as she might, she couldn't ignore him, couldn't avoid watching him. His profile was dark, his expression impassive. Rachel sighed and set her cup down on the table. She moved her chair closer to his, her heart catching a little.

No going back.

But did she really want to move forward? She closed her eyes and waited for common sense to return, to drag her back to sanity. She had made so many reckless decisions when it came to relationships. Worse, she had tried to make people love her.

Her hand was on his shoulder, the knotted muscles were tense beneath her touch. She opened her eyes and he turned, his expression questioning. The words from the other night came back, that he wasn't ready.

After a long moment he reached for her hand and pulled it forward. With her pulse fluttering at the base of her throat, he brushed the back of her hand with a sweet kiss. "Good night, Rachel."

"Good night?"

"Yeah, time for you to go." He smiled at her. "I think we both need space and maybe fresh air. Alone."

She couldn't move.

"Rachel, this is me being a gentleman and not a rogue cowboy. This is me making the right choice for both of us. I'm not sure what to feel right now and I don't want to hurt you."

"Not sure?"

He shrugged. "Until recently I still felt married to a woman who isn't coming back. I still have a lot to work through and I don't want to hurt you."

"I'm not going to get hurt. I'm a big girl."

He smiled at that. Her hand was still in his. He squeezed her fingers lightly and let go.

"I know you are, but I'm not willing to be the one who hurts you."

Rachel picked up her cup but she didn't move from her seat. He was telling her to go, but the look in her eyes said something else. She knew, of course, to back off, to not take things where they shouldn't go. She moved her chair away from his, giving them both space.

"Wyatt, what was she like?"

He stared off into the night and didn't answer right away.

"I'm sorry, I shouldn't have asked."

"No, it's okay, I'm just surprised." Wyatt sighed. "I can talk about her. For a long time I couldn't, but now, it's been eighteen months and I can talk. I can tell you that she loved our girls. Man, when we had Molly, Wendy glowed. She loved that baby."

"I'm sure she did."

"She loved her, but..." He stared out at the night, away from her. "She left us. She held Molly, she fed her and sometimes she laughed. When we had Kat, Wendy disappeared inside a shell. She stopped taking care of herself. She didn't take care of the girls. I took her to doctors, to counseling..."

"I'm so sorry."

He nodded. "Yeah, me, too. I had some pretty wonderful years with a woman that I thought I'd spend my life with."

"I think she probably wanted the same thing." Rachel didn't know what else to say. She had seen his pain, but hearing it made it all the more real.

It put everything into perspective.

She stood and he looked up, smiling. Her hand trembled as she reached to touch his cheek. His eyes closed and he leaned into her touch. Her heart couldn't decide if it should fast-forward or pause.

"Good night, Wyatt."

As she walked through the door she heard him sigh and she echoed the gesture. Walking away was something every girl, every woman should know how to do.

And sometimes, she knew from experience, it wasn't easy. Sometimes there was a cowboy on the other end of the emotional tightrope.

She closed the door and bolted it. She pulled the curtain closed and locked the connecting door between their rooms.

The phone rang. She picked it up, glancing quick at the girls. Kat slept on, Molly's eyes fluttered a little.

"Hello?"

"It's me." His voice was soft, not sweet, not this time.

"I kind of knew that."

He laughed. "Yeah, well, I wanted to apologize. I just wanted to say that I'm trying not to lead you on."

"I'm not going to let you." She sat on the edge of the desk and held the phone with her shoulder. "Wyatt, I'm…"

"Rachel?"

"I was a really wild teenager and I made a lot of mis-

takes, mistakes I regret and that I've worked to get past.
I'm almost thirty years old. I know what I want. I know
what I'm waiting for. I'm not chasing you."

She closed her eyes and told herself how stupid that
sounded. She'd spent the last few years thinking that
God would send someone if there was someone for her.
And now she was telling this man she wasn't going to
chase him. Stupid, stupid, stupid.

"Rachel?"

"Yeah?"

"I think you're amazing." She could hear his smile.

Amazing. Right. He didn't know that she was trembling from her head to her toes. Fear?

"Thanks. Good night, Wyatt."

She put the phone in the cradle, her hand on it, waiting. It didn't ring again.

Wyatt pulled up the drive to his house. The girls were
sleeping in the backseat of the truck. Rachel hadn't said
much on the drive home. He hadn't pushed her. After
last night it seemed like a good idea to keep quiet.

Breakfast had been a quiet affair on the balcony of
their hotel. The girls had eaten cereal from room service, Rachel had eaten fruit and yogurt. He'd felt pretty
guilty eating biscuits and gravy. They'd had lunch at
the hospital cafeteria.

The twins were doing great. Amelia was breathing
on her own now. Wyatt breathed a sigh of relief over
that situation. At least that, if only that, was going right.
He, on the other hand, had a big mess to clean up. He
had a woman sitting next to him and he didn't have a
clue what to say to her or how to fix things.

How did a man move on when, until eighteen months

ago, he'd planned on spending his life with one woman, raising their children, growing old, serving God? And then it had all changed. Yeah, move on. That's what people were telling him. Time to move on, Wyatt.

He stopped the truck and just sat there. Rachel opened her door but she didn't get out. He shot her a look and she didn't smile. Of course she didn't. He hadn't given her a lot to smile about. He really wanted her to smile.

He really wanted to explain to her how it felt to try this moving on stuff. It hurt like crazy, deep-down hurt. It hurt the way it had when people had tried to tell Wendy to just get over it, take a shower, go for a walk. And she hadn't been able to do those things.

He sat there for a second, thinking. Maybe it didn't hurt as much as he'd thought it should? The thought hit like a ton of bricks, the knowledge that getting over his pain could hurt, too. He sure hadn't planned on that.

"I'll carry the girls in for you." She stepped out of the truck and looked back in at him.

Oh, no way was she doing this.

"I can take the girls in, Rachel." He got out and opened the back door to reach for Molly. She woke up enough to crawl into his arms. "Come on, kiddo, you can take a nap inside."

"I want a pink cake for my birthday," she whispered close to his ear.

"A strawberry cake?" He held her close, his ribs hurting like crazy.

"No, just pink. A pink cake." He carried her up the back steps. Rachel followed with Kat.

"Well, then, we'll find you a pink cake."

"I can make her a cake." Rachel had opened the other door and reached in for Kat. "If you want."

"I think she'd like that. We usually buy one from the store."

Last year they hadn't had much of a party. It had been the three of them and a store-bought cake. Her third birthday and he'd put candles on her cake and later, after the girls had gone to bed, he'd stood outside and bawled like a baby. He'd had a fight with God, then he'd shifted his anger to Wendy.

The dog ran around the side of the house, wagging his tail, glad to see his people home. Wyatt carried Molly up the back steps and into the house. Rachel was behind him with Kat. He opened the door and nodded for her to enter first.

"Do you want me to fix something for dinner?" Rachel asked as she carried Kat through the house to the living room.

"No, I'll take the girls to the Mad Cow. Why don't you go on home? I'm sure you have a life that doesn't include us."

She shifted her arms and placed his daughter on one end of the sofa. When she turned, her smile was vague. He placed Molly on the other end of the sofa. Her eyes opened and she smiled.

"I'm not tired, Daddy."

"You don't have to sleep, honey." He turned and Rachel had found an afghan and was covering Kat with it. "Seriously, though, if you have things to do…"

"I actually do. My mom needs help with some things."

"They're lucky to have you."

"I'm lucky to have them. They've always been there for me. Now it's my turn to be there for them."

She picked up her purse and he walked out with her. They'd left her car in the carport, but it was still covered with green pollen. He waited while she dug through her purse for her keys. When she found them, he opened the car door for her.

"Rachel, if you need a couple of days off to get other things done, I understand."

"I might. There's something…" She sighed. "Never mind. I'll see you tomorrow."

"Are you sure?"

She got in the car and he rested his arm on the vinyl top and looked in.

"I'm sure. I'll see you tomorrow. We have a lot to do before Molly's birthday Saturday."

"Okay, I'll talk to you later." He closed the door and backed away from her car. As she backed out of the carport, he waved and she smiled.

It seemed normal enough, but it didn't sit right. Whatever she had started to tell him mattered and he wanted to know what it was.

Chapter Fifteen

Boxes lined the walls of the living room and Rachel didn't want to empty the contents of the room into the brown cardboard. She sat down on the footstool and stared at the bookcases, the curio cabinet and the pictures on the walls. She loved this room with its pine-paneled walls. She loved the hardwood floors and the big windows.

She loved this house.

"The boxes won't pack themselves."

She turned and smiled at her mother. It was a good week. Maybe the excitement of the move had given Gloria Waters the extra energy. Or maybe her immune system was in check. Either way she had accomplished a lot in the two days since Rachel had been gone.

Twenty-nine years old, Rachel shouldn't be having this conversation, about moving, about starting over with her parents. She pulled a few books off the shelves and held them. Her mom walked into the room and sat in the rocking chair across from her.

"Rachel, don't go. Stay here."

"That's out of the question." Rachel stacked the

books in the bottom of a box. "I'm not going to stay here when the two of you are going to Tulsa."

"Are you afraid?"

Afraid? Rachel looked out the window. Across the road the neighbors were mulching their garden. Down the street a new neighbor had moved in. Her dad had already invited them to church. A church that would soon lose its pastor. She thought about that church, her teen girls, her Sunday school class and the nursery.

Rachel always became involved in her dad's ministry. The new church was larger, had quite a few paid staff, he'd told her. She didn't know what that meant for her. But the real reason she would go would be to help her parents. She cooked when her mother didn't feel up to it. She kept the house clean.

Afraid?

"Afraid to jump out there, find someone and fall in love. Are you afraid? I know that Tanner hurt you, but it was a long time ago."

Rachel didn't know how to process what her mother had just said. Tanner. She hadn't really thought about him in years. They had dated when she was twenty.

"It isn't about Tanner." About a man who had dated her for a year and then decided he couldn't handle her faith.

"I wonder sometimes. I know he hurt you."

Rachel smiled at that. "It hasn't hurt in a long time, Mom. I'm here because I want to be here, to help you and Dad. And I guess because I haven't found anyone to spend my life with."

"You will, honey."

"Will I?" She shrugged. "I don't know if I will. If I don't, it's okay."

have ignored the doctor and went ahead with whatever he needed to do.

Now he had the girls to think about. He glanced behind him. They were on the swing, not going very high but jabbering nonstop. He started to turn back to the horse but caught a flash of red on the road. Rachel.

She'd taken yesterday off. The girls had missed her, moping around the house because he had fed them some kind of casserole he thought would be an easy fix. He'd been pretty wrong about that. His cooking skills, with or without Etta's cookbooks, were not improving.

The red car eased up his driveway. He hadn't expected her today either. There were a lot of things he hadn't expected but he didn't want to dwell on them. The girls jumped off the swings and started across the yard. He would have yelled for them to stop, but they paused a good distance from the driveway and the car that was pulling up.

He gave a quiet command and the horse stopped, waiting for him to walk up to it. He left the rope on the ground and the horse remained steady in the spot where he'd come to a halt. Ears forward, the animal turned its head toward him.

"Good job, boy. Real good." He unsnapped the lunge line and replaced it with a lead rope. "Let's get you out to pasture and see what's going on."

He led the horse to the gate and turned him loose. The animal went off at a fast trot, shaking his head. After a few minutes he burst into a full run, bucking his back end into the air. Wyatt turned and walked back toward the house and the girls. And Rachel.

"What are you doing here?" He opened the gate that led to the yard.

"Thought I'd stop and check on the girls and find out if you've heard anything about the twins."

"The twins will probably be home by the first of next week." He picked up Kat, wincing a little at the catch in his ribs. "Sis, you're getting heavy."

Kat shook her head no and rested her chin on his shoulder.

Rachel smiled at the girls and not at him.

"So, what's really up?" He put Kat on the ground. "You girls run and play."

Kat and Molly started to protest, but he shook his head. They ran for the swings, forgetting to be upset. He smiled as he watched Molly help Kat onto the lower swing.

Rachel stopped walking. She watched the girls, her eyes a little misty. "I came over to bake the cake for Molly's party tomorrow. But before the party and before church Sunday, I want you to know something. I want you to hear it from me."

"Okay." He pulled off his hat and waited.

"My dad is taking a church in Tulsa. My mom needs to be closer to the doctors there. They want to be closer because they're getting older and they feel like it will be better for them."

"I hate for the church to lose your dad." He waited, wanting to hear that she wouldn't leave. He glanced in the direction of the girls, wanting it to be about them. "Rachel, the girls love having you here."

"I know. I love them."

Unsettled shifted to anger. "You're trying to tell me that you're going, too, right?"

"I am." She continued to watch the girls play, but her

eyes filled with tears. He watched one slide down her cheek and then the next.

"I'd like for you to stay. We could work something out if you wanted to work for me full-time."

"I can't." She wiped the tears away, one finger across her cheek. "My brother and sister live so far away. I'm the only one here to help my parents."

"I see." He rubbed the back of his neck and couldn't think of a thing to say that didn't sound crazy.

He didn't want to hire another housekeeper. Joint cream and therapeutic socks were no longer appealing. He kind of liked butterflies, country music and the smell of wildflowers.

The thoughts were pretty dangerous and he didn't want to go there. He'd taken his ring off. Now he was contemplating how to keep Rachel Waters in his life. No, in his girls' lives.

That's why he needed Rachel. She made Kat and Molly smile again. She made them happy. And that made his life a lot easier.

"Would you think about it? Just consider it. If you don't want to leave, the job is yours."

"Thank you. And I will think about it." She smiled and the gesture trembled on wild cherry lips. He was about as confused as a man could get.

"Well, I guess you have to make this decision. I need to feed the girls lunch."

"I can help."

He brushed his hand through his hair and settled his hat back on his head. "If you have things to do, I can handle it."

"I came over because you need help. I'm going to

fix lunch and then I'll get something in the oven for dinner."

"Right, that works." He leaned against her car and he couldn't look at her. "Man, this is rough."

"I'll be around for the next month. I can even help you find someone."

"No, I don't want to do this again." He managed a smile. "Maybe you can teach me to cook before you leave."

"I can do that. And for the next couple of days, we have a lot to do to get ready for Molly's party."

"Yeah, her birthday. She's counting on you for that. I can't braid hair and I sure can't decorate for a little girl's birthday."

"I'm not going to miss her birthday, Wyatt. I'll go ahead and bake the cake today. I'll decorate the cake and the house tomorrow before her guests arrive."

"Thanks, that'll be great."

She nodded, her smile still soft and trembling. "I'm sorry. I love the girls. I don't want them to be hurt."

"Yeah, but they will be. I know you have to go. I get that. But the girls are my priority."

"That's the way it should be."

"Well, I have to get back to work."

"I'll take the girls inside to help me with the cake."

He nodded and walked away.

This wasn't the way he'd expected his day to go. He'd almost prefer to get kicked by a horse. At least with a horse he knew what to expect.

Some things in life were honest and easy, always what you thought they'd be. And sometimes one choice changed everything. Jackson Cooper's words wormed their way into his mind. Rachel had definitely gotten under his skin.

But worse, she'd made Kat and Molly pretty happy. For the first time in a long time they'd felt whole, the way a family should feel. Because of her.

And now they were back to square one.

The cake baked in the oven, making the kitchen smell like strawberry. Rachel had explained to Molly that pink cakes sometimes had flavors and since they were using a mix, pink happened to be strawberry. The little girl had stopped being offended after a small taste of batter confirmed that pink was not only a pretty color, it tasted good, too.

"What now?" Rachel leaned on the counter across from the two girls who sat on stools sharing a plate of cookies.

"We should draw pictures," Molly informed her, dipping a cookie in her cup of milk.

"Or play with frogs." Kat nodded her head, milk dripping down her chin and a circle of chocolate around her mouth.

The back door slammed shut. Rachel straightened and waited for Wyatt to join them. She heard him in the laundry room and then he was there, tall and lean, his jeans faded. He must have hung his hat in the laundry room because the crown of his hair was flattened from having worn it all day.

"How about the Mad Cow, girls?" His smile didn't include her. Rachel didn't blame him.

"Rachel is making omelets." Molly picked up her cup to drink her milk. "Because eggs are good and we have stuff to do."

"What stuff?" This time he did look her way, his brow arched in question.

"Party stuff. We're going to decorate for tomorrow." Molly clasped her hands together and leaned toward her daddy. No way would he deny that little smile.

"I tell you what, you girls decorate. I'll order from the Mad Cow and bring it home for us." He shifted to face her. "If you write down what the three of you want and call in the order, I'll run upstairs for a quick shower and a change of clothes."

In a month, life would be ordinary again, missing them, missing Dawson. Rachel smiled because it didn't do her or the girls any good to let those thoughts take over.

He smiled back and then he left. She watched him leave, wondering how much pain he was in. He hid it well, his pain. The girls were tugging on her, asking questions about the cake and ice cream that she promised to make. Homemade, with strawberries, of course.

The oven timer went off. She grabbed an oven mitt and pulled out the cake. Strawberry pink. She put it on the top of the stove. The aroma filled the air, even stronger than when it had been baking. Both girls were off their stools and standing a short distance away.

Rachel wanted cake. She wanted chocolate. She really wanted to not be this new person she'd created, the one who jogged instead of eating cheesecake when she was depressed.

"It's going to be good." Molly grinned big.

"It is going to be good. And we'll put pink icing on it and pretty stuff."

"Flowers? And a ballerina?"

Rachel smiled. "Yes, flowers and ballerinas. We bought those in Tulsa, remember?"

"Bought what?"

Wyatt stood in the doorway dressed in khaki shorts and a T-shirt. His feet were bare and his hair still damp from the shower. His tanned skin looked darker thanks to the white T-shirt.

"Decorations for the cake." Rachel ached inside because something had happened, something was gone and she knew she'd miss it for a long, long time after she left Dawson.

The thin thread of connection they'd shared had been broken. Because she was leaving and he didn't want his girls hurt. She didn't want them hurt either.

She was torn. Did anyone get that? She felt so responsible for her parents. She loved this town. She smiled at Kat and Molly. She loved them.

"Did you make the list of what we want to eat?"

She picked up a pen and grabbed a tablet from the basket on the counter. "Okay, what does everyone want?"

She didn't look at him and she hoped he wasn't looking at her. Kat jumped up and down and said, "I want fries."

"More than that, Kat." Wyatt smiled at his daughter.

Rachel wrote down the rest of the order. "I'll call Vera."

"Okay, let me know how long it'll be. I promised the girls they could ride their pony for a few minutes."

Both girls shouted and started to jump around the room. Wyatt smiled, watching them. And Rachel watched him. Molly and Kat ran into the laundry room to pull on boots and hats. And suddenly Rachel didn't know what to do, didn't know where she fit.

She knew she never wanted to leave here. The thought settled deep, like most bad thoughts. How many times had she moved as a kid? She'd lost track.

But she wasn't sixteen looking for a place to start over. She was nearly thirty and some unseen clock was ticking an unfamiliar beat, one she hadn't expected.

Once again her gaze traveled to that cowboy. It was his fault, that much was obvious. It felt pretty good to blame him for making this difficult.

Kat and Molly returned wearing their boots and with cowboy hats on their heads. She smiled at little faces that were starting to tan. They had matching braids that stuck out from beneath their hats. Cowgirl hats, Molly had informed her, were important for cowgirls. They had bought one for Rachel, too.

She didn't look as cute in a cowgirl hat as they did.

She wouldn't need one in Tulsa. She turned away from the happy scene and started dishwater for the few mixing bowls and spoons she'd used to make the cake.

Footsteps behind her. She felt him close, felt the warmth of his exhaled breath, inhaled the spicy cologne he wore. His hand touched her arm.

"You okay?" His voice was close to her ear and she nodded, looking out the window at the barn, at fields with grazing livestock, at the dog sleeping under the shade of an oak tree.

"Yeah, I'm good."

"No, you're not."

She shook her head. She wasn't at all good. She was breaking inside, not just her heart but all of her. Because she loved them. She loved the girls and she loved him and for a few brief weeks she'd been a part of their lives, a part of their family. She didn't want to leave them, or Dawson.

She closed her eyes and waited for an answer, even a whisper. Nothing. Of course nothing, God knew. He had known this plan and He knew the rest of the untold story. He knew how much it hurt.

"I'm going to take the girls outside." His hand dropped from her arm. "You were good for us."

She closed her eyes and listened to him walking away from her. She wanted him to beg her to stay. Of course he wouldn't do that. He wanted her help finding a replacement because she really was just the housekeeper and the nanny. She wasn't a part of his family.

She wasn't… She opened her eyes and watched him with the girls, watched him hug them, watched him pick Kat up and set her on his shoulders, grimacing just a little as she settled.

She wasn't the woman he loved. How could she stay here working for him, feeling the way she felt? How could she stay here when she knew that her parents needed her?

In the end it was easier to walk outside and pretend she wasn't leaving. It was easier to watch the girls laugh as Wyatt led them on the pony and pretend she would always be in their lives.

Chapter Sixteen

The birthday party had been a pretty big success thanks to Prince the pony. Wyatt sat back in the lawn chair and watched some of the last visitors leave. He smiled at the sight of the poor pony with pink and purple ribbons in his mane and tail. That had been Rachel's idea. It had seemed pretty goofy to him, to do that to the poor pony. The kids had felt differently about it. Little girls loved ribbons. He'd have to remember that.

Little girls loved pink cakes and balloons. They loved pretty dresses and dolls, even when they were cowgirls with ponies and stock dogs. Rachel had taught him that about his daughters. She had taught him a few things about himself, too.

Someone sat down next to him. He turned and smiled at Robert Waters, Rachel's father. The older man smiled back and stretched long legs in front of him. He wore his customary slacks and button-up shirt.

Wyatt glanced down at his own khaki shorts and leather flip-flops. He smiled at Rachel's dad.

"Glad you were here." Not so glad to hear that you're

leaving. Since that wasn't common knowledge, Wyatt didn't mention it.

"Wyatt, Rachel told me that she shared with you that we're leaving. The elders know and a few others. I'll make the announcement tomorrow."

"I'm sorry to hear that you're going." Wyatt let out a sigh and shook his head. "The church hoped you'd stay a long time."

"You know as well as I do that we can never make plans for God." Robert crossed his left leg over his right knee, still relaxed, always relaxed. He was about the calmest man Wyatt had ever met.

"Yeah, things do happen without our permission."

"Have you given any more thought to the youth ministry? When I asked you to do that, I didn't know we were going to be leaving. I guess God did."

"I've thought about it. And yeah, I think I'm ready. I still have moments when I question God. He could have stopped her."

"No one blames you for that. I imagine we could all put together a list of things we question God over. Why someone we loved died in a car accident or why someone had to die young. And the only answer is that sin entered the world and we are allowed free will. We make choices that change lives."

Wyatt fought a real strong urge to say something about this move and if it was really what God wanted or was he giving Pastor Waters freedom to choose, right or wrong. But he knew that Robert Waters was a praying man. He didn't make hasty decisions. He followed what he felt God wanted for him.

He didn't want this man to leave. But maybe it really had been God's plan to have Pastor Waters in Dawson for this season to do the things he needed to do here before moving somewhere else where God had another plan.

"This isn't going to be an easy move for us." Pastor Waters sighed at the end of the sentence and shook his head. "Rachel loves Dawson. She loves taking care of your girls."

"They love her, too."

Pastor Waters glanced his way and smiled. "I guess you've asked her to consider staying?"

"I have, but she won't."

"No, I didn't figure she would."

Family issues, everyone had them. For Wyatt it was all about making his girls his first priority. His parents had never made that a rule. For his parents, life had been about parties and what made them happy. Their two boys were pictures they showed when they wanted to brag about something other than money or the land they owned.

He'd never be his parents. He ran the family business from a distance and his girls came first. Especially now.

Across the lawn Violet and Rachel were cleaning up the leftover party favors, the empty cups and paper plates that were blowing off the picnic table. They talked in quiet whispers like two old friends.

That scene made him a little itchy on the inside, so he turned to search for his girls. They were swinging, feet dangling and party crowns still on their heads. Molly had the biggest crown, the queen crown. And each girl had pink satin ballerina slippers.

He'd never seen so much pink in one place.

"I think I'll go check on my girls." He pushed himself out of the chair, wincing a little at the catch in his ribs and the pull across his lower back. He'd never been so glad to see a horse go as he had been to watch that buckskin loaded into the trailer yesterday afternoon.

He would have kept the animal around if Ryder had been able to take over training for a week or two. But they both had different priorities now.

"Molly, did you have a good birthday?" He stood behind his daughters, pushing one and then the other.

"The bestest one ever." Molly looked back at him, smiling big.

His gaze traveled the short distance to Rachel Waters. The bestest ever. He decided to feel a little angry with her and with God because she was going to leave them empty again.

Last night he'd had to tell the girls. They'd both cried and Molly had begged him to make Rachel stay. She wouldn't, he'd explained. She had responsibilities. Molly asked him what that word meant. He'd had to find a way to explain it to a four-year-old.

Things that matter. Responsibility is the things that we have to do because they matter, they come first. Family, the farm, a job. Those were responsibilities. Molly wanted to be Rachel's responsibility.

The things that come first.

Rachel laughed, the sound carrying. He tried to picture this yard, this house and their lives with her gone.

They'd be empty again.

He gave Kat an easy push. No, they wouldn't be empty. They would still have each other. And they'd have something else. They had the ability to move on and to laugh.

* * *

Two weeks after Molly's party, Rachel walked through a ranch house on the outskirts of Tulsa, just a few blocks from her dad's new church. The church was larger than any he'd ever pastored. The benefits were clearly the best. It was something wonderful for her parents. It meant having a real retirement and security.

It meant great medical care.

It meant Rachel moving into a small bedroom with purple carpet and green walls. Obviously a teenager had been here. Rachel felt a little dizzy, standing in the center of that room.

"It's a nice little house." Her mother stood at the window looking out at the tiny little yard. Rachel didn't want to look. She knew what she'd see outside that window. She'd had views like this before.

She would see other houses, back to back, side to side. She would see privacy fences and manicured shrubs. There would be a patio and eventually patio furniture. Her dog would go on a leash and they'd take walks around the neighborhood. They would talk to strangers who would possibly become friends.

They would adjust. They always did.

And she would live this life until? Until her parents no longer needed her. She smiled at her mom, who hadn't looked this happy in a long time. The idea of a big church with a large staff had taken a burden off her mother.

Gloria Waters wouldn't feel guilty, as if she was letting her husband or his congregation down because she couldn't take a more active role in the ministry. Rachel wanted to tell her mother that they had her, she took that burden. She carried that weight for them.

Cynthia, her sister, had called that morning as they drove into Tulsa. She had given Rachel a lecture about being a martyr because she didn't want to take chances in life. It was easy to stay with their parents, to not get involved in real life.

Rachel had ended the conversation with a blunt "Goodbye."

It was easy for Cynthia. Life had always been easy for the pretty blonde with the stick figure and the outgoing personality. Cynthia had married her college sweetheart. She'd never been rejected.

Her dad stuck his head around the corner. "Nice room."

Rachel smiled. "Love the colors."

"I thought you would." He stepped into the room. "You can paint if you want."

"I know." She smiled, pretending to love the idea of painting another room.

She would be thirty in a few months. Thirty and living with her parents. What did people think? Did they think she was somehow defective? Did they get that she wanted to be here to help?

"Let's take a walk around the neighborhood." Rachel's dad reached for her hand. "I think there's a pool down the block."

"Dad, I'm not fifteen."

He laughed a little. "Yeah, I know. But swimming is great exercise. You can jog one day and swim the next."

She remembered this from her teen years. Her parents always broke the news about moving by telling them how great the new place would be. Eventually Rachel stopped caring. She stopped seeing the moves as an adventure. It became about having to learn a new school, make new friends and reinvent herself each time.

She no longer reinvented.

But she did go for a walk with her dad. He held Wolfgang's leash and they took their time, letting the dog sniff all of the new scents.

"Rachel, have you prayed about this move?"

"What do you mean?"

He stopped while the dog took particular interest in a sign post. "I mean, have you prayed for yourself? Is this move what you're supposed to do?"

"Dad, we're here. I'm here."

Her dad continued to walk and she stayed next to him, whistling to get the dog's attention when it appeared a little too interested in a neighbor's cat. That wouldn't be a good way to start this new life.

"Rachel, I want you to make a decision based on what *you* want."

"What I want is to be here helping you and Mom."

"I'm not sure about that. I kind of wonder if you aren't sacrificing your own happiness because of some sense of duty to your mother and me."

"You've been talking to Cynthia." Rachel took Wolfgang's leash because she needed to control something. Her life was obviously out of the question.

"I talked to Rob and Cynthia. They're both concerned that you're giving up what you want because you feel as if we need you."

"That's nice of them." The brother and sister who visited once a year suddenly knew what was best for her and for their parents.

The thought was unfair, but at the moment she didn't feel like being fair.

"Rachel, I'm about to do something I should have done a long time ago. I'm pushing you from the nest."

"Pushing me?"

She wasn't stupid, but seriously, where had this come from?

"Rachel, years ago God called me to this ministry. He called me. He called your mother with me. We had children. Now our children are grown and it is time for you, my daughter, to find your own place. Your mother and I can take care of ourselves. We took care of you. We really are able to handle life."

"But when Mom is sick…"

He smiled and she felt ten again. "Rachel, I'm her husband. I can take care of her. Go and live your life, make your own choices. When I took this position I knew it was right for me, right for your mother. I think you have to pray about the right place for you."

"Here." She held tight to the leash and fought tears that burned her eyes.

"If that's what God's plan is, fine. With us, in Tulsa, or back in Dawson, it doesn't matter as long as you know it's the right place for you." He kissed her cheek. "Go do something for yourself, Rachel. Eat chocolate, find something you love. Or *someone* you love. Stop using us as an excuse to avoid your own life."

"Ouch."

He laughed a little. "Sorry, but the truth can hurt. You pray and if, after you pray, you honestly feel like it is God's will for you to move here, then I'll accept that."

"I'm starting to get a very big hint." The hint that her parents would like to be alone.

"I thought you might."

Right, so where did that leave her?

* * *

Wyatt backed the trailer up to the corral gate, watching the side mirrors as he eased back. He stopped when the open gate hit the back of the trailer. Perfect.

The dog that had followed next to his truck started to bark. Wyatt turned off the truck and watched Rachel's car easing up the drive. He let out a shallow breath, still not taking deep breaths because his ribs wouldn't give that much. He stepped out of the truck and waited for her to get out of her car.

He hadn't expected her today. For the last week she'd been packing, loading boxes and getting the church staff ready to take over her many jobs. They didn't have a new pastor, not yet. Wyatt and a few other men had prayed about the decision. For now they'd take turns preaching, just until they could find the right man.

The dog left his side and ran to hers, tail wagging. Rachel reached to pet the animal. It followed her back to him. He glanced toward the house. Violet was inside with the girls. She'd been interviewing housekeepers. So far he and the girls hadn't liked any of the candidates.

"I didn't expect to see you today."

She shrugged one shoulder and didn't look directly at him. Her brown hair blew around her face and her expression seemed a little lost to him.

"I hadn't expected to stop. I missed the girls and wanted to give them something I bought in Tulsa."

"They've missed you, too." He almost included himself, but he wasn't going there.

What did he miss? Her pancakes, coffee that didn't taste bitter, or music blasting as she cleaned?

"Do you mind if I go in and see them?"

"No, go ahead. I have to load some calves that we've sold." The reason he'd backed the trailer up to the corral. The bawling calves were huddled in the far corner of the corral.

"I could help you."

"I can get it." He tried not to move like someone who needed help. She laughed at his attempt.

"Let me help. I'll miss this." The faraway look returned. "We're moving into a neighborhood where our view is of the neighbor's back door."

"I've lived in those neighborhoods. It works for a lot of people. I guess it's a good thing we're all different."

"Yeah. So I can help?"

He pointed her to the gate. "I'll head them this way. You make sure they don't squeeze through there."

She nodded and headed for the spot he pointed to. She wasn't country at all, just wanted to be. That was okay with him. He enjoyed watching her standing there in her denim shorts, a T-shirt and sandals. Not exactly a picture of a cowgirl, but he didn't really know what a cowgirl was supposed to look like. He'd seen a few in his time that looked like anything but.

The calves moved away from him. His dog circled, keeping them together and moving toward the trailer. One angus steer tried to break from the group, the dog brought him back, nipping quick at the steer's hooves.

Ahead of him, Rachel stood next to the gate, her hand shading her eyes as the sun hit. He didn't smile, couldn't. He was picturing her in that house surrounded by neighbors.

The calves ran through the opening into the back of the trailer. He swung the trailer door, swinging the latch in place. The calves moved to the back of the trailer.

Wyatt slid through the gate. Rachel moved out of his way.

"You don't have to go."

Her eyes widened and she stared, waiting. He didn't know what to say other than what he'd said. He lifted a hand and rested it on the side of the trailer.

"I kind of do have to go. I don't have a home here. My parents are moving."

"Rachel, the girls don't want any other nanny. They already miss you and you're not gone."

"Of course, I know they'll miss me. I'll miss them, too. But I feel like I need to be close to my parents. If my mom gets sick, I need to be there."

"It isn't that far. What is it, just under two hours to their new church?"

"Something like that. But if she's sick, she needs daily help, not a visit."

"Right, you're right." He let it go because he did understand her loyalty to her parents. He got it.

"I'm going to go see the girls. I want them to know that I'll visit."

He smiled and tipped his hat. "Yeah, visits are good. I have to get these steers on down the road."

She turned and walked away. He watched her walk through the back door of his house and then he climbed in the truck and cranked the engine. He eased forward, watching in the rearview mirror as the corral gate swung shut. The trailer shifted as the cattle shifted.

In the house Rachel was telling his girls goodbye. Why did he have the sudden urge to hit something? It combined with a pretty nasty urge to turn the truck and stock trailer around.

And do what? Beg Rachel to stay? What would he

tell her? He could tell her that his girls were happier with her in their lives. *He* was happier.

After that, what then? He would have her in their home as a housekeeper and nanny. She would cook for them, clean their house and hug the girls. He'd still have to deal with moving on.

Last night he'd pulled out photo albums. He'd glanced through pictures of Wendy in college. They were young and in love. Crazy in love.

He rode bulls and roped steers. She spent weekends working at a homeless shelter. They'd picked youth ministry together. After college they'd gotten married.

The pictures stayed happy for a few years, until after Molly's birth. That was when the story of their lives changed. He'd looked at those pictures and tried to figure out what he could have done.

But he couldn't change things. He couldn't undo them now. What he had was a future with his two little girls and memories of their mother. Someday he'd share the good memories.

None of that fixed the situation right now. Rachel was going to leave and Violet was hiring a new housekeeper. She'd talked about a lady named Thelda Matheson. He hoped she wore joint cream.

Chapter Seventeen

Rachel stood in the green-and-purple bedroom staring out a window without a view and knowing this was all wrong. She was in the wrong place, in the wrong life. It felt like wearing someone else's shoes.

Her parents were drinking coffee in the new kitchen, sitting in front of patio doors at a table they'd had for years. Same table, same parents, different kitchen. Same life. Their life.

She joined them at that table. They looked up, not asking questions. She got up to pour herself a cup of coffee and then she joined them again.

"You're right, this isn't my place anymore."

"What does that mean?" Her mom put her cup down and glanced at Rachel's dad. The two seemed to always know everything she was about to tell them.

When she had been sixteen and rebellious, nothing ever seemed to surprise them. They always seemed to know what trouble she'd gotten herself into.

"I left my ministry." Rachel wiped at tears that were rolling down her cheeks. "I left my home."

"Dawson?" Her dad smiled, as if he'd planned it himself.

"Yes, Dawson. The teen girls. My Sunday school class. Molly and Kat. I left it all because I thought you needed me here. But God called you to make this move, not me. It's just that I'm stubborn or afraid, I'm not sure which."

"And you thought I needed you." Gloria patted her hand. "Honey, I will always need you, but I'm really okay."

"I know you are. Maybe I wasn't. Maybe I've needed you."

"I think we just got into the bad habit of letting you take care of us." Her mom smiled. "What do you plan on doing?"

"I think I'm going to call Etta and see if I can still take her up on the offer to stay at her house. I'll call the church and ask if I can keep working with the kids."

"It feels good, doesn't it?" Her dad grinned big.

"Yeah, it kind of does feel good. This is right, Dad."

"I think I tried to tell you that the other day. Time to fly, Rachel. Go find your future."

She carried her still-full cup to the sink. "I think I'm going to start packing."

The one thing she wouldn't do was make this move about Wyatt. He'd hired a new housekeeper. The girls needed to get settled with the person he'd found. Rachel needed to make sure she was where God wanted her, not jump back into what felt comfortable and easy.

She needed to wait because she didn't want a broken heart her first day back in her new life.

Wyatt drove past the parsonage a few days after Rachel's last visit. It was empty. He let out a sigh and kept on going. She was gone and Mrs. Matheson had taken her place. He didn't like the lady. No reason, he just didn't like her. He didn't like her sensible shoes or the smell of eucalyptus that hovered over her as she moved through the house.

Kat and Molly weren't crazy about her either.

He pulled up the drive and parked inside the garage. Violet was still at the house. She assured him she would be leaving in the morning. They'd be fine without her.

Of course they would. He walked out of the garage and across the yard to the barn. The stallion he'd bought from the Fosters whinnied from the small corral at the side of the barn. Wyatt walked up to the fence and the big bay, his dark red coat gleaming, trotted up for a treat. Wyatt pulled an apple snack out of his pocket and the horse sucked it up, barely grazing his hands.

The back door banged shut. He turned. It was Violet. She walked toward him, her high heels sinking in the yard that was still soggy from last night's rain. He wondered if she would ever try to fit into these surroundings. He doubted it.

"Did you see Rachel before she left?" Violet stood next to him, holding her hand out to the horse but withdrawing it before the horse made contact.

"No, I didn't see her. I think they left last night."

"Right." Violet stepped back because the horse stuck his nose out to her.

"What is it you want to say, Violet?"

She smiled up at him. "Don't let her go."

"What does that mean? I offered her the job, she turned it down. How can I change that?" He really wanted to walk away from this conversation. "I've hired someone. Remember?"

"Don't be ridiculous, I'm not talking about hiring her as a housekeeper. I'm talking about what you seem to be ignoring or avoiding. You love her. It's obvious she loves you. Why in the world are you letting her go?"

The mother of his wife, pushing him to—what?

"Violet, this isn't the conversation I want to have with you."

"No, I'm sure it isn't. But I think I'm the best person to tell you that Wendy would want you to move on. She'd want it to be with someone like Rachel, someone who loves you and your girls. This kind of love doesn't happen often. For most people it happens once. You're blessed to have it happen twice. Don't let this get away."

"It's too soon." He pushed his hat down on his head, tipping the brim to shade his eyes.

"Who says?"

"I say." He backed away from the fence, from the horse, from Violet. "I say it's too soon."

"You can't control that. You're trying to hold on to her memory and the love you shared. I get that. But you can't say it's too soon. Not if the right person has entered your life and you're on the verge of losing her. If you haven't already lost her."

"I have to go for a drive."

"Fine, go for a drive. But if I was you, I'd spend time praying about this. I don't believe in chance, Wyatt Johnson. It was no accident that she was here, in your life and in the lives of your daughters."

"Violet, let it go."

She drew in her lips and shook her head. "Wyatt, you're stubborn."

He walked away, back to his truck, back to a few minutes alone. As he drove down the drive, he thought back to her words. He remembered telling Rachel that he wasn't ready.

He hadn't planned on ever being ready.

And Rachel had made a choice. He'd asked her to stay and she'd made the decision to go.

Because he hadn't asked her to stay for him. He called himself every kind of fool because he knew he'd asked the wrong question.

Fly, little bird, fly. Rachel smiled as the wind whipped through her hair. The radio blasted Sara Evans and she sang along to a song about suds being left in the bucket and clothes left hanging on the line.

Rachel Waters was finally leaving home. After the conversation with her parents a few days ago, she'd taken time to figure out exactly what she wanted. She knew it wasn't Tulsa. As much as she loved the city, she didn't want to live there.

And it had been pretty obvious her parents didn't need her. It had been more obvious that maybe they were a little relieved to hear that she planned on moving out.

She'd watched them together, watched her mom and dad taking care of each other, unpacking, planning. She'd watched herself on the outside of their circle, trying to be helpful, trying to take care of them. And all along they could take care of themselves.

She'd stopped taking risks. A long time ago she'd decided safe was good. Well, today was a new day. Today included giving in a little, maybe even giving in to temptation.

So on the way out of Tulsa she'd gone through a drive-through for a frozen coffee drink full of calories and a cookie laden down with chocolate chips. Take that, thighs.

Rachel Waters was done controlling her life. She planned on finding her path, her future, her today. With God in control.

Today. No more waiting for tomorrow. No more fear of taking risks.

She had called Etta who'd been overjoyed with the idea of Rachel staying with her for a while, helping on the farm and with her business. Vera had answered the next call and agreed to give her a few lunch shifts during the week.

Rachel cruised through Dawson, slow, taking it all in. Home. She smiled, loving that word. The one place she had loved more than any other and now it was her home. Her choice. She had a place to go and a nice savings account. It felt good. It felt better than good.

It felt pretty close to perfect until she drove past Wyatt's and saw the girls on the swing. It shouldn't hurt, that he'd offered her a job. But it did. He wanted her in their lives, but only as the person who cooked meals, gave hugs and went home at the end of every day.

She wanted more than that.

The old convictions were still strong, the belief that God would bring the right person into her life. As she got older she wondered if maybe that wasn't His plan. Not everyone had the same destiny. There was a point in time when a person just accepted what his or her life was and made peace with it.

Etta's house was a welcome sight. The big, yellow Victorian glowed in the setting sun. Rachel pulled up the drive and parked. When she walked around the corner of the house, Etta met her on the sidewalk.

"Well, aren't you a sight for sore eyes." Etta grabbed her in a tight hug.

"It's only been a few days."

"Longest days of my life, wondering if you'd get it right."

Rachel laughed and hugged Etta back. "I got it right."

Etta slid an arm around Rachel's waist and they walked up the steps to the porch. "At least partially right."

"How much more right do I need to be?"

Etta turned at the sound of a car coming down the road. No, it was a truck. Rachel's heart froze in place, refusing to pick up where it left off. She took a deep breath and her heart did the same.

"Hmm, someone else must be trying to get it right."

"No, Etta." Rachel refused to watch the truck drive on by.

"Oh, you kids. I tell you what, in the last year, I've had it up to my neck with silly young couples who take forever to get it right. It was simpler in my day. The man knew what he wanted and he went after it. The woman knew it was the right thing to do and she stopped running. Happy ever after."

Rachel wanted to laugh but she couldn't. The truck didn't go on down the road, it pulled into Etta's drive.

Etta chuckled a little. "Don't run, Rachel. I'm going inside and you let yourself get caught."

"I have a job. I'm going to work for you. He found someone else to watch the girls."

Etta had walked inside. The screen door closed behind her.

"Oh, honey, you are clueless."

Rachel stood on the porch waiting for Wyatt to get

out of the truck and join her. He walked a little easier than he had the previous week. It hadn't been that long, she reminded herself. But honestly, the last week had felt like a lifetime.

"So this is where you went to." He walked up the steps. He took off his hat and held it in front of him, raising one hand and running it through dark hair flattened to his head.

She'd been right about him, he was heartache and she didn't need heartache, not even if it came in a package with lean, suntanned cheeks and a smile that nearly became a caress.

"I came back." She eased the words out.

"I know. I've been in Tulsa."

"What? Why?"

"To talk to your dad."

"Oh."

"And to see you." He stepped closer. His dark eyes held hers captive.

"Really?" Her heart took a hopeful leap forward but she pulled it back, reined it in. Maybe the new housekeeper hadn't worked out.

"Yeah, really." His smile was sweet, it melted in his eyes and melted her heart. Wasn't that the same heart she was trying to keep under control?

For some reason it wasn't working, that control thing.

"How are the girls?"

He reached for her hands. "The girls miss you."

"I miss them, too."

He tossed his hat on a nearby chair. "I miss you, too."

"I see."

"No, you don't. Rachel, I got up this morning and walked around a house that has never felt more empty.

I realized what was missing. You." He teased her with another one of those smiles. "I realized I asked you the wrong question."

She didn't know what to say.

"You are the thing missing from our lives. From *my* life. I went to Tulsa because I wanted to see you. I wanted to tell you that I don't want you in our lives as a housekeeper or a nanny."

Her heart wouldn't let go of hope. It wouldn't stop its crazy beat inside her chest. She couldn't move, couldn't breathe.

"Rachel, I want you in our lives because we love you. I love you."

"You do?" She loved him, too, but she was afraid to say the words, afraid to believe this moment was happening.

He grinned and brushed a hand across her cheek. "I do. While I was in Tulsa, I asked your dad to do me a favor."

"What's that?" Was that her heart melting, pooling up inside her?

"I asked him if he would do the honor of officiating at a wedding."

"Oh."

"I told him I'd like to date his daughter for a few months." He pulled her close, touching his lips to hers, sweet, seductive and then gone. "And I asked him if he would walk you down the aisle and then step behind the pulpit and marry us."

"Wyatt." She whispered the word close to his ear and he turned, brushing his cheek against hers.

"So now I need to ask you, Rachel Waters, if you'll be the wife of one very hardheaded cowboy. This isn't about being ready to move on. This is about being ready to love you for the rest of my life."

Rachel closed her eyes, replaying his words, the words she'd been waiting for, wanting to hear. She'd dreamed of those words and how it would feel at this moment. And now she knew. She knew that shivers would tingle up her arms and down her spine. She knew that her heart would twirl inside her chest.

She now knew that he would lean and his hands would cup her cheeks as he dropped the sweetest kiss on her lips.

But in her dreams it had never been this wonderful.

"Rachel, will you marry me?" Wyatt whispered the proposal again after kissing her long and easy.

She nodded and tears pooled and slid down her cheeks.

"Of course I'll marry you."

Wyatt held his breath as she said the words he'd been waiting to hear and then he released his hand from hers and fished the ring out of his shirt pocket.

"I was hoping you might say yes." He grinned, his face a little warm. "So I stopped at a jewelry store on the way home and told them I needed the most beautiful diamond for the most beautiful bride."

She stood in front of him, sweeter than cherry soda on a hot summer day and everything he wanted in life. He reached for her hand and slid the ring onto her finger. The diamond glinted, winking the promise of forever.

"I love you," he whispered.

He held her close, thankful to have her in his arms

again. She felt good there, in his arms. She felt right. This felt right.

This was something only a fool would let go of. He wasn't a fool. He might be a hardheaded cowboy, but he knew what he wanted and he knew when to hold on to it.

She moved her hands to his shoulders and then to the back of his neck as he captured her lips in a kiss that promised forever.

"I love you, too," she whispered close to his ear and he held her tight.

No way would he ever let her go.

Epilogue

❧

Wyatt walked out of the barn and saw his wife and kids in the backyard. Ryder stood behind him. The two of them had been working cattle all day, giving immunizations and taking care of other details that had to be dealt with. Little bull calves were now steers. Ears were tagged.

The two of them were dirty and pretty close to disgusting.

Ryder slapped his back. "Brother, that's a nice little family you've got."

Wyatt smiled and he couldn't agree more. But he wasn't going to give Ryder room to gloat. He knew where Ryder was going with this conversation. Wyatt counted to three and waited for it.

On cue Ryder spoke, a big smile on his face. "Wasn't it just a couple of years ago that I said something about needing a boy in our family to protect all of these girls?"

Wyatt continued to ignore his little brother. Listen to Ryder, or watch his family playing together in the backyard. He picked ignoring the pest at his side. Even if he was right.

"Yep, that's one cute little baby boy you've got." Ryder, loose limbed and way too sure of himself, took off across the yard. Andie had the twins in a big play-pen, keeping the "little fillies" as Ryder called his girls, corralled.

Wyatt smiled when Rachel turned to find him. She was more beautiful today than she'd been on their wedding day. That day, dressed in a cream gown and walking down the aisle with her dad, that had been a day.

But today, with their little boy tucked safe in the pouch that hung around her neck, today she glowed. Today, just looking at her knocked him on his can.

He choked up a little, thinking about Rowdy's birth. He had feared losing Rachel. He'd been afraid she'd slip away.

Now those thoughts were pushed aside. He had a wife, two beautiful daughters and one handsome little guy.

"Are you going to come and push your daughters?" Rachel called out, bringing him back to earth.

"On my way." He hurried across the lawn. When he got there he kissed her first, holding her close for a minute, loose in his arms. And then he kissed the dark head of his little boy.

God had brought her to Dawson and then brought him home. Good planning, God. He smiled as he pushed Molly high and gave Kat a lighter push.

Good planning.

* * * * *

Dear Reader,

Welcome back to my favorite fictional small town; Dawson, Oklahoma. I love Oklahoma. I've never lived there, but if I had to move, that's the direction I'd head. Oklahoma has history, horses, ranches…and let's not forget: cowboys.

I hope you enjoy Rachel and Wyatt's story. When Wyatt Johnson first arrived back in Dawson, I knew that his story had to be told. It is a story about healing and moving past our pain.

It is also about trusting God with where we are in our lives.

It was obvious that Wyatt would need a woman who could handle his pain and stand up to him when he was hardheaded. Enter pastor's daughter Rachel Waters. As you read Rachel and Wyatt's story, I hope it touches your life. And if you're dealing with your own pain, I pray that God heals your heart.

Brenda Minton

THE COWBOY'S
HOMECOMING

He that dwelleth in the secret place of the most
High shall abide under the shadow of the Almighty.
I will say of the Lord, He is my refuge
and my fortress: my God; in him will I trust.
—*Psalms* 91:1–2

This book is dedicated to all of the strong women out there, and to the women wanting to be strong, that they find their strength.

Chapter One

People were never who or what you thought. That's a lesson Beth Bradshaw knew from experience and she had the scars to prove it.

She had even learned things about herself that took her by surprise. Like the fact that she could be strong. She didn't always have to do what pleased others. Sometimes she did what pleased her.

The fact that she was the person sitting on a horse in front of Back Street Church, determined to talk Jeremy Hightree out of his plans for the building was a big moment for her. It was a mountain climbed. It was a fear tackled.

Someone had to do it. So, shaking in her boots, remembering the last time she was here, she sat and contemplated the confrontation.

The horse beneath her shifted, restless from standing. She waved at flies buzzing the animal's neck and ears but her gaze remained on the run-down church in front of her. Things changed, that was part of life. She'd obviously changed since the years spent attending this little church with her mother.

Jeremy Hightree had changed. She knew he'd changed because only huge changes could bring him back to Dawson, Oklahoma, with the plans he had for this building.

The church had been untouched and neglected for too many years. The lawn had grown into a field of weeds. The exterior had faded from white to gray and the paint was chipped and flaking off. After one hundred years of service, the tiny church with the tall steeple had become a forgotten piece of the past.

So why should she care what Jeremy planned on doing to a forgotten piece of Dawson history? The question rolled through her mind as she dropped to the ground and led the chestnut gelding up the sidewalk, metal hooves clip-clopping on concrete. She looped the leather reins around the handrail and walked up the crumbling concrete steps to the porch. The door stood wide open but she didn't go in. She glanced around, looking for Jeremy, her heart hammering a chaotic rhythm, afraid she'd see him. Afraid she wouldn't.

But this wasn't about seeing Jeremy. Her heart did a funny skip forward, asking her to rethink that last thought. But she wouldn't. She couldn't. This had to be about the church, not schoolgirl emotions.

She took a hesitant step inside the church. It took her eyes a minute to adjust to the dim interior. Filtered light from the dirty stained-glass windows caught dust particles that floated in the air. A bird glided through the building and landed on the pulpit. Her great-grandfather had made that pulpit. The wood was hickory and the stain was natural and light. A cross had been carved into the front.

Her history in this town was tied to this church. And

she had ignored it. She took a deep breath, breathing in dust and aging wood. For a minute she was eight years old again and unscarred, still smiling, still believing in fairy tales and happy endings.

Jeremy was still the little boy who pulled at the ribbons on her new dress and teased her about the freckles on her nose.

But she wasn't eight. She was twenty-eight. Her mother had been dead for eighteen years. And Jeremy wasn't a little boy. He was the man who planned on destroying this church.

Eighteen years of pain tangled inside, keeping her feet planted in the vestibule. The little room where they'd once hung their coats was now draped in spiders' webs, and mice ran from corner to corner. The old guestbook still rested on the shelf where it had been placed years ago. She flipped through the pages and stopped when she got to her name written in a child's penmanship. She remembered her mom standing behind her, smiling as Beth scrawled her name, proud that she'd learned to sign it in cursive.

Too many memories. She didn't need all of them, she just needed to know the truth. If it was true, she would find a way to stop him. She walked down the aisle of the church, her booted feet echoing in the tall ceilinged building. She stopped and waited for everything to settle, for the memories to stop tugging at her. In this memory, her mom was next to her, singing. The piano rocked to a Southern gospel hymn. And behind her...

"Bethlehem Bradshaw, I'll tell on you."

His voice was soft in the quiet sanctuary. She turned, amazed that he could still unsettle her. He stood in the doorway, sunlight behind him, his face in shadows.

She didn't need to see his face to know him. She knew that he had short, light brown hair and eyes the color of caramel toffee. She knew his smile, that it turned the left side of his mouth more than the right and always flashed white teeth. He walked with a swagger, his jeans hanging low on his hips and his T-shirt stretched tight across the shoulders of a man.

He was no longer a boy. He was lethal and dangerous. He had plans to destroy something that she wanted to protect.

"Why would you do this?" She hated that her voice shook. She despised that she wanted to run out the back door. The closer he got, the harder it was to breathe, to stand her ground.

She wanted to pound her fists against him and beg him to stop, to leave town and forget this church and whatever he had against the people of Dawson. Instead she stood, frozen, unable to do any of those things. Weak. She hated being weak. And afraid.

"Why would I do what? Tease you?" Jeremy Hightree stopped at the second pew from the front of the church, the one where she'd sat with her mother so many years ago. He leaned against it, hip against the side of the wooden bench.

He had always teased her, she wanted to remind him. He would sit behind her and pull ribbons from her hair. He'd once dropped a plastic spider in her lap during Sunday school.

And he had picked a ragged bouquet of wildflowers the day of her mother's funeral and pushed them into Beth's hands as she walked out the doors of the church with her brother Jason and her father. His brown eyes had been rimmed with red from crying and she had wanted to hug him because her mother had always hugged him.

Her mother had defended him. He was the son of her best friend from grade school. Other people had called him a dirty mess. Her mom had called him a little prince.

Beth's feelings had fallen somewhere in between.

She stepped down off the stage, closer to him. One thing was for certain, he wasn't the dirty little boy anymore. He was a man who had traveled. He had won two world championships; one in bull riding and another in team roping. Little girls had posters of him in their bedrooms and little boys wanted to be him when they grew up.

He'd built a business from nothing.

So why this? Why now? It took a few minutes to gather her thoughts, to know how to respond to him. She needed the right words, the right emotions.

"Why the church, Jeremy? You could buy any piece of land you wanted. You could leave the church and never think about it."

One shoulder lifted in indifference. Instead his gaze shot away from her and his jaw clenched. He was anything but indifferent.

"Let's talk about something other than this church. Funny how people have neglected it for years and now everyone wants to talk about it. It was a public auction, Beth. Anyone could have bought it. I was the only one who showed up to bid."

"I know. I guess we all thought someone else would take care of it." She hated admitting that to him and then begging him to let go of his plans.

He moved a few steps closer and Beth stood her

ground. She didn't back away. She wouldn't let him get to her. And he could. She shivered and remembered. The memory was soft, sweet, jagged with emotion.

It was the briefest moment, the briefest memory. Yet she'd never forgotten. They had as much history as this church. They'd grown up together. They'd shared a childhood.

"I'm sorry how things turned out with Chance." His voice changed, got a little rougher, a little less velvet than before.

"You couldn't have known." No one would have guessed the abuse Chance was capable of. But it was over. The divorce had been finalized fifteen months ago.

Jeremy must have known something. He had tried to warn her what Chance was like. The day she left town, he'd seen her waiting at the park and he'd tried to tell her. But she had been desperate to escape.

"Beth?" His voice pulled her from the memories, from the darkness, back to the present and the problem at hand.

"I don't want to talk about Chance."

"I understand. And I don't want to talk about the church. It isn't personal, you know. It's a business decision."

"Is it really? It seems personal to me."

He crossed his arms over a muscular chest. "Maybe it is a little personal. I'm tired of this memory and I'm tired of this church standing like a beacon on this hill."

"That's a little drastic, don't you think? This church hasn't been a beacon in a dozen years."

One shoulder lifted again. "I don't know, maybe. But it's my story, not yours."

"This church meant so much to…" She wasn't going to beg him. She breathed deep, willing herself not to cry.

"It meant a lot to your mother."

His tone had changed again. The rough edges were gone. She looked up as he stood straight again and took a few steps in her direction. His steps were slow, calculated.

Had she really thought she could talk him out of this? A shared moment gave her no claim over him. Memories didn't give her a right to assume he would listen. His story in this church mattered to him, not the memory of a kiss they shared a dozen years ago.

"Yes, it did mean a lot to her." But Beth had only been inside the building a handful of times since her mother's funeral. Eighteen years. After her mother's death her father had caught her here once and dragged her home.

Jeremy watched her. His smile faded a little. His eyes narrowed as he stared hard. His Native American heritage was evident in the smooth planes of his face, tanned a deep brown from working outside. But almost everyone in Dawson shared that heritage, that ancestry. Redheads, blonds, brunettes; hair color and eye color didn't dictate a lack of Native American ancestry. The people of Dawson were proud of that heritage, proud of their strength and resilience.

They were known for bouncing back, for not letting the past get them down.

The past was tied to everything, though. It was the shadow of pain in Jeremy Hightree's eyes. It held her own heart captive. It was the fear that clawed at her chest and woke her up in the middle of the night.

"I'm not sure what to tell you, Beth. Your mom meant a lot to me. But this church is…"

"What? Tell me what this church ever did to you?" She pinned him with a stare, hoping to make him squirm. Instead his expression softened, as if he understood her pain, and was hiding his own behind anger.

She remembered the boy with the bouquet, the one she'd wanted to hug. She couldn't allow herself to compare him to that boy. "Tell me, Jeremy, what will revenge do for you?"

Well, now, the kitten had grown some claws. She stood in front of him, pint-size with dark eyes that flashed fear and fire simultaneously. Her dark brown hair hung in pigtails. She picked that moment to lick lips that trembled. He smiled and for a few minutes he didn't quite know what to say to her, because he was picturing her as a cornered kitten, shaking in her boots but ready to swipe at him. He had a lot of questions for her. He had questions about her life, about Chance Martin, about Dawson.

Instead of asking questions he shook his head and considered walking away. She'd mentioned revenge. He really didn't like that word.

And when she'd said it, his decision didn't feel as good as it had even an hour earlier when he'd stood outside picturing this hill without this church, without the memories that had been chasing him down, biting at his heels.

"It isn't just about revenge." He shrugged and smiled at Bethlehem Bradshaw. He'd always been a fan of her full name, not the shortened version. The full name had meant something to her mother. And her mother had meant a lot to him. She'd done more for him than people would ever know.

That loyalty struck a raw nerve with him right now. Because Bethlehem's mamma was gone and here was her daughter begging for something that woman would have wanted. She would have wanted this church to remain standing.

But he thought she would have cried at its condition now, because it hadn't been used in years and no one had cared to keep it maintained. She wouldn't have wanted that either.

Of course she would have told him to forgive.

Forgive his mother for being the town drunk. Forgive Tim Cooper for a tiny indiscretion more than thirty years ago and not owning up to it. As far as Jeremy was concerned, Tim Cooper didn't need his forgiveness. That was between Tim and Mrs. Cooper.

Jeremy had a truckload of bad memories. He'd learned early to fight for himself and his little sister. At eight he could make a mean box of mac and cheese. By the time he was ten he could sign his mother's signature on school permission slips. He learned to braid his little sister's hair and wash her clothes.

His sister, Elise, was married now. She and her husband owned a convenience store in Grove. They sold bait to fishermen and coffee mugs to tourists. Elise was big on forgiveness, too.

"It looks a lot like revenge." Bethlehem's soft voice intruded into his memories, shaking him up more than a green Oklahoma sky on a stormy afternoon.

"Bethlehem, I'm not sure what you want me to say."

"Say you won't do this."

"I can't say that." For the first time since he'd bought

the church, he had the biggest urge to forget his plans. Because of Beth.

"Why not?"

Jeremy shook his head to clear the thoughts. "I have plans for this piece of property."

He needed a bigger shop for the custom bikes he'd turned from a hobby into a business, an extension of the chain of motorcycle dealerships he owned.

"Do you have plans or are you just angry?"

He leaned in and then he regretted the move that put him a little too close to Bethlehem, close enough to see the flecks of gold in her brown eyes, close enough to get tangled in the soft scent of her perfume.

Man, she was summer sunshine. She was sweet, the way she'd been sweet at sixteen. A guy couldn't forget a kiss stolen along a creek bank on a summer night.

Time to think fast and get the kid he'd been back under the control of the man he now was. And she wasn't making that an easy thing to do.

"Let me ask you a question. How many times have you been to church in the last dozen years or so?"

She turned pink and glanced away from him. "We're not talking about me. And I do go to church."

He smiled at that. "Yeah, we weren't talking about you. But now we are."

Because there was a scar across her brow. It ran into her hairline. A matching scar ran jagged down her arm. She shifted, uneasy, and crossed her arms in front of herself. This church wasn't the only thing he'd like to tear down. If he ever got hold of Chance Martin, he'd probably do the same to him.

But he doubted Chance would ever show his face in Dawson, not if he wanted to live. Because Jeremy figured he probably wasn't the only man in town that wanted to get hold of that coward.

Beth's arms dropped to her sides and she took a few steps toward the door, her eyes shifting from him to the exit. He got that she needed to breathe, and he let her have the space.

At the door she turned to face him again.

"Don't do this. Please." A tear streaked down her cheek.

He let out a sigh and shook his head. "Bethlehem, I'm sorry. I know why this church means something to you. It means something different to me."

"I know and I'm sorry."

"Right."

"I'll buy it from you." She spoke with renewed determination, her dark eyes flashing. "You don't need this land. Do you even plan on staying here?"

"No, I'm not staying here, not full time. I have a home in Tulsa."

"Then don't do it. What will it accomplish? Who do you want to hurt?"

He brushed a hand over the top of his head, over hair cut short, and moved it down to rub the back of his neck.

"I'm done with this conversation, Bethlehem."

"It's a building. It didn't do anything to you."

He looked around, remembering. She was wrong about that. This building tied into a lot of anger. That anger had pushed him to battle it out on the backs of bulls. It had put him on a motorcycle, racing through the desert at speeds that would make most guys wet themselves like little girls.

When he looked at this building, there wasn't a good memory to hang on to. He glanced away from her, away from the second pew where her mother had sat, and he called himself a liar.

Good memories included potluck dinners when he got to sit with Bethlehem and her mother. He had other good memories, like the smile she gave him when she was fifteen and he'd just won a local bull-riding event. She'd smiled and then hurried away with her friends, giggling and shooting glances back at him. Hers had lingered longest and when he'd winked, she'd turned pink and nearly tripped.

"Bethlehem, I am going to tear this church down."

"I feel sorry for you."

"Yeah, lots of people do." But he didn't want her to be one of them.

"I'll do what I can to stop you. I won't let you tear it down."

"What would you do with it, Beth? Open it back up, sing songs on Sundays, serve potluck once a month? It's an old building. It should probably be condemned."

She shrugged and smiled a soft smile. He knew he was in serious trouble then. He got a feeling she was about to pull a one-two punch on him.

She stepped close, her smile pulling him closer.

"Don't you feel it, Jeremy? After all these years, don't you feel it?"

Yeah, he'd seen it coming. No other woman had ever set him on his heels the way she could. Because he knew exactly what she meant and, yeah, he felt it. He felt the past. He felt God. He felt faith. All the things he'd been ignoring and it hit him every single time he walked into this building. He felt hundreds of prayers that had been said, probably most of them for him, his little sister, and his mother.

He remembered Sunday school teachers who had brought him cookies. The pastor back then, Pastor Adkins, and his wife had bought Jeremy and his sister school clothes and Christmas presents.

But all of those good memories got lost, tied up with the bad, when he remembered Tim Cooper on the front pew with his family. Each Sunday they'd showed up in their van, wearing new clothes and happy smiles. When he'd been about six years old there were only a few Cooper kids. As the years went by, the clan grew. The Coopers had about a half dozen kids of their own. They added about a half dozen adopted children.

Jeremy had sat two pews back across the aisle, without a family to have Sunday lunch with, without a dad.

"Sorry, Bethlehem."

He turned and walked away, knowing there would be tears streaking down her cheeks, knowing she'd nearly collapse with sadness and frustration over his stubbornness.

As he walked out the back door his phone rang. He shielded the display and shook his head. He really didn't want to deal with this today. Bethlehem had just about done him in.

But if he didn't answer she'd call again. And again. There was always a crisis in his mother's life.

"Hi, Mom, what do you need?" He held the phone to his ear and walked across the overgrown lawn to the RV that he'd been living in.

Horse hooves on pavement caught his attention. He turned to watch Bethlehem ride down the road at an easy trot. Her hand came up and he knew she was wiping tears from her eyes.

That made him not much better than Chance Martin.

"Jeremy, this is Carl Duncan." A county deputy on his mom's phone. Great.

"What can I do for you, Carl?"

"I'm sorry to bother you but we've got your mamma down here at the jail. Someone called her in for a disturbance."

"Did she have clothes on this time?" He brushed a hand across his head and looked down at the ground, at his scuffed work boots and at a little black snake slithering a short distance away.

"Yeah, fully clothed but drunk enough we're considering sending her to the E.R."

"Do what you have to do and I'll be there in about thirty minutes."

He slid the phone back into his pocket and turned. His attention landing on the eyesore that used to be Back Street Church. The steeple still stood and a cross reached up, tarnished but intact.

It bothered him, that Bethlehem had made him remember more than he'd wanted to. She'd forced him to recognize other things about this building, this church. She'd made him think about the good things that had happened here.

But it didn't matter. He'd bought this land to raze a church and build a business. He wasn't going to give up on his plans, his dreams, not for Bethlehem or anyone else.

Next week Back Street Church was going to be nothing but a memory.

Chapter Two

The horse flew up the driveway, hooves pounding the ground and neck stretched forward. Beth leaned, reins in her hands, her legs tight around the horse's middle. They flew past the house, past the garden and the barn. She pulled the horse up at the fence and then just sat there on the gelding, both of them breathing hard.

"Take it easy on that colt." The gruff voice didn't lecture, just made a statement.

Beth turned to smile at Lance, her dad's ranch foreman.

"He's barely winded."

"He's needed a good ride, that's for sure. Where you been?"

"Riding." She slid to the ground, the reins still in her hands. Lance took the horse and led the animal to the barn. She followed. The ranch foreman was getting older but he was still burly and fit. He hitched up his jeans with a piece of twine and his shirt was loose over a T-shirt. He glanced back, his weathered face so familiar she wanted to hug him just for being in her life.

"Your daddy has been looking for you. He said he called your phone three times."

"I didn't have a signal."

"The only place in Dawson with a weak cell signal is Back Street." Lance turned, his gray eyes narrowed. "You weren't up at the church, were you?"

"I'm twenty-eight, not twelve."

"I think I know that. I'm just saying, you don't need to mess around up there. And you aren't going to be able to stop Jeremy Hightree from doing what he plans on doing."

"Someone has to stop him."

"Well, the city of Dawson is trying to take care of that. Let them."

"I'm afraid I'm just going to have to help them."

She took the horse's reins from the ranch foreman and led the gelding down the center aisle of the barn. She grabbed a brush off a hook and crosstied the horse. Lance flipped the stirrup over the back of the saddle and loosened the girth strap.

"You can't stop him, Beth. He's got thirty years of mad built up in him."

"He needs to get over it."

"Right, and men always listen when a woman tells them to just 'get over it.'" He said it in a girly voice and shook his head. It was funny, that voice and big old Lance with his craggy, weathered face. Lance had always been there for them. He'd always managed to make her smile. When she was a teenager and thought the world hated her, and she hated it back, Lance had been the one who teased her out of the bad moods.

The horse stomped and Beth ran a hand down the deep red neck. The animal turned and nibbled at her arm before lowering his head to enjoy the loss of the saddle and the feel of the brush across his back.

"I think I'll ride him next weekend in Tulsa."

"He isn't ready for barrels."

She brushed across the horse's back and then down his back legs. "He'll be ready."

"You're as stubborn as your dad. Maybe Jeremy has met his match."

"What about Jeremy?" This voice boomed. The horse jumped a little to the side.

Beth bit down on her bottom lip and then flashed a smile, as if she hadn't been talking about anything important. "Nothing, Dad."

"Right, nothing. I saw you racing up the drive on that horse. Where have you been?"

Her dad walked a little closer. She stood straight, the brush in her hand, and faced him. She'd been backing down all of her life and she couldn't be that person anymore.

"I went to talk to Jeremy Hightree about the church. I have to stop him from tearing it down."

The harsh lines around her dad's mouth softened and he looked away, but not before she saw the sorrow. It still felt like yesterday. Shouldn't it be different? Shouldn't eighteen years soften the pain? She'd been without her mother longer than she'd been with her. There were times that her mother's smile was a vague memory. And more times that she couldn't remember at all.

But her dad missed Elena Bradshaw more than all of them. And missing her meant he disliked Back Street Church as much as Jeremy.

"Dad, she loved that church." Beth had never been

brave enough to say it, to put it out in the open. This was the new Beth Bradshaw, the woman who took control. The woman who wasn't afraid. Much.

Her dad raised a hand and turned away, his profile a dark shadow against the bright, outside light. She'd always thought of him as the strongest man in the world. What little girl didn't think that way? As a child she'd tried to match her steps to his. She'd always tried to please him. She had never wanted to hurt him.

"Please, Dad, we have to stop him."

He shook his head and walked out the door, away from her, away from memories. She took a step to follow him, to get him to help. Lance's hand on her arms stopped her.

"Let it go." He released her arm. "Let him have his memories. That church has been empty for years. It isn't all you have of your mom."

"I know it isn't. It's about more than her memory. It's about Jeremy's anger at a building. It's about..." She sighed. It was about her mom.

"Yeah, it's about that building. Everyone in town is talking about it. They all have a reason they think it shouldn't be torn down, Beth. The truth is, they could have done something to save it."

Beth watched her dad walk across the driveway to the house and then she turned to face a man who had been a second father to her. Lance was her mother's second cousin somehow twice removed. He'd taught her to come home strong after the third barrel, to not be afraid as she rushed toward the gate. He'd taught her to rope a calf. He'd taught her to let go of pain. He'd tried to keep her in church, having faith.

"I don't have anything to remember her by, Lance.

Everything is boxed up and hidden. Her pictures, her jewelry, and even the quilts she made. He boxed it all up. I don't know if he burned it, gave it away or threw it in the Dumpster."

"He shouldn't have done that. Sometimes a person hurts so bad they don't know what else to do. They box up the pain and I guess your daddy boxed up his memories right along with it."

"She loved that church."

"She sure did. And she loved her family. She'd want those memories unboxed." Lance untied the horse and led him down the aisle of the barn. A horse whinnied from somewhere in the distance. The gelding, Bob, whinnied a reply.

It had been years since Beth thought about the day her dad had started packing everything into boxes. He'd been crazy with grief, pulling pictures off the walls, yanking quilts off beds. Everything that reminded him of Elena Bradshaw had been packed up and hauled off while Beth cried and Jason stoically helped their father.

Lance placed a strong hand on her shoulder.

"I'll feed this horse for you. I think it's about time you talked to Buck about the box she left you. It's yours, Beth. She'd want you to have it." He put the horse in a stall and latched the gate. "And you know this horse isn't ready for Tulsa."

She nodded, still fighting tears, still fighting mad that everyone else always seemed to have answers, to be in control, and she always seemed to be fighting to be strong.

It was a fight she planned to win.

"Yeah, I know."

"Go talk to your dad."

She walked out of the barn and across the dusty driveway toward the house. A lone figure in the garden bent over tomato plants that were just starting to flower. She stopped at the edge of the garden.

"I'm not going to help you save that church." He bent to pick a few weeds.

"I'm not here to talk about the church. I'd like the box my mother left for me." She shoved her hands in her pockets, no longer brave. The deep breath she took did nothing to calm nerves that were strung tight. "If you don't mind."

Her dad turned. He stood straight, his hat tipped back. He was tall and broad, his skin weathered by sun and time but he was still strong.

"What brought that up?" her father asked.

Beth had imagined anger, not a question like that. She didn't really have an answer. "I think it's time. I want to have something to remember Mom by."

"It's just a box of stuff." He shrugged. "I'll bring it down from the attic."

She wanted to rush forward and hug him, but he turned back to the tomato plants. She'd won the battle but it didn't feel like a victory. She whispered "thank you" and her dad nodded. After a few seconds she walked away.

As she entered the house, she remembered the day her mother had sat them down in the living room and explained that she had taken her last treatment. The memory was followed by one of the day they took Elena off life support.

Beth stood in the living room for several minutes and then she walked back out the front door. She pulled keys out of her pocket and headed across the yard to the garage and her truck. It was starting to make sense, why Jeremy would want to do this. Even if she didn't want him to, maybe she understood. Her dad had shoved his pain into boxes and stored them in the attic. She'd run away. Jeremy needed to see that church gone.

As much as she understood, she still planned on finding a way to stop him.

The police station was a long, rectangular building with metal siding that looked more like a forgotten convenience store. In an area like this, they didn't need much for a police station. The occasional robbery, traffic violation or intoxicated driver, those were the extent of the crimes. His mom had probably committed each one, more than once.

Jeremy pulled his truck into a parking space next to a patrol car and he sat there for a long minute because he dreaded going inside. Why had he come back to Dawson? Oh, right, for revenge.

He'd been running from this life for years. He'd done a good job of putting it behind him. He had a successful business building customized motorcycles. He had two world championships. He'd done commercials for cologne and they'd made posters of his ugly mug to sell at rodeo events.

No matter how far he'd gone or what he thought he'd done right, one person knew how to pull him right back into the gutter. A shadow moved in front of the door. On the other side of the glass deputy Carl Duncan waved and motioned him inside.

He'd been fifteen when he bailed Jane out the first time. He'd used his money from lawn jobs and he'd borrowed a car from a neighbor. Back then Carl had been his age, just a kid trying to make a better life for himself. The cop at the time had been Officer Mac. He'd retired years ago.

That was a memory that made him smile. Officer Mac had been a farmer who carried a badge for extra money. When he'd seen Jeremy in that car, he shook his head and told Jeremy he was going to pretend he didn't see an underage driver behind the wheel.

Jeremy pulled the truck keys from the ignition and shoved them into his pocket as he got out of the vehicle. At least he had his own car these days.

He walked across the parking lot, stopping to glance up at the sky, another way to kill time. There were a few dark clouds, nothing major.

Carl pushed the door open. A woman screamed from somewhere at the back of the building. That would be Jeremy's mother. He knew that awful sound and knew that her eyes would be red, her hair a wild mess. They'd been through this more than once.

"What did she do this time?" He grabbed a seat from behind one of the desks and sat down.

"She was in the convenience store trying to convince them you've stolen all of her hard-earned money."

"That would get me a cup of coffee."

They didn't laugh. Carl sat down on the edge of the desk and shrugged. "She's coherent. Sort of."

"Right. So what do I do with her, Carl?"

"Take her home." The cop shrugged. He didn't have answers, either. "Maybe put her in a home. I don't know, Jeremy. I'm real sorry, though."

"Me, too." Jeremy loosened his white cowboy hat and then pushed it back down on his head. "Yeah, maybe a home. She might actually get sober."

"Right, that would be good. She looks a little yellow."

Her liver. He didn't know how it had held up this long.

"Do I owe you anything?" He pulled the wallet out of his back pocket and Carl shook his head.

"No, there weren't any charges. I just brought her in to keep her from doing something crazy. Are you really going through with the church situation?"

It always came back to that. The people in this town ought to be thanking him for getting rid of that eyesore, not questioning his motives. Considering that the church had been one step away from being condemned, he didn't know why everyone had a problem with his plans.

His mother screamed again. "Get me out of here! I didn't break any laws. I'll get a lawyer."

Jeremy laughed, shook his head and stood. "I'd better get her home before she hires a lawyer."

Carl nodded and headed down the narrow hall. He stopped at the farthest door and pulled keys from his pocket. "Mrs. Hightree, I'm letting you out now. Can you settle down for me or do I need to keep you overnight?"

"You can't keep me overnight. I didn't do anything wrong."

"Public intoxication." Carl slid the key in the lock. "Or public nuisance."

He unlocked the door and she stepped out of the room, a pitiful figure in a housedress, gray hair sticking out in all directions and a gaunt face. Her attention quickly turned to Jeremy. She frowned and stomped her foot.

"I'm not going with *him*."

"Mrs. Hightree, you don't have a choice."

She flared her thin nostrils at them and shook her head. "I have choices. I can walk out of here. I can head on home without his help."

Heat crawled up Jeremy's cheeks. After a lifetime of this, a guy should be used to it. It wasn't as if her behavior took people by surprise. What did surprise him was how old she looked, and how bad. He'd seen her less than a week ago and she hadn't looked this old.

She had been a pretty woman twenty years ago. Thirty-one years ago she had obviously turned some heads. He pushed that thought aside because now wasn't the time to get caught in the muck.

"Mom, we're going home."

"Janie, my name is Janie."

He grabbed her arm, loose flesh and bones. "Right, Jane."

He hadn't called her mom since he was ten and he'd found her passed out in the yard when he came home from school. That had been enough to take the word "Mom" right out of his vocabulary.

"You don't have to hold me. I'm not going to run."

"No, but you might fall down."

She wobbled a little, as if to prove his point. "There's nothing wrong with me."

Jeremy shot a look back at Carl. The cop stood behind them, sorry written all over his face. "Thanks, Carl. You're sure there weren't any expenses this time?"

"Not this time. Do you want me to call the hospital in Grove? Maybe she should be seen?"

"I'm fine, I said." She jerked her arm free from his hand. "I don't need either of you holding me or telling me what to do. I just need to go home."

"I'll take her home." Jeremy opened the door and motioned his mother through. "See you later."

"Yeah, we'll see you around. Maybe we can meet for lunch at the Mad Cow tomorrow?"

"Right, and you can try to talk me out of what you all think is a big mistake." Jeremy smiled, and Carl turned a few shades of red, right to the roots of his straw-colored hair. "I'll meet you for lunch, but if everyone was so worried about this church, why didn't you all do something sooner?"

"Yeah, I guess you've got a point there, Jeremy. Maybe we just thought it would always be there."

"It would have fallen in, Carl."

Carl stood in the doorway while Jeremy held on to his mother to keep her from falling off the sidewalk. "My grandpa goes up there once a month to check on the place. I think a lot of the older people in town would love to have it opened up again, but nobody had the money and the younger families have moved away."

"Call me and we'll talk over burgers at Vera's."

Carl nodded. "I'd appreciate that."

Jeremy escorted his mom out the door and down the sidewalk. She weaved and leaned against him. Tires on pavement drew his attention to the road. Tim Cooper. Yeah, they'd have to face each other sooner or later. They hadn't talked since the day Jeremy learned the truth. The day Tim Cooper wrote him a check, because it was the right thing to do.

Jeremy opened the door on the passenger side of the truck. Jane wobbled and her legs buckled. When he tried to lift her up she swatted at his hands.

It took a few minutes but he got her in the seat and buckled up. They headed down the road, toward Back

Street but then turned east. The paved country road led to a tiny trailer surrounded by farmland. It had two bedrooms and a front porch that was falling in. More than once he'd tried to get her to move. But this was her house and she didn't want his money.

It was the only thing she'd ever owned. This trailer was her legacy. He shook his head as he drove down the road. He thought about how he'd envied the Coopers and their big old ranch house.

His mom choked a little and leaned. Great. Her body went limp and she fell sideways. He eased into the driveway of the trailer and pulled the emergency brake. He put the windows down and waited while she got sick on the floor of the truck.

Maybe they would head for the hospital. He pulled her back in the seat and wiped her mouth with the handkerchief he pulled out of his pocket. "Mom, are you with me?"

She shook her head and mumbled that he was as worthless as his father. Yeah, she was with him. He shifted into reverse and glanced in his rearview window. A blue truck pulled in behind him. Great, what he didn't need was a big dose of sympathy in brown eyes that dragged his heart places he didn't want to go.

But that's what he was about to get.

"Leave me here," his mom mumbled without moving from her prone position on the seat next to him.

"I can't leave you here. You need help."

"Since when do you care?"

"I don't know, since forever, I guess." And he'd proven it time and again. His mom passed out as Beth rapped on his driver's side window.

* * *

Beth shouldn't have stopped but she'd seen Jeremy's truck at the police station. She'd watched in her rear-view mirror as he helped his mother down the sidewalk. For a few minutes she'd listened to the smart Beth who insisted she should drive on home and forget it. But the other Beth had insisted she put her heart on the line. And that's why she was looking through the window of his truck into eyes that were slightly lost and a lot angry.

His window slid down. "Imagine seeing you here."

"I thought you might need help."

"No, we're fine. I'm taking her to the hospital."

In the seat next to him his mother made a grunting sound that resembled a negative response. Obviously she didn't want Beth around and she wasn't interested in going to the hospital.

"Do you want me to ride over there with you?" She regretted the words the minute they were out. No one in their right mind would volunteer. But she had gone and done it.

His mother leaned to the floor again. Jeremy groaned and reached in the backseat of the truck for a towel that he tossed on the floor. "You wouldn't happen to have a bag or a bucket in your truck, would you?"

"Give me a sec and I'll check." Beth hurried back to her truck. She pushed through the contents in the toolbox in the bed of her truck and found a small bucket, a roll of paper towels and a spray bottle of window cleaner.

She returned to the passenger side of Jeremy's truck and opened the door slowly, carefully. Jane Hightree was passed out, leaning toward her son. Beth handed him the bucket and then she sprayed the floor down and covered it with paper towels.

"Beth, you don't have to do this." His voice was quiet and a little tight with emotion. She glanced up as she pulled on leather gloves.

"I don't mind. I'm good at cleaning up messes."

"Yeah, well, I usually clean up my own messes."

She ignored him and cleaned, tossing it all in a bag she'd pulled out from under her truck seat.

"I appreciate the help." Jeremy reached for the passenger seat belt, pulling it around his mother, even though she remained prone on the seat. "I'm going to take her to Grove."

"Do you want me to go?"

He shook his head and then looked up, smiling at Beth. "I can handle this, but thank you." He released the emergency brake and his hand went to the gearshift.

She nodded. "Let me know what happens with your mom."

"I'll do that."

Beth closed the door and walked back to her own truck. As she climbed behind the wheel he backed out of the drive and headed down the highway. Beth went the opposite direction, toward her brother's house because being strong on her own wasn't easy. When she'd confronted Jeremy at Back Street Church she had meant to talk him out of something, not put herself in his life.

She had to keep her focus on what was important. The goal wasn't to get tangled up in his life, it was to save the church.

Chapter Three

Beth finished her phone call and sat down at the table with a cup of coffee. After helping Jeremy with his mother the previous evening, she'd had a long talk with her brother Jason about ways to save Back Street Church. Thanks to his wife Alyson they had a very clear idea of how to accomplish their goal. They'd learned that the building had turned 100 the previous year.

They were still digging but it was possible the building could be saved by having it listed on an historical registry. The phone call Beth had made would set the plan in motion.

And she didn't know how she felt about what she'd done. As much as she didn't want the church torn down, she also didn't want to hurt Jeremy.

It seemed that no matter what, someone would get hurt. Either Jeremy or the people in town who cared about the future of the church. He had plans for a business. Beth saw the church as a connection to her mother. Others in town had similar stories and reasons for wanting the building to remain standing.

She took a sip of her coffee and reached for the box sitting on the table in front of her.

Her dad had finally given it to her the previous evening after she'd gotten home from visiting Jason and Alyson. Now that she had it, though, she didn't know what to do with it. She'd left it sitting on her dresser last night, untouched. Thirty minutes ago she had carried it into the kitchen. She'd been staring at it while she ate her cereal and then made the phone call to the historical society.

She let out a shallow, shaky breath and reached for the box. It was just a plain metal box. Her mother had intended for her to have this eighteen years ago. Eighteen long years, with so many mistakes, so much heartache in between.

Would her life have been different if her mother had lived? Would Beth have made different choices, taken a different path? Those were questions that would never have answers.

She lifted the lid of the box and a sob released from deep down in her chest. Tears followed as she lifted her mom's Bible from the box. Her mother's most prized possession. Of course her dad wouldn't have wanted Beth to have that Bible. He would have seen it as the root of all their problems; the same way he blamed Back Street Church for her mother's death.

He had needed to blame something, or someone. He had picked the church Elena turned to when the doctors told her there was nothing they could do.

Beth opened the Bible and stared through tear-filled eyes at her mother's handwritten notes in the margins. Reading those notes, it was as if her mom was there, teaching her about life. There were notes about faith, sermons, and verses that were her favorites.

She closed the Bible and placed it on the table. There were other things in the box. Her mother's wedding ring. A book of devotions. Her journal.

The journal was leather bound. The pages were soft, white paper that had yellowed with time. The writing had faded but was still legible. Beth flipped through the pages. The last half of the journal was blank. But the final entries, pages and pages of entries, were written to Beth.

She skimmed several but paused on the one dated August 5.

Dearest Beth, you're barely ten and I know this isn't going to be easy for you, but I want you to know that I love you and God has a plan for your life. Don't give up. Don't forget that your daddy, even if he's hurting and angry, loves you. And don't hurry growing up. It'll happen all too soon. Love will happen. Life will happen. Don't rush through the days, savor them. Love someone strong.

Love someone strong. Beth closed her eyes. She didn't know if she'd ever really been in love. Chance had been a mistake, an obvious mistake. He'd been her rebellion and a way to escape her father's quiet anger. Now she realized her dad had been more hurt than angry. But at eighteen she hadn't cared, she had just wanted to get away from Dawson and the emptiness of her life.

Her life was no longer about Chance. It couldn't be about what she'd been through. Instead it was about what happened from this day forward.

Jeremy Hightree didn't understand that. He still saw the church as a connection to his troubled childhood.

Maybe her mother's words could change his heart. She put everything back in the box but she didn't replace the lid. She wouldn't do that. It was a silly thing but she couldn't put the lid back on the box. Instead she carried it down the hall to her bedroom and placed the box on her dresser.

She walked out the French doors of her room, onto the patio that was her own private sanctuary. She stood in the midst of her flowers and the wood framed outdoor furniture that blended with the surroundings.

When she came home a short year and a half ago this had been her healing place. She'd planted flowers and she'd hidden back here, away from questions and prying eyes. In this garden no one questioned the jagged cut on her face or the arm that had needed to be reset.

This morning she was escaping from other emotions. Her mother's memory, Jeremy's plans for the church, her own fears.

She really needed to slow down. Everything was coming at her in fast forward. It was time to pray and plan her next move, before she rushed forward and did something she would regret.

At last she had fallen to sleep. Jeremy stood at the door of his mother's room and waited for her to move, to wake up and yell again. She'd done a lot of that since the previous evening when the hospital had transported her to the long-term facility a short distance from Grove, and only five minutes from Dawson.

She'd done so much screaming this morning that the nursing home staff had called him to see if he could calm hÁer down. Surprisingly she had calmed down immediately when she saw him.

He sighed and turned to go.

"Jeremy, how are you?"

Wyatt Johnson walked down the hall. Jeremy shrugged one shoulder and turned his attention back to his mother's room, to the bed, and to the thin figure covered with a white blanket.

"Do you need anything?" The two had gone to school together. They'd ridden horses together and roped calves together. Wyatt's horses and Wyatt's calves. They'd been friends, even though Jeremy hadn't been a part of Wyatt's social circle. They'd traveled to rodeos together and fought their way out of a few corners together.

"No, we don't need anything. It looks as if she'll be here for a while." For the rest of her life. Her liver was damaged from years of alcohol abuse. Her brain wasn't much better.

There must have been a time when she'd been a good person. He really tried to remind himself of that; of the reality that she had fed him and cared for him.

Or he liked to hope she had.

When he thought of gentle touches, it sure wasn't his mother he thought of.

"I'm sorry." Wyatt leaned his shoulder against the doorframe. "Guess there isn't much more a person can say."

"Nope, not much, but thanks." Jeremy turned from the room and headed down the hall, Wyatt Johnson at his side. Jeremy stopped at the nurse's station. The woman behind the desk looked up, her glasses perched on the end of her nose. "I'm leaving."

"We'll call if there are any problems."

"Right." He stood there for a minute, wondering if there was something else he should say or do. The nurse continued to stare at him. She finally lowered her gaze to the papers she'd been reading.

He guessed that was his cue to move on. So he did. Wyatt moved with him. When they got to the door Jeremy punched in the code and pushed the door open.

"Wyatt, I don't want to talk about the church. Not now."

"I hadn't planned on bringing it up."

An alarm sounded. Wyatt reached past him and pulled the door closed. He pushed other buttons on the keypad.

Jeremy stared at the closed door, at his truck in the parking lot and then shifted his attention back to Wyatt. He couldn't be mad at a guy who'd gone through the things Wyatt had gone through; losing his wife, raising two little girls on his own. And then falling in love with a preacher's daughter. At least Wyatt's situation had a decent ending.

The single life was good enough for Jeremy. He dated women who wanted nothing more from him than a decent meal and a dozen roses to end things. That philosophy kept his life from being complicated.

He hadn't seen too many happy relationships in his life and figured he was a lot better off than the friends who'd started believing they needed to settle down and have a family. Wyatt didn't look too worse for wear, though.

"Looks like it might storm." Jeremy nodded toward the southern sky. It was Oklahoma, so there was always a pretty good chance it might storm.

"Yeah, looks that way. We're under a tornado watch

until this evening. No warnings, yet." Wyatt pulled keys out of his pocket.

"Yeah." Jeremy ran out of things to say about the weather.

Wyatt grinned and tipped his hat back. "I know you don't want to talk about the church, but you bought it and you had to know that'd stir up a hornet's nest. I've known you a long time and you've always been fond of a hornet's nest if you could find one."

Jeremy told himself not to respond to his friend's baiting. He smiled and kicked his toe at the ground. Yeah, he wasn't going to ignore it.

"Wyatt, the church was for sale and I bought it. If people in Dawson are suddenly attached to a building they've neglected for years, that's their problem. Someone else could have bought it."

"Someone else could have," Wyatt said. "No one did."

"Right. I bought it and I plan on building a business that might give a few people in Dawson the jobs they need."

"That's a decent idea. But you have two hundred acres across from the church. Why not build your business over there?"

"I'm building a house on that side of the road and I'm buying cattle."

"Yeah, I saw that they finished framing the house yesterday. It's pretty huge for one guy. Are you actually going to live in Dawson?"

Jeremy stopped at the edge of the sidewalk. "I'm going to be here part of the time."

"The church means a lot to a lot of people. I know it doesn't seem that way."

"No, it doesn't and I kind of wonder why everyone suddenly realizes the church means something to them." Jeremy glanced at Wyatt.

"Pastor Adkins kept me in church after my dad's big indiscretion. I guess Back Street is what got me where I am today."

"Gotcha." Jeremy processed the story with the others he had been told. "Sorry, Wyatt, I have to get back and get back to work."

"Work?"

"Business doesn't stop because the boss is out of town." He gave Wyatt a tight smile. "I'm managing my business from a laptop in the RV and trying to help Dane with a flaw in a bike we're designing."

Jeremy had partnered with Dane Scott in team roping years ago. And more recently in the custom bike business.

"I'd like to come by."

"If you want a cup of coffee or you'd like to see the bike we're building, stop by anytime."

"And don't bother hitting my brakes if I'm there to talk to you about the church," Wyatt added for him.

"Sounds about right." Jeremy touched the brim of his hat and walked across the drive to his truck.

When he pulled up the drive of Back Street Church, Beth Bradshaw was sitting in front of his RV. He hadn't expected her to be the one pounding his door down trying to save this church. But why wouldn't she be the one?

Maybe, more than anyone, Beth needed to fight this battle.

He joined her on the glider bench outside his RV. She scooted to the edge, as far from him as possible.

He tried real hard not to let that hurt his ego. He figured she had a lot of reasons. One might be that she hated his guts.

That didn't sit well with him, the idea of her hating him.

He pushed the ground and the glider slid back and forth. Sitting there on the glider with her kind of felt like courting the old-fashioned way. The only thing missing was lemonade. She probably wouldn't see the humor in that, but he did. The two of them as nervous as cats sitting on a glider, what else could he think?

He had to lead the conversation in another direction, away from courting Bethlehem.

"I kind of thought you might thank me for tearing this church down, Bethlehem."

"Stop calling me that."

"It's your name."

"No one calls me Bethlehem and you know it."

He started to remind her that her mother had called her Bethlehem. Neither of them needed that memory. He glanced at the box on her lap. She had her hands around it, like a little girl holding on to a treasure.

She glanced at him, a cowgirl face with straight brown hair in twin braids and eyes that pinned him to the spot. She'd have him questioning everything about himself if she didn't stop looking at him like that.

"Why would you ever think I'd want this church torn down?" Her words were soft, matching the look in her dark eyes.

He shook his head and reined in the part of him that wanted to give her everything.

"I don't know, I guess I thought it was tied to a lot of memories that you'd want to be rid of, not memories you'd want to hang on to." He eyed that box again, wondering why in the world she'd brought it here and what it would mean to him.

Jeremy's words played through Beth's mind. She settled her gaze on the church. It was weathered and beaten down, forgotten. She'd been riding past this church her whole life, and since she'd come home from California those rides had resumed. Sometimes she even stopped and sat on the front steps.

As a teenager, when she'd felt the most alone, she'd found peace here. He wouldn't understand. He would think she was weak if she told him that she'd hidden here, trying to find answers, to find a way past the pain of losing her mom.

She cleared her throat.

"I brought you something." She reached into the box and handed him her mother's Bible. She had no idea why she wasn't keeping it for herself.

He needed it more? Maybe because she hoped something in there would stop him. He wasn't going to listen to her or anyone else.

Maybe he would listen to her mom. Her heart trembled a little, afraid of his reaction, afraid of her own reaction. He took the Bible from her hands.

"Beth, this isn't fair."

"It was my mother's."

"I can't take this."

"She would want you to have it. I think she would want you to know what she thought of you." Her hands trembled as she reached, flipping the pages of the book in his hands. "There are prayers in here, for Jason and me. Also for you and Elise."

He let out a shaky breath and she waited. He didn't react. After a few minutes he stood and walked away, still holding her mother's Bible. She considered going after him, trying to talk to him.

Her feet wouldn't move in that direction. Besides, she knew when to let a man be. This was one of those times. He walked across the church lawn, head down, the Bible in his hands. He climbed the steps and walked into the church, closing the door behind him. It didn't take a genius to know he didn't want to talk.

Guilt flooded her. For years Chance had used God's word to beat her into submission. She didn't want to do that to Jeremy. She considered going after him and apologizing.

She watched the door, waiting for him to come back out. The wind picked up. The southern sky was dark. She shivered a little and watched as clouds moved. A band of gray on the horizon meant rain and it was getting wider. Before long she'd have to hightail it for home.

A truck rumbled down the road and pulled into the crumbling parking lot that hadn't seen this much traffic in years. Jason's truck.

Her brother parked and got out. He walked toward her, his smile familiar. The one person to hold her life together, her brother. He'd always been there for her. He'd done his best to make her smile during their mother's illness and after they'd lost her. He'd been the one sending money to California as her marriage fell apart.

"What are you doing here?" He looked from the church to her and then at the darkening sky. "Did you know there's a tornado watch and a severe thunderstorm warning?"

"I heard on the news earlier that we could have storms today. It's May in Oklahoma, what's new? What are you doing here?"

He sat down next to her. "Same as you. I thought I could talk him out of it. Or maybe offer him enough money that he'd walk away."

"He doesn't need money."

"No, I guess he doesn't."

"He needs closure." She bit down on her bottom lip, letting that thought settle in. "He's a lot like dad. They both blame this church for their pain. Dad kept us away. Jeremy wants to tear the church down."

"Interesting." Jason crossed his left leg over his right knee and relaxed, as if it was just a pretty summer day and they were sharing iced tea on the front porch. Instead they were both casting cautious glances toward the southern horizon. "Where is he?"

"Inside the church."

"Hmm." Jason smiled, the way Jason did. He'd always been the one finding ways to make everyone laugh, to make them smile when they didn't feel like smiling. When he'd stopped smiling, God had sent Alyson and she'd helped him find his joy again.

He'd learned that he didn't always have to be the one lifting everyone else up. Beth loved her sister-in-law for doing that for him.

Sometimes she was jealous, that everyone seemed to be able to find someone to love them, to keep them safe. Her memories of a relationship were of abuse and fear, not safety or security. She had memories that no one would understand, so she didn't share.

"Beth, be careful."

"It's a storm, Jason. I've been through a few."

He shook his head and his smile faltered. "That isn't what I mean and I'm pretty sure you know that. Jeremy has a lot going on in his life."

"Right, and I'm not the best judge of character."

"I just don't want to see you hurt."

"I know." She smiled, for Jason. "I won't get hurt."

The wind picked up and in the distance jagged lightning flashed across the sky. Thunder rumbled and the humidity in the air was heavy. Jason pulled out his phone.

She glanced at the radar he'd pulled up on the screen. The big red blob was lingering over their area of the satellite map.

"Great." She watched the darkening clouds and trees leaning and swirling with the wind. "I guess this might be a good time to pray."

A sprinkle of rain hit her arm. Beth looked up at the sky and then at the dusty, dry ground as the raindrops hit. It had been so long since it rained that the droplets bounced and didn't soak in, not immediately.

Faith. She'd been through a drought, a long man-made drought, but faith was seeping back into her life. Her spiritual life had been a lot like hard, cracked earth, devoid of moisture. When faith started to return it was that same earth but with a trickle of water streaming through it, soaking into the dryness.

"We should probably go." Jason stood, pushing his hat back from his face as he studied the sky. "This doesn't feel right."

"What, you don't love that green sky?"

"Not particularly."

She loved the rain. She loved storms. On the drive over a DJ on the radio, probably trying to be a comedian, had played the Jo Dee Messina song, "Bring on the Rain." Beth found herself singing one line from that song, that she was not afraid.

The front door of the church opened. Jeremy stepped out on the porch. He was still carrying the Bible. Next to her, Jason made a noise and she shot him a look to silence anything he would say.

But he said it. "Is that Mom's Bible?"

"It is."

"Dad gave you the box?"

"He did."

"And you brought the Bible to Jeremy Hightree?" Jason's voice was tight, not really disapproving.

"I did. I just thought…"

"You might have pushed too far, Beth."

"Maybe. But I don't think so." She met her brother look for look. "If this doesn't work, I'm moving on to step two, and then step three."

"I knew I shouldn't have told you about the historical society." Jason murmured, then smiled and waved to Jeremy.

Jeremy Hightree walked down the steps of the church. He glanced at the sky, watched for a minute and headed in their direction. He looked relaxed, in jeans, boots and a deep red shirt. But casual was a facade on this cowboy.

Rain was misting down on them and the wind was picking up.

"Jeremy." Jason held out his hand. Jeremy took it, a quick handshake and then his gaze dropped to Beth.

She waited. And wished she was tall because then he wouldn't have to drop his gaze to meet hers. She could face him, head on, eye to eye.

He held out the Bible. "I can't keep this."

"She cared about you."

"I know she did, but this is something she wanted you to have."

"We should go." Jason shot a quick look at the sky. "Now!"

Her brother took hold of her arm and started to pull her toward the parking lot and their trucks. Her gaze shot to the southern horizon. Wind blew against them, slowing their progress and the rain hitting Beth's face stung like ice against her skin.

A slow, loud warning siren sounded in the distance and she heard Jeremy yelling at them to stop.

Chapter Four

The tornado siren sounded as Jeremy watched Beth heading for her truck, Jason at her side. She turned to say something. Her words were lost in the strong gust of wind that hit, blowing leaves across the church lawn and small limbs from the few trees.

Jeremy scanned the horizon. A warning didn't necessarily mean a tornado on the ground. Sometimes a warning was just a warning.

This time, though, things were a little different. He could feel the energy, the hum of the storm, the vibration of it. The deafening roar echoed in the distance.

"We should head for the basement." Jeremy watched the sky as he yelled, cupping his mouth to get the sound across the wind.

Jason nodded and started back, his cell phone in his hand. Jeremy guessed he was probably calling his wife. Beth stood frozen a few feet behind Jason.

"Beth, come on."

She nodded but she didn't move. She was watching the sky, the wind blowing her hair. A gust caught her hat. She pushed it back down and held on.

Jeremy raced across the crumbling parking lot and grabbed her arm. "This is not the time to stand and watch."

The roar increased in intensity. To the south the clouds were now tumbling and rolling, a dark mass of swirling destruction.

"Hurry." He had hold of Beth's arm and she was fighting him, pulling away.

"I can make it home."

"Beth, head for the church," Jason yelled as he pushed his phone into his pocket and turned, glancing at the dark clouds and then at his sister.

Jeremy cursed under his breath and picked her up. She was light in his arms and her protests were weak. Her arms went around his neck and he didn't know if it was rain or her tears that soaked his shoulder.

"I can walk." Beth struggled a little, and he held her tight.

"I know you can but…" He shook his head, not wanting to get stuck in the storm while she watched the clouds.

As they raced to the church, pieces of insulation fell from the sky. Jeremy ducked his head into the wind. That put his face pretty close to Beth's. And she smelled so good he decided carrying her was about the best idea he'd had in a while. Or maybe the worst.

Jason was ahead of him, jerking the door of the church open. They raced through the building to the door at the back of the sanctuary. The basement was dark. The steps were narrow.

He hadn't turned on electricity to the building. There hadn't seemed to be a reason.

Jason pulled out his cell phone and lit up the steps

with a patch of blue light. Jeremy held Beth tight and followed the other man down the steps. The basement held two classrooms and a kitchen/fellowship area that had seen better days.

"The back room," Jeremy yelled, and he didn't have to. The deafening roar had been left behind. The basement was pretty quiet, and a whole lot eerie. Jason glanced back and nodded. The room in the corner was the smallest and safest.

"Let me down." Beth came back to life, fighting in his arms.

"Not until we're in that room and safe. I'm not going to let you freeze up now, or have you head back upstairs to chase tornadoes."

"I didn't freeze. I just didn't…" She shuddered in his arms. "Don't grab me again."

"I won't. Once you're safe I'll never touch you again."

Man, that wasn't a promise he wanted to keep. As much as he didn't want to admit it, she felt good in his arms.

He put her down in the corner of the room and slammed the door shut behind him. The windowless room cut them off from the rest of the world. Buried beneath the ground, it was nearly soundproof. Their cell phones glowed an unearthly blue.

He turned, surveying their shelter, flashing his cell phone around the darkness. He'd had Sunday school in this room as a kid. It had been painted white, to dispel the dark, windowless gloom. Posters of Jesus had hung on the walls to add color. There had been an easel with a felt board in the corner for paper cutouts of Jesus and the disciples.

Now the room was draped with spiderwebs that

clung to his clothes. He brushed a strand from his face and hoped the resident hadn't remained behind.

Back then he'd been a kid who knew how to pray. Man, he didn't have a clue where that kid went. Somewhere along the way he'd started taking care of things on his own.

Lot of good that had done him.

He scanned the room looking for the flashlight he thought he'd left down here a few days earlier, when he'd been poking around in the old building, stirring up dust and memories. He'd left it in the kitchen.

"I have a flashlight out there." He yanked the door open and ignored objections from Jason and Beth. The flashlight was on the counter next to an old avocado-green fridge. He grabbed it and raced back to the shelter of the classroom.

Jason shook his head when Jeremy walked in, flashing the light around the room. Jason had taken a seat on the edge of an old table.

"How long do we stay down here?" Beth sat on the stool in the corner of the room, shivering, her bare arms damp from the rain that pummeled them as they ran for the church. He flashed the light in her direction and she glanced away.

Jeremy pulled off the plaid shirt he wore over his T-shirt. He tossed it to her, as if it didn't matter. But it did. When she held it in her hands and smiled it mattered a lot. She slipped her arms into the shirt and pulled it around herself.

He turned away, listening, waiting. Jason stood next to him, his cell phone up to his ear. Jason bowed his head, leaning against the wall. Jeremy put a hand on his shoulder, squeezing tight. "She's fine."

"Of course she is." Beth smiled, her words sunny and bright in the dark room. "She's Alyson and she's probably in the basement praying like crazy for everyone else."

"Someone has to pray." Jeremy looked up, listening for any signs of distress in the old church. It sounded as steady and solid as ever. He could barely hear the wind that he knew roared around them.

Or maybe the storm was done, blown over. Maybe the massive, gray funnel hadn't been a funnel. Now *that* was wishful thinking. There was only one way to find out for sure.

"I'm going up." He opened the door.

Beth choked out a sound. He turned the flashlight in her direction. Her fingers were curled around the cuffs of his shirt and she shivered.

"I don't think you should go." Her voice broke a little. Mascara streaked down her cheeks.

His hand was still on the doorknob.

"What do you suggest? Stay down here indefinitely?" He handed the flashlight over to Jason and pulled his cell phone back out of his pocket.

"Well, until we know for sure if it's over." Beth wrapped her arms around herself; his shirt swallowed her. He couldn't help but think about how her scent would linger with his on his shirt.

He needed to get his business going and leave this town as soon as possible. He was starting to doubt the wisdom in building a home here, even if it was meant only to be a weekend home, a place to escape to.

"I think it's probably over." He answered her question, smiling a little.

"It might not be."

"Beth, it's a tornado." Jason sighed and sounded more than a little frustrated. It took a lot to get Jason to that point. "They don't linger, they move on."

Jeremy nearly walked away from the door, back to Beth. He considered crossing the room and taking her in his arms until she stopped shivering.

And then he considered the fact that he might be losing his mind.

He walked out and closed the door behind him and tried not to worry about what he'd find when he got upstairs. The church could be flattened. His RV could be gone. His barn and his livestock were across the street. Who knew what had happened to them as the storm moved through.

In the basement, nothing had been disturbed. The few small windows were intact. He hurried up the stairs and opened the door to the sanctuary. The church was untouched. The air around him was still. It was silent.

It was eerie as anything.

The birds that had taken up residence in the building swooped and landed on the hanging overhead lights. He no longer needed the cell phone for light so he dialed his sister's number. She had a scanner and if her phone was working she'd be able to tell him what was going on.

The cell didn't work. He opened the front door and stepped out on the porch. His RV still stood at the edge of the parking lot. The trees were still standing. Across the road his house was no longer framed. He had to stand there for a minute, take it all in.

He took a deep breath and whistled. After a few minutes he walked off the porch and looked around. He pushed his hat back and looked up, at the building that had sheltered them during the storm. And yeah, he got the irony in that.

The church was untouched. The lawn was littered with tree limbs and debris from other people's homes, barns and businesses. Not one shingle had blown off the church roof. Not one window had been cracked.

Footsteps on the floor behind him dragged his attention back to the church and the two people who had gone through this storm with him. Jason Bradshaw was punching buttons on his phone and frowning.

"No cell service," Jeremy offered, knowing it wouldn't help Jason feel any better.

"Yeah, I have to get home and check on Alyson."

"Right. I'll make a drive through town."

Jason's steady look landed on his sister. Beth stood at the edge of the porch. She still wore Jeremy's shirt.

"Are you staying here or going with Jason?" Jeremy stood at the bottom of the steps looking up at her. Somehow he'd managed to sound casual. That wasn't easy when she was standing there with his shirt swallowing her petite frame. Once, a long time ago, she'd worn his jacket on a cool night. He remembered her scent had lingered on it, floral and citrus. That took him back to places he didn't want to go. Or maybe he did. That was the problem.

"I'll go with you." She walked down the steps and stood next to Jeremy.

Jason shook his head as he shoved the useless phone back in his pocket. "Obviously the phone towers have been hit. There could be power lines down across the roads."

"Jason, we'll be careful." Beth smiled at her brother. Jeremy wasn't part of a "we." He'd never been part of a "we." He'd have to explain that to her. He'd managed to live a whole life on his own. But now wasn't the time for that discussion.

Instead he found himself as part of a "we."

"We've been through a few of these storms, Jason." Jeremy winked at Beth. "We'll be careful."

Jason's ever-present smile faded. "She's my sister."

"Right, I get that. I'm going to try and make it to the nursing home to check on my mom. I also want to make sure this didn't hit Grove."

Beth smiled at him, and then a softer smile for her overprotective brother. "Jason, go check on Alyson. We'll be safe."

Jason rubbed a hand across his forehead and grinned a little easier. "Yeah, okay, I'm cutting the apron strings, sis."

"Good, they were getting a little tight." She took a few steps and stopped in front of her brother. Rising to her tiptoes she kissed his cheek. "You're the best."

"Yeah, I like to think so. I'll be back soon or meet up with the two of you later." Jason walked across the lawn toward his truck. He stopped once and leaned to pick up an envelope in the lawn.

Typical of a storm, debris from other locations landed miles from home. Jeremy let out a sigh and surveyed the landscape that two hours earlier had been whole.

The church hadn't been touched. Beth smiled and started to point that out to Jeremy. Instead she let it go. No use stating the obvious. And Jeremy had walked away. He was studying the debris in the yard.

Beth turned her attention to the property across the street. The frame of his house was gone. The barn was missing a piece of sheet metal from the roof. She shook her head and walked back to Jeremy's side.

"I'm sorry about your house."

He shrugged and smiled. "It missed the church."

"It would have saved you a lot of time if it hadn't."

"Yeah, I guess it would have saved some explaining, too. People would be a lot more forgiving if it got torn down during an act of God, and not by me."

"Maybe God is trying to tell you something." Beth had meant to tease, but it hadn't come out that way.

"I doubt that, Beth. The church has to go. I have plans for a building. I have a guy already selling his house to move here and manage things."

"I think you should have an alternate plan."

"What does that mean?" He stood in front of her, tall, his eyes pinning her down.

"I'm still going to stop you."

He grinned, slow and easy and she had a moment of serious doubt. "You're pretty sure of that, aren't you?"

She matched him with a smile of her own. "I'm very sure."

"Let the games begin. Because as much as you don't want that church torn down, honey, I do."

Sirens in the distance ended the dance. Jeremy walked to the edge of the church parking lot and she followed. Beth stopped next to him and closed her eyes. She let the soft words of a prayer fill her mind, a prayer for her community, for the injured if there were any, for homes and businesses lost. For strength. It had been more years than she could count since the area was hit by a tornado.

She opened her eyes and looked up at Jeremy. He

gave her an easy smile. Her heart did the two-step, obviously forgetting that they were on opposing sides.

A police car pulled into the church parking lot, a county deputy that she didn't know. They'd probably called in reserve officers to handle the situation. The car stopped behind Jeremy's truck.

"Checking to make sure everyone is okay." The officer got out of his car. It was the normal routine after a storm like this, to go through the area making sure people weren't trapped or injured. Or worse.

"We're fine." Jeremy slid his fingers through hers and they walked across the debris-strewn lawn toward the officer.

"How bad is it?" Beth asked, wanting to know but a little afraid to hear the answer.

"Pretty bad. Estimates are that it stayed on the ground for about twenty miles. There's a small area of Dawson that was hit pretty good. It leveled a few homes, more are damaged and Dawson Community Church lost part of its roof. The school sustained some damage so we're going to have to find somewhere to set up a shelter."

"What about the nursing home? Was it damaged?" Jeremy held tight to her hand and she gave his a little squeeze. His mom had never been there for her kids, but she was still his mom.

"Nursing home is fine. They have a backup generator and no damage."

"And Grove?" Jeremy's sister lived in Grove.

"Grove didn't even get a thunderstorm and the cell is breaking up now."

"Where will people go?" Beth couldn't imagine her

town without the Community Church, or with friends moving because houses had been destroyed.

"Not sure yet. With the school and the Community Church out of commission we're pretty limited on suitable shelters." The officer got back into his car. "Folks might have to go to Grove or even to Tulsa if they don't have family to stay with."

"What about here?" She didn't look at Jeremy. "I'm sorry, it isn't mine to offer, but the church is intact. There's plenty of room."

"Beth." Jeremy's voice was soft, raspy.

She forced herself to meet his eyes. She wouldn't be afraid. Nope, she'd just plow through and suffer the consequences. Jeremy's jaw clenched and he glanced away, back at the church.

"Sir?" The officer was in his car, window down and the engine idling quietly.

Jeremy looked at Beth and then he shook his head and smiled. "They can use the church as a shelter."

The officer nodded and then the patrol car backed away, turning and pulling out of the drive. It cruised down Back Street toward town, lights flashing but no siren.

Jeremy looked down at her, shaking his head. Beth waited, because he still had hold of her hand. Her mind flashed back a few years, to Chance, to the times when she'd pushed him too far. "Beth?"

She shook her head. "I'm sorry. It wasn't my place to offer the church."

"No, it wasn't. You win this round, but we're not finished." He reached for her hand. "And stop looking so worried. As mad as you make me, I'd never hurt you."

He leaned close, pulling off his hat and raising her

hand to hold it close to his chest, close to the steady rhythm of his heart. His gaze locked with hers. "I've never hit a woman and I don't plan on starting now. Even if you drive me crazy. I won't hurt you."

"I…" What did she say to that?

Before she could think of anything to say, he moved closer.

He touched her cheek and then his lips settled on the scar above her eye. And she didn't pull away. As his kiss trailed down to her cheek she fought a shred of panic. She fought the confusing urge to fall into his arms. She fought tears that burned her eyes because for a long time she'd felt like pieces of a woman and she longed to be whole.

Jeremy stepped away from her, and she could breathe again. She could think.

"We should drive into town and see what needs to be done. And I'd like to find a way to check on my mom." He sounded as if he was looking for a way out of this moment, too. As if he too needed space to breathe.

Beth nodded because for the moment she couldn't gather words to respond.

She looked back at the church as he opened the passenger door of his truck for her to get in. The church had a reprieve. But for how long?

"The church is safe, Beth. It's still standing and tonight if people need a place to stay, it'll be here."

"I know." She climbed into his truck and he closed the door.

Back Street intersected with Main Street. Main Street ran north and south. Tulsa was over an hour away. Dawson Crossing, the town had been named back in the

1800s. Folks had shortened it to Dawson and it sometimes got confused with a larger community close to Tulsa.

Today Dawson looked as if someone other than Jeremy had been turned loose with a dozer. On the outskirts of town several homes were demolished. Nothing remained of those homes but foundations with scattered, splintered lumber. Home after home had been damaged. Trees were down, power lines hung from broken poles and roofs were partially gone. In town the convenience store had lost the roof over the gas pumps and the windows were shattered.

The Mad Cow Café didn't look too worse for wear. There were shingles missing, but other than that, Vera looked happy to still have her business. She stood out front, her apron tight around her waist. When she saw Beth and Jeremy, she waved. Jeremy stopped his truck and backed up.

"Is the café okay, Vera?" Jeremy leaned forward and Beth leaned back in the seat, giving him a clear view of the Mad Cow's proprietor.

"It sure is. I have a generator on the way so hopefully I won't lose all my groceries. But I'm one of the lucky ones."

"Is there anything we can do?" Beth asked.

"Not yet, Beth. I did hear that Jeremy's going to open the church as a shelter. Do you need blankets?"

Jeremy blinked a few times at how quickly word traveled in this town. He was all for letting people stay in the church. The word shelter implied a lot more than he had really planned.

"I haven't thought about it, Vera. I just planned on

leaving the door open for anyone who needs a place to stay."

"Bless your heart." Vera stepped off the sidewalk. Her dark hair was shot through with gray and her skirt and blouse were not as crisp as usual. She walked up to the truck and leaned in the window. "Honey, you need to move the pews and make room for cots. Wyatt Johnson has quite a few in storage at the Community Church. They also have blankets and other emergency supplies. The Red Cross will be showing up, too."

Go Wyatt. Jeremy just smiled.

Beth jumped into the conversation. "We'll need flashlights and plenty of bottled water."

Vera patted her arm. "Already taken care of. Jason was through here earlier and he's going to bring a tank of water and set it up at the church."

Jeremy accepted that the church wouldn't turn itself into a shelter. But people in Dawson were prepared the way they were always prepared. People here knew that in the space of a heartbeat, life brought change. He'd experienced plenty of change in his own life.

In the last few weeks he'd gone from being a guy with a plan to the guy everyone wanted to stop. And now this. He shook his head and he let it go because his plans being halted were nothing compared to people losing their homes.

"I guess we should get on the road and see if there's anything else we can do." Jeremy shifted into gear. "See you later, Vera."

"Okay, but be careful. And don't worry, I'll bring up a big batch of barbecued pork for sandwiches to feed anyone that shows up this evening."

"Thanks, Vera." Beth reached through the window and gave Vera's hand a squeeze.

"Do you mind riding along with me while I check on my mom?" He shifted his truck into gear and peered to the left, at a field littered with debris, including what looked like it might have been part of someone's roof.

"Of course not."

He slowed as they neared emergency vehicles, lights flashing. A first responder in an oversize coat stepped out to stop them and then walked up to his window. Jeremy waited.

"Got power lines down in the road, Jeremy. I can't let you drive through." The volunteer was young, maybe in his late teens. Jeremy wasn't sure if he should know the kid or not. But the kid knew his name so he guessed he must.

"I need to get to the nursing home to check on my mom."

"Yeah, there isn't a way to get there right now. Part of the Lawtons' barn is in the road up here, and farther up there's a big old tree across the road."

"Thanks, I'll try again this evening."

The volunteer in his gray jacket with neon stripes nodded. His safety helmet was loose, a little large on his head. The jacket swam around his thin frame. But in a small community, it took everyone to pitch in when disaster struck.

Jeremy backed his truck into a drive that led to someone's field. He pulled around and headed back to Dawson. Beth leaned back in her seat and sighed. He glanced her way.

"I can drive you back to your place," he offered,

slowing as the truck got close to a side road that would lead them to the Bradshaw ranch.

"I'm not in any hurry."

Yeah, neither was he. Even at thirty, he didn't want to meet up with Buck Bradshaw. Beth's dad was a big man and probably still willing to take care of business if anyone messed with his little girl.

"Remember your sixteenth birthday?"

She turned pink, so he knew she remembered.

"I remember."

He'd kissed Beth on her sixteenth birthday. They'd been at a rodeo and her friends had teased her for smiling at him. Later he'd led her to the creek and held her close, enjoying the feel of her in his arms. He hadn't been quite eighteen. She'd been so far out of his reach, it had been like grasping at a star.

And her dad had caught them down there. Man, he'd cussed Jeremy a blue streak.

"Jeremy, watch out." Beth's scream coincided with Jeremy hitting the brakes as a woman rushed into the road right in front of them.

The woman waved her arms, panic etched into a pale face. A trickle of blood on her cheek smeared when she brushed her hand across her face.

"What in the world?" Beth was unbuckling her seat belt. "That's Keira Hanson."

"Hang tight, Beth." Jeremy pulled to the side of the road. The woman ran to the passenger side of the truck, stumbling through the grassy ditch to get to them. She was trembling and the blood oozed from a cut on the side of her face.

"Keira, what's wrong?" Beth already had her door open. "Get in and we'll drive you up to your place."

"It's Mark. He was in the barn when this hit and part of the building collapsed." She sobbed, leaning into the truck. "I couldn't call for help and I couldn't get him out on my own."

"Beth, I'm going to run on up there. You take my truck and drive back to that roadblock. Tell them to get help up here."

Jeremy unbuckled his seat belt and set the emergency brake. Beth was already scooting over and he opened the door and stepped out of the truck as she slid behind the wheel. He watched as she adjusted the seat and shifted into gear.

"Be careful." Her voice was soft and her eyes tore him up. And he thought maybe no one else had ever cared about him as much as Beth and her mamma.

He watched as she turned his truck back in the direction they'd come from and then he started up the long dirt and gravel drive.

He didn't know what he'd find when he reached the Hansons' barn, but he prayed that Mark would be alive. It had been a long time since he'd prayed. And he was thankful that God had a good memory.

"Jeremy will find him, Keira." Beth shifted and hit the gas to speed down the paved road. "He'll be just fine."

"I keep praying that's true, Beth. But what if…"

Keira pushed her hands against her eyes and Beth shot a quick look around the cab for something Keira could hold against the cut on her face. She slowed down and reached for the glove box. It opened to reveal napkins from fast food restaurants.

"Keira, grab those and hold them against the cut to stop the bleeding."

Keira nodded and reached into the glove box.

"What if he's…" Keira sobbed and neither of them needed for her to finish that sentence.

"He isn't." Relief flooded Beth when the flashing lights of first responders came into view. She pulled up to Kenny Gordon, the kid who had been directing traffic minutes earlier.

"Beth, the road's still closed." The kid grinned.

"I know, Kenny. Listen, we need help up at Keira's place. The barn collapsed and Mark is inside."

Kenny got serious. He lifted his two-way and told someone on the other end that they needed a team to head up to the Hanson place. He finished the call and leaned in the window.

"They'll be up there in five minutes, Keira. We'll find him, don't you worry."

Keira nodded and a fresh batch of tears streamed down her face, mixing with dirt and blood.

"Kenny, do you have a first aid kit?"

The kid nodded. "Got one in the truck over there. Hang tight a sec and I'll get it for you."

Beth reached for Keira's hand. "Keira, we'll find him."

"I'm really trying to pray, Beth. The only thing I can get out is, 'God, don't let him die.'"

"I think that's a prayer." Beth had been saying plenty of her own prayers since all of this started. She didn't think God was expecting long prayers, not at a time like this.

Kenny was back with the first aid kit. He had already taken out a few wipes, salve and a Band-Aid.

Beth tore the top off the antiseptic wipe and pulled it out for Keira.

"Clean the wound and then we'll put this on it."

Keira nodded. She gasped when the wipe hit the cut, but she cleaned it and the side of her face before taking the Band-Aid from Beth.

"Thanks, Kenny."

"Maybe you all should stick around here until the responders can get up there and clear things up a little." Kenny's gaze shot past Beth to Keira and Beth knew what he meant. She wondered if that was his idea or the idea of one of his supervisors, someone who didn't want Keira on hand when they found her husband.

"We have to go back." Keira's voice was shaky. "Kenny, thank you for thinking of me, but I have to be there."

Kenny handed Beth the first aid kit. "In case you need it."

Beth backed the truck up the same way Jeremy had earlier. She turned and headed back in the direction of the Hanson farm.

And she prayed, because God wasn't the dictator that Chance had wanted her to believe. God hadn't forced her to stay in a marriage that kept her prisoner to a man who beat her and locked her in the bathroom when she talked about leaving.

God hadn't wanted that for her. And now she was free. She was free and she knew that God heard her prayers.

Sirens behind her warned that the emergency crews were on the way. She pulled to the side of the road and allowed the big yellow truck and first responder rescue unit to pass. She followed them up the long, rutted driveway that led to the Hansons' place.

When they pulled up to the barn, Keira jumped out of the truck. One of the first responders stopped her. She fought against him, wanting to get close to the barn.

Beth hurried to her side. "Keira, let them find him. If we stay back, they'll be able to work more quickly."

Keira slumped against Beth's side. "I can't do this. I can't stand here and I can't breathe."

"Sit down." Beth eased the woman to the ground. "Slow down, breathe easy so you don't pass out. When they find Mark, he needs to see you here, waiting for him. He's going to need for you to be calm."

Keira nodded but she was still gasping, still sobbing. And Beth wasn't going to tell her she shouldn't be upset. She would be frantic if it was someone she loved in that barn.

She scanned the area, looking for Jeremy. She spotted him, pulling boards off the building. He'd pulled on leather work gloves and he ripped at metal from the caved-in roof. He turned, as if he knew she was watching. His smile was weary, his T-shirt soaked with perspiration. She curled her fingers around the cuffs of the shirt he'd given her.

He pulled off more boards and then went down on all fours and crawled into the hole he'd made. Beth wrapped her arms around a sobbing Keira and held her close.

"They'll find him," Beth whispered, to herself and to assure Keira.

Seconds ticked by and then minutes. Beth glanced at her watch. The tornado had hit more than two hours earlier. She tried not to think about how seriously injured Mark might be and what that amount of time meant to him. She closed her eyes and prayed they'd find him soon.

Boards and metal scraps were being tossed aside. Men worked with crowbars and anything else they could find to move the rubble of the barn. Neighbors had shown up to help.

"Here he is." Jeremy shouted the alarm from somewhere under the pile of lumber.

Keira jumped up, wobbling. Beth held on to her arm.

"Keira, we have to stay back."

They watched as several men ran to join Jeremy, who had backed out of the tunnel he'd made in the rubble of the barn. An ambulance pulled closer. Its blue lights flashed. The crew moved silently, pulling medical equipment and a stretcher from the back of the vehicle.

The first responders continued to remove the rubble that covered the area where Jeremy had found Mark Hanson.

"He's going to be fine." Beth held on to Keira, who was a few years older than herself. Life hadn't been easy for the Hansons. Keira had suffered three miscarriages in the last few years. Mark had lost his job.

Beth swallowed, pushed aside doubt. And then there was a shout. They had Mark. They were talking to him. And then they were easing him out of the mangled pile of wood and metal that used to be their barn. As he lay on the ground, he turned, looking for his wife.

Keira tore loose from Beth's arms and ran to her husband. They hugged and Keira kissed his face, kissed his head. The paramedics stabilized his leg while Keira held his hand. And Beth wanted to laugh and cry, all at once. Salty tears trickled down her cheeks and she wiped them away with the back of her hand.

Faith. A couple that held on to each other.

Beth searched the crowd for Jeremy.

Jeremy pulled off his gloves and walked toward Beth. He smiled at the tear-stained face and wavering smile that greeted him.

"Looks like he has a broken leg, but he'll be fine."

Beth sniffled. "Yeah, but how can they take one more blow? They've lost babies, lost his job. What if they lose this farm, too?"

"It looks to me like they'll be happy to have each other."

"I get that, but seriously, how many times can a couple get knocked down?"

Boy, she was going for the jugular. "I don't know, Beth."

"No, you don't. I'm sorry."

"Look, I know you're upset about the church. But I can give Mark Hanson a job when I get the shop built. Once he's recovered, I can put him to work."

She looked up at him, her brown eyes huge and tears spilling out again, running down her cheeks. "You're cut and you're limping."

"I got tangled in some sheet metal when I was digging through that mess. And the limp is old news and nothing a few aspirin won't fix."

Beth reached for his hand and led him back to his truck. He thought about pulling away from her, but he didn't listen to his good sense very often. This time he completely kicked it to the curb.

If good sense meant cutting loose from Beth Bradshaw, he didn't need it right now. There'd be time for regret later.

She opened the door of his truck and pulled out a first aid kit. While he stood there like an idiot, she wiped his cuts. Her fingers were gentle, touching his arm and then his cheek. She pulled out a butterfly bandage for his arm, the deeper of the two cuts.

"It's just a scratch on your face, but the cut on your arm might need stitches."

"I'm sure it's fine." He swallowed as she settled the adhesive strip in place.

"There, all done."

"Thank you."

Her hand was still on his arm, her touch sweeter than honey. She sniffled and stared up at him. "You'd really give him a job?"

"Beth, I know this might be news to you, but I'm not the enemy." He let out a heavy sigh. "I'm not the enemy."

He brushed his fingers across her cheek and wiped away the tears that had spilled out again.

"I know you're not. But the church…"

He rubbed his hand across his face and waited. He could walk away. He could tell her he didn't want to discuss this with her. But those big brown eyes were looking up, intent, searching. She was all kinds of trouble he hadn't expected.

"I know it doesn't make sense, Beth. But I'm a long way from being that poor kid that went to Back Street. Then again, I'm not. I'm still the kid who stole vegetables from neighbors' gardens, and worked until bedtime to buy what we needed."

The words kind of surprised him because he'd never

said them aloud to anyone. She had stripped away his control with soft questions and tear-filled eyes.

Jeremy reached into the truck for his hat and pushed it down on his head, calling himself a few choice names. Beth was standing in front of him, teary-eyed and tired. She didn't need an info dump.

"Beth, I'm sorry."

She shook her head. "No, I am. It was my fault for pushing you."

"No, it wasn't. You said what everyone else has been thinking and maybe you're right. But I guess that doesn't mean I'm going to change my mind."

"I know and I do understand." And then she smiled, bright as summer sunshine after a storm. A storm like the one they'd just been through. "But I am going to stop you."

"I don't know how. It's my land and I'm all set. I just have to get the final permit from planning and zoning."

Her brows shot up and her expression changed, making him wonder. He had a bad feeling. No one knew small-town politics better than he did. He'd been dealing with the city of Dawson for weeks, trying to get things squared away so he could move forward.

"We should go." Right, they should go. And he figured he should plan on a battle for the church.

"I can drive you to your house now, if you want."

"My truck is at the church."

"Gotcha."

The ambulance was pulling away. As it headed down the drive, a few trucks pulled up. Jeremy knew it was time to hit the road as Tim Cooper and several of his sons got out of one of their big Ford F-350s.

"Let's hit the road." Jeremy walked around to the

tailgate of his truck. He'd left tools out that he needed to store in the box before they left.

Before he could get them all in the toolbox, someone called his name. He turned as Reese Cooper headed in his direction. Tim Cooper stood next to the truck Reese had gotten out of. Jeremy nodded at the other man. They shared DNA, that was it.

The day after Jeremy's mother interrupted services at Back Street Church to tell the world who her son's father was, Tim Cooper had offered Jeremy a big check. Not an apology, just a check. Jeremy had ripped the paper into pieces and walked away. He'd made the grand announcement that he'd do just fine on his own. He'd gotten a scholarship to ride on a college rodeo team. He'd already made some money riding bulls. He didn't need anything the Coopers had.

He skipped another glance in the direction of Tim Cooper before he switched back and focused on Reese. At one time he had needed family. By the time he turned eighteen that need had been left in the dust.

Reese stopped in front of him. Younger by just a couple of years, Reese was one of the more serious members of the Cooper clan. He didn't have Jackson's attitude or ladies'-man personality. He wasn't a clown like Travis. He wasn't full of himself like Blake. He wasn't nearly as likable, in Jeremy's opinion, as Jesse.

"How's Mark?" Reese rocked back on his heels a little.

"Broken leg."

Reese nodded. He shot a nervous glance in the direction of his father and then landed his direct gaze back on Jeremy. "Need some help getting a shelter set up at Back Street?"

Jeremy shrugged. "I don't have a clue, Reese. I'm not sure who all will be there or what needs to be done. I'm heading that way now to see where to start."

"We'll be over to help." It was a statement, not a question. The younger man didn't leave room for objections. Jeremy smiled a little easier. Reese Cooper was his half brother. He respected him for cowboying up and not backing down.

"That's fine, Reese." Jeremy shot a look past Reese, in the direction of Tim and a couple of his sons. "Tell your dad he can stay home."

Reese opened his mouth and closed it pretty quickly. "Sure, I'll tell him. Hey, I joined the army. I'm going to basic next week."

Respect. Jeremy slapped Reese on the back. "That's amazing."

"Yeah, well, a friend of mine from Tulsa went over a few years ago. He didn't make it back."

"You'll make it back, Reese." Beth stepped into the conversation. She hugged Reese tight. "We'll have a big party when you come home."

"I'm counting on that, Beth." Reese stepped back from the two of them. He tipped his hat in farewell and walked back to the Coopers.

"Girls." Jeremy twirled his fingers in the end of Beth's brown hair, letting the silken strands slip through his hand. He wanted to bury his fingers in the dark strands and taste the gloss she'd pulled from her pocket and swiped across her lips just moments earlier.

She wrinkled her nose at him, the way she'd done way back when. It should have undone thoughts of kissing her, it didn't.

"Girls?" She smiled and her left brow arched a little higher than the right. "What does that mean?"

"Yeah, girls. You're sappy and sweet, and you smell good." He leaned in a little, proving to himself that his words were right on the mark.

She was wearing his shirt and she smelled like some flowery shampoo, making this feel a lot more complicated than he'd expected.

"That isn't what you used to say." She whispered the words so softly it snagged his heart.

"Yeah, I was a dumb kid who thought girls were gross."

"I remember."

She walked away, glancing back over her shoulder. He laughed a little and followed her to the truck. She already had her door open and was climbing in when he got there.

"Beth, someday I hope you'll forgive me."

She cocked her head to one side as she buckled the seat belt. "Jeremy, I hope you'll forgive yourself and a lot of other people."

He closed the door and as he walked around to his side, he glanced across the lawn to the group of Coopers who were busy cleaning up the debris-strewn lawn. Yeah, he had people to forgive.

The driveway up to the Bradshaw ranch was lined with trees, all of which were still standing. Jeremy turned and headed up the long blacktop lane toward the big brick house where Beth had grown up. Halfway to the church Beth had asked to stop and check on her family.

"You can relax," she said, dimples in her cheeks

punctuating a smile that hit him in the midsection. Sweeter than a speckled pup; he'd once heard an old-timer use that expression about his wife when he'd met her.

"Relax?" He rolled his shoulders and tried to pretend he didn't have a clue what she meant by that.

"You're all tense. Do you think my dad is going to jerk you out of the truck and tell you to stay away from his little girl?"

He glanced her way and winked. "The thought did cross my mind."

He was a dozen years beyond that scraggly kid with the holey jeans and the secondhand boots.

"He'll be too distracted to think about it." She smiled and rolled down the truck window. "He's dating someone, I think."

"I guess that's good." He slowed to a stop in front of the house. "Here we are."

He was acting like a kid on his first date. They both knew where they were, and this was anything but a date. The knots in his gut weren't about Beth Bradshaw. That twisted-up feeling was about the turn of events that had put his plans on hold.

Back Street Church had been spared. No way was he going to think that it had anything to do with Beth, the prayers of Dawson's well-meaning citizens, or anything God wanted from him.

Beth didn't move real fast to get out of the truck. Her dad was standing in front of the barn with Jason and Alyson. Buck Bradshaw glanced in their direction, his mouth settling in a firm line. Jason said something and their father shook his head.

"I thought you said there wasn't anything to worry about?"

Next to her, Jeremy's tone teased as he asked the question. She smiled and opened the door. "There isn't."

She was out of the truck and heading toward her dad when Jeremy caught up with her. She glanced sideways. He was tall and all lean muscle. He walked with the slightest limp that she only noticed when he moved faster than his normal casual swagger. He'd broken his leg a few years ago. She remembered hearing folks in the Mad Cow talking about it for weeks. A bad break that had nearly ended his career.

"Have you been to town?" Jason asked as they approached. His hand was on his wife's waist. Alyson was four months pregnant; the baby bump barely showed beneath her shirt.

Jeremy pushed his hat back. Beth watched him glance from her dad and back to Jason. She settled her focus on her dad.

"The road to the nursing home is blocked, but they said it didn't suffer any damage. I guess you know about the houses on the west side of town?" Jeremy reached to pet the collie that had strayed onto their place a few months ago.

"I heard that you're going to open the church up for a shelter." Jason shifted his attention to Beth. "That's going to help a lot."

"Yeah, I guess it will. If you all start calling this an answer to prayer, I'll…"

Beth smiled at him, "What, take it back?"

"Yeah, maybe."

Alyson cleared her throat. "I have piles of extra blankets and I'll box up snacks and cereal."

That's when Beth's dad spoke up, his voice raspy and a little gruff. "I've got extra cots in the barn and a small generator that I can bring over."

Beth shot Jason a surprised look, because their dad had steered clear of all things Back Street for a very long time.

Beth's heart squeezed a little as she watched her dad come to grips with something inside himself. Eighteen years was a long time to hold on to anger. It had aged him beyond his sixty years.

"The cots and blankets will help, I'm sure." Jeremy pulled off his hat and ran a hand through short, brown hair. "I really don't have a clue what they're going to need. I'm letting them use the building, that's about all I know. And I guess I'd better head that way to see what I need to do."

"I should go with you to get my truck. And I can help get things set up," Beth added.

"I'll take you in a bit. We have a few things to do around here." Her dad's words stopped Beth's departure.

She could go with Jeremy. Or she could let her dad protect her. She understood, so this time she smiled a goodbye to Jeremy who nodded and walked away.

Chapter Five

Jeremy drove back to the church alone. But man, it still felt as if Beth was in his truck. Her perfume had taken up residence in the fabric, in his mind. He rolled down the windows and let fresh air blow through the cab of his truck, trying to rid himself of her presence.

The tornado didn't seem possible, not now with the blue sky and the sun streaming down. It looked like a perfect spring day. But blue skies or not, Dawson had been hit hard. The flattened outbuildings, the damaged homes, the flashing lights of emergency vehicles scouring the area, it was all part of the sickening reality.

The parking lot of Back Street Church was no longer empty. There were a couple of cars, a church van from the Community Church and a pickup truck with the Cooper Ranch logo on the doors.

And there was a big yellow bulldozer. He'd forgotten he'd arranged to have it delivered this week. Talk about bad timing. Jeremy pulled up next to the thirty-foot RV he'd been living in and parked.

His gaze settled back on the Coopers' truck parked a short distance away. He'd avoided the Coopers like the plague since he'd gotten back to town and today they were crashing into his life from all sides.

He pocketed his keys and stepped out of his rig. There were people on the wide front porch of the church. Jeremy headed that way, not real thrilled that his space had been invaded. His plans had been changed. A quick glance up at the sky and he really had to wonder what God was thinking.

One of the men on the church porch turned toward him. The cowboy hat slanted low over the man's eyes didn't hide his identity. Jackson Cooper. He wore his ranch money like old jeans. He was comfortable with his life, with his family. Jackson was the Cooper most likely to speak his mind, most likely to fight for a friend and the most likely to get knocked in the head on any given day.

Travis stood behind him. Lean and a little cagey, Travis had been adopted from somewhere in Eastern Europe when he was about five. Jeremy remembered the little kid in church, jabbering in Russian. Everyone liked Travis, when he wasn't getting on their nerves.

"What are you two doing here?" Jeremy walked up the steps, a little slower than earlier. A sharp pain in his left leg reminded him of pins and metal that kept things together these days.

"Here to help, bro." Travis grinned and tossed Jeremy a bottle of water. "We came bearing gifts."

"I'm not your bro." Jeremy set the water on the floor of the porch.

Jackson shot Travis a look and the younger brother sauntered off. Jackson stepped forward, acting as if he was going to play older brother to Jeremy, as well. That would be the day. Jackson took off his hat, swiped a hand through shaggy hair then grinned.

"Do you need me to knock that chip off your shoulder?" Jackson was no longer smiling.

"I don't think you could." Jeremy picked up the water bottle. "I need to see what's going on in there."

"They're moving pews and setting up cots. Wyatt and Ryder brought supplies."

"Good, we can have a revival later."

Jackson laughed, "Yeah, I'm with you on that. We'll let them play church. But helping neighbors isn't just for the church crowd. Helping family isn't, either."

"We're not family." This was getting real old. Jeremy shot Jackson a look that he hoped conveyed that sentiment.

"Jeremy, let me tell you something." Jackson stepped closer. "I might not agree with everything my family does. I don't join them on Sundays for church. But I can tell you this, the Cooper family sticks together. *All* of us."

Time for a reminder. "Jackson, no one would even know I was a part of the Cooper family if my mom hadn't gotten drunk and showed up at church to announce to the world that Tim Cooper owed her."

A grin split Jackson's too-handsome mug. "Yeah, that was about the best day in church I've ever had."

"Yeah, I can imagine that it was exciting for everyone."

"You and I both know that Dad should have come to you sooner. It was a big conversation between my folks, that Dad should have done something."

"Your mom is a forgiving woman."

"Yeah, she is that." Jackson shoved his hat back on his head. "She's always asking about you."

"Tell her I'm doing fine. You can tell Tim the same."

"Right, you've made a lot of money and you can buy your revenge." Jackson nodded in the direction of the dozer. "So, you plan on taking out the plaque up front that dedicates the church to the people in the community? You know, our great-grandfather donated this land. Funny that you own it now and you're going to tear down what he helped build."

Jeremy hadn't known that, and he didn't really want to hear it right now. He let the anger roll off his back. He wasn't going to punch Jackson Cooper, not right here on the steps of the Back Street Church. He also wasn't going to let him get under his skin.

"Since you probably haven't darkened the door of any church for years, don't think you can give me a Sunday school lesson on forgiveness."

"Right, I guess I can't. I guess we both have to get past this. But for right now, there are people needing help. Our help. That's what the Coopers do, we help our community."

"Last time I checked, I'm a Hightree."

Jackson leaned in close. "You're a Cooper. You look in a mirror, buddy, and you tell me you aren't a Cooper."

"Do you guys think you can give it a rest and help us set up cots?" Wyatt Johnson stood in the door of the church. "Later we'll get out the boxing gloves and the two of you can fight it out."

"I don't need gloves." Jackson slapped Jeremy on the back.

"Right, me neither." He shrugged it off. "What do we need to do?"

Wyatt motioned them into the church. Shop lights had been placed around the room, hooked from electric cords to an extension cord to the generator that hummed outside the building. The lights were bright inside a building that hadn't seen electricity in a few years.

For the first time Jeremy looked around at families he had grown up with. In the corner of the church a young mom sat with her little girl on her lap. A boy played at her feet. The mom glanced up at him, her eyes wide in a pale face.

They'd lost their home. He shoved off his anger with the Coopers and called himself a few choice names. Community mattered. He should know that. Man, he'd been on the receiving end of this town's charity more times than he could count. As a kid he'd had shoes and he and his sister had warm coats because of this church and the people in this town.

He'd been able to rodeo because Wyatt and Ryder Johnson hadn't minded loaning him a horse. Clint Cameron had taught him to ride bulls.

Tim Cooper had offered to pay him off when the news broke that Tim was his dad. By that time, Jeremy had been too angry to take a dime from the Coopers. He'd let Tim put money in the bank for Jane, because she deserved something. She'd blown through the money in no time flat.

The woman in the corner of the church looked away from him, because he'd been staring. He started to turn but the plaque Jackson had mentioned caught his attention. How he'd missed it before, he didn't know. It was wood and brass, but too far away for him to read. The plaque was a reminder of more than the history of this church. It meant he had a whole set of ancestors he hadn't thought about, and more ties to this church than he'd ever dreamed of. Because he was a Cooper, no matter what his last name.

He pulled himself back to the moment at hand and turned to find Wyatt Johnson.

"What about food? Do you have everything you need?"

"Vera brought soup and sandwiches," Wyatt replied. "We need clothes for these kids, though."

"I can help you there." Jeremy glanced around, at the kids, their parents. "If you get sizes I'll make a trip to Grove and get whatever you need. Or I can get gift cards that we can hand out so they can get what they need."

Wyatt nodded, his smile tight. "That will be good."

A car honked as they were setting up a few more cots. More people had arrived. Families milled in the yard, looking lost, looking empty. Kids sat quietly on the porch playing with a few scattered toys.

The empty, forgotten Back Street Church had suddenly been remembered. Ironic, Jeremy decided. They needed it again and suddenly it was an important part of the town.

The car horn honked again. He walked outside to see what was going on. Jason Bradshaw's truck pulled into a parking space. Jason jumped out, leaving the engine idling and the lights on. Through the windshield Jeremy could see Beth in the passenger seat. Jason hurried across the lawn. Jeremy walked down the steps to meet him. Jason was frowning, which wasn't a good sign.

"What's up?" Wyatt must have seen Jason, too. He walked across the yard, bypassing Jeremy.

"The McCormicks can't find Darla."

"Who's Darla?" Jeremy figured he was probably the

only one who didn't know. Jackson had left the church and joined them in the yard. Travis was coming down the stairs.

Boy, when something happened in Dawson, it really was a situation of calling in the cavalry. The good ole Western kind of cavalry. The kind that brought cowboys in worn boots and familiar smiles, and concern in eyes that usually teased.

"What's up?" Jackson quickly shed his normal "who cares" attitude.

"Darla McCormick was walking home from a friend's house this afternoon when the storm hit. Her parents can't find her."

"Where do we start looking?" Jeremy looked to Wyatt, because it seemed to be his call.

"We can each take a section of land," Wyatt said. "On foot, not horseback. We need to check every inch of pasture and even the roadside."

For miles, Jeremy thought. He'd picked up mail from areas that were miles away. That's what a tornado did. Man, if he had a kid, he'd be going crazy by now. He'd be racing through the countryside like a madman. Where were Darla's parents?

"Where's her family?" He'd gone to school with Mark McCormick.

"They're with their pastor. She's just ten," Jason answered.

"We need to pray now and then join the search." Wyatt took off his hat. Jeremy looked at Jackson. The two of them took off their hats and Jeremy held his against his heart. He'd prayed for friends when they'd taken a hard hit on a bull. It wasn't like he didn't believe. He'd just had a real dry spell when it came to faith.

But he knew that prayers got answered.

A kid was lost somewhere and she could definitely use some of those answered prayers. He closed his eyes and it wasn't about anger, the past, the Coopers. It was about a little girl named Darla McCormick. And it was about finding her safe. Amen to that.

Beth hitched her backpack on her shoulder. She had a first aid kit, water, snacks and a flare. She listened as the men planned. But she didn't want to stand around planning. She wanted to get on the road. She wanted to find Darla.

"Let's go, Bethlehem."

She looked up, met Jeremy's eyes. He smiled a real smile, not the teasing smile. "What?"

"We're a team. Didn't you hear Wyatt?"

"I was thinking." And obviously Wyatt wasn't thinking or he wouldn't have done that to her. He would have paired her with Jason. Or even Travis Cooper.

"Let's go. We're taking Wyatt's far twenty."

"Okay. Let me get my dog." She headed for Jason's truck and Jeremy was behind her.

"You're taking your dog?" Jeremy caught up with her.

"She's great at tracking. We couldn't find a calf last week and she led us right to him."

"Right, that isn't really tracking, it's just a dog that follows trails. And she's riding in my truck?" Jeremy pulled keys out of his pocket and held them up.

"You don't have to drive, I can." She had her own truck, it was still there from earlier. They didn't even have to ride together.

"We can take the dog in my truck." Jeremy looked

down at the collie and Beth smiled because the dog was already licking his hand and he reached to scratch it behind the ears. No one could resist… Well, the dog didn't even have a name yet. Everyone just called her "the dog."

Beth whistled and the dog followed her to Jeremy's truck. She opened the door and the dog hopped in, situating herself on the seat between them. Her pretty collie face broke into a smile. Jeremy opened his door, shook his head and climbed behind the wheel.

The collie whined and lay down, head on Beth's lap. Beth ran her hand over the fawn-colored head, sinking her fingers into thick, soft fur. She'd bathed the dog the previous evening and she still looked shiny and clean. Her limpid eyes stared up at Beth, seeking affection.

"What's the dog's name?" Jeremy pulled onto the road.

"She doesn't have a name."

"That's pretty sad, Beth. A dog should have a name."

"Do you have any ideas?"

"Yeah, Lucky."

"That's a horrible name. And it isn't a girl dog name. Why would you pick Lucky?"

He grinned. "It isn't as if you've come up with something better."

"Every stray shouldn't be named Lucky. I think she's a Petunia."

He laughed, white teeth flashing in his suntanned face. He glanced her way and then back to the road. The sun was going down and he took off his sunglasses. Beth hated that they were going to be searching in the dark. It would have been so much easier if they'd gotten started in daylight.

"You wouldn't do that to the dog." He shot her another look and then focused on the road. "Name it Petunia, I mean."

"Petunias are lovely flowers and they smell good."

"Fine, name the poor thing Petunia. But seriously, it sounds like a name for a pet skunk."

Silence washed over the cab of the truck for the next few minutes as they drove through town and into the country, past the Johnson ranch and down a dirt road to the back field that would put them in a direct path from where Darla had been walking in the direction the storm had traveled. Beth didn't want to think about that little girl getting picked up in that screaming vortex.

She wanted to believe that God would answer prayers and Darla would be found safe. She wanted to make deals with God. She would go to the mission field, or maybe give everything she had, if He'd help them find the child. But she knew better. She knew that God didn't need her promises or deals. She knew that prayer didn't work that way.

Jeremy parked. He glanced her way and she didn't want to get out of the truck. Fear knotted in her stomach. She looked out the window at the silent field, a breeze blowing the grass in waves. In the distance coyotes were yipping and howling. Darla was out there somewhere.

"Please help us find her," she whispered.

"In order for God to help us out, Beth, we need to start looking."

"I know." She opened her door and got out, stepping into the deep grass at the side of the road. Petunia hopped out of the truck behind her and followed her as she walked around the vehicle and met Jeremy. He had a .22 pistol in a holster at his side. She eyed the small-caliber handgun and he shrugged.

"You never know. A coyote, a snake, it pays to be prepared."

"Right." She'd grown up here. She knew that a person never knew what they'd encounter in a field, whether at night or during the day.

"We'll walk in the ditches first, down to the gate. One of us on either side. And then I think we should walk back and forth through the field. If we use the fence as a guide and go parallel from end to end we'll know we aren't skipping anything."

"Sounds like a good plan." Beth scanned the field, looking for anything out of the ordinary, anything remarkable. Nothing stood out. There was a hay barn and a crumbling foundation; leftovers from a forgotten farm.

They walked separately for a while, down the ditches on either side of the road. Beth felt choked with fear. What if they found Darla? What if they didn't? It was getting dark now. She wondered if Darla was afraid of the dark.

She met Jeremy at the gate to the pasture.

Jeremy reached for her hand. She hesitated, then accepted his strong hand holding hers tight.

"What did he do to you?" Jeremy's question was spoken in a soft voice as they walked along the fence line. They took careful steps in the dark and kept their attention focused on the ground, on clumps of weeds and brush that hadn't been cut down. The beams of their flashlights swung back and forth. The sun was now just a deep red glow in the dark violet evening sky.

"Jeremy, not now."

"Right, of course." He held tight to her hand. "I wish I could have stopped you that day. I wish I had gone to your dad and told him what you were planning."

She shook her head. "Stop."

Stop having a velvet-and-sandpaper voice that set her nerves on edge. Stop saying everything right.

She didn't want to have this conversation with Jeremy Hightree, a man who skated in and out of lives, who left broken hearts scattered like leaves in the fall. She'd already been broken. Now she was healing.

Her sense of self-worth had been stripped away, and she'd been putting herself back together piece by piece with the help of people who loved her and cared about her. It didn't make sense for Jeremy to be a part of the healing process.

So she kept walking and so did he. The dog stayed close, but always with her nose to the ground, sniffing, whimpering.

After an hour of walking back and forth across the field, Beth was starting to give up. She was starting to fear the worst. "Why don't you call and see if the others have had any luck?"

"They would have called us." He pulled his phone out anyway. Beth waited next to him.

Petunia ran ahead of them. Jeremy was dialing the phone, then suddenly Petunia was barking. The high-pitched yips filled the dark and silent night.

Chapter Six

"She found something."

Beth grabbed Jeremy's hand. Before he could slip the phone back into his pocket, Beth pulled him in the direction of the barking dog. Her flashlight beamed across the field, searching for the dog.

"It could be a skunk, Beth."

"I know, but it could be Darla."

Jeremy wanted to pull back, to tell her to calm down and to be realistic. An entire day had gone by and the girl hadn't been seen. If she were here, just a half mile from her home, why hadn't she gone home?

"I know what you're thinking." Beth slowed her headlong rush to get to the dog. The collie's barks had turned frantic and high-pitched. In the distance a coyote howled.

Jeremy's hand went to the gun that he'd slipped into the holster before he left the RV. It could be that the dog had a skunk cornered. It could be anything. Or anyone.

"Petunia. Dog," Beth called out in a quiet voice, "come here."

The dog continued to bark at the crawl space under

the old foundation. That meant it was probably a rodent of some type. A skunk. Maybe a coon or opossum.

Or maybe the girl was there and prayers had been answered. He hoped prayers had been answered. He remembered years ago when Beth's mom had come to church, giving them all the news that nothing could be done. She'd fought for years but the battle with cancer had been lost. Her hair was gone. Her clothes hung on her body. She was ready to go home, but she would appreciate prayers. Maybe God would give her the healing the doctors hadn't. If not, she wanted peace.

And she'd left them. He'd been twelve and more angry than he'd ever been in his life. Beth's mom had been a mother to him. She'd left Beth alone.

He sucked in a breath, and Beth's hand touched his arm. He glanced down, unsure of what he should feel for the woman at his side.

He held the flashlight in one hand, Beth in the other. The dog was barking, loud, sharp barks. They reached the old homestead and the dog looked up at them but kept barking.

He leaned, crawling close to the hole in the foundation.

"Darla?" He waited. He could hear a scurrying sound. Just as he thought, rodents of some kind. One more time, though. "Darla, kiddo, people are looking for you."

And then a sob. He listened, making sure it wasn't Beth. The sound came from inside the crawl space. He couldn't fit through the hole. He flashed the light around the darkness, spotting rocks, old posts, concrete blocks. "Darla?"

"I'm calling for help." Beth was pushing buttons on

her phone and then talking, asking for an ambulance, for support.

"Darla, you have to say something. Are you okay?"

"I'm here."

At the sound of her voice he exhaled a sigh. And he knew that one family would have a happy ending.

"Are you hurt?"

"My ankle." She sobbed again. "I want out of here. I just want to go home."

"Okay, now you have a light and we're going to get you home. Can you crawl toward me?"

He heard movement, rocks shifting, scraping. She cried out a little but she kept moving. And then he saw her, a dark-haired kid with big eyes in a pale face. There was a cut on her head. Blood had dripped down the side of her face and dried. Dirt smudged her cheeks.

"Darla, have you been sleeping? Or dizzy?"

She nodded a little. "I was running and something hit my head. I crawled under here, though. I knew about the old house because we play here sometimes."

"Good thing you knew that." He reached for her hand. Beth was behind him, her hand on his back, her face close to his. She trembled against him. His insides were jumbled together.

"I really want to go home." The child crawled out of the hole and into his arms. He sat back, holding her tight. Thin arms wrapped tight around his neck and held on. Beth's arms were around them both.

"Let's take a look and make sure you're okay." He set the girl on the foundation of the house. She had knobby knees and long legs.

"My ankle really hurts." She stretched her leg and he eased the shoe off her foot.

Next to him Beth was rummaging through that backpack of hers. She pulled out a bottle of water and a package of snack crackers. Jeremy stopped her from handing them over to the child.

"Nothing in your stomach hurts, right?" Jeremy held the child's shoeless foot and touched the swollen ankle. She flinched and then shook her head.

"My stomach is okay." Her big eyes were locked on the water and snacks that Beth still held. "I'm just really hungry."

He nodded and Beth handed the snacks to the child, first taking the lid off the water. She reached back into her pack and pulled out sterile wipes and bandages of all sizes. He grinned up at her. She was definitely prepared.

"I knew we'd find her." She smiled that beaming smile of hers.

"Right." A prayer answered. He was okay with prayers being answered for this girl and her family.

In the distance he heard sirens. The coyotes, silent for a moment, started in again. Their howls joined family dogs up and down this stretch of road. Darla shivered.

"It's okay," he said with a wink, and she smiled.

"They've been really close. I was afraid they would find me."

"I don't think they could have found you and they aren't real fond of people." He teased her with a grin and a wink, making her laugh.

Beth held out a sterile wipe. He handed her the flashlight and she held it up, giving him a clear look at the gash on the child's head. It was pretty deep and still oozing. He wiped at it, and Darla shuddered. Tears ran down her cheeks, turning dirt stains to mud.

"Sorry, kiddo, this might hurt but we need to clean

this cut." He glanced back at Beth. "Do you have another bottle of water? We can wash it out for now and the paramedics can take care of the rest."

She handed him water. He tilted Darla's head to the side and rinsed the wound, wanting to get out the gravel and dirt embedded in the gash before he applied pressure to stop the bleeding. He wasn't a first aid expert, but he'd been around enough cowboys to know the basics.

Darla cried out when he pushed the gauze compress against the wound. "Hang in there. And think of all the stories you'll be able to tell the kids at school. You never know, you might even get interviewed by the newspaper."

That got her attention and she smiled. "Do you think?"

Lights flashed across the field from numerous vehicles lining up on the road next to the property. Someone must have opened the gate to the field because in moments the long line of cars, trucks and emergency vehicles were heading across the field. Jeremy shined the light to signal their location.

"They're almost here." Beth sat down next to the child, holding her close.

This night was nearly over. Jeremy needed distance. He needed to get his head on straight.

What had made him believe that coming to Dawson would be easy? He watched as Beth continued to talk in quiet whispers to the frightened child. When he'd planned this venture, the pros and cons of tearing down Back Street Church, he hadn't counted on Beth.

First responders and a half dozen others, probably including the girl's parents, were jumping out of vehicles and heading toward him. For a few minutes he could be distracted. His gaze shot back to Beth and Darla. Yeah, maybe not so distracted.

As the crowds pushed in, Beth lost track of Jeremy. She moved out of the way of the medical crew and the family members that were surrounding Darla. In the dark, with the dozens of people circling the area, it was easy to slip to the edge of the crowd, to watch and not be involved.

Her brother found her, though. He broke from the crowd and spotted her.

"You okay?" Jason slipped an arm around her shoulders and gave her a loose hug.

Beth nodded. "I'm good. Tired, though. This day has lasted forever."

"It has been a long day. You and Jeremy did good."

"Yeah." She watched Jeremy move, watched him stay in control. "What makes someone want to destroy something and yet, at the same time, go out of his way to keep someone safe?"

"It isn't about destroying the church, Beth." Jason shrugged. "It's about dealing with his past."

Yes, the past. No matter how much he said it was about building a business, the real motivation was Tim Cooper. He'd been an elder in the church, a pillar of the community, the man a kid like Jeremy would have admired. He would have wanted someone like Tim Cooper as a dad. And if things had been different, he would have been.

"Don't get that look in your eyes," Jason warned.

She smiled up at him. "It's dark, you can't see a look in my eyes. There isn't a look."

"Fixing him won't fix this problem. The church is still standing, Beth. Pray and give it time."

"I will." She watched the crowds surrounding people. "But I do have a plan and I'm not giving up."

"You called the historical society?"

"I did."

Jason sighed. "Beth, I know you want to save the church. I get that. But…"

"But what?"

"Nothing. I just don't want you hurt."

"I'm not going to get hurt."

"You're playing both sides of the fence."

Now what was that supposed to mean? "I'm not."

"Yeah, you are. You care about the church and you care about Jeremy Hightree. When push comes to shove, who are you going to choose?"

She didn't have an answer for him. Jason touched her shoulder. "Do you want to ride home with me?"

Beth watched as Darla was placed on the gurney, her mother holding her hand on one side, her dad on the other. "No, I'll ride back with Jeremy. We're parked down the road about a half mile."

Jeremy stood at the edge of the crowd, near Wyatt. He turned in her direction. As he approached, Jason gave one last warning. "Be careful."

"I will. I am."

"I'm heading back." Jeremy nodded at Jason as he spoke to her. Beth watched her brother, saw him bristle a little like their stock dog did when someone pulled up the drive.

Beth stood on tiptoe and kissed her brother's cheek. "I'll call when I get home."

"Make sure you don't forget." Jason hugged her, said

something low, probably just a goodbye to Jeremy, and he left.

"It's always good to feel liked." Jeremy chuckled, the sound vibrating in the silence that followed the departure of the huge crowd that had been there just moments earlier. Taillights reflected shades of red as the long line of vehicles left single file, out of the field and then down the road. The lights on the ambulance flashed in the dark night.

They stood there for a long moment, the two of them alone again. Beth drew in a deep breath of clean night air. A light breeze blew around them, pushing the long grass in swirls and picking up leaves that had fallen from the trees during the storm. The storm that hit her heart at that moment rivaled the one that hit Dawson that day.

Had it only been a day? Was she really standing in this dark field with a sliver of moonlight cutting a path across the green grass and Jeremy Hightree standing in front of her, watching her?

Where was fear? She'd battled it for so long, she'd forgotten what it meant to be strong, to not worry about the next moment, the next day, the next crisis.

Jeremy tugged his hat low and smiled a smile so cute that everything she'd been thinking scattered like dandelion seeds in the wind. He stood in front of her, tall and strong and with hands that she knew were gentle. He was wearing a dark blue T-shirt. She still had his long sleeved shirt.

"Beth, are you okay?" His voice was soft but strong. His eyes stayed with hers. Connected. She loved his eyes. They were warm caramel.

"I'm fine."

How long had they been standing there? Two minutes or five? Was he starting to wonder about her sanity? Her fingers curled into the palms of her hands. He stepped closer, his expression shifting from gentle to determined.

She closed her eyes. He touched her cheek and she looked up at him, at his cowboy smile that melted her down to her boots. He looked good in a cowboy hat. She felt warm in his shirt.

"It's been a long night." His words were drawn out, soft.

"It has."

"I'm going to hold you."

What did she say to that? Shivers of apprehension trickled down her spine. Apprehension or anticipation? She nodded a little.

"It wasn't an order, Beth. I thought that maybe we were both wrung out after this day."

He stepped close and his arms went around her, pulling her lightly against him, holding her close. She froze and started to pull back. His arms didn't lock around her. He didn't force her to stay. She didn't want to move.

"Holding you feels better than just about anything," he whispered near her ear. His cheek brushing hers was rough, his lips on her temple were warm.

She nodded and breathed deep. The fear and tension from the incredibly long day melted and she felt safe. It would take time to process that information. Jeremy Hightree made her feel safe.

"You okay?"

She nodded and instead of breaking the connection she moved farther into his embrace, into strong arms that held her close. She breathed deep and relaxed, her cheek against his shoulder.

"My legs are shaking," she admitted, holding tight, her hands on his arms.

"It was a long day and longer night. It's okay now."

She nodded into his chest. "Yeah."

When she looked up, his face was close to hers. Her lips parted on a sigh and she moved her hands up his arms to his shoulders. Jeremy pulled back, smiling.

"Not tonight, Beth."

She closed her eyes. No, not tonight. Her heart thudded, racing fast. Not tonight. Or tomorrow night. Not ever. What had she been thinking?

A soft embrace shouldn't distract her, but it had. Maybe Jason was right; she couldn't stand on both sides of this fence. Jeremy on one side, the church on the other.

She took his hand and they started across the field, toward the paved road where he'd parked his truck. She reminded herself that there was a dozer parked at the church, and tomorrow the historical society would be paying a visit to Back Street Church.

And Jeremy wasn't going to be happy.

Chapter Seven

Lunch was being served from tables set up on the front lawn of the church when an SUV bearing a county license plate pulled into the parking lot. Jeremy had eaten a sandwich that Vera pushed into his hand, while telling him that Chance Martin had rolled through town that morning. For whatever reason, Vera thought Jeremy should know.

It was going to be another long day on too little sleep. After watching Beth drive away the previous evening, he'd sat for hours on the glider outside his RV. Lights had glowed inside the church and he'd heard the soft murmur of voices as people settled in. He'd called his Tulsa dealership and asked his manager to get partitions out of storage and haul them to Dawson so the sanctuary could be divided.

As Jeremy crossed the lawn he eyed the dozer sitting on a trailer close to his RV and then his attention drifted to the group of people getting out of the SUV. Probably officials from the county or state emergency management team. He headed for his RV and his laptop. He was expecting a file from his partner, Dane Scott.

The group of people cut him off, stopping him at the edge of the parking lot. Two ladies and three men. Two of the men wore suits, one played it casual in dress slacks and a button-down shirt. They all had "official business" stamped on their smiling faces and Jeremy had an officially uneasy feeling in his gut.

"I'm not the guy in charge." Wyatt was in the church and he pointed them in that direction.

"Are you Jeremy Hightree?" the casually dressed guy asked.

"Yeah, that's me. I'm not in charge of the shelter, though. The man you need to talk to is Wyatt Johnson. He has names, family situations, all of the specifics."

"We're here about the church." One of the women stepped forward.

"Excuse me?"

Casual guy took over again. "Mr. Hightree, we received a nomination for this church to register it as a historical building."

Right, of course. He made eye contact with the balding man in a suit, the one who had yet to say a word. He was on the county planning and zoning commission, so Jeremy had seen him before. He should have expected this.

"What qualifications does the church meet to be registered as a historical building?" Jeremy had hoped to have a building started on this spot by now. Instead he was going to have to jump through small-town hoops.

"Well, sir, the church is one hundred years old."

"This is Oklahoma, a lot of buildings are that old. They can't all be deemed historical landmarks."

"Mr. Hightree, we are doing research on the building and how it came to be. This is only the beginning of our investigation."

"Right, so put me off and put off my business another few months. Maybe, if you're lucky, I'll get tired of waiting on you and walk away. But then this church will go back to being run-down and forgotten."

"We're just doing our job."

"Well, I have a job to do, too. I'm sure I'll hear from you soon." Jeremy walked around the group and into his RV.

When he walked out with the printout from his computer, they were gone. Kids were playing and a few people had set up lawn chairs under a tree. The men staying in the shelter had left right after lunch. Most of them had property that needed to be cleaned up, debris to haul off, and homes to rebuild or repair. A few of the people staying in the shelter just needed a place to stay until their electricity came back on.

One family had left already that morning. Someone had loaned them a generator.

Wyatt told him that there might be people in the shelter for a week, possibly two. Maybe by then the historical society would be done with their research.

The bike Jeremy was working on was in the barn. He walked across the road and opened the barn door. One of the horses he'd brought with him walked from the corral into the open stall to watch, and probably hope for grain. He'd been fed a few hours ago, so the gelding was out of luck.

He rolled the bike out of the stall and into the center aisle of the barn. Working on the motorcycle would help him clear his thoughts. That's how he'd started in this line of work. While he'd been recovering from the broken femur and torn-up knee, he'd built a bike for himself, then for a friend. It had been good therapy during his rehab. Within a year it had become a business that kept him busy. And then it had become a business that kept several guys busy.

With the motorcycle in front of him he could pretend that the only thing he had to worry about was building the perfect bike. The perfect chrome for the fenders. The perfect paint job. He straddled the seat and reached for the handlebars. The handlebars had to be perfect, just the right height for his customer. A custom bike was just that, custom. Every inch of it was designed specifically for the person who ordered it.

A truck came up the road. He glanced out the wide double doors and watched as Beth pulled in. She had parked in the church parking lot and as she got out she waved at the two little boys playing with toy fire trucks. She ruffled the blond hair of one boy and high-fived the other.

He climbed off the bike and reached for a rag to wipe his hands. But he sure wasn't going to go rushing across the road to follow her around the way the kids at the church were doing. He had a little self respect.

Not a lot, obviously, because he was definitely thinking of excuses for heading back over to the church.

His attention drifted to the leveled house. Working on it would keep him busy and keep his mind off the one thing he hadn't been able to shake since yesterday—the way it felt to hold Beth. He walked the short distance across the field to the foundation that was all he had left of a house. He picked up a few boards, nails jutting out, and tossed them on a pile of debris.

The best way to clean was probably to pile up the

wood and burn it. He'd try to salvage what wasn't broken into pieces or splintered. Maybe he'd put the good wood in a pile for anyone who needed it for small repairs.

A truck pulled into the drive next to the house. Jackson Cooper stepped out, waving and then turning back to the truck. When he turned back toward Jeremy he was pulling on leather work gloves.

"Need some help?" Jackson picked up a few loose boards on his way over.

"Not really."

Jackson laughed and continued to pick up boards. "Too bad. Everyone is getting a helping hand. You're included in that."

"I think we should concentrate on people who really need to get their homes back in order. This is just a frame, or was. I have a place to live."

"Yeah, well, we have to start somewhere, right?"

Did he mean as family, or did he mean start somewhere on the house? Jeremy let it go, which wasn't easy for him.

"I guess so."

"I heard about the historical society paying you a visit."

Jeremy threw a board onto the growing pile of usable lumber. "Word travels fast in a small town."

"Yeah, it does. You had to know someone would do something like that."

"I guess I hadn't really considered it." But now he knew that everyone had a story about Back Street. Today one of the families using it as a shelter had told him about their wedding. Twenty years ago they had walked down the aisle at Back Street. Eighteen years ago their son was dedicated and later baptized at Cooper Creek.

"Remember when we carved our names under the back pew?"

Jeremy threw a few splintered boards into the burn pile and walked away. Jackson tossed another question at him. Jeremy turned. "I remember."

Jackson grinned at him. "Kind of gets you right here," he slapped his heart, "doesn't it?"

"Yeah, that's where it gets me."

And coming across the road was Beth Bradshaw.

She was a complication that he hadn't planned on. He'd honestly thought he'd get this done before anyone really noticed what was happening. He hadn't expected Dawson to have a planning and zoning commission. He hadn't planned on permits and signatures. He really hadn't thought that anyone would care.

He looked past her to the faded church. Two days ago he'd seen an eyesore that no one should miss. Today he saw a place where lives were changed. The stories he'd been told were fresh in his mind, pushing his own story aside because the other stories weren't as painful.

Jackson walked up and slapped him on the back, hard enough to knock him forward a step. "You might want to get that look on your face under control, little brother."

"There's no look on my face."

"Yeah, there is. It's the 'end of the road' look a guy gets when all of a sudden being single doesn't seem like so much fun. So what, you've dated senator's daughters and heiresses. Nothing compares to a cowgirl with cherry lip gloss and a smile like that."

"I have to go."

Jackson shrugged and pulled off his gloves. "Me too. I'll be back later to help you clean up this mess. Might want to put on some aftershave and take her to dinner."

"You might want to stop playing big brother."

"No, I don't think so. This is kind of fun."

Jeremy shook his head and walked away. Fun wasn't the word he would have used for his relationship with Jackson. But then again, it wasn't all bad. Beth walked up the driveway. Her smile was shy and he was always surprised how it made him want to take care of her. She made him want to be an Old West cowboy, the kind of guy that tossed his jacket on a mud puddle for the woman to step on to keep her feet dry.

On top of that pile of emotion was something else he had to deal with.

"You called the historical society?"

She nodded. He had hoped she'd deny it. Instead she came right out and admitted her guilt, or at least her part in trying to stop his plans.

"You brought in a dozer." She countered with a little shrug of slim shoulders.

"Yeah, I did." He watched Jackson get in his truck and back down the drive. Jackson tipped the brim of his hat and laughed.

"I'm sorry, Jeremy, but I had to do something. This seemed like the only answer. This church has been here for a long time. If it gets registered as an historical building I can get grants to help maintain it."

"Beth, is it really about money? People in this town could have come together and done something."

"I think that time goes by and we all get used to the way things are and think that nothing will change. We didn't know that the trust for the Gibson land, this land, had a limit and that if the church wasn't used would revert back to their family. The kids who inherited live in Kansas City. They didn't care about a church in Dawson."

"Well, plenty of people care now." His phone buzzed and he pulled it out of his pocket. "Sorry, I have to take this."

She nodded and walked away. He watched her go as he answered the phone. She knew how to twist a guy inside out, and he didn't think she realized she was doing it. He'd just about give her anything if he could, but he couldn't let go of his plans for the church.

He thought about the look in her eyes last night, when she'd been in his arms smiling up at him. He tried to block images of how she'd look at him when the church was gone.

As Beth crossed the road, Angie Cooper pulled into the parking lot. Beth shot a look over her shoulder and saw Jeremy walk back into the barn. He had to have seen Angie, and of course he was going to ignore her.

Beth had other things on her mind today, other plans to put into action. If the historical society couldn't stop Jeremy, she had a plan B. She would get signatures and go to planning and zoning commission with a petition to stop the building of a commercial business inside Dawson. She'd been doing research and there wasn't a current ordinance to stop Jeremy, but that didn't mean she couldn't try to get one put on the books.

She stopped at her truck and grabbed the clipboard and pen she'd brought with her. When she turned, Angie Cooper was standing behind her. Beth wanted to be Angie someday. A doctor's daughter from Oklahoma

City, Angie always managed to look put together. She was cool under pressure. Her clothes were never wrinkled and her shoes always worked.

How did a person get to be Angie Cooper? Maybe because she'd survived. Angie had survived a dozen kids. She had survived learning that Tim Cooper was Jeremy Hightree's father. Some said she had always suspected.

"How is he?" Angie waited for Beth to close the truck door and fell in next to her as they walked toward the church.

"He?"

"Jeremy? This can't be easy for him, coming home after so many years, and now this."

Why would Angie ask her about Jeremy's wellbeing? "I think he's okay."

Or he was until she'd turned the historical society loose on him. And how would he be when he saw the petition? She swallowed misgivings.

"What is that?" Angie indicated the clipboard with a nod of her head.

"It's a petition. I'm going to try to stop him from doing this."

Angie looked at the church and sighed. "I'm not sure if that's the best thing to do, Beth."

"Why wouldn't it be? This church is a part of our community. We can't walk away from it and let him do this."

Angie slipped an arm around Beth's waist. "People have reasons for doing what they do, Beth. From the outside it looks like he's doing this for the wrong reasons. But it isn't all about the past. We all work through our anger in different ways."

The biggest reason to be like Angie Cooper, she was a forgiving woman. She was a class act.

"He'll regret this."

"Maybe, but we learn from our regrets. We learn to do better the next time."

Beth realized she had a long way to go before she would be like Angie Cooper. "I know you're right."

Angie laughed a little. "But you're still going to stand between Jeremy and this church."

"If I have to tie myself to the porch to keep him from dozing it down, I will."

A few minutes later she was explaining the petition to the Johns family and they were signing it. Of course Jeremy would pick that minute to walk into the church. He walked down the aisle, toward her and then with a shake of his head he turned back toward the door.

Beth followed him out the door, where he stopped at the top of the steps. He stared straight ahead, giving her only his unshaven profile and strong jaw to look at. When she reached him, he shook his head a little and looked down at her.

"Beth, do you have to be the one doing this?"

"I'm sorry."

He shook his head and walked down the steps. "I'm sure you are. If anyone asks, tell them Scrooge is helping the Matheson family clean up their farm."

"Jeremy, I am sorry."

He walked across the churchyard, stopping to talk to one of the little boys playing under the oak tree.

Beth watched him leave and she held on to the clipboard knowing that some things you couldn't take back.

Chapter Eight

The Matheson farm had taken a pretty hard hit. Jeremy stood next to the pile of debris that had been a barn and shook his head. People around here didn't let a little thing like losing everything chase them off from their homes and the town they'd grown up in.

Since he'd been born and raised here, he knew a thing or two about standing his ground. He regretted that it had to be Beth he came up against in this battle. When he thought about Bethlehem Bradshaw he remembered her in his shirt, her in his arms. Now he had the image of her with that stupid clipboard full of names.

He pulled his gloves back on and grabbed the wheelbarrow he'd been using to cart old shingles and pieces of metal that were scattered around the yard. A chainsaw buzzed in the background as the trees that had been toppled were cut up.

He'd give this job another hour and then he needed to head for Tulsa where he still had a business that needed his attention. He had three custom bikes going out next month and a dealership that was receiving a shipment of new bikes next week.

The other thing he needed to do was talk to his lawyer about the trouble brewing with the building. That didn't sit well with him. Yeah, he wanted the business built on a site that already had utilities, water and septic, but he wasn't interested in a legal battle that would tear the community apart.

As long as the church served as a shelter, he had time to think about what he should do and how to move forward. For the most part, people were thankful that he had opened Back Street as a shelter.

Reese Cooper had slapped him on the back earlier and told him that it meant a lot to the community.

He rounded the corner and Ryder Johnson jumped out of the way. He raised his hands and grinned. "Watch out, it wasn't me."

Jeremy tried to smile. "Well then you're probably the only one."

Ryder walked with him to the pile of debris that they'd burn after everything was cleaned up. "It's been a rough couple of days in good old Dawson."

"Yeah, it has." And they weren't going to talk about the church. Jeremy would have said thank you, but that would have brought it up. "Did Rob Matheson get an appointment in Grove?"

"Yeah, he headed that way about two hours ago. It'll probably take all day, but he has to do something. He didn't have insurance on his tractor. The insurance on the barn won't cover what was inside it."

"That's a tough break."

"It is. He's in a mess of trouble if he doesn't get temporary funds to keep him going."

"We might have to do some kind of fundraiser to help out the folks in town who don't have enough insurance to cover everything." Jeremy had talked to Wyatt about the same thing.

"Yeah, that's what Wyatt said. Maybe the idea of a rodeo would work."

"Might, if we can get participation from outside Dawson. Wyatt is going to work on it."

Ryder pulled gloves out of his pocket. "I'm going to get back to work. Sara is on her roof over there, nailing down tarps. Their kid is helping, but I think he's only ten."

Jeremy followed the direction of Ryder's gaze. Sure enough Sara Matheson had climbed up on the roof of her old farmhouse. She had blue tarps stretched over the roof that covered the back rooms of her house.

"Later, Ryder."

Ryder nodded and walked off. Jeremy went back to work with the wheelbarrow.

After hauling a few more loads from the house to the burn pile, Jeremy pulled off his leather gloves and headed for the table that had been set up with cold drinks and coffee. He poured himself a paper cup of sweet tea and took a long drink.

Vera walked over to stand across the table from him. The owner of the Mad Cow seemed to be everywhere, helping everyone.

"Vera, I don't know how you do it all."

She took his cup and refilled it. "You do what you have to do, Jeremy. You know that. We know how to survive here in Dawson. We've been through more than one tornado. We've been through more than one crisis. Folks always find a way to bounce back."

"Yeah, but you're giving away more than you're taking in right now."

"Now, Jeremy, you know that God will take care of me. He always has. Remember when my house burned down years ago? My neighbors were there before the fire trucks. They helped me clean up and rebuild."

"Yeah, I remember." He hadn't been very old, maybe thirteen. He and some of the boys in town had helped her out at the Mad Cow for a few days after the fire.

Vera winked and handed him a sandwich. "Most of us understand about the church, Jeremy. We don't want it gone, but we understand."

He hadn't expected that at all. Sara Matheson walked up though, ending the conversation.

"You doing okay, Sugar?" Vera poured Sara a cup of iced tea.

"We're going to make it, Vera." Sara took the tea and smiled at Jeremy. "Thanks for all your help today."

"I'm sorry you all got hit this hard."

She'd shrugged it off but a tear trickled down her cheek. She brushed it away and smiled. "It could have been worse, Jeremy. We weren't here. None of us were hurt. I even found my wedding ring. Actually, Wyatt found it in the yard this morning."

"I'm glad to hear that." Jeremy tossed his cup in the trash. "I'm going to get more work done before I have to leave. Let me know if you need anything."

As he walked away, Jackson followed him, his hat pulled low and dirt streaking the front of his T-shirt. Once, years ago, they'd been told they looked like brothers. At sixteen, Jeremy had laughed and said he wasn't near as ugly as Jackson.

But when he'd looked in the mirror that night, he'd

seen what that other person had been talking about. It had spooked him back then, made him wonder things about the dad he'd never known, the guy his mom had told him had just been passing through.

It had been tough, growing up, being the man of the house from the time he could pull on his own boots. It had been tough, trying to model himself after men in the community that he'd looked up to, men like Tim Cooper. Man, he'd been modeling himself after his own dad.

"This is a mess." Jackson picked up a piece of sheet metal and tossed it in the wheelbarrow Jeremy pushed across the lawn.

"Yeah, it is."

"Dad wants to talk to you."

Jackson as the family messenger. Jeremy would have put Blake, the older, more mature Cooper in that role. Jackson, though, he was easy to talk to. Blake had his own life, his own problems.

"Nah, I don't think I want to do that." Jeremy toed his boot into the dirt and looked off to the west.

"You should. This isn't going away, Jeremy."

At that, he laughed. "The only thing that doesn't seem to be going away is you. Every time I turn around you're there. It's getting kind of old."

Jeremy started to walk away. A hand grabbed his arm and stopped him. He turned, looked at the hand that held him without giving. He shook loose but Jackson didn't back off.

"Jackson, I don't need more history lessons. I'm tired of the past."

"Then why are you acting like you're still living there?"

"I didn't think I was until I came back here and found out how much you people hold on to it."

Jackson grinned big. "Yeah, we do have a thing for holding on to the past. Most of us don't have a dozer aimed at a church."

"When did you start caring about church, or about what happened to Back Street?"

Jackson shrugged. "I never stopped caring about church. I went all my life. I guess I kind of figured I had it handled. I'm okay with God. And that church didn't do a thing to you."

"No, it didn't."

"Have a talk with him, Jeremy."

"Right, I'll think about that." And he'd think about jumping in front of Jim Pritchard's big black Angus bull, too. Never.

Jackson slapped him on the back. "You know how I know you're a Cooper?"

"How's that?"

"That stubborn streak. Yeah, that's Cooper through and through. No way can you possibly be wrong. Am I right?"

"I guess so, you're a Cooper."

Jeremy walked off with Jackson's amused laughter ringing in his ears. He tried not to think about growing up alone when he'd had brothers just a mile down the road. Jackson, Reese, Blake, Travis and Jesse. Yeah, it would have been nice to be a part of their lives.

Stubborn. Yeah, that stubborn streak was a mile wide.

Wyatt Johnson, present at nearly every cleanup Jeremy found himself at, turned from the foundation that had been a barn until just a few days ago. Jeremy wondered how the guy did it all.

"Jeremy, how's it going at Back Street?" Wyatt stepped back and stood next to Jeremy.

"I imagine as well as can be expected. What about you, Wyatt? Burning the candle at both ends, aren't you?"

Wyatt grinned. "Both ends and in the middle."

"Don't you have a pretty new wife at your house?"

"Yeah and I couldn't do this without her."

"What, run a ranch, pastor a church and tend to the entire town of Dawson like it's one of your kids?"

Wyatt didn't seem bothered by the observation. He shrugged, still smiling. "This is our community, Jeremy. And you feel the same way. If you didn't, you wouldn't be doing everything to help out."

Jeremy turned to watch the group of men, a few women and even kids that had showed up for this cleanup at the Matheson farm. There was a list at the church. Each home or business that needed help was on the list and volunteers signed up to be there.

"Yeah, this is our town."

Wyatt laughed. "Isn't that a country song? Isn't there something about a girl whose name he painted on the water tower?"

"I never painted anyone's name on a water tower." Never. And it had never bothered him before. Today, for whatever crazy reason, it did.

His heart felt kind of like a lonely old dog left on the side of the road. He laughed. That wasn't a country song, but probably should be.

"I think I'm going to take a drive."

Wyatt tipped the brim of his hat. "Don't be climbing no water towers, Jeremy."

"Why, are you the town cop on top of everything else?" Jeremy managed a smile and even laughed a little at the idea of Wyatt with a badge and a Bible.

"Nope, not the town cop. But I know the guy who will take you down if you hurt his sister."

"Yeah, I'm not planning on going there."

But on the way through Dawson his eyes did stray to the old gray metal water tower. He grinned, remembering Wyatt's words and the reality that he'd never painted anyone's name on anything. He'd never thought about settling down.

And yet, he had a strange urge to buy a can of spray paint on his way out of town.

Jeremy had been gone for two days. Not that Beth kept track of his whereabouts, but the RV had been strangely quiet. A town that had been without him for several years now seemed quiet and lonely without him there.

Beth knew that her actions might have driven him away. Maybe not permanently, but at least for a few days. The historical society was still researching Back Street Church and the planning and zoning committee were looking into zoning for commercial businesses. The wheels were all set in motion and Beth regretted her part in it.

Beth spent day three after the tornado delivering sandwiches to work crews in the area and to families that were toughing it out in damaged homes with no electricity. It had turned hot and humid, making it more miserable for everyone involved.

She had turned off the main road onto a dirt road that led down to the creek where she'd spent a lot of her childhood playing in the cold, clear water. It would feel good, to take off her shoes and wade in the creek, to forget everything going on in Dawson.

She parked her truck in the grassy clearing and pulled the keys out of the ignition. As she walked down the trail a tiny shard of apprehension slid through her middle. Or maybe it was common sense telling her to be careful. She walked a little farther and stopped. The creek bubbled along, a rushing, energetic sound. In the distance she heard the steady hum of a tractor engine and on the road the crunch of tires on gravel.

She walked a little farther, closer to the creek, deeper into the woods. The air was cooler and a soft breeze rustled the leaves in the trees. When she reached the creek she leaned against a tree to kick off her shoes.

The sound of shattering glass stopped her. Birds flapped over head and flew among the branches of the trees.

Beth froze, her breath holding in lungs that refused to cooperate. The sound of metal and glass. And then the sound of a vehicle starting and racing off.

Her legs shook and refused the order to run.

She couldn't run back to her truck. What if someone was still up there? What if it hadn't been her truck, hadn't been what she thought? Maybe someone had been in a wreck? Or perhaps tossed something out a window?

But no matter what, she couldn't force herself to walk back up the path. She was frozen in that spot, stuck in the past and in memories of Chance's abuse.

The old Beth stood there, afraid to move, afraid of

what he'd do next. It had been that way for so many years. Always the fear of what would push him to lose his temper.

She edged down the path, to a spot that allowed her a clear view of her truck and the reality that someone had indeed been there, and she had been the target. The windows were cracked and splintered. A dent creased the door of the truck.

What now? She wasn't going to cower. She wasn't going to cry. She was going to be the new Beth, the one that took charge of her life. The one who didn't shake in her shoes. If only she could convince her legs of that fact.

For a long moment she stood on the shadowy path, surrounded by trees and things that scurried in the fallen leaves. She listened for the return of the car or truck that had driven away. Whoever it had been probably wouldn't return. But she wasn't going out on that road, either.

The creek sparkled, clear and cool. She had wanted to wade in the water, to cool off the way she had when she'd been a kid. Instead she remained on the path and kept walking. Several hundred feet down the trail she slipped through strands of sagging barbed wire.

The sound of the tractor she'd heard earlier was louder now. The field she was walking through belonged to the Coopers. Ahead of her, probably another ten or fifteen minutes of walking, was Back Street. She could make it to the church and someone would give her a ride.

She slipped through another fence, onto the land Jeremy Hightree had purchased months ago. The grass had been cut and was drying in the warm sun. He must have decided to bale it for hay.

The sweet smell of clover brought back so many memories of childhood picnics and playing in the field. She walked a little slower, feeling a little calmer now. She was close to people, close to help.

Ahead of her the tractor circled. The grass, nearly two feet high, fell beneath the blade of the mower. Tomorrow or the next day he'd rake the hay into rows to bale. She looked up, searching for clouds. Rain always put a damper on hay season. Grass had to be dried before it could be baled.

The big, green tractor turned the corner. She kept walking but the tractor slowed and stopped. Beth waved and Jeremy waved back. And then she realized he was motioning her in his direction. She glanced to the south, saw the steeple of Back Street Church. She shifted her gaze back to the tractor and to Jeremy.

She remembered him sitting in the park all of those years ago, telling her to be careful, to rethink her decision to leave town with Chance. He'd told her then that he'd give her a ride home. She could pretend it never happened.

She could no longer pretend. Chance had happened. Her life with him had happened.

The image of her truck at the side of the road, glass shattered and a dent in the door, reminded her that Chance could still control her life. Even if he hadn't done that to her truck, the fear she'd felt, the memories it had brought back, were because of Chance.

She turned in the direction of the tractor. Thirty feet away from her it stopped, and Jeremy opened the door. He stepped out, his ball cap pushed back, giving her a full view of his face, the full effect of his smile. The white T-shirt made his tan look deeper, darker. His teeth flashed white in a smile that nearly made her stop and rethink this decision.

She was running to safety and for a moment it felt like anything but.

"You're pale." He reached down and pulled her up. "Where's your truck?"

Beth glanced back toward the road. From the perch on top of the tractor she could see Back Street. She could see the church and the cars in the parking lot.

"Bethlehem?"

She slid into the cab of the tractor. It was cool in there and Jeremy pulled the door closed, capturing them in the tinted interior where the radio played a Brad Paisley song and the engine of the tractor idled, vibrating the big machine.

"Someone trashed my truck. I parked to walk down to the creek and someone pulled up and vandalized it."

"What the…"

She bit down on her bottom lip and wished the tears away. His expression softened and his arms slid around her waist. Holding her close.

"You're okay?" His voice trickled down her spine like warm water. And then it wasn't a question, it was reassurance. "Beth, you're okay."

She nodded. The tractor wasn't meant for two so she had to sit close. His arm around her waist held her on the narrow seat.

"We need to call the police." He pointed the tractor in the direction of his barn and shifted gears.

"No."

"No?"

He braked and the big machine rumbled to a halt.

"Jeremy, I don't want to start this over again. I'm here. Chance is in California. But I don't want this to be my life."

"He's in Dawson."

Jeremy's words shook her from the daze she'd been in.

"How do you know?"

"Someone saw him drive through town."

"Maybe he didn't do it."

"You really think that?"

She glanced out the gray tinted window at the half mowed field. "I don't want my life to be about police reports and fear."

"Then do something about it. Don't let him bully you. You need to make it clear to him that you're not afraid."

"But I am."

"Beth, he hurt you. He was a coward who took you across the country so you wouldn't have anyone to turn to. You're not that girl anymore. You're stronger than that. You have family and friends who will back you up."

More regret. "I can't believe you're even talking to me after what I've done to you."

Jeremy leaned close and he smiled, "Yeah, so am I. You're going to end up costing me a lot of money because I am going to fight this."

"I know." She wiped a finger under her eyes. "And I'm sorry."

"But it's a battle you have to fight. I get that."

The tractor lumbered forward. He steered with one hand on the wheel. His other arm was around her, keeping her next to him. A few minutes later he parked the tractor next to the barn.

They sat for a second. Jeremy's arm was still around her. She closed her eyes and leaned against his shoulder. It felt good there, with his arm around her. It felt safe.

"Jeremy, thank you."

"For what?" he whispered. His breath was soft. His lips brushed close to her ear.

"For being my friend."

His arm tightened. He took off his hat and dropped it on the gearshift. He brushed his hand across her cheek, rough and gentle at the same time.

"Beth, you're beautiful. Stubborn but beautiful."

He leaned, holding her close. She touched his shoulder, afraid to breathe, afraid to interrupt the moment. Her heart had been waiting for this, longing for it. His lips brushed her temple first, and then her cheek while his right hand cradled the back of her head.

When his lips touched hers, tears slid down her cheeks. His lips on hers were tender, forcing old memories from her mind and replacing them with something new and wonderful. Her heart soared, reaching for his. This kiss took her back and suddenly she was sixteen again, standing on the creek bank with a boy who wanted to be a rodeo star.

That kiss had been the kiss of a boy. This time she was being held by a man, a man who made her feel everything all at once, and beautiful. His arms held her close and his lips were firm, sweeping her away from reality and into a world where she believed in fairy tales again.

And then he pulled away, too soon.

He touched his forehead to hers. "I don't want to be

the next person to hurt you. And I don't want the church between us this way."

"What?" Her voice shook. A moment like this shouldn't end with words that sounded like him putting distance between them.

"You deserve someone safe, someone who isn't going to hurt you."

"You mean the church?"

"The church, yeah. And me. Beth, you deserve someone steady."

"Right, of course." She slid from his embrace. Standing, she reached for the door of the tractor. Lights flashed in the corner of her eye.

"The police are here. Someone probably spotted your truck."

She nodded and opened the door to step out. "I have to go."

"Let me park this thing and I'll go with you."

She smiled back at him. "I can handle it."

She had to handle it because she had drawn the line between them and he had drawn another line. She walked toward the church and wondered how it had become the battleground.

If she had to choose between Back Street and Jeremy...

She wouldn't let herself think that thought, not now. A deputy was getting out of a patrol car and her truck had been vandalized. That should be enough to think about for one day.

Chapter Nine

Jeremy parked the tractor and hopped down, landing hard on his left leg. Big mistake. He winced, inhaling a deep breath, pushing past the jarring pain. As a kid he'd been told all of those falls from horses, and the bull wrecks, would catch up with him. In the last couple of years he'd become a believer.

His injuries were catching up with him. He was starting to feel like an old man. He watched the retreating back of Bethlehem Bradshaw. Other things were catching up with him, too. He grinned at that thought and even laughed a little. He'd played pretty fast and loose over the years, thinking he'd never get caught.

But she wasn't the type of woman a man walked away from. She was the type of woman a guy had kids with, maybe a minivan. Or a big old SUV, the kind with three rows of seats and movie screens that dropped down from the ceiling.

If he'd been a settling-down kind of guy, it would have been with someone like Beth.

He limped across the road to the church. A crowd had gathered. Jason had arrived; so had Beth's dad.

They were standing with her as she spoke to the deputy. Jeremy walked to the back of the group and waited. He listened as Beth explained what had happened.

He listened when the deputy told her that Chance was in town visiting his family. Of course that wasn't enough to charge the guy. If she'd seen a vehicle, or there had been witnesses… There hadn't been.

Jeremy watched the color drain from Beth's face, saw her glance around, looking for something or someone. Her gaze latched on to his. He smiled and winked. He didn't know if he could convey in a look that he wouldn't let anyone hurt her, but he hoped she understood.

He would do his best to keep her safe from Chance. He wouldn't be the one to hurt her, either. And he didn't know if she really got that message. She needed someone better than him. She needed a man who planned to stick around, not a cowboy who had never held on to a woman long enough to get attached.

He walked back to his RV and eased his way up the steps. Man, he was tired of living in two rooms. He had a big house on the outskirts of Tulsa. If he'd been there he'd have taken a swim to work the kinks out of his leg.

Instead he grabbed a bottle of water out of the fridge and opened the lid on a bottle of aspirin. A few of those and putting his leg up for a minute, he'd be as good as new. Or as good as he was going to get.

He walked past the door and glanced out. Beth was talking to her dad. She wiped at her cheeks and looked away. She looked in his direction again. He was the last person she needed to look toward. Man, he'd hurt more women than he could remember. He wasn't anyone's hero.

The Bible on the table caught his attention. He sat down in the half-size recliner and kicked back, his legs stretched out on the footstool. He set his bottle of water on the table and picked up that Bible.

"Yeah, I remember." He remembered being a kid in secondhand clothing two sizes too small and coming to Back Street to feel safe.

He remembered taking his Sunday school lessons so seriously he would've fought anyone who teased him for going to church.

His stories were a lot like the ones that people had shared with him. People's pasts were connected to Back Street Church. His own past was connected to this church.

This morning there had been a message on his cell phone from the head of planning and zoning. They had a list of names on a petition, people who were asking that the land the church was on not be zoned for commercial use.

That was Beth's handiwork. He kind of admired her pluck, even if it was going to cost him a bundle to fight it.

A knock on the door interrupted those thoughts. He put the Bible down and looked up. Beth peeked in through the screen.

"What's up?"

She stood on the outside looking in at him. "Nothing. Are you coming out?"

"Yeah, in a sec." As soon as he could convince himself to put the footstool down. "You can come in."

She opened the door. "You're sitting still? In the middle of the day."

He nodded in the direction of the kitchen. "Grab a bottle of water if you want."

She did and then she turned, her face still a little pale. Her eyes huge and rimmed with dark smudges. "They're going out to talk to him. It'll make him mad."

"Beth, that's how he controls you, by making you believe you have no power."

Should he remind her that they were in a battle over Back Street and yet here she was in his RV? No, he wouldn't, because she needed someone to talk to.

She sat down on the sofa. "I know. I do know that. But it isn't easy being strong. If I turn him in, he threatens to do worse when he gets out. If I call the police, he makes me feel guilty. How can I do that to someone I love?"

"Do you love him?" He thought his voice sounded strained.

Beth opened her water. She didn't look up. And he had a long minute of wondering why she had to think about the answer to that question. Finally she shook her head. He pretty near sighed with relief.

"No, I don't love him. I think he killed any love I had for him a long time ago. The only thing left is fear, and I'm working on that."

"You're a lot stronger than you think. You walked away."

She smiled, her expression soft. "I stayed. For a long time, I stayed."

"I know.

"He had me convinced that I wasn't worth anything. He made me believe that no one would want me but him, and that I was lucky to have him."

Jeremy forced himself to relax, to take a deep breath

and unclench his fists. He put the footstool down and leaned forward, because he couldn't sit back and have this conversation with her. He wasn't worth much, but he'd never hurt a woman the way Beth had been hurt.

"Beth, he's a sick individual with a big problem. And you aren't the cause. Man, any guy would be lucky—no, blessed—to have you."

She smiled one of those smiles that knocked a guy backward. It hit him full force. It made him want to stand in front of her, protecting her forever. It made him want to jump in his truck and drive over to the Martin place.

He tried hard not to think that he'd just said blessed. God talk felt like a foreign language. But what else could he say, other than the truth?

Beth's smile dissolved a little. She held the bottle of water in both hands and looked up.

"Jeremy, I've been to counseling. For the last year I've had to work through those feelings. Chance tore at my self-esteem to keep me a prisoner in our relationship. I've been rebuilding myself, my faith, my life." She stood up. "And now I'm going to get you a bag of ice."

"Ice?"

"For whatever you injured jumping out of that tractor. I saw you limping across the road like some old dog that had been hit and was coming home to lick his wounds."

"It's my knee and the pins holding my leg together. Too bad they don't have bionic parts, I'd be worth millions."

"They wouldn't put bionic parts in a cowboy that can't stay off the back of a bull." She laughed, "Or *stay on* the back of a bull. I guess that's where the problems start, when you fall off."

"Thanks."

"Don't mention it." She opened a drawer and found a plastic bag. After she dumped a tray of ice in it she brought it back and dropped it on his knee.

"Thanks." He winced and moved the ice. "I really don't need it. I took aspirin."

"You can take care of yourself, right?"

"I'm a long way on the other side of fifteen, Beth."

"So am I." She kneeled next to him. "Don't take over. Promise me you won't do that. I need to be strong."

He tangled his fingers in brown hair that slipped through his fingers like strands of lavender-scented silk. She leaned and he brushed the back of his hand against her cheek. Soft. He sighed and pulled his hand back, because this wasn't where they needed to be going.

She needed to be strong. That was her way of warning him to step carefully and to not invade her life.

"I know that you're strong." He also knew that if he caught Chance Martin anywhere near her, Jeremy wouldn't be responsible for what he did to the other man.

He would let her be strong. He wouldn't let her get hurt. Not even by him.

Beth stood and then she leaned to kiss Jeremy on the cheek. It should have been an easy gesture between two people who had known each other since childhood. An innocent kiss on the cheek. But she paused in the moment, breathing in his scent, his warmth. His hand moved, to her neck and he held her there, her lips against his cheek, her breath catching and then releasing in a quick sigh. He turned and their lips connected.

But she was being strong, not afraid. She was in control of her life. She was in control of this kiss, her heart melting, her world spinning. She opened her eyes and released herself from his grasp. As she stepped back, he stood, still holding her hand.

He looked apologetic. Oh, no, that wasn't what she wanted. She touched her finger to his lips.

"Don't say it. Please don't say how sorry you are. Remember, rebuilding self-esteem here."

He grinned. And he didn't say anything.

Beth backed toward the door. "I'm going home now. Jason is taking me, since my truck is unfortunately out of commission."

"Jason is out there? Waiting for you? He knows you're in here?"

The questions came fast and she laughed at the way his eyes darted to the door. "Yeah, he's out there. He gave me five minutes and said if I'm not back he's coming in."

"Oh…"

"Don't say a bad word."

He shot her a look and ran a hand through hair that was a little spiky on top. She should let him off the hook, but what fun would that be?

"Beth, seriously, I respect Jason. You're…"

"Off limits? Haven't I always been? Wasn't that the problem when I was sixteen? My dad caught us together. Jason made a threat against your person. You were a chicken."

"I'm a lot of things but…"

"But you're not a chicken? Really?"

He took a step toward her, barely grimacing, she noticed. His brown eyes glinted in the shadowy interior of the RV. She didn't smile, wouldn't smile. Her heart had needed this, had needed him. And she wasn't going to think about the past, or why he was there.

"I'm not afraid of your brother."

She laughed. "Jason is helping in the church. He told me to take my time and let him know when I'm ready to go. He also said to tell you there's a community picnic here tomorrow."

"Yeah, I think I knew that. And thanks for scaring ten years off my life."

"You aren't afraid. Remember?"

He snaked an arm around her waist. "Not at all."

Beth reached for the door. Game over. "Yeah, neither am I."

"Chicken?" He whispered close to her ear.

"Not at all." She stood on tiptoes and kissed him, pushing the limits because he whispered her name into the kiss and backed away.

She walked down the steps of the RV and across the parking lot calling herself every kind of fool. She was playing with fire. She was playing with her heart and his. Why? To prove she wasn't afraid? To prove to herself that a man could find her attractive, maybe even love her?

Or because she liked the man in question? Maybe she more than liked him. When she'd been fourteen and running barrels she and her friends would twist apple stems to find out the first name of the man they'd marry. One twist for every letter of the alphabet. She'd always made the stem of her apple twist off at the letter J.

Rather than finding Jason she walked to the back

of the church, to an old tree that still shaded the lawn. She'd played here as a kid, under this tree. She'd had plastic horses and cowboys. Her gaze drifted back to the RV. Jeremy had played with her.

And she'd had faith. She'd had a mom who taught her to believe and to pray. Her mom had been so strong—a fighter who battled cancer until she couldn't fight another battle.

At the end she'd turned to this church because she wanted her last weeks to be peaceful, spent with her community and her family. She'd attended church with her head wrapped in scarves and her body frail. Jason and Beth had been at her side. And their father had stayed at home, angry with God.

His anger had spilled over on this church. Today she'd watched him look at the building, his eyes still sad. He connected this church with the wife he lost.

This church. She shaded her eyes with her hand, blocking the bright, afternoon sunlight. This church, faded and worn, had sheltered them. It had provided stories of faith, people who loved one another, songs about Jesus.

Jeremy on one side, the church on the other. Beth rubbed a hand across teary eyes. She wanted to save this church for the memories that were made here and for her mother who had held on to faith here.

And she wanted to back away from the battle for Jeremy.

The answers were no longer simply black and white.

Cancer had taken Beth's mother. Alcohol and bad choices had stolen Jeremy's childhood. This church had been there for all of them. And how long had it taken her to see that? She had wanted to preserve it for her mother's memory, but it was faith she needed to hold on to.

Jason walked around the side of the building. He must have seen her walk this way, or had looked out the window and saw her standing beneath the tree. She smiled at her brother and met him halfway.

"Ready to go?" Jason pushed his hat back and lifted it before settling it into place again.

"Yeah, I'm ready. Is there anything else to do here?"

"No, they have it covered. Jeremy has brought in partitions so the families who are left have their own little areas inside the sanctuary. Did you know that?"

No, she hadn't, but she wasn't surprised. He had watched those people sign her petition and he was still taking care of their needs while they were living in the church.

The church was quiet. Several of the families had moved out. The few that remained were working on the homes they wanted to move back into.

Jeremy walked down the steps of his RV and looked at the big building with the faded paint and the tall steeple. Years ago an old van had picked him up each Sunday, driven by Teddy Buckley. As he got older, Jeremy made sure his little sister was up and ready. Even if they couldn't find her shoes, he took her to church.

Church meant breakfast and sometimes lunch. Church meant a break from his mother passed out on the couch. Or her crazy manic moods when she cleaned and cooked, as if everything was right in their world. He'd never taken a drink in his life, because he wouldn't take the chance of becoming his mother.

He'd always had a plan to get away from her. It was

his one real skill set. He was good at sticking to his plans. He had planned a world championship in bull riding and he'd made it. It had taken ten years, but he'd done it. He also had a world title in roping.

He'd planned to build a motorcycle dealership that thrived. He'd done more than that. He'd built a custom bike shop that was doing better than he'd ever dreamed. He wasn't Midas, but he'd done okay for himself. And for his family. He'd helped Elise and her husband. He'd taken care of his mother.

He was still taking care of her.

It was hard to fathom, loving her, even after all she'd done to them. He shook his head and turned away from the church. In the field across the road, cattle were starting to sound the dinner cry. A horse whinnied. He breathed in deep, enjoying the clean smell, the familiar scents. Man, this was home.

He had tried not to let that be his thoughts about this place, but as hard as he tried to push it back, it kept on coming back. This was home. Tulsa was a big house that impressed people. It was traffic, business, playing the right games.

It wasn't home.

He walked across the road to the barn, to the corrals and fences. Pain throbbed lightly in his leg, reminding him of the crazy things he'd done to earn money to buy this place. A dozen years fighting it out on the back of bulls in arenas packed with fans.

It would be a lie to say he hadn't loved that life. He'd loved the traveling. He'd loved the fans. He'd loved the money.

He walked into the big old barn that had been on this land for more years than he could remember. He'd done some repairs, but the place was still in good shape. Better shape than the house he'd been trying to build. It wasn't good for much more than kindling, thanks to the tornado.

A truck slowed and turned into the driveway of the barn. Jeremy groaned. Too late to pretend he wasn't here. Too late to head out the back door. He guessed it would have to happen sooner or later. He leaned against the side of the barn and waited.

He tried to look casual, arms crossed and hat tipped low. He guessed he probably looked more like an Old West gunslinger than a guy trying to pretend he just didn't care.

"Saw you out here, thought I might stop and see how you're doing." Tim Cooper, otherwise known as his dad, walked up to the barn. He wasn't the young father of a dozen kids anymore. His hair had grayed. The lines in his face were deeper.

Jeremy looked for a reflection of himself in that craggy, suntanned face. Maybe in the light brown hair or the shape of his mouth. Man, maybe it was his walk and the way he managed to look like he really didn't care. But he did.

Or at least Jeremy did.

"I'm doing okay." Jeremy turned to look inside the barn. "I just came out to feed."

"Right. I can help. Or if you need help getting that house frame back up, we can help."

"I can do it."

Tim nodded and took a few steps closer. "I have twelve kids. No, make that thirteen…"

"Are you sure there aren't a few more out there?" The low blow didn't feel as good as Jeremy thought it might. If he'd been Tim Cooper, he probably would have punched him right then and there.

Tim just rubbed his jaw with his thumb and then he smiled. "I guess I had that coming. But yeah, I'm sure there are no more out there. I messed up, Jeremy. There's no excuse for what I did. I'm not going to blame it on anything other than pure stupidity. When I met up with your mom in Grove, I should have went on home. I didn't. I'm not going to blame it on her, either."

"Then no one is to blame?"

"That isn't what I'm saying. I'm to blame. I hurt a lot of people. I hurt myself, my wife, my kids. That includes you. I should have realized."

"I'm not sure what that means." Jeremy's heart was beating a little faster, a little harder. He walked into the barn, away from a man he wanted to hurt.

"Jeremy, it means you were my son. If your mother would have told me the truth, I would have been there for you."

Jeremy jerked the feed door open. He was thirty years old. He had been kicked, stepped on and head-butted by some of the baddest bulls in the country. He'd never felt this way. He'd never thought he would be this old and still want this man to be his dad. Tim Cooper was a man who admitted his mistakes and tried to do right. Yeah, even Jeremy could see that.

He pulled a bag of feed out and hefted it over his shoulder before glancing back at Tim Cooper. "I guess you'll have to give me the whole story because the only one I have is the one I witnessed and that was my mom screeching in church that you were my dad and you looking pretty stinking embarrassed."

Tim turned a little red. "Yeah, that was a bad day all around."

"I guess that's an understatement." Jeremy walked out the back door of the barn and pushed through the half dozen head of cattle milling around. He pulled a pocketknife out of his pocket and slit the top of the feed bag.

"When I saw that your mother was pregnant, I approached her and asked if you were mine."

"And she didn't tell you the truth."

"She told me there was no way I was your dad."

Jeremy poured the feed into the trough. "That let you off the hook, didn't it? You didn't have to tell your wife. You didn't have to help raise me."

"I would have." Tim stood a short distance away, his gaze shifting from Jeremy to the church. "I should have. I guess I knew. I watched you grow up and I knew. And that was my biggest mistake."

Jeremy shouldered past Tim Cooper. "Yeah, well, it's a little too late now, isn't it?"

"I know that's how you feel."

"Right, you know." Jeremy walked back into the barn. A horse had walked through a stall door and stood in one of the empty stalls. It stuck its nose out at him and he rubbed the animal's face.

"I can't undo the past." Tim Cooper grabbed a flake of hay from the bale in a wheelbarrow.

"None of us can." Jeremy settled into the fact that he was a lot calmer than he thought he'd be. He'd thought about this moment and it had always included his fist connecting with Tim Cooper's smug face.

But Tim Cooper wasn't smug.

And the mad had all drained out of Jeremy.

"I guess Elise isn't yours?" Jeremy turned a five-gallon bucket and sat down. Tim did the same, grabbing an empty bucket and turning it next to Jeremy's.

"No, she isn't." Tim stretched his legs in front of him. "I didn't make a habit of cheating on my wife. I love Angie. I hurt her and I've had to live with that."

"She's a good woman." He absently rubbed his leg and he didn't look at Tim. "If you're doing this because you think it'll make me change my mind about the church, you're wrong. I do think it is pretty sad that you all neglected it all these years and now you suddenly care."

Tim sighed. "We didn't neglect it. We accepted that our community was changing. Years ago, people stayed in Dawson. They farmed. They raised their kids here. They went to church here. That meant every church in town was full. Life changed, people moved or they wanted bigger churches. It's hard to get a pastor to come to a church like Back Street in a town the size of Dawson. It isn't as if we had a lot to pay."

"Yeah, I guess I can see that." Jeremy glanced to the left, across the street to the church.

"That church didn't hurt you. I did."

"You're right about that." Jeremy pushed himself up from the bucket and wished he hadn't sat on something so low to the ground. He grimaced and flexed his leg. He figured it was probably going to rain pretty soon. For the sake of those recovering from the tornado, he hoped it didn't.

"Jeremy, I'd like for us to spend some time together."

"Let's not push it, Tim. It wasn't that long ago that you tried to buy me off."

"You misunderstood. I was trying to make up for what I did, not..."

"Yeah, we have a different memory on that."

"I hope you'll give me a chance. We're having a birthday party for Heather. Maybe you could join us."

Heather Cooper was one of the nicest girls Jeremy knew. He had defended her once, in high school. Now he realized he'd been defending his little sister. He should have known.

It took him a minute to process thoughts that hadn't sunk in before. When he'd been busy being mad he hadn't thought about how this connected him to people he'd always known. Yeah, Jackson had been in his face, but that was Jackson.

Heather Cooper was his little sister. The man standing in front of him was his dad. It took time for all that to sink in. He'd spent the last dozen years running from it instead of working through it.

"I'll think about it."

"Bring a date if you want." Tim waved and walked out of the barn. "The party starts in two hours."

Right, bring a date. The whole "welcome to the family" wagon might be pushing things. It wasn't that easy, to just move on and suddenly be a Cooper. But Jeremy was willing to give it a try.

Chapter Ten

The box was open on Beth's bed. It shouldn't make her feel this way, as if her mother had just left. Opening the box was like opening up the past, the forgotten pain. Beth brushed at her eyes and sat down on the bed. Why had her dad waited so long? Had he been afraid she couldn't handle the memories? Or had he been unable to handle seeing her with these things of her mother's?

She lifted the ring box from among the contents and lifted the lid. Emotion clogged her throat and tears burned her eyes. Her mother's wedding ring. The diamond glinted in the overhead light, sparkling in the gold setting.

Beth slid the ring on her finger, the one where she'd worn Chance's ring for eight years. She'd hocked the ring the day she left him because she'd needed money to run, to hide. Now she smiled, because it was ironic that the ring was the one good thing he'd done for her in their marriage.

She picked up the journal that had been hidden in the box all these years. It was yellowed with age and smelled a little musty. But it was her mother's story.

Five years of battling cancer and having faith. Beth felt a healthy dose of shame. Her mother had never lost faith. Beth had. A few battles and she'd jumped ship and tried to manage life on her own.

It hadn't worked out so well.

Things were getting better, though. Her faith was getting stronger.

She opened the journal to one of her mother's shorter notes, a day when she'd felt defeated. And she'd ended the short entry by quoting Psalm 91. *He who dwelleth in the secret place of the most high, shall abide in the shadow of the almighty. And I will say of the Lord, He is my refuge and my fortress. My God. In Him will I trust.*

In Him will I trust.

Beth put the journal on her nightstand and placed the lid on the box. A light knock on her door, tentative and cautious. She wiped at her eyes and took a deep breath.

"Come in."

The door eased open. Her dad peeked in. "I have that new gelding down at the stable. Do you want to try him out?"

His gaze slid to the box and to the journal. He inhaled sharply and glanced away.

"Dad, she would have wanted you to move on, to…"

"No." He shook his head, gray hair thinning and weathered lines creasing his face. "Beth, we all deal with things in a different way. I've dealt with this nearly your entire life."

"I know." Because they'd found the cancer soon after Beth's birth. Had he ever blamed her?

"How's Lorna?"

Her dad didn't smile. And then he did. "I guess she's

doing fine. Come on down and see if you think this gelding will suit you."

"I'll be down in a few minutes."

She picked up the note she'd gotten from the historical society that day. They hadn't found a real reason to register Back Street Church as an historical building. She folded the piece of paper and shoved it into the pocket of her jeans.

When she got to the barn the horse was already saddled. It was a good-looking roan, brown and sprinkled with gray and hints of chestnut. The horse turned, ears twitching at Beth's arrival.

Beth's dad walked out of an empty stall. She smiled because his step was lighter these days. She'd come home. He said that had made things a lot easier for him. But Lorna was the one responsible for the lighter step, the easier smile.

"Want to try him in the arena?" Her dad unclipped the lead rope from the hook on the wall.

"Sure." She took the reins and led the horse out the door and to the arena. The white boards of the arena needed painting. She'd have her dad pick up the paint and she'd do that next week, when things settled down a little.

Her dad opened the gate to the arena and she led the gelding through. He side-stepped a little and she pulled him close, brushing a hand down his neck. Probably a good idea to lunge him a bit before riding him, but she hadn't brought a rope out with her. She glanced back, sometimes there was a long line wrapped and hanging on the corner post. Not this time.

She led him once around the arena instead and then she slipped her foot into the stirrup and swung her right leg over the horse's back. As she settled into the saddle a truck pulled up the drive. She reined the horse around and watched Jeremy get out of the big Ford. He was dressed in a polo and jeans. He'd left his hat at home. Did that mean he was going out, or was he leaving? Did he know about the historical society decision?

He was a little overdressed for a neighborly visit.

No sense dwelling on what might happen. Or might not. She loosened the reins and nudged the horse forward. The gelding broke into an easy trot. She moved her hand and gave him another light nudge with her heels. He moved into an easy lope around the arena. She neck reined him to the left, leaning the reins lightly against the right side of his neck. He took the lead and circled in a tight circle. Nice.

She tightened her legs and he slowed to a walk, just the lightest pressure on the reins. Her dream horse. She smiled as she rode back to her dad. He was standing next to Jeremy.

"Dad, he's great."

"He's off a little," Jeremy answered. He opened the gate and walked in.

"No, he isn't." She eased the horse back and he tucked his head against the pressure and backed up. She released and he stepped forward and stopped.

"Yeah, he is." Her dad rested his arms on the top of the gate. "Right leg, Jeremy."

"Yes, sir." Jeremy ran his hand down the horse's neck. He touched the horse's rear leg and eased his hand down. "Pretty warm, Beth."

"Well, that's just wrong." She slid off the horse and walked around to the side where Jeremy was lifting the horse's rear leg. The gelding pulled a little but Jeremy leaned into his side and held the leg up.

"He might have pulled a tendon in the ride up from Oklahoma City. Or maybe he hit it against the trailer." Her dad walked through the gate and closed it behind him.

"It's a little swollen." Jeremy released the leg. "Doesn't look like anything serious, but I'd call Joe."

"Yeah, I will." Her dad shook his head. "He's a nice animal."

"I'll take him in and put him in a stall." Beth took the reins from Jeremy. "What are you all dressed up for?"

Jeremy looked down, as if he hadn't noticed the jeans, or the unscuffed boots he was dragging through the dusty arena.

"I'm on my way to Heather's birthday party."

He said it like he went to birthday parties at the Coopers' every day of the week. But Beth wondered. She glanced back as she walked toward the gate with the gelding. He smiled, a tight smile, a little tense.

"It'll be fun." She led the gelding through the gate. The men followed.

"Let me take him. We'll wrap that leg up and call the vet." Her dad took the reins.

"Would you like to go with me?" Jeremy rubbed the back of his neck and shifted a nervous look at Buck. Jeremy was thirty and afraid of her dad.

"Sounds like a good idea." Her dad stopped and the horse stopped next to him. The big roan hung his head, looking for all the world as if he thought he'd let them down. Beth ran a hand over the horse's soft, sleek neck.

"Go with you to the Coopers'? I don't know, that might be a little awkward."

"Tim said to bring a date."

Beth smiled then. "A date, huh?"

"Well, yeah."

A date. She looked down at her own faded jeans and the T-shirt she'd put on earlier, after cleaning house. "I would have to get ready."

Jeremy glanced at his watch. "We don't have to be there for thirty minutes. I'll unsaddle the horse and help your dad get him settled."

"I'll hurry."

Jeremy held the gelding while Beth's dad wrapped the animal's leg. He'd already called the vet and so now it was down to putting the horse in a stall and waiting.

"She's been through a lot."

Jeremy had been stroking the gray flecked neck of the horse and he looked down, meeting the serious gaze of Buck Bradshaw.

"Yes, sir, I know she has."

This had to be one of those conversations when the father was asking about intentions toward his daughter. Jeremy didn't have an answer. He couldn't tell Buck that he'd come here with a definite plan, part revenge and part business. He'd known day by day what to do and how to go about doing it. But now, his life was minute by minute and things just kept changing.

Beth was one of the unknowns in his plan. He remembered something in science about unknown properties. Yeah, Beth had definitely changed the equation and he had a feeling she might change the outcome.

Buck Bradshaw stood and patted the horse on the rump. He was a big guy, burly. Maybe he was getting older, but he was still solid. He could probably still hurt a guy.

"So?" Buck pushed his hat back and looked Jeremy square in the face.

"I'm thinking she's a wonderful person and I'm glad she's a friend."

Buck's chin dropped and inch and he stared. "She went through a lot with Chance."

"I know she did."

Jeremy wanted to remind Buck that Chance was back in town, staying at his parents' place. He was being investigated for damage to Beth's truck. Jeremy wasn't going to hurt Beth. And he'd sure make sure no one else did.

But he didn't know what that meant about his plans.

"Keep her safe." Buck stepped out of the stall and closed the door.

"I intend on doing just that." Jeremy walked out of the barn with Buck. The sun was low on the horizon and a few hazy clouds turned the sky pink and lavender.

Beth walked across the yard, her dark hair loose. She had changed into jeans that were rolled up above her ankles, and a button-down shirt. The boots she'd worn had been replaced by glitzy little sandals. Gloss shimmered on her lips, drawing his gaze when she smiled.

"Ready?" He cleared his throat and tried again. "Ready to go?"

"I'm ready. I hope this isn't a dressy event."

"It's taking place in Tim and Angie's backyard."

"Right." She looked down and shrugged.

"Beth, you look fine." He wanted to comment about the distressed jeans with the tiny holes above the knees and the bright red of her toenails.

He nodded a quick goodbye to her father and led her to his truck. He didn't hold her hand. She didn't reach for his. He opened the door and she climbed in, smiling as she clicked her seat belt in place and he closed the door.

It was a five-minute drive to the Coopers'. He'd never been one to get too worked up, but this case of nerves rolled around inside him. Beth glanced his way and smiled. He was focused on the road when her hand touched his arm.

"They're the same people you've known all your life." Her words were spoken softly as they turned up the driveway that led to the big Georgian-style home.

"Right. But growing up they were the family I always wished I'd had."

They were the family he hadn't had. It made bitter a real easy pill to swallow.

"I guess we have to let go of the past and all of the regret, the things we wish we'd had or wish we'd done differently."

He smiled at Beth and after shifting he reached for her tiny hand. It slid into his, fingers interlaced. She knew about regret. She knew about loss.

"Thanks for coming with me."

"Because you couldn't have done it without me?" She smiled and gave his hand a light squeeze before letting go and slipping her hand from his.

"I think that's probably what I would have said."

He parked and stepped out of the truck. Beth was out before he could reach her side. They walked up to the house together, her fingers brushing his as they walked side by side. He didn't reach for her hand. Tha would have connected them and they didn't need connections right now.

The front door opened as they walked up the steps. Angie Cooper wore an apron over her jeans and T-shirt. She smiled and waved them inside.

"I'm so glad you're here." She hugged Jeremy and then Beth. "Tim is manning the grill out back. I hope you're hungry."

"Starving," Beth said.

She eased her hand into his and smiled up at him, in a way that set him on his heels because it reached deep inside and forced him to be someone different, someone a lot stronger than he'd ever been before. Maybe someone a lot more forgiving.

He stopped in the two-story entryway. Angie had continued down the hall expecting them to follow her, probably to the kitchen and out to the patio. Jeremy rubbed the back of his neck where tension had settled in the muscles.

"Jeremy?" Beth slid a finger through his belt loop and pulled him close. "Relax. This is your family."

"You two coming?" Angie had reappeared. She stood in the hall and beckoned for them to follow.

Jeremy took a deep breath. "Yeah, we're coming."

Beth exhaled, as if she hadn't been sure. That made two of them.

The patio ran the entire length of the house. A covered outdoor kitchen at the far end, complete with a grill, sink and fire pit, seemed to be the popular meeting place. Jeremy glanced around, noticing that the visitors were all family. Of course with the Cooper clan, that meant a couple of dozen people, give or take.

Reese, Jackson, Travis, Jesse, even Blake was there.

They were sitting around the pool, iced tea in hand. Maggie Cooper Jones was trying to corral her three kids. Lucky was sitting with his wife. Their daughter was in her early teens and she'd just dived into the pool.

Heather was at a patio table with Mia. There were a couple of kids missing.

He was a member of this family. As a kid he would have jumped in without thinking. Today he stood back and watched because as an adult he questioned how they felt about him being there, in the middle of their family. If it had been him, he might have been a little angry.

But they were all long past being teenagers. They'd been dealing with this for the last twelve years, same as him. They just hadn't dealt with it together. That's where Jeremy had made the choice, one he couldn't undo.

Jackson nodded in his direction and stood up. That started a migration.

"Everyone, look who's joining us, Jeremy and Beth." Angie touched his arm and smiled.

She knew how to take in kids, even the grown and angry kind. He had his past, she'd had her own to deal with. She'd had to deal with finding out about him. That made her one of the strongest women he knew.

The Coopers didn't give him long to think about his past or what Angie had been through. They didn't give him a chance to worry about his reception. As he stood there getting his bearings, the Cooper family stampeded. The girls, his half sister and adopted sisters gave him hugs and they cried.

His brothers slapped him on the back and gave him fisted man-hugs. Tim manned the grill and smiled at his wife and then at Jeremy.

This was the closest thing he'd ever had to a family, a real family. He'd had his church family when he was a kid. He'd had the guys he traveled with when he rode bulls. He'd taken care of his mom and his sister.

"Want a glass of iced tea?" Heather smiled and led him to the stainless steel fridge under the counter that connected to the grill. "Sorry, we can be overwhelming."

"A little."

"I'm sorry, you know, that we didn't get to grow up together." And then she shrugged. "But in a way, I guess we did. Back Street kept us all connected."

"Heather, let's not talk about the church. Not tonight."

She looked startled and then she nodded. "I didn't say that as a prelude to a 'please don't tear it down' conversation."

"You'll have to forgive me if I say that it sounds like a few of the other conversations I've had lately."

"It probably does and I'm sorry. Let's forget it and join the party. Beth is talking to Jackson."

That stirred an emotion a little different than the one he'd just battled, and a lot more confusing.

Tim caught him before he could make it to Beth's side. He flipped steaks on the grill and offered Jeremy a bottle of water.

"I'm good."

"I'm glad you came."

Jeremy looked around, at this family, his family. "Yeah, so am I."

He'd let the last twelve years of running keep him from being here with them. That was just about the craziest thing he'd ever done. Because in the last week they'd proven over and over again that it might have been nice to have them all involved in his life.

Even if Jackson was on the big side of being a pain. And at that moment he was leading Beth over to the flower gardens.

Tim slapped him on the back and laughed. "You might want to hold on to her. I think Jackson is starting to think about settling down."

"She's a free woman." Jeremy's words sounded tight to his own hearing.

"Yes, she is. She's thrown you a curveball on this church situation."

"That she has."

"I hope you don't let that come between the two of you."

Jeremy shrugged it off because it was better if something did come between them. Might as well be the church.

Tim shook seasoning on the steaks. "These are nearly done. You know, if this becomes a legal battle for you, it might be cheaper to let it go and build elsewhere."

Yeah, that made sense. But he hated to back down from a fight.

Beth knew that Jackson was messing with Jeremy, even before he whispered that his brother's brown eyes were starting to turn kind of green. He shouldered against her and laughed. She laughed, because Jackson had always been the flirt, but never the guy she was interested in dating.

"I should go sit with him." She shot a look in Jeremy's direction. He'd taken a seat next to Reese and was pretending to drink water and not glare. She reached into her pocket where she'd stuck the note before leaving the house.

She could at least give him this. It might make him frown less.

"If he hurts you, I'll take care of him." Jackson walked with her, away from the flower gardens that Angie Cooper tended herself.

"He isn't going to hurt me."

Jackson shrugged. "He's never been much of a settling-down kind of guy."

"A little like his older brother?"

Jackson laughed at that. "I guess you got me there. But if the right woman came along, I might just give up my single ways."

"It happens that way, Jackson."

"Yeah, it does."

They were at the table where Reese and Jackson were discussing the army and Reese leaving for basic training. Jeremy pushed out the chair next to him. Reese made some kind of crazy excuse why he had to leave.

"Nothing like matchmaking, is there?" Jeremy leaned close to her and she loved that he smelled like the outdoors and clean soap.

"It isn't my favorite thing in the world." She pulled the note out of her pocket. Keep it to herself or show it to him?

"What's that?" Jeremy reached and she handed him the note about the historical society's ruling.

"You win this battle." She met his caramel gaze and held it, wanting him to smile. "They voted against the church becoming a historical site."

He read the note and he didn't smile. "I don't want this to be a battle. I never wanted that."

"I made it a battle, didn't I?"

He smiled then and leaned to kiss her cheek. "You did. And I'm afraid there won't be any winners."

No, there wouldn't be winners. She thought about telling him he could walk away, but what if he did? What if he gave up and left?

Chapter Eleven

Back Street Church on Sunday morning was full to capacity with members of Dawson Community Church and various other residents of Dawson. A few came out of curiosity, others were there to say "thank you" to God for sparing them, others were steadfast members of the community church who needed a place to go on Sunday morning until their church was repaired.

Speaking of repairs, Beth stood in the yard and looked up at the church. Some repairs had taken place at Back Street. The people using it as a shelter had helped. And so had Jeremy. She'd seen him on a ladder that morning, repairing loose gutters on the roof over the porch.

A door closed. She glanced to her right and watched him walk down the steps of the RV, a little less gimpy than a few days ago. Last night after Heather's birthday party he'd driven her home. He'd walked her to the door. He hadn't kissed her good-night. As a matter of fact, he hadn't said much after she'd shown him the note. And she was kind of sorry she'd given it to him if that's how he was going to act.

Like a sore winner.

She glanced his way again. He smiled and nodded. She walked up the steps, greeted Wyatt Johnson at the door and walked into the building.

It no longer smelled like dust and age. The inside had been polished and cleaned. The windows had been washed and sunlight lit up the old stained glass. The sanctuary glowed with warm light and the warmth of a hundred people. Beth stopped in the vestibule and took a deep breath. This was how it felt to come home.

She'd been attending Dawson Community Church for several months, but this church was home. Today it looked like it had years ago. It wasn't shadowy and empty, draped with spiderwebs.

Her heart wasn't empty. Faith had been returning, seeping in through the cracks in her heart.

God wasn't a bitter father pushing her from what was familiar and comforting. He wasn't an angry husband, using his word to beat her into submission.

He was God the father, compassionate, merciful and offering grace to a broken life. Her life.

"We'll walk in together."

Her dad stood next to her, surprising her. There were two people she didn't expect to see in this service. He was definitely one of them. And next to him, Lorna. A public acknowledgement of their relationship.

"I haven't been in here in years." Buck Bradshaw shook his head. "Your mom and I were kids in this church, and then we were teens. And then I got busy with the farm and she kept coming. I guess that happens."

"It can." Beth reached for his hand, rough and strong. He'd always been strong. They walked down the aisle together. Beth stopped at the second pew from the front, the pew where she'd always sat with her mother and brother. The third pew was where Jeremy sat with their Sunday school teacher.

Her dad didn't move. He held tight to her hand and looked at the carpet runner that covered the center aisle. Dark brown, faded and worn. Someone had found it in a closet and unrolled it.

"I didn't want to lose her. I wanted God to heal her." He looked up, his brown eyes watery.

"Dad, we don't have to do this." Beth let go of his hand and sat down. She slid down the pew and made room for her father and for Lorna. It pulled at her heart a little, to see Lorna next to her father.

After so many years it should have been easier. But it felt as if they had all gotten stuck in time, not moving forward, because they had avoided church, and sometimes they'd avoided one another. They had avoided honest discussion.

Her dad sighed as he took his seat.

"No, we don't have to," Buck's voice rasped. "But we should have done this a long time ago. I should have told you how much I loved her and didn't want to lose her. I should have told you how much I prayed."

Beth leaned against him, shoulder to shoulder. "Dad, it's okay."

He shook his head, "I let her down. I told her I would hold us together."

"We did the best we could. How were you supposed to know how much it would hurt?"

"No, I guess no one ever knows." A tear trickled down his cheek.

Wyatt Johnson took the place behind the pulpit. He smiled at the crowd and shook his head.

"Disaster has a way of bringing us all together. The important thing is to keep that unity after the healing is done."

The rest of the sermon was lost because Beth looked back and saw Jeremy enter the church. He removed his hat and stood at the back of the building. Her heart beat in double time and her eyes overflowed.

Her dad pushed a box of tissues into her hands. "Might need those."

She sniffled and nodded. She had failed to change Jeremy's mind. Maybe God could do what she couldn't. Back Street Church still had a purpose. She hoped she wasn't the only one who saw the need.

Jeremy left before the service ended. He made eye contact with Wyatt, slipped his hat back on his head and walked out. The sunlight was bright. The sky was bluer than blue. He stood on the front porch of the church and stared out at the field that he'd baled the day before. The big, round bales dotted the pasture. His cattle grazed among the bales.

His cattle. His land. His church. That last part didn't feel as good as the rest. What had started as a simple plan now knotted inside his gut like the worst idea he'd ever had. Maybe he'd always known he wouldn't be able to do it.

The dozer was still sitting on the trailer.

So what did he do now? Head back to Tulsa? He glanced back into the church and his gaze attached to the back of Beth's dark head. She turned and smiled, as if she'd known he was there, watching her.

Last night had changed things and he still didn't know how. He didn't know if he'd given up on the church or if he'd given up on being here because he didn't know how to be a Cooper, a citizen of Dawson or a man in Beth's life. He didn't even know why that last part was in the equation.

If he went back to Tulsa, he could slip back into his old life. He kind of liked that life. It was definitely a lot less complicated. He could keep this land, build his shop and let someone else manage the place. That had been his initial plan. He'd never considered living here full time. He'd planned on building a house where he could stay once in a while.

He was Jeremy Hightree, not Jeremy Cooper. He could climb on the back of a bull and never break a sweat, never get lost in fear or the battle for the championship. Cool on the back of a bull, that was what they'd said about him.

Yesterday he'd bought a basketball net. Actually, he'd bought two. He shook his head as he walked across the parking lot to his RV. Impulse shopping. He'd also bought a cheap volleyball set. He'd been planning activities for the community picnic that they were holding today on the grounds of Back Street Church.

He was starting to see that he was in a real crisis. He looked up and shook his head. He'd always heard that a guy couldn't outrun God.

Well, a guy could sure try.

But today he was going to finish putting together a basketball net, because the kids deserved something to do. He pulled his toolbox out of the back of his truck and grabbed one of the folding chairs from in front of his RV.

When the church bell rang, signaling the end of the service, the basketball net was finished. He lifted it and went for the sand that he'd use to fill the base. A truck drove by. He didn't recognize it. But he recognized the man behind the wheel and seeing him set Jeremy's blood to boiling. Chance Martin. Obviously he hadn't gotten the message about staying away from Beth.

Jeremy stopped walking and watched the other man slow down and glance in the direction of the church. It would be a cold day in a hot place before Jeremy would let that man lay one hand on Beth.

People were streaming out of the building and down the steps. Jeremy watched for Beth. He glanced back, saw that Chance had stopped his truck.

Where was Beth? And why in the world would Chance choose today, in front of this crowd, to cause problems?

Maybe he wouldn't. Jeremy liked the thought that the other man would pull on down the road and leave well enough alone. It was Sunday. Jeremy didn't want to have to hurt this guy, not today, not on Sunday.

Beth walked out the front door of the church, talking to Rachel Johnson, Wyatt's wife. The two were laughing, totally oblivious to Chance's presence. Jeremy put the sandbag he carried on the base of the basketball net and started toward Beth.

A truck door slammed. He glanced toward the road and saw Chance heading across the lawn of the church, pushing through the crowd. Jeremy picked up his pace. He reached the steps of the church right after Chance. Jeremy wasn't alone. More than a dozen men had noticed the situation. Including Jason Bradshaw who was fast-tracking toward his sister.

Beth stood on the porch, her eyes large, focused on Chance.

"Chance, I think you should leave." Jeremy took a step forward, putting himself on the steps of the church.

"Jeremy, I'd recommend you stay back from my wife." Chance turned to face him. He'd been a skinny kid back in school. He'd outgrown that phase.

"I'm not your wife, Chance." Beth walked down the steps. Jeremy wanted to stop her, but man, she looked determined. She looked like a woman who wasn't backing down. Maybe she'd done too much of that in the past.

"Yes, Beth, you're my wife. We were married legal and binding and that divorce document doesn't mean a thing to me."

"I'm not afraid anymore, Chance. I'm not going to let you quote verses to scare me. I'm not going to let you use God as an excuse for hurting me. I'm not afraid."

Jeremy wanted to cheer her on, but he could only stand there and wait. She was beautiful and strong, but he could see her legs trembling. She sneaked a glance in his direction and he smiled.

And then Chance rushed up the steps and grabbed her. Taken by surprise, Jeremy was a stupid moment too late. He watched as Chance's hand came up, connecting with Beth's face. And then he took the steps two at a time and made it just in time to grab Chance Martin as he fell backward, groaning in pain.

Jeremy held Chance by the arms. The other man was fighting mad and Beth stood there trembling but okay, rubbing the fist that had punched Chance. A bruise was already turning her cheek blue. That bruise went all over Jeremy. He pulled his hand back and spun Chance around. A hand grabbed his fist.

"Bad idea." Jackson shook his head and grinned. "There's a deputy pulling up. Why don't you let me take Chance to meet his destiny?"

Jackson grabbed Chance and Jeremy watched them walk away. He took a deep shaky breath and turned to find Beth still standing on the steps of the church. Jason had a protective arm around her and Buck had turned and was headed in the direction of the patrol car.

"You okay?"

"I'm good." Her chin came up a notch. He recognized someone trying to be strong. He'd made that same move too many times to count. It had started when he was a kid and some well-meaning grown-up would ask if he needed anything.

He was always good.

Even when he was a kid and scared to death.

"Yeah, I know you are." He didn't reach for her hand. Instead he changed the subject. "Want to see what I've been doing while you were in church?"

The cop was putting Chance in the back of the patrol car.

She smiled a wavering smile. "You were in there, too."

"Yeah, I was there, too."

Jason moved, let his sister go. "Take a walk, sis. This will blow over and everyone will calm down."

She nodded and joined Jeremy. He didn't reach for her hand, didn't put his arm around her. Instead they headed for his RV and the parking lot, not touching but walking side-by-side.

They didn't make it far. The deputy caught up with

them, tall and purposeful, his hand on his sidearm, probably out of habit. Domestic abuse ranked as one of the most dangerous calls a cop could make.

Beth hugged herself and watched the officer approach. How many times had she lived through similar moments? She weaved a little. So much for being strong. He wrapped an arm around her waist and held her close.

"Beth, do you want to press charges?" Officer Hall stopped in front of them. He was an older deputy. Jeremy remembered him from years ago. He'd been to their house more than once. A few times, along with caseworkers from family services.

"I…" Beth glanced at the patrol car. How many times in the past had she said no? "Yes. I do want to press charges."

"It's what you need to do, Beth." Jason Bradshaw joined them. He smiled at his sister. "You aren't alone anymore. He doesn't have a right to hit you."

"I know." Finally she nodded. "I want to press charges."

Jeremy stepped away and he watched Beth talking to the officer. He watched her fill out a form on the clipboard she'd been handed. Once she glanced his way. Did she want him to stand next to her, to be there with her as she did the one thing she'd always feared doing?

He pulled his keys out of his pocket and walked to his truck. All around him the good folks of Dawson were having fun. They were having a picnic on the grounds of Back Street Church. The kids were already shooting hoops and someone had set up the volleyball net. It leaned precariously to the east and the girls playing were laughing and having a great time with the cheap ball and net.

He suddenly flashed back twenty years, when he was a kid of ten, tossing a ball to one of the Cooper boys while Tim talked to the pastor. Jeremy shook free from the memory and climbed into his truck.

Beth finished filling out the complaint against Chance. She glanced in the back of the patrol car. His head was down. He looked contrite. In a moment he would smile at her. He would mouth an apology and ask her to forgive him. She knew because this was a scene that had played out too often in their marriage.

"Beth, don't let him make you feel sorry." Jason was at her side. She smiled up at him.

"Not this time." She looked away from the car, back to the church and to the people she'd known all of her life. "No, I'm not going to feel guilty for what he did."

She'd done that too many times in the past. She'd changed her mind, told the officer she wasn't pressing charges. Her husband was sorry. He hadn't meant to hurt her. Now, remembering, her heart shook. She had been the victim but each time the police came, and he had made her feel as if she deserved the abuse. She had deserved the bruises.

In the end, the broken arm.

But she hadn't deserved it. She had been a victim who didn't know how to walk away. She had believed him when he told her the abuse was her fault.

"He has a problem." She was proud of herself for being able to make that statement. She knew it had to be a huge first step in being strong and moving on with her life.

Step two would be convincing herself that someday someone could love her without seeing all of her flaws.

Eight years of being told no one else would want her had left scars far deeper than anything he could have put on her body.

She smiled up at her brother. "I'm worth more than that."

Jason's strong arms wrapped around her in a giant brother-hug. "I'm glad to hear you say that."

"Thank you for all the times you tried to convince me to leave."

"I'm your brother, I wanted to do more."

"You gave me the way out."

"I guess I would have done anything to get you back home safe."

She nodded and wiped at her eyes. Their dad was still talking to the deputy. He walked away and joined them, his smile a little fierce. He hugged Beth tight, holding her against him in a choking hug that buried her face against his shoulder.

"Dad. Can't. Breathe."

His laugh was shaky and he let her go. "I'm glad we're all together."

"Me, too." Beth glanced toward the RV and the empty parking space. Jeremy's truck was gone. He was gone.

"He left a few minutes ago." Jason sighed. "Let's get back to this picnic. Our town could use a little bit of a break. So could we."

"Vera brought a dozen pies." Buck Bradshaw had bought the pies. Beth would keep that secret for her dad. He often did little things for people in the community and rarely did anyone find out that he was the person responsible.

When Camp Hope had hit a financial snag last year,

her dad had been a factor in keeping the camp going. He said it was a good thing to give kids a place to go in the summer.

It all felt a little empty when she thought about Jeremy leaving the picnic. When she thought about him leaving at all.

"Do you think he feels guilty?"

Jason stopped walking. "Chance?"

"No, Jeremy. Do you think it bothers him to watch people enjoying the church when he's planning to knock it down in a matter of days?"

Jason shrugged. "I don't know. I guess it would bother him. Or maybe he's changed his mind."

"I don't think he has." But last night she'd given him the note and he hadn't been as happy as she would have thought.

An old sedan pulled in the parking lot. Jason raised a hand in greeting. "I'm going to help Etta. She went home for some clothing Alyson's mom sent to help out."

"That's nice of her. How's Alyson feeling?"

"Very pregnant." He grinned. "Want to help me grab this stuff from Etta's car?"

"Sure." But her mind tripped her up. Because she'd always wanted a baby of her own. She had always wanted to be a wife, a mom. But it was easier to help Jason than to think about the future, or about Jeremy walking away. Jeremy shouldn't be in her dreams of forever. But she had a hard time erasing those thoughts.

Chapter Twelve

Jeremy left Tim Cooper's on Monday and drove down the narrow paved road to the trailer he'd grown up in. He'd always known the truth about this place and his upbringing, but seeing it after being at the Cooper ranch made it seem all the smaller, made his childhood a little sketchier.

He walked into the dingy single-wide that had been his home for the first eighteen years of his life and he let out a deep breath, whistling as he looked around. He should have come sooner. He'd just been putting off the inevitable.

Ten feet wide, fifty feet long. Two bedrooms and a bathroom with a floor that sagged. He stood in the tiny living room and tried hard not to go back in time, to sleeping on that old, plaid sofa every night.

He wasn't here for a trip down memory lane, he was here to pack. He'd met with his mother's doctor that morning and the nursing home director. She wouldn't be returning home.

He glanced around the room with the fake wood paneling and carpet from the 1970s. Maybe one of the families that had lost their home could use this place until theirs was repaired. He'd talk to Wyatt.

As much as he didn't want to take a trip back, the trailer did it for him. He walked down the narrow hall, past the room where Elise had slept. It wasn't any bigger than his walk-in closet. It had room for a twin bed and a dresser, but not much else.

It should have been easy to put this behind him. He should cowboy up and let it all go. But it wasn't that easy. He could tough it out on the back of a bull, ride through his injuries, but this place held a lifetime of bad memories.

Too much of the past included how this place treated his sister. A guy could pull on a pair of jeans and a T-shirt and let it all be good. A girl, not so easy.

Elise had cried as they stood at the edge of the yard waiting for the bus. She'd cried because she was cold. She'd cried because her jeans were too short. And too many times she'd cried because she was hungry. It hit him deep, because as a kid he hadn't been able to do anything about it.

His mother had been drunkenly oblivious to his little sister's pain.

He slammed his palm against the wall. The first time didn't do it. The second time helped. The sting bit through the skin of his palm, but it didn't lessen his anger with this past. He walked back down the hall and out the front door.

The porch sagged and a couple of the boards were splintered. The handrail had long since fallen off. Jeremy jerked off his hat and swiped his arm across his face. Man, it was hot for so early in the summer. He walked down the steps to his truck. He had boxes from the convenience store in the back. Not that there was much in this place to pack up.

A truck turned the corner and eased up the road, stopping at his driveway. He shook his head and leaned against the bed of his truck. Beth didn't know how to leave well enough alone.

He grabbed the boxes out of the back of the truck and leaned them against the back tire. Beth pulled in the drive and stopped. She didn't hurry to get out of the truck she'd been driving. One of her dad's old farm trucks. She smiled through the tinted window.

Was she waiting for an invitation?

Yeah, probably. He nodded and she jumped out of the truck. What he didn't get was why in the world did this all get a little easier when she showed up?

"What's up?" She slowed her pace as she got closer, as if she suddenly doubted the decision to stop. Second thoughts. Yeah, that made two of them.

"I need to pack. I guess maybe someone could use a temporary place to stay."

"That would be nice." She glanced at the trailer and back at him. "What about your mom?"

"She won't be coming home."

"I'm sorry."

"Yeah, well, that's the way life is." He picked up the half dozen boxes and walked toward the trailer. Beth followed, her pace a little quicker to keep up with his.

He slowed.

"I'll help you." She followed him up the steps.

Jeremy stopped at the screen door, held it open and turned to look at the woman behind him. The memory of Chance going after her flashed through his mind.

That fresh anger pushed the past to the far recesses of his mind. He couldn't change the past.

No reason to dwell there, either. At this point he sure didn't know what the future held.

Beth took a step back and nearly fell backward when her foot hit one of the broken steps. His hand shot out and he pulled her back up.

"Maybe this wasn't a good idea. I'm not sure what I was thinking."

"Beth, stay."

He touched her cheek, the place where Chance's hand had connected with soft skin. The blue and green of the bruise had spread out across her cheekbone. She flinched when his fingers touched the area.

Something shook loose inside him. He pulled her close and held her tight. When she relaxed against him, he kissed the top of her head, getting lost in her, in the sweetness of her hands on his arms, the soft scent of her, the way her head fit against his chest.

"I would never hurt you." Jeremy whispered the promise and he knew it shouldn't matter so much. How did he keep a promise like that when nearly everything he had planned would hurt her in some way?

She pulled back and looked up at him. "Let's get stuff packed."

With a nod he opened the screen door again. He grabbed the boxes and held the door open for Beth to take that first step into the home where he'd grown up. He hadn't brought anyone here as a kid, not as a teen, not ever. Most kids wouldn't have wanted to come here. Most parents wouldn't have allowed it.

He watched her expression, saw the flicker of emotion in her eyes. He glanced around, seeing what she saw. The living room and kitchen, dirty dishes still in the sink and empty bottles of booze on the counter. The trash overflowed and flies swarmed.

"Where do we start?"

He smiled. Was that all she had to say? He handed her a box. "I guess we pack up all this junk my mom called her 'collectibles.'"

"Do you have tape?" Beth grabbed one of the flattened boxes and pulled it into shape.

"In the truck." He walked to the door. "Thanks for helping."

"Jobs like this are easier with a friend."

He nodded and walked out the door. Man, he'd never needed fresh air so badly in his life. He needed space. He stood in the yard and scanned the field, the neighboring farms. He'd lived here his whole life but he'd never seen it like this, as a place he didn't want to run from.

And inside the trailer, Beth was packing up junk from his past. He needed to get his head on straight and remember his plan. It was getting a little easier with the ruling from the historical society in his favor. In a few days the planning and zoning committee would make a decision on the petition, to zone or not zone the property for commercial use.

Too bad he no longer knew what his plan was. Yeah, the church, the business; but Beth had changed everything, right down to his old resentments that had driven him to bring that dozer to Dawson. Revenge wasn't quite as sweet as he'd once thought it would be, back when it was all about him.

He kind of missed the old Jeremy, the one who knew how to let go and not take relationships too seriously.

Beth was the type of woman a guy married, had babies with, grew old with. She'd already been hurt. She deserved a lot better than a guy with his kind of baggage. That was one thing her dad had been right about. When he'd caught him by the ear that summer at the rodeo ground, he'd told Jeremy that Beth was worth way more than some kid who didn't have squat to his name.

Jeremy wasn't that kid anymore. He jerked off his hat and ran a hand through his hair.

The tape gun was in his truck. When he walked into the living room of the trailer a few minutes later, Beth had taken pictures off the walls. He glanced at the school pictures in cheap frames and shook his head. He'd always been surprised that his mom bought the school pictures each year and framed them.

"This is you when you were ten." Beth held up one of the photographs and smiled. "I remember that black eye."

"Yeah, me too."

He'd been fighting with Jackson Cooper at church. Tim had pulled them apart and given them both a sound talking-to. He still remembered being a scrawny kid looking up at Tim Cooper with that eye swelling shut and Tim seeming like the biggest man in the world. That's what he thought back then.

He'd wanted a dad real bad.

"Your mom has all of your school pictures."

Jeremy nodded and reached for one of the boxes and the tape gun. "Yeah, she did that. She always tried to dress us up that one day. And that year she tried to convince me to put makeup on my eye. I didn't."

"Of course you didn't."

He took the picture from her hands and set it down.

He didn't want to think about that day and his mother telling him not to fight with Jackson. Because she'd known that Jackson was his brother. He grabbed newspaper and wrapped the picture.

"Was your mom always…" Beth bit down on her bottom lip and one shoulder lifted in a shrug. "I'm sorry."

"Beth, I'm thirty years old, not fifteen. Yeah, there are memories here, but I'm not a little boy who needs Band-Aids and lollipops. My mom is an alcoholic. And yeah, most of our lives she was drunk."

"But our mothers were friends in school."

"Yeah, they were. I think my mom was okay as a kid. She was raised by an aunt. But for some reason her aunt left when my mom turned about fifteen."

And then her high school boyfriend had been killed in a car accident.

Life hadn't been easy for Janie Hightree. She'd done her best to pass that legacy on to her kids, to keep the cycle going. He and Elise had pulled it together somehow, some way. He hadn't thought about it before, how they'd survived and actually done something with their lives.

Beth stopped asking questions. Jeremy grabbed a box and walked into the kitchen. He looked around and shook his head. She understood why. The room was a disaster. Dishes in the sink, empty bottles and cans, the trash overflowed and flies swarmed. The place had a stench worse than any barn she'd ever been in. It smelled more like the county landfill.

"I think the only way to deal with this mess is to throw it all in the trash." He shuffled through cabinets and pulled out a box of trash bags.

Beth couldn't agree more.

"You know, I don't really need help. This is more than you expected and I really can do it alone."

Beth wrapped another photograph and placed it in the box. She walked into the tiny kitchen and pictured him there, a boy trying to take care of a mom and a little sister. As a teenager, even from the time he was eleven or twelve, he was always working odd jobs around town. Vera had put him to work washing dishes. Buck had hired him to clean stalls in exchange for riding lessons. Until Beth had been caught making eyes at him, and then he'd been sent packing.

She smiled, remembering him in that barn, faded jeans, worn-out boots and a threadbare T-shirt. She hadn't seen any of that. She'd seen a smile that set butterflies loose in her stomach and eyes that always looked deep into hers, as if he really cared what she had to say.

Even then he'd been different. He'd been two people—the tough kid and the sweet guy. Now he was the man who made her forget fear, forget all of those years thinking she wasn't worth anything.

And he was the man most likely to hurt her.

"I don't mind helping. I can even wash the dishes."

"No, these are going in the trash." He had already filled one garbage bag.

"What about the bedrooms?"

"There are two. Elise's room is cleaned out. Mom probably sold what she could, if there was anything to sell."

"And your mom's room?"

"More stuff to throw away. I went to the store the

other day and bought new clothes for her to wear. The stuff in there isn't worth taking to her or giving away."

"So pack it all in garbage bags unless we find something worth keeping?"

He stopped stuffing trash into the bag. "There won't be anything worth keeping."

Okay, she knew when to let it go. She grabbed a trash bag and headed for the back of the trailer. The floor had weak spots that sagged and the paneled walls were dingy and stained by years of dust and nicotine. The bedroom at the end of the hall was a little bigger than the first, but not enough to count. A double mattress on a frame was pushed against one wall, the sheets a jumbled mess, an old quilt thrown over the whole mess. The closet was full of old housedresses, worn polyester pants and shirts.

The dresser held more of the same. The drawers didn't pull out straight and the top of the dresser was covered with books, papers and old dust collectors that had obviously done their "dust collecting" for years. She hated to throw away the figurines, thinking that at one time they had meant something to Janie Hightree.

As adamant as Jeremy was that it should all be thrown away, she wondered if Elise would feel the same way. These were her mother's few possessions. Beth grabbed an old shirt and dusted a few of the figurines. One was porcelain and dated. Had Janie kept it for a reason?

She placed it in a box and as she dusted, she added several more to the collection. Ten minutes later she was shoving clothes into a trash bag when booted footsteps came down the hall. She glanced toward the door as Jeremy walked into the room. He walked over to the box and picked up one of the figurines.

"What's this?"

Beth shoved the last of the clothes into the bag and pulled it closed.

"I don't know, I guess I just thought that Elise might feel differently. She might want some of these. Or perhaps you could put them in your mom's room."

Jeremy exhaled a sigh and put the figurine back in the box. He shook his head. "I don't really want that and it won't mean anything to Elise."

"Okay." She knew when to let it go. Sometimes.

Jeremy turned out to be the one who didn't let it go. He leaned against the dresser, his gaze traveling around the dingy, tiny room.

"Hard to believe this was her life." He shook his head and then looked up. "It could have been my life, or Elise's life. Somehow we escaped."

The moment stretched between them, silence hanging over the room. Beth stepped close. She put a hand on his cheek, felt the raspy five-o'clock stubble, and then his lips moved to brush across her palm. His hands moved to her hips.

Beth closed her eyes as his lips touched hers, sweet and gentle. She sighed into a kiss that moved her to new places, stronger places. He whispered her name at the end of the kiss and shook his head lightly.

"I'm not sure what we're doing here." He rested his cheek against hers and she wanted him to hold her close for a long time.

"I don't know either, but does it have to be wrong?"

And then she was cold and lonely because he moved to the doorway. How did she tell him that he changed things? He shifted her heart from broken and lonely to hopeful.

He made her feel safe.

How did she tell him something that important when he didn't know what they were doing here? She took that as her cue to leave.

Chapter Thirteen

Saturday night at the rodeo. That's what Jeremy needed after the week he'd had. He'd packed up his mom's trailer at the beginning of the week, gone to a planning and zoning meeting a couple of days later. He'd managed to steer clear of Beth because he needed time to get his head on straight.

He unlatched the back of his trailer and backed his horse out. The big gray stepped onto firm ground and lifted his head, ears alert as he took in the surroundings. The animal was so excited he was almost to the point of trembling.

The horse had needed this as much as Jeremy. They both loved the smell, the sounds and the action of the rodeo. He ran a hand down the light gray of the animal's neck and then led the horse to the side of the trailer to tie him while Jeremy got the saddle and bridle out of the tack room of the trailer.

"Hey, bro, how's it going?" Travis walked up, long-limbed and all energy. His dark-framed glasses didn't manage to give him a serious expression, not with the big grin on his face.

"Going good, Travis. What about you? You bull-fighting tonight?"

"Nah, no bulls tonight. It's a ranch rodeo. What are you going to do?"

"I didn't know it was a ranch event." Teams of four or five guys doing events that were similar to work done on the ranch. Sorting calves, loading and simulated branding.

He hadn't really talked to Wyatt since a few guys started planning the rodeo. It was meant to be a way to raise funds for some of the folks in Dawson who were still struggling to get back to normal after the tornado. People had to be reminded that even though they were back to everyday life, quite a few of their neighbors were still in limbo. Several were living in campers. A few had moved to apartments in Grove. A couple of families were still at the church.

But the rodeo required a team and he didn't have one. He shoved his saddle back in the tack section of his trailer. So much for letting loose and burning energy tonight.

"You can take my spot on the Cooper Clan team," Travis said.

"No, that's okay." Jeremy brushed a hand down his horse's back. Travis got a little closer and eyed the gray gelding.

"Nice horse."

"Yeah, he's been real good for me."

Travis nodded. "Yeah, I think you should ride with Jackson, Reese and Dad. I'd give anything for a night off."

Travis glanced toward a trailer where a girl in dark jeans and a tank top was saddling a pretty bay mare.

"I bet you'd like a night off." Jeremy laughed at the younger man. But he got it. He'd also been searching for a face since he pulled into the rodeo grounds fifteen minutes earlier. He'd seen the Bradshaw trailer parked at the end of the row. So far he hadn't seen Beth. It was a ranch rodeo, but they'd still have barrels.

And then Jackson was strolling toward them. Jeremy shook his head. It was really about time to head for Tulsa.

"You don't have a team, do you?" Jackson Cooper spoke as he reached down to buckle his bright orange chaps. Yeah, that took some self-confidence. His shirt was orange, too. Kind of a peachy orange.

"No, I didn't realize it was ranch night." Okay, enough explaining. He needed to load his horse and leave.

Leave, as in straight back to Tulsa.

The lights flashed on around the arena. Jeremy untied his horse and Jackson was still standing there in his way.

"Where you going?" Jackson looked puzzled enough.

"Home. I'm not planning on running barrels and I'm not on a ranch team."

"I told him he could take my place on the Cooper Clan Team." Travis grinned big.

Jackson shrugged. "Works for me. Travis can't sort calves for nothing."

Because Travis couldn't stay in one place long enough to sort calves. It was easy. There were ten calves in one section and the team of riders had to sort the calves in order, bringing one calf at a time across the line to the other side of the arena. If a calf slipped over the line out of order, the team was done.

Travis liked constant motion and sitting on a horse long enough to keep calves from crossing a line probably wouldn't be his thing.

"If you take my place, they might really win." Travis jerked the number off his back and handed it to Jeremy. "Have at it, bro."

"Right." Jeremy looked at the number and he felt like he'd been picked by the cool guys to play on their ball team.

"Better get that horse saddled." Jackson slapped him on the back and walked away. "Glad you're one of us."

Jeremy tied his horse and reached for the bridle. And then he saw Beth heading his way, a country girl in faded jeans, a T-shirt and dark pink roper boots. He couldn't picture her in California, in a city. She belonged in Dawson.

He thought about that for a long moment and refused to think the same about himself.

"You riding?" She sat on the wheel well of the trailer and watched him saddle Pete, the horse.

"Yeah, I guess I'm riding with the Coopers."

"That's great."

He glanced her way before reaching under his horse to pull the girth strap tight. The horse stomped as the strap tightened under his belly.

"Yeah, I know, Pete." He lowered the stirrup back into place and then ducked under the horse's neck so that he was on the same side as Beth. "You riding tonight?"

"I'm trying that roan Dad bought." She pulled off her hat and smoothed her hair. "I guess it's quiet at your place since there are only a couple of families left in the church."

"Yeah, it's quiet." What else could he say?

"I should go take care of my horse." She stood up. Next to him she was tiny. He could imagine holding her close, lifting her in his arms. He couldn't imagine anyone striking her, ever.

Every time he looked at her this way, he wanted to run a finger over that scar on her face. He wanted to ask her if it still hurt, the deep-down-inside pain of the past.

She was healing.

He didn't want to hurt her all over again. He wasn't thinking about the church, he was thinking about him and that look in her eyes that said she wanted something more, something that lasted.

"I'm going to loosen Pete up a little and then find out what I'm supposed to do. I've watched ranch rodeo a few times but I'm as green as they get."

"You've been team roping a lot lately." She made the comment as she moved a few steps away from him.

"Yeah, with Dane Scott." Dane had a degree in engineering. The two of them were partners in the custom bike business. Dane didn't look like an engineer or a computer genius. He looked like a biker, the kind of guy that scared people when they met him in the dark.

He was the same guy who warned Jeremy that God wouldn't look too kindly on his plan to tear down Back Street. Jeremy figured he had Dane's prayers to thank for everything that had happened since he got to Dawson.

"Well, good luck tonight." The look she gave him, all innocence and sweetness, was a lot like the look she'd given him years ago. It teased and tempted. It left him staring after her like his brains had been scrambled.

She fast-walked back to the Bradshaw trailer. It held

four horses, tack and living quarters. The Bradshaws went big wherever they went.

He watched as she untied the dusky roan and mounted. He watched as she nudged the horse from a walk to a trot and then an easy lope away from the crowd.

"You going to admire the scenery or ride?" Jackson Cooper rode up on a big black gelding. The horse tossed his head and backed up, nervous energy already causing perspiration to soak his dark coat.

"Yeah, I'm riding. But don't forget that I've knocked that grin off your face before."

"And got a black eye for your trouble."

Good point.

Beth kept the gelding in control, holding the reins tight as the big animal trotted along the back of the rodeo grounds, bobbing his head up and down, wanting to break into a run. She eased him into a walk and turned him toward the trailer where Jason was tying his horse and talking to their dad and Lance. The other members of their team were standing at a nearby trailer.

As she rode up the driveway she thought about all the times in her life that this was normal. This was where she'd grown up and where she belonged. But Chance had convinced her that they could see the ocean, live a dream life and escape the country. Escaping the country had been what he wanted and she'd followed.

This would always be home. A dark, humid night with millions of stars sparkling in the sky, arena lights, hamburgers on a grill and the citizens of Dawson in the bleachers of the tiny rodeo arena that was Dawson's main form of entertainment—this was her life.

The horse beneath her jogged a little and pulled at the reins. She couldn't give him his head. He'd get to run soon enough. But he was raring to go. She loved the energy. After years of not riding, not barrel racing, she was glad to be back.

"Beth." Jenna Cameron rode up on a palomino mare. "You riding tonight?"

"I am." The two had been friends in school. They were closer now. They both suffered from mild post-traumatic stress disorder. Beth from years of abuse and being under Chance's control. Jenna had been injured in Iraq. She'd lost her leg from the knee down in a roadside bomb attack.

They had shared stories about fear, captivity, and being whole again. Beth smiled at her friend, who was one of the strongest women she knew.

"You know I'm going to beat you, right?" Jenna laughed, her smile bright. She had a lot to be happy about. She had Adam MacKenzie for a husband, twin boys and a baby girl.

Beth would have those things someday. She was starting to dream again. To hope.

"I'm willing to wager a steak dinner that you don't." Beth pulled the roan to a stop and Jenna stopped next to her. The palomino, creamy yellow in the bright lights, pawed at the ground.

"I'll see your steak dinner and raise you a cheese-cake."

"Great, now I'm too hungry to run barrels."

"That was my plan."

The announcer called for the invocation. The two women turned their horses toward the arena. Team Cooper rode past. Big men, big horses and lots of cowboy ego. Jeremy was with them, riding with his family. He nodded in her direction and she smiled.

"Interesting," Jenna murmured and then bowed her head as the prayer was said.

Beth waited until amen. "Nothing interesting, just a lot of imagination and speculation."

"Right." Jenna laughed. "Beth, how long have we been friends? I think you loved Jeremy even when you were twelve and he was teasing you in this very arena."

"That wasn't love, that was aggravation." But she couldn't help looking at him as Team Cooper was called and the men on horseback rode into the arena, discussing their strategy. At the far end of the arena a line had been drawn with flour. The calves to be sorted were on the other side of that line.

"Let's go see how they do." Jenna led the way. The two rode near the arena and watched. Jeremy went into the herd of calves, found number five and cut him from the herd. The calf ran across the line and Jeremy went back for calf six. The other riders kept the herd from crossing the line.

People were cheering. Jenna stood in her stirrups to get a better view. And Beth realized she was holding her breath. He was a Cooper. Her heart picked up a few beats and she moved her horse closer.

A loud bang exploded in her ear. Beth's horse jumped forward. She grabbed at the reins, getting control as the animal started a series of bucks that jarred her teeth, her head, her neck. She heard Jenna yell for her to hang on.

That wasn't optional. It was hang on or land on the ground.

As the horse jerked forward, taking a few running

leaps away from the arena, she heard her dad yell something about firecrackers.

The horse finally calmed down. He stopped, trembling, breathing hard. She stayed in the saddle, her own breath coming hard and fast as her heart slowly returned to a normal rhythm. She turned, and the horse took jerky steps, nervous, ears twitching.

"What happened?" Jeremy rode out of the arena straight toward her.

"Someone threw a firecracker," Jenna volunteered, her face a little pale.

Beth's dad led his horse up to hers. He grabbed the reins.

"Get off him."

"Dad, we're both fine."

"I'm not going to have a horse that can't be trusted."

"Someone threw a firecracker at his feet. You'd jump, too."

Buck Bradshaw's jaw worked, clenching and unclenching. "I wouldn't have put you on him if…"

"Dad, I'm a grown woman, not a child." She held the reins tight. The horse stood calmly, or as calmly as he could considering the arena, the lights, the crowd and the deafening noise that had startled them both out of ten years.

Jeremy rode up close to her. He opened his mouth and Beth raised a hand to stop him.

"If you're going to repeat what my dad just said, save your breath."

He grinned, luscious, heart-stopping and handsome. "I was going to tell you that was some pretty great rodeo."

"Funny." She swallowed and clenched the reins hard,

not to hold the horse steady but to hide her trembling hands.

"I'm going to find the kids with those firecrackers," her dad grumbled and walked away. More like stormed. She watched him go and then turned back to Jeremy.

He leaned close. "You okay?"

"I'm good." She rode her horse in a tight circle that put a few feet between herself and Jeremy. "You did great out there tonight."

Couldn't she think of anything better than that? Shouldn't she tell him that she resented that he'd still tear down Back Street after everything the community had been through? Shouldn't she tell him she wouldn't let him break her heart?

Instead she'd complimented his riding skills.

"I need to cool this horse off before barrels. I can't stand taking a crazy horse into the arena," Beth said.

"Doesn't he have a name? You keep calling him 'horse.'" Jeremy reached down and patted the horse's neck.

"Yeah, his name is Trigger. How's that for sappy?"

"Cute. Call him Trig for short?"

"I guess."

And then he did the unexpected. But if a person always does the unexpected, shouldn't it become the expected? He rode up next to her and, before she could react, he was out of his saddle and sitting behind her. They'd done that a lot when they were kids riding in trail rides or just around the arena. He had one foot out of the stirrup and over her horse, pulling the two together and then sliding behind her saddle.

Trig hopped a little and then settled. Jeremy's arms were around her waist.

"What are you doing?" She glanced back but then faced forward again because he was close behind her, so close she could feel his warm breath against her neck.

This was why he'd kept all the girls talking when they were teenagers. Because he always knew what to do, what to say to make a girl fall.

"We're going to cool this horse down a little," he answered. He had the reins of his horse in his hand and the poor thing followed behind, ears back.

"I'm not sure this is a good idea."

She felt him shrug behind her. "Yeah, it probably isn't. But since when do we make the best decisions?"

"I know this is hard for you to believe, but I've been working on that."

"Are you saying I'm a bad decision?" He leaned close, his chin near her shoulder.

She inhaled and regretted it immediately, because he smelled so good. Her senses, the ones meant to derail bad choices and the ones that were tuned into the world around her, were all mixed up and colliding with a mess of other emotions.

The sharp scent of his cologne mixed with the mint of his gum. Combined with the rough feel of his hands on her arms and the warmth of his breath, she nearly came unraveled.

"Jeremy, what are we doing?"

He didn't answer for a second. "Beth, I'm not even sure."

Great, that made two of them. And she really needed for one of them to be sure of something.

"I think you should go."

He leaned back. His hands were on her waist and he

rode loosely behind her. "And yet you're riding farther and farther from the arena."

Hmm, he had a point. And yet she kept going. Behind her he laughed and she smiled. "I'm going crazy. That has to be what is happening to me."

He reached and took the reins from her hands, trapping her between his arms, brushing his raspy cheek against her neck.

"I think crazy is okay once in a while, as long as you don't do something you regret." He kissed her on that spot beneath her ear and she closed her eyes for a brief second.

"Maybe."

"But I'm going to go ahead and take your advice and say goodbye. You do mean go as in get off your horse, not go back to Tulsa, right?"

"I think that's what I mean." She smiled back at him and he turned the reins back over to her. She pulled the horse to an easy halt next to his gray gelding and he slid a leg over, settling back into the saddle. Beth watched him ride away, then turned and rode back to the arena.

Two years ago she'd told herself she wouldn't travel this path again. She wouldn't open her heart up just to have it broken. Shouldn't it feel a little broken now?

Instead her heart felt as if the pieces were being put back together. By Jeremy Hightree.

And he had the ability to break it all over again. Either he'd leave, or he'd tear down the church. Both pointed to heartbreak.

So shouldn't she put her emotions in check and make a break from him before either of those two things happened?

Common sense was pointing to yes.

Chapter Fourteen

Monday after the rodeo Jeremy sat in his lawn chair looking at Back Street Church. They'd had services again yesterday. But by next week Dawson Community Church would be repaired and open once again.

Back Street would be forgotten. Again.

A truck pulled into the parking lot and pulled up next to his. Tim Cooper got out. Tim took his hat off and pulled out one of the spare lawn chairs. He shook it open and sat down.

"Nice day for sitting."

Jeremy nodded. "Yep."

Tim glanced across the road. "Saw you on that monster bike yesterday. Is it yours?"

"No, we built it for a customer. I'm hauling it to Tulsa tomorrow." The bike was already on the trailer attached to his truck.

Tim nodded. His gaze strayed to the church and he sighed. "It's been here a lot of years. I guess we did sort of let it go."

"Yeah, but it was here when people needed it."

"You mean after the tornado?"

Jeremy nodded. It didn't sit well with him, that the people in town were done with the building. It had served its purpose—again.

It had served a purpose when he was a kid. He didn't really feel like sharing that with Tim Cooper. It was good that he had stopped by and all, but they weren't ready for long discussions. But Jeremy had realized something about himself, and about this church.

The other day at his mom's trailer he'd caught himself wondering about how he and Elise had survived their childhood. Now he realized he hadn't survived on his own. Elise hadn't survived on her own. Man, it was hard to look at that church and think about tearing it down. He and his sister had survived because of this church and the people who had attended it.

He let out a sigh and shook his head. "I have a lot of memories tied to this building."

"Yeah." Tim cleared his throat. "I guess we all do. That's why I'm here. Joe Eldridge from the planning and zoning commission called me. He said they voted in your favor this morning."

"In *my* favor, huh?"

Tim let out a long sigh. "Yeah, you have your zoning. You can go ahead with the demolition of Back Street Church."

Months of working, fighting and waiting. Now that it was over, he didn't know what to think. The people of Dawson were done with Back Street. The last family had moved out of the shelter that morning. He could move forward with his plans.

"I guess I'm not going to tear it down." Jeremy glanced at Tim, his father. "I guess I thought it would make me feel better."

"Sometimes a man has crazy thoughts."

They both laughed. "Yeah, like dozing down a church. Like that dozer could really do the job."

"So, what are you going to do with it? And what about the business?"

"I don't know. I think I'm going to head back to Tulsa. And Back Street Church can go back to being a monument to the people in this town. Maybe they'll need it again someday."

"I hate to see you not build a shop here. There are people in town who need jobs."

Yeah, he knew that. He just didn't know if he could stay here any longer. Yesterday he'd watched Beth leave church with her dad and brother and he hadn't known how to deal with how he felt for her. He still didn't know what in the world name to put on it.

He'd never been in love before. He'd made a lot of bad choices and been in a lot of relationships that had meant nothing to him. He'd walked away from women who claimed they loved him and he hadn't felt a thing for them.

A few had told him he was breaking their hearts. So what was he going to do? Break Beth's heart? He'd rather cut off his right hand than hurt her.

"That tree over there looks like it got shook loose in the storm." Tim nodded in the direction of a soft maple that shouldn't have been planted so close to the building in soil as sandy as this.

"Yeah, I noticed that the other day. The roots are exposed and some of the leaves are starting to turn. It'll have to come down."

"I'm supposed to be picking up a gallon of milk from the convenience store. I just wanted to stop by and see how you're doing." Tim stood up. "I guess you'll be around?"

"I'll be around. I'm keeping this land."

"Right. You can take a guy out of Dawson but it's sure hard to keep him away."

"Something like that." Because Vera had the best pies in the state and people here were friends for life. And family.

He stood up and held his hand out to Tim Cooper. Tim took it and held it tight.

"Any man would be proud to call you son."

"I appreciate that."

Tim stood there for a long minute. "I guess we'd like for you to keep coming to our family dinners, even if you decide to leave us for Tulsa."

"I think I'd like that, sir."

"That's good."

Tim tipped his hat down, turned and walked away. Jeremy watched him get in his truck and then he turned back to that tree. Time for it to come down.

Beth had saddled up for a ride through the pasture but she'd changed her mind. She hadn't seen Jeremy, hadn't really talked to him since the rodeo. And that left a lot unsaid. She didn't even know what needed to be said at this point.

She knew that he had the go-ahead to demolish Back Street Church. She knew she couldn't stop him. She knew it would hurt. It would also hurt him.

It took her fifteen minutes to get to Back Street. As she got close she heard the dozer. Her heart tightened and she urged the horse forward, into a steady gallop.

They rounded the corner and the dozer was heading for the church.

She leaned and the horse stretched his legs and ate up the ground. As they raced across the lawn of the church she saw the dozer, saw Jeremy in the seat. She headed the horse toward the church, and positioned herself at the steps, between Jeremy and the building.

The dozer chugged to a stop.

"Beth, what in the world are you doing?" He leaned out, his hat shading his face.

"I'm stopping you from making the biggest mistake of your life."

He sat there, staring. And then he shook his head. "You like to think the best of me, don't you?"

She couldn't stop trembling. And seeing red didn't begin to describe how mad she was at him. "I do believe the best in you. I also know that I'm not going to let you do this."

"Beth, listen to me…" He jumped down from the dozer.

Beth remained on her horse. She backed the gelding up a couple of paces and made like she was a lot stronger than she felt. She wasn't backing down.

"You can get off that horse."

"No, I'm not going to. I'm going to stay here until you change your mind."

He snorted and shook his head. "You're the most stubborn female I've ever met."

With that, he walked away. Beth watched from her position in the saddle as he walked into his RV. All was quiet. The dozer was silent. The RV was silent. A few minutes later he walked out with a suitcase. He saluted and walked to his truck.

At the truck he stopped. "It's all yours, Beth. The paper is on the table in the RV. I'll be back in a few weeks to get my stuff. But try believing in someone. Just try believing that there are people out there who won't hurt you."

He tossed his suitcase in the back of the truck and drove away. Beth dismounted on shaky legs. She stood next to the gelding who turned to rub his head against her arm. She rubbed his face and leaned against him.

She waited for Jeremy to return. Years ago she had waited for Chance to return, but that had been different. She had awaited Chance's return with fear, wondering what he'd do next. She'd wait, wondering when he'd unlock the bathroom door and let her out. She'd waited, finally, for her chance to escape.

She'd come home on a bus, bruised, broken and afraid she'd never trust or love again.

As she sat on the church steps, her heart truly broke. She felt it tighten with pain and crumble into pieces. Her throat tightened with emotion and regret. Tears, cold and salty, coursed a trail down her cheeks. The horse grazed at the end of the reins, chomping as the bit clicked. She shouldn't let him do that. She should pull him up.

Instead she sat on the steps and waited.

A truck finally did come down Back Street. Jason turned into the parking lot and got out. Her brother walked across the lawn with an easy gait, a smile on his face.

"What are you doing over here?" He studied her face and she turned away.

"Trying to decide if my first mistake was trusting him or falling in love with him. I'm trying to decide if my second mistake was pushing him from my life or if that was the best thing to do."

"Gotcha." He sat down next to her. "So, where is he?"

"Packed a suitcase and left. He said the church is mine."

"Interesting. But he left?"

She nodded and a fresh wave of tears and pain swept over her. She pulled up the collar of her shirt and wiped her eyes. She was so done with crying, so done with feeling empty.

Jason got up. "I'll be right back."

She nodded and continued to cry. The horse pulled on the reins. She pulled him back and tied him to the handrail. His ears flicked this way and that but then went back to show his displeasure because he'd been enjoying a patch of clover.

Jason returned, a paper in his hand. "He signed it over to you. Do what you want with it, he says. And there's a P.S."

"What?"

Jason grimaced as he read the note and then looked at her. He shook his head. She wanted him to read it. She wanted him to get it over with. "Jason, please?"

"He was only going to knock down the tree. But..." Jason shrugged and handed her the note. "You read it."

She took the paper and held it tight. The words wavered and her eyes overflowed. "He was only knocking down that tree before it fell over and hit the church. And he didn't feel like defending himself." Good going, Beth. She closed her eyes. "I didn't give him a chance to explain."

Jason grinned at that little revelation and cleared his throat. "You were hardheaded?"

"It does run in the family." She should have trusted him. He'd never given her a reason not to trust. "I just automatically think the worst. I don't want to be that person."

Jason sat back down. "You're not that person. And Jeremy Hightree has a lot to work through. Maybe he's trying to work through his feelings, or yours."

"Mine?"

Jason leaned back and gave her a long look. "I'm not sure if he's ever had anyone love him the way you do. That's a lot for a guy to deal with."

She started to deny that she loved Jeremy, but that was a pointless argument. She wouldn't be sitting there on the church steps bawling like a baby if she didn't love him.

"What do I do?"

"Give him time, Beth. He'll be back."

She glanced back over her shoulder at the church. The paper was in her hand, telling her that it was hers. Her church.

"What do I do with the church?"

Jason shrugged. "I don't know. You offered to buy it before. What would you have done with it if you'd bought it?"

The ridiculous situation dawned on her and she started to laugh. She laughed until she cried, but not sad tears. "Who gets a church from a guy? Other women get roses, jewelry, candlelight, romantic dinners. I get a church."

"Alyson always tells me not to buy her flowers because they wilt. She'd rather have plants for the flower garden."

"I have a church." She sighed and stood up, facing

the building. The horse walked up behind her, pushing his head against her shoulder. "I'm not sure what to do with it."

Jason had stood. He untied the horse from the handrail and slipped the reigns over the animal's head. "Pray about it, Beth. I can't help but think God had a hand in bringing this all about. This church has sat here empty for the better part of the last ten years. It's time for it to be used and you're the person to decide how."

She nodded and slipped her left foot into the stirrup. As she swung into the saddle her gaze went to the building. Again she sighed, because it was too much for one day. Jeremy leaving, the church, it settled heavy on her heart.

"I'll pray about it." She held the reins loosely in her right hand and smiled at her brother. "Thank you."

As she turned the gelding toward home she heard a basketball bouncing on pavement. Two boys were walking across the parking lot, heading toward the basketball nets Jeremy had put up.

Beth smiled and watched the two kids as they started a game of horse. A few minutes later another boy arrived with his skateboard.

As she headed home, plans began to whirl through her mind. She didn't have to urge the horse forward; he was ready to get home. They seemed to be in the same mood, both a little lighter and a little more free.

Chapter Fifteen

Jeremy walked through his Tulsa dealership studying the way the manager had arranged motorcycles. It was late June and the weather was great. Several customers milled around, probably dreaming of the perfect day and a bike to ride country roads. Yeah, he knew that dream. He'd spent the last couple of weeks, since he'd left Dawson, taking advantage of as many days like that as he could.

Today the bikes looked perfect. They were polished until the paint gleamed and the chrome could reflect images. In the far corner were a few custom bikes, for customers who wanted something out of the ordinary.

"Jer, you got a minute?" Dane Scott walked out of his office, a big guy with bleached hair, a goatee and a heart of gold. He was raising his sister's two kids because she'd never been able to get her act together.

"I have a minute and we have a fresh cup of coffee." Jeremy headed toward his own office and knew that Dane would meet him there with his mug that said THIS IS THE DAY THE LORD HAS MADE. Jeremy kind of laughed because the mug and the man didn't match, not unless you knew Dane.

Dane walked into the office, holey jeans and a short sleeved button-down shirt, loose tie around his neck. He kicked the door shut, poured himself a cup of coffee and sat down. Jeremy stood behind his desk, waiting, because he had a feeling this was going to be good.

"Get out of here." Dane's words were soft, easy, and pretty stinking determined.

"What?"

"You're driving us all crazy. I don't know who you left behind in Dawson, but man, I've never seen you like this. And it's starting to get on my nerves."

"I don't know what you're talking about." Jeremy loosened his own tie and sat down behind his desk. The big chair was leather and soft. It fit him like a glove. This office fit him. It got under his skin that Dane would tell him to leave his own business.

Dane leaned forward, muscled arms folded on the desk. He grinned big. "Buddy, I've known you for years. We team rope together. We play golf together. We chase women together. We're confirmed bachelors and we love it."

"Right, that's us." Jeremy leaned back in the chair and worked real hard at casual.

"Yeah, it *was* us. When was the last time we went out? When was the last time you had a date? Have you taken Paula out since you got back from Dawson?"

Paula. A woman busy with her career and not interested in long-term relationships. She was lively conversation at dinner and even played golf.

"No, because we've both been busy."

"No busier than usual. As a friend, I'm telling you to

take care of whatever is eating at you. I think we both know that it has something to do with Dawson and that church you didn't tear down."

"I told you, we're building on the five acres where my mom's trailer used to sit."

"Right, that's a good location, not in a neighborhood. Perfect. What happened to the church?" Dane grinned and leaned back in this chair.

"You prayed for me and my plans fell apart. Thanks for that." He sighed and shook his head. "I mean it, thank you."

"Not a problem. God and I were looking out for you, keeping you from making a huge mistake. And now I'm telling you, don't make another decision you're going to regret. You have good people here. You have a manager who makes sure each location is on target. You don't have to live in this dealership."

"This is my business."

"And you're going to chase away the customers if you keep stomping around frowning. Look, playing the field is all good if it's what you want. But if you stop wanting that, if you start thinking of picket fences and baby cribs, then it's time to let it go."

Jeremy laughed at that image. "Right, that's me, a picket fence and baby crib kind of guy."

Dane shrugged. "Kids aren't all bad. I mean, girls, yeah, they're kind of a pain when they get all moody and emotional, but they have moments when you see the person they're going to be someday."

"Right." Jeremy stood up and stretched. He looked out a window that faced a busy street. In the distance he could see the downtown businesses, the tall buildings reaching up. He could watch planes take off.

He loved his place on the outskirts of Tulsa.

He had planned on living his life here, away from Dawson. He had planned on never settling down. Man, he had a lot of plans. And lately, none of the plans fit. His plans felt like cheap boots, a little tight, uncomfortable and ready to be kicked off.

The day he'd left Dawson he'd felt good about leaving. He'd been saving Beth from being hurt by him. He didn't do long-term relationships and he cared about her too much to play that game with her.

Today walking away felt like the worst thing he'd ever done, not the most chivalrous.

"So?" Dane still sat in the chair watching him, a cheesy grin on his face. "Do you need to go buy a ring?"

Jeremy glanced down at his friend. He thought a lot of things about Dane right then. Some of it wasn't too PG. And then he thought that not many people would sit him down and force him to look at his life the way Dane could.

"Yeah, I need to buy a ring." Because he realized then that he'd played the field and never fallen in love because he'd been in love for years. With Bethlehem Bradshaw.

Back Street Church Community Center. Beth stood back and watched as Ryder Johnson helped her brother put the sign in place at the edge of the lawn. She smiled at them, and at the newly painted building. The church was no longer empty and forgotten.

It was now a place for the people of Dawson to gather for family reunions or special events. It was a shelter. It was a place for kids to hang out. Twice a week after school snacks would be served and homework help provided. There were basketball hoops, volleyball nets and a homemade baseball field.

The community had something worthwhile, because of Jeremy Hightree. She glanced across the street at the empty barn, the forgotten foundation of the home he'd given up on. Only one family had left town after the tornado. One family, and Jeremy.

It hurt to think about that day, about watching him drive away.

"Kind of empty over there without his livestock." Jason walked up, work gloves in his hand. He shoved the gloves into the front pocket of his jeans.

"Yeah, a little." She smiled up at her brother. "I should have trusted him more."

"Maybe. But sometimes we go by what we see even when we know that faith is evidence of things unseen."

She nodded and wiped at eyes that overflowed far too easily these days. She had always loved Jeremy in some little way. She'd loved him as a kid because he'd been hurting and tough. She'd loved him as a teenager because he'd been that guy that always knew the right thing to say, the right way to smile and flirt.

As an adult? She loved him because he made her feel strong, not afraid. Because he made her heart feel a little less fragile. She loved him.

And because she hadn't trusted, he was gone.

"I keep praying that he'll come back," Beth admitted. "I want him to see what I've done with the church."

Jason laughed. "Yeah, that's the only reason you want him back."

"I want to apologize for doubting him," she admitted. It wouldn't do any good to admit she was in love with Jeremy. He wasn't a man looking for a wife and a home to settle down in.

"Right. You keep telling yourself that, sis." He hugged her. "I have to get home. Ryder already left. Andie called and said he had to get home and help her corral the twins."

Beth nodded and her heart did a little dance thinking about those twin baby girls of Andie's and Ryder's. "I'm going to make sure the lights are off inside the church and lock up."

"Will you be okay here alone?"

She looked at the church and nodded. "I'm fine here."

He was asking because of Chance. But Chance had left again. His dad had driven up to the ranch and apologized for his son. He'd told Beth that Chance was moving to Oregon. He'd met a girl.

If only Beth could warn the poor thing. Online Chance was probably a perfect man. He was handsome, educated, wealthy. He was everything a woman wanted, online.

Online he could be whoever he wanted to be. In person he was a different story.

"I'll see you tomorrow." Jason kissed the top of her head.

"Give Alyson my love."

Jason nodded and walked away. She watched him leave and then she headed for the church. She remembered that day weeks ago when she'd walked through the doors of Back Street and felt lost and alone.

It was no longer a rejected, forgotten building. The inside glowed with promise. The windows were clean and cobwebs were gone. The kitchen in the basement had been remodeled. One of the rooms was now a nursery and the pantry held emergency supplies.

She stood in the sanctuary and said a silent "thank you."

"Bethlehem Bradshaw, I'll tell on you."

The voice was velvety soft and a catch of emotion punctuated the words. She didn't turn, couldn't. Her heart froze and then hurried to catch up.

Finally she turned. He stood in the doorway, a cowboy in faded jeans, a T-shirt and worn boots. His hat was cocked to the side. When he smiled her world tilted a little.

"What are you doing here?"

He took a few steps forward. "I had some unfinished business here. By the way, I like what you've done with the place."

She bit down on her bottom lip and waited to hear what his unfinished business was. Her gaze slid down, to the Bible in his right hand. Her mother's Bible.

Should she say she missed him? Or maybe ask if he wanted the church back? She should ask about his mother or if it was true that he was building his business where his mother's trailer had been.

Instead she stood there unable to say anything at all. He took a few more steps, his smile so sweet she wanted to melt into his arms and ask him to never let her go.

Chapter Sixteen

Jeremy didn't want to rush this. For two days he'd been thinking about what he'd say. He'd thought about it when he put his place in Tulsa up for sale. He'd thought about it when he bought the townhouse that would be his place to crash when he checked on his business in Tulsa.

He'd thought about it when he went shopping.

Now he had it all in his head, and even in his heart, but he didn't want to rush it. What if he was wrong and she wasn't interested? What if he was thinking that his bachelor days were over and she had no intention of settling down with a guy like him? A thousand "what-ifs" played through his mind, scaring the daylights out of him.

All of a sudden his plans were tossed out the window when one of his surprises came wobbling into the church, fat-bellied and short-legged. He knew it was there before he saw it because Beth's gaze dropped and her mouth opened and then turned to a smile.

"Aw," she cooed.

He looked back and he was right. There it was, wobling down the aisle. He reached to grab the German shepherd pup before it peed on the newly polished floors of the church. It struggled a little and then went to town licking his face.

"It's adorable."

He handed the puppy over to her. "I saw him in a pet store window and he looked like a guy that needed a bigger home."

She took the puppy that looked like a bear cub and held him close. His licking went into overdrive. Jeremy watched, and he felt as if he'd done at least one thing right. Who needed a bouquet of flowers when they had a puppy? He'd actually thought about the flowers, but the ones at the convenience store in Dawson were pretty wilted and brown.

So now what? He'd stalled for at least three minutes. Beth looked up and her eyes sparkled a little. Was she glad to see him, or was it the puppy that put that smile on her face? For a guy who had dated his fair share of women he realized he really knew very little about them.

"Beth, can we talk?"

She raised her face. The puppy squirmed in her arms, still trying to zero in on her cheeks.

"Of course we can." She bit down on her bottom lip. "Jeremy, you haven't changed your mind, have you?"

"My mind?"

"About the church. I mean, you left the letter and ran with it. There were kids here every day, playing basketball, riding skateboards. I realized that there are churches in Dawson, but nowhere for the kids to hang out. People complain the teenagers in town are causing problems. I just thought if they had somewhere to go…"

He took her free hand and lead her out of the building. "Beth, I'm not taking the church from you. I gave it to you. It's yours to do whatever you wanted with."

"Thank you."

"I have other unfinished business." He led her down the steps. He didn't know where they were going, but somewhere.

"Unfinished business?"

He kept walking. There was a bench under one of the big trees in the front lawn of the church. He led her there but they didn't sit down. Beth put the puppy down and it walked around the bench and then plopped down in the grass.

Unfinished business. She was far more than that. He held up the Bible that had been her mother's. Her gaze drifted from his face to the book he held. She shook her head.

"I don't understand. You didn't have to bring it back."

He smiled, and he could no longer resist touching her. He touched her cheek and then slid his hand back. His fingers tangled in the silky strands of dark hair. Beth's eyes lowered and she moved closer.

"I missed you," he whispered, and he couldn't imagine ever being away from her again.

Beth opened her eyes to those words. Her hands rested on his arms, as if they had a mind of their own. He had backed away, though.

She had missed him, too. But she didn't want to say it, not yet. She didn't want to go where she might get hurt. Living near the lake, she'd always been taught not to jump into the water unless you knew what was beneath the surface. It was good advice. And in this case, she didn't know, not yet.

Jeremy held up her mother's Bible. He flipped through the pages and handed it to her, open to the back section.

"I've been reading and I found something that I think might be a problem." Jeremy pointed to the page he'd opened to.

She shook her head because she didn't get it. This wasn't what she wanted, a discussion about her mother's Bible. She wanted to know that he was back to stay. She wanted to hear him say something about them.

"Jeremy, I don't understand."

He grinned, his eyes sparkling with that old mischief and humor that she'd known since childhood.

"Look at this page, Beth. The page where weddings and births are recorded."

"Right?"

"It isn't filled out."

She looked down, wanting to understand because he obviously wanted her to get it.

"No, it isn't." She sighed and touched the pages. She should write Jason and Alyson's wedding details on these pages.

And then she saw what he was trying to point out to her. The page was marked with the blue ribbon that her mother had used to keep the place where she was reading. Tied to the end of the ribbon was a ring.

Beth's breath caught and she didn't know what to do. Crying seemed good, or the laughter that bubbled up. Her heart couldn't catch up with Jeremy.

"Beth, your mother never got the chance to record weddings." He grinned. "Or the births of new children.

I think we should take care of that for her. I think we should put our names on this page. Jeremy Hightree and Bethlehem Bradshaw, married..." He touched her cheek again and this time his lips touched hers and he held her close, as if he never meant to let her go. "I don't know, what day do you think we should write on the date line? It's getting close to the end of June. Maybe August. Or September?"

Her words refused to spill out in a way that made sense. She had an answer, she really did. He was smiling at her.

"Beth, I'm putting my heart on the line here." He spoke softly, his mouth close to hers. "Do I need to kiss you again?"

That made perfect sense. She nodded and he captured her mouth with his, a persuasive kiss that explored what her heart had been trying to tell her for weeks. He pulled her close and she wrapped her arms around his neck.

She wanted this, forever. She pulled him closer and he kissed her more. And then he stepped back. He took off his hat and sighed.

"Bethlehem Bradshaw, will you please marry me?"

She nodded and tears flowed down her cheeks. "I will marry you, Jeremy. Today, if you want."

He smiled that big cowboy smile of his and he lifted her up off the ground and twirled her. The puppy barked a fierce puppy bark and Jeremy set her back on the ground.

"I love you." He kissed her again and she tried to whisper that she loved him back. She had always loved him and she always would.

Epilogue

Two months later

Bethlehem Bradshaw stood at the front of Back Street Church. Wyatt Johnson held her mother's Bible. Behind him was the pulpit her great-grandfather had built. Her family sat on the pew where she'd always sat with her mother. And instead of sitting behind her, Jeremy Hightree stood next to her. He smiled down at her, and she couldn't believe this gorgeous man in his Western tuxedo was going to be her husband.

That morning they had recorded their wedding in her mother's Bible. Jeremy Hightree married Bethlehem Bradshaw, August 28, a Sunday afternoon. Witnessed by family and friends. Her father gave her away. Her brother was the best man. Her sisters-in-law, Alyson and Elise, were her bridesmaids.

Wyatt Johnson smiled at the two of them. "I now pronounce you husband and wife. You may kiss the bride."

The church erupted in applause. Jeremy pulled her close. His ring was on her hand, joined with her mother's wedding band. He smiled as he whispered that he loved her. The kiss was sweet and easy and another round of applause cheered them on as he held her in his arms. And then he lifted her and carried her out of the church.

Next year they would hopefully fill in the next page in the family registry, the page for births. She closed her eyes and dreamed about a family with the man holding her close, carrying her out the door to a stretch SUV limousine.

Jeremy and Bethlehem Hightree. She now knew how it felt to be loved by someone strong. She had engraved the words from her mother's journal on the wedding page in the Bible.

Love will happen. Life will happen. Don't rush through the days, savor them. Love someone strong.

* * * * *

Dear Reader,

Welcome back to Dawson! Readers have emailed me on occasion to ask when certain characters will get their story, their romance. One of the characters people have asked about is Beth Bradshaw, sister to Jason Bradshaw in *The Cowboy's Courtship*.

I was only too happy to give Beth a story. When she first showed up in Dawson, I realized she'd been through a lot and she was going to need a special man, someone strong and caring. Along came Jeremy Hightree, a cowboy who'd left town years ago and is back only to tear down one of Beth's most beloved childhood memories.

Jeremy and Beth join forces when a tornado hits Dawson and Back Street Church is needed as a shelter. Thrown together, they find love and healing. I hope you'll enjoy their story.

Brenda Minton

SPECIAL EXCERPT FROM

Love Inspired®

*Widowed single mom Rebecca Mast returns to her
Amish community hoping to open a quilt shop. She
accepts carpenter Daniel King's offer of assistance—but
she isn't prepared for the bond he forms with her son.
Will getting closer expose her secret—or reveal the love
she has in her heart for her long-ago friend?*

Read on for a sneak preview of
THE WEDDING QUILT BRIDE
by *Marta Perry*,
available May 2018 from Love Inspired!

Do you want to make decisions about the rest of the house
today, or just focus on the shop for now?"

"Just the shop today," Rebecca said quickly. "It's more
important than getting moved in right away."

"If I know your *mamm* and *daad*, they'd be happy to
have you stay with them in the *grossdaadi* house for always,
ain't so?"

"That's what they say, but we shouldn't impose on them."

"Impose? Since when is it imposing to have you home
again? Your folks have been so happy since they knew you
were coming. You're not imposing," Daniel said.

Rebecca stiffened, seeming to put some distance between
them. "It's better that I stand on my own feet. I'm not a girl
any longer." She looked as if she might want to add that it
wasn't his business.

No, it wasn't. And she certain sure wasn't the girl he
remembered. Grief alone didn't seem enough to account

LIEXP0418

for the changes in her. Had there been some other problem, something he didn't know about in her time away or in her marriage?

He'd best mind his tongue and keep his thoughts on business, he told himself. He was the last person to know anything about marriage, and that was the way he wanted it. Or if not wanted, he corrected honestly, at least the way it had to be.

"I guess we should get busy measuring for all these things, so I'll know what I'm buying when I go to the mill." Pulling out his steel measure, he focused on the boy. "Mind helping me by holding one end of this, Lige?"

The boy hesitated for a moment, studying him as if looking at the question from all angles. Then he nodded, taking a few steps toward Daniel, who couldn't help feeling a little spurt of triumph.

Daniel held out an end of the tape. "If you'll hold this end right here on the corner, I'll measure the whole wall. Then we can see how many racks we'll be able to put up."

Daniel measured, checking a second time before writing the figures down in his notebook. His gaze slid toward Lige again. It wondered him how the boy came to be so quiet and solemn. He certain sure wasn't like his *mammi* had been when she was young. Could be he was still having trouble adjusting to his *daadi*'s dying, he supposed.

Rebecca was home, but he sensed she had brought some troubles with her. As for him…well, he didn't have answers. He just had a lot of questions.

Don't miss
THE WEDDING QUILT BRIDE by Marta Perry,
available May 2018 wherever
Love Inspired® books and ebooks are sold.

www.LoveInspired.com

LIEXP04

Inspirational Romance to Warm Your Heart and Soul

Join our social communities to connect with other readers who share your love!

Sign up for the Love Inspired newsletter at **www.LoveInspired.com** to be the first to find out about upcoming titles, special promotions and exclusive content.

CONNECT WITH US AT:

Harlequin.com/Community

 Facebook.com/LoveInspiredBooks

 Twitter.com/LoveInspiredBks

LISOCIAL201

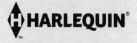

Reward the book lover in you!

Earn points from all your Harlequin book purchases from wherever you shop.

Turn your points into *FREE BOOKS* of your choice
OR
EXCLUSIVE GIFTS from your favorite authors or series.

Join for FREE today at
.www.HarlequinMyRewards.com.

Harlequin My Rewards is a free program (no fees) without any commitments or obligations.

MYR1